LOVING A
LOST LORD

**Center Point
Large Print**

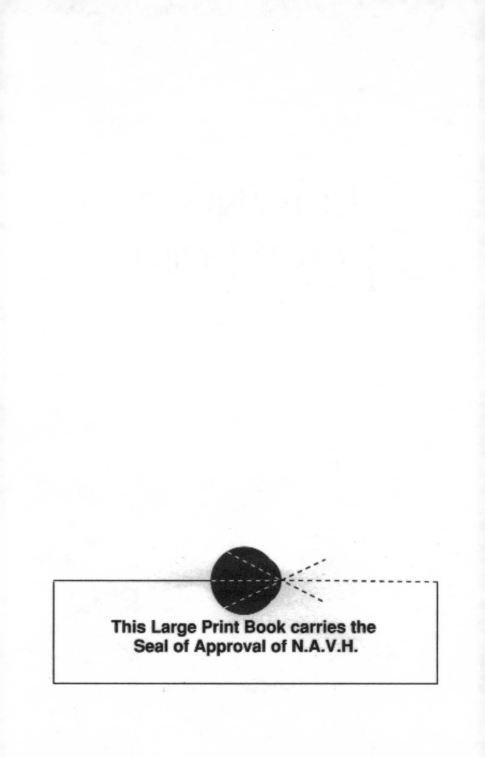

**This Large Print Book carries the
Seal of Approval of N.A.V.H.**

LOVING A
LOST LORD

MARY JO PUTNEY

CENTER POINT PUBLISHING
THORNDIKE, MAINE

This Center Point Large Print edition
is published in the year 2009 by arrangement with
Kensington Publishing Corp.

The text of this Large Print edition is unabridged.
In other aspects, this book may vary
from the original edition.
Printed in the United States of America.
Set in 16-point Times New Roman type.

ISBN: 978-1-60285-531-1

Library of Congress Cataloging-in-Publication Data

Putney, Mary Jo.
  Loving a lost Lord / Mary Jo Putney. -- Center Point large print ed.
    p. cm.
  ISBN 978-1-60285-531-1 (lib.bdg. : alk. paper)
  1. Large type books. I. Title.

PS3566.U83L68 2009
813'.54--dc22

2009016712

*To all those teachers who helped me
learn to love books and education.
Thanks for your patience!*

Acknowledgments

My special thanks to Shobhan Bantwal, author and expert on all things Hindu. Any mistakes are my own.

As always, thanks to the Cauldron members for the brainstorming and support. And a special thanks to Kate Duffy, an editor who knows how to make authors purr.

Chapter One

Kent, 1812

Late-night visitors were never good news. Lady Agnes Westerfield woke to banging on the door of her private wing of sprawling Westerfield Manor. Since her servants slept two floors above and she wanted to stop the racket before it woke her students, she slid into her slippers and wrapped herself in a warm robe.

Her candle cast unsettling shadows as she made her way to the door. Soft, steady rain hissed against the windows, punctuated by two deep gongs from the hall clock.

Among the quiet hills of Kent, robbers were unlikely to knock on her front door, but she still called, "Who's there?"

"Randall." Recognizing the familiar voice, she swung the door open. Her heart sank when she saw the three tall young men on her front steps.

Randall, Kirkland, and Masterson had been part of her first class of students—her "lost lords" who needed special care and education. There had been six boys in that class, and they had become closer than brothers. One had been lost in the chaos of France; another was in Portugal. Having three of the others show up with anguish in their eyes did not bode well.

She gestured them inside. "Is it Ballard?" she asked, voicing a worry she'd had for months. "Portugal is a dangerous place with the French army running amok."

"Not Ballard." Alex Randall stepped inside and removed his rain-soaked cloak. He limped from a wound he'd received on the Peninsula, but he was still ridiculously handsome in his scarlet army uniform. "It's . . . it's Ashton."

Ashton was the sixth of their class, the most enigmatic, and perhaps dearest of them all. She braced herself. "Dead?"

"Yes," James Kirkland answered flatly. "We learned the news at our club and immediately rode down here to tell you."

She closed her eyes, despairing. It wasn't fair for the young to die when their elders lived on. But she had learned early that life wasn't fair.

An arm went around her shoulders comfortingly. She opened her eyes and saw that it was Will Masterson, solid and quiet but always knowing the right thing to do. "Did you come together to support me if I went into shrieking hysterics?" she asked, trying to be the calm headmistress they had known for so many years.

Masterson smiled wryly. "Perhaps. Or perhaps we wanted comfort from you rather than vice versa."

That was the underlying truth, she guessed. None of her young gentlemen had had decent mothers, so she'd taken that role in their lives.

A yawning maid appeared and Lady Agnes ordered food for her guests. Young males always needed feeding, especially after a long ride from London. When they'd hung their dripping cloaks, she led them to the salon. They all knew the way, for they had been frequent visitors even after finishing their schooling. "We all need some brandy, I think. Randall, will you pour?" Lady Agnes said.

Silently Randall opened the cabinet and drew out four glasses, the lamplight shining on his blond hair. He was taut to the point of shattering.

She accepted a filled glass and sank into her favorite chair. The brandy burned, but it sharpened her wits. "Tell me what happened. An accident?"

Kirkland nodded. "Ashton was never sick a day in his life." He looked a decade older than usual. "Is Miss Emily here? She will need to know, too."

Lady Agnes shook her head, wishing that her longtime companion and friend was present so they could mourn together. "She is visiting family in Somerset and won't be back for a week. General Rawlings is also away."

She contemplated her glass, wondering about the propriety of drinking herself senseless. She never had, but this would be a good time to start. "He was my first student," she said softly. "If not for Adam, there would be no Westerfield Academy." She didn't notice that she had slipped into using the late duke's personal name rather than his title.

"How did that happen? I never heard the story.

You know how Ash was. When it came to his private life, he'd make an oyster look chatty." As Masterson spoke, the maid returned with a heavily laden tray.

The young men fell on the sliced meats, cheese, bread, and pickled vegetables like wolves. Lady Agnes smiled as she poured claret for everyone, glad she could do something for their bodies if not their spirits.

Randall glanced up. "Tell us how it all began."

She hesitated, then realized that she wanted—needed—to talk about how she'd met the very young Duke of Ashton. "Emily and I had just returned from our traveling years. Though I loved visiting so many faraway places, it seemed like time to come home. My father was unwell and . . . well, there were other reasons, but they don't matter.

"After three months back in England, I was champing at the bit, wondering what to do with myself. I'd already sorted out the steward here at Westerfield Manor, and I needed a challenge. A pity women aren't allowed in Parliament."

Kirkland looked up from his sliced beef with a smile. "I would love to see you speak to the House of Lords, Lady Agnes. I daresay you'd sort them out in no time."

"I found a better use for my energy. One day I was strolling through Hyde Park and wondering what to do with myself when I heard a whip cracking. Thinking someone was beating a horse, I went into the shrubbery and found a dreadful little man cursing up a tree. Perched on one of the branches over his head was Ashton, clutching the most indescribable puppy."

"Bhanu!" Masterson exclaimed. "I still miss that dog. How on earth did Ashton get him up a tree?"

"And *why?*" Kirkland asked.

"The man was Ashton's tutor, a fellow called Sharp. To be fair, Ashton was driving the man to distraction," she said judiciously. "He refused to speak English or look anyone in the eye. His only friend was this filthy puppy he'd found some-where. Sharp ordered the puppy killed, but the groom assigned the job couldn't bear to do that, so he released Bhanu in Hyde Park. When Ashton found out, he ran away from Ashton House to find his dog."

"And he wouldn't quit until he succeeded," Randall murmured. "Stubbornest man I ever met."

"*You* should talk!" Kirkland exclaimed.

Laughter at the comment lightened the atmos-phere a little. Lady Agnes continued, "When I appeared and asked what the trouble was, Sharp poured out all his frustrations on me. He'd been assigned the task of preparing the boy for Eton.

"After a fortnight of being driven mad, Sharp was convinced that the new Duke of Ashton was a lackwit who couldn't speak English and certainly couldn't attend Eton. The boy was a vile limb of

13

Satan! He was the wrong duke; the title should have gone to his decent English cousin! But the boy's fool of a father had been a cousin who never thought he'd inherit, so he married a Hindu slut while stationed in India. When the other heirs died, our Ashton ended up with the title, to the horror of everyone in the family."

There was a collective gasp around her. "I'm amazed Ash didn't go after his tutor with a knife," Masterson breathed.

"I was tempted to take the whip away from Sharp and use it on *him*." Instead, she'd gazed into the tree and seen stark misery on the boy's face as the tutor raved. The child understood every word and knew that he was despised.

In that moment, he'd captured her heart. Lady Agnes knew a great deal about being different—an outcast in the society to which one was born. This small boy with the startling green eyes needed an ally. "Ashton had been treated with contempt by those around him ever since he was taken from his mother in India and shipped back to England. No wonder he was hoping that his horrible new life could be wished away."

Her gaze went to each of the men in turn. "And that, gentlemen, was when inspiration struck and the Westerfield Academy was born. I used my grandest voice to announce that I was Lady Agnes Westerfield, daughter of the Duke of Rockton, and that I owned an academy for boys of good birth and bad behavior. I also claimed to have learned ancient methods of discipline during my travels in the mysterious Orient.

"Sharp was intrigued, and we struck a bargain. If I could get Ashton out of the tree and behaving civilly, Sharp would recommend to the trustees that the boy be sent to my academy rather than Eton. So I chased the man out of earshot, dredged up the Hindi I'd learned during my time in India, and asked Adam to come down." She smiled fondly at the memory.

"Of course he spoke perfect English—I was sure he must have learned the language from his father. But since I made the attempt to address him in Hindi, he decided that it was time to come down from the tree and deal with the world around him." He'd had tears on his face when he'd reached the ground, but that she would never tell anyone. "Though I spoke the language badly, at least I was trying. He and I struck a bargain of our own. He was willing to come to my new school if he was allowed to keep Bhanu and continue the study of mechanics, which he'd begun with his father.

"I thought that sounded perfectly reasonable. In return, I would expect him to apply himself to all his studies and learn how to play the role of English gentleman." She had also promised that his private thoughts would be his own. Torn from the land of his birth and his mother, he had needed to know that.

15

"Then I went in search of other students. You all know how you came to Westerfield." The English peerage had no shortage of angry, frustrated boys who didn't fit the pattern expected of them. Randall, for example, had managed to get himself expelled from Eton, Harrow, and Winchester, the three most prestigious public schools in Britain. She believed that his feat was unmatched.

The parents and guardians of her first class had been grateful to find a respectable school that would take their problem boys. Lady Agnes's sprawling estate was well suited to become a school, and her high birth had been a powerful lure. So was her recruitment of General Philip Rawlings. The general's military reputation was stellar, and parents assumed he would rule with an iron hand.

Instead, the general shared her belief that violence should never be a first resort with children. Bored by his retirement, he had accepted her offer with enthusiasm. With her connections among the beau monde and his ability to command boys without ever raising his voice, they had created a unique school.

Within a year, other parents were begging for places at the school, and subsequent classes were larger. Lady Agnes had become expert in alluding to her mysterious oriental ways of creating well-educated and well-behaved young gentleman.

In fact, her methods weren't at all mysterious,

though they were unconventional. When she first met with a boy, she found out what he most wanted, and most hated. Then she arranged for him to have what he wanted, and not be forced to endure what he found unendurable.

In return, she required her boys to work hard at their studies and learn how to play the game of society. Once her students realized that they could play the roles expected of them without losing their souls, they did well.

Kirkland topped up everyone's claret, then raised his glass in a toast. "To Adam Darshan Lawford, seventh Duke of Ashton and the finest friend a man could have."

The others raised their glasses solemnly. Lady Agnes hoped the tears in her eyes didn't show in the dimly lit room. She didn't want to ruin her reputation.

After the toast, Kirkland said, "Now his cousin Hal is the eighth duke. Hal is the one who notified us, actually. He found us dining at Brooks, because he knew we would want to know as soon as possible."

"Hal is a good fellow," Masterson observed. "He was broken up by the news. Inheriting a dukedom is all very well, but he and Adam were friends."

Lady Agnes had met Adam's cousin Hal. He was indeed a decent fellow, though conventional. Life, and the Ashton title, would go on. She wondered if there was any special young lady who should be informed of Adam's death, but he'd never expressed interest in a particular woman. He'd always been very close about his private life, even with her. Well, the news would be public soon enough.

Realizing she hadn't heard the full story about Adam, she asked, "What kind of accident did he die in? Was he riding?"

"No, he was testing his new steam yacht, the *Enterprise*, up near Glasgow," Randall replied. "He and his engineers were making a trial run down the Clyde. They ended up steaming quite a distance. They had just turned to head back when the boiler exploded. The boat sank almost immediately. Half a dozen engineers and crewmen survived, but several others didn't make it."

Masterson said gloomily, "Ash was probably in the engine room tinkering with the damned thing when it exploded. That . . . would have been quick."

She supposed that if Ashton could choose how to die, he'd be pleased to go this way. He was surely the only duke in England with such a passion for building mechanical devices. But he was unusual in many ways.

Then she stopped and considered what had been said. "Has his body been found?"

The young men exchanged glances. "Not that I've heard," Randall said. "Though our information might be incomplete."

He might be alive! Though she wanted desperately to believe that, she knew her thought was hope, not likelihood. And yet . . . "So there is no proof that he is dead."

"With the fire and the sinking of the boat in such difficult waters, his body might never be recovered," Masterson said quietly.

"But he *might* have survived." She frowned as she considered. "What if he was injured and came ashore some distance away? In one of his letters, he told me how strong the currents are around the Scottish and Cumberland coasts. At the least, his . . . his body might have been carried such a distance that it wouldn't be connected to a steam boat explosion many miles away."

"It's possible, I suppose," Randall said, his brows knit.

"Then why are you here instead of looking for him?" Lady Agnes snapped.

They all stiffened at her sharp tone. There was a long silence before Masterson banged his wineglass down on the table. "That's a damned good question. I was so shocked at the news that my brain ceased working. I'm going to head north and find out what happened. The survivors will be able to tell us more. Maybe . . . maybe there will be a miracle."

Randall said grimly, "Not bloody likely."

"Perhaps not, but at the least I'll learn more about his death." Masterson rose, swearing under his breath as he wavered from a combination of exhaustion and drink.

"And I'll go with you," Kirkland said flatly. He and Masterson turned their gazes to Randall.

"It will be a fool's errand!" Randall exclaimed. "Grasping at false hope will just make the truth more bitter in the end."

"Not for me," Masterson retorted. "I'll feel better for knowing I tried. Granted, it's unlikely he survived, but there is some chance that his body will be found."

Randall scowled. "Very well, I'll join you. Ashton deserves our best efforts."

"Then it's decided, gentlemen. You may spend the rest of the night here and take fresh mounts from my stables." Lady Agnes rose and caught their gazes, one after the other. Voice steely, she commanded, "And if Adam is alive, I expect you to *bring him home!*"

Chapter Two

Cumberland, Northwest England
Two months earlier

By the time her tour of the house reached the drawing room, Mariah Clarke was giddy with happiness. "It's wonderful!" She spun in a circle with her arms out and her blond hair flying as if she were six years old, rather than a grown woman.

Her father, Charles, moved to the window to admire the Irish Sea, which glinted along the western edge of the estate. "Finally we have a home. One worthy of you." He glanced at her fondly. "As of today, you are Miss Clarke of Hartley Manor."

Miss Clarke of Hartley Manor. That sounded rather intimidating. It was time to start acting like a young lady. She straightened and tied a loose knot in her long hair so she would look closer to her twenty-five years. Like Sarah. As a child, she had often been alone, so she'd imagined that she had a twin sister called Sarah, who was always available to play. Always loyal. The perfect friend.

Sarah was also a perfect lady, which Mariah wasn't. If Sarah were real, she would be impeccably dressed with never a hair out of place. There would be no missing buttons or grass stains from sitting on a lawn. She would always ride sidesaddle, never shocking the countryside by riding astride. She would be able to charm everyone from cranky infants to curmudgeonly colonels. "I shall have to learn the art of supervising a large household. Can we afford more servants? The three here aren't really enough for an establishment this size."

He nodded. "The same card game where I won Hartley Manor also yielded a nice amount of money. With care there will be enough to staff the estate properly and make improvements. If the manor is managed well, it will produce a respectable income."

Mariah frowned, not liking the reminder of how her father had acquired the manor. "The gentleman who lost the estate, was he left destitute?"

"George Burke comes from a wealthy family, so he won't starve." Charles shrugged. "He shouldn't have gambled if he couldn't afford to lose."

Though she could not be as dismissive of Burke's fate as her father, she didn't pursue the subject. As a small child, she'd lived with her great-grandmother, who had gypsy blood. After Granny Rose's death, Charles had taken Mariah with him everywhere. Though she loved her father, she'd never enjoyed their life on the road, where his charm and skill at cards had produced a sometimes erratic living.

When Charles's wallet was particularly flat, Mariah had told fortunes at village fairs, a skill she'd learned from her grandmother. Mariah couldn't see the future, but she was good at reading people, so they left feeling happier about their lives and prospects.

Fortune-telling was not a pursuit that Miss Clarke of Hartley Manor would ever admit to! Luckily, she wouldn't have to do that again. "I'll look for the estate account books so I'll understand our finances better."

"My practical little girl," Charles said with amusement. "You'll have this place in order in no time."

"I certainly hope so." She pulled a holland cloth cover off the nearest piece of furniture, revealing a wing chair upholstered in blue brocade. Like most of the furniture left in the house, it was worn but serviceable. Every room and wall had gaps where George Burke had removed the more valuable pieces. No matter—furniture and paintings could always be replaced. "With so few servants, neither house nor garden were as well cared for as one might wish."

"Burke preferred spending his money on a fashionable life in London." Charles looked at her with the regret revealed when he thought of the mother she couldn't remember. "You will be a splendid lady of the manor. But I'd best warn you now that as soon as we're settled, I must leave for a few weeks."

She stared at him, dismayed. "Is that necessary, Papa? I thought now that we have a home, we will stay in it."

"And so I will, Mariah." His mouth twisted wryly. "I am not so young as I was, and the thought of a comfortable home is very appealing. But I have . . . some family business to take care."

"Family business?" Mariah said, startled. "I didn't know we had any relatives."

"You have whole clutches of them." Her father's

gaze shifted away from her to contemplate the sea again. "I was the black sheep and my father disowned me. With justice, I might add. Now that I have achieved respectability, it's time to mend fences."

Family. What a very strange concept. "You have brothers and sisters? I might have cousins?"

"Definitely cousins. Not that I've met any of them." He sighed. "I was a very wild young man, Mariah. I didn't start to grow up until I became responsible for you."

She tried to imagine what it would be like to have family beyond her father. "Tell me about your—our—family."

He shook his head. "I will say no more. I don't want you to be disappointed if I am still forbidden the family home. I really have no idea what I'll find there." His expression was bleak.

"Surely at least some of your relations will welcome you back." She tried not to sound wistful when she added, "Perhaps I can visit them?"

"I'm sure that even relations who still disapprove of me would be pleased to meet Miss Clarke of Hartley Manor." He grinned. "Now let's visit the kitchen. I've found that Mrs. Beckett is a most excellent cook."

She followed happily, ready for some of the bread she'd smelled baking. It would be worth missing her father for a fortnight or two to finally have a family.

Mariah awoke with a ridiculous smile on her face, as she did every morning now. She slid from the bed, wrapped a robe around herself, and padded to the window to look out at the shimmering sands that bordered the sea. She still had trouble believing that this lovely estate had become her home. Granted, much work needed to be done, but every day there was some improvement. When her father returned, he would be surprised and pleased by her efforts.

A gentle rain drifted across the landscape, soft and magical. The dampest corner of England wouldn't have been her first choice for a home, but no matter. Now that she was here, she loved every raindrop and twist of fog.

Hoping that she would receive a letter from her father today, she dressed, doing her best to look like her dignified imaginary sister. She began to comb out her hair while mentally listing her tasks for the day. After breaking her fast, she would go into the village. First she would call on the vicar, who had promised to suggest men who might make good outside servants.

Her thoughts lingered on the vicar. Mr. Williams was single and attractive, and she had detected warmth in his gaze whenever they met. If he was looking for a wife, he would want a Sarah, not a Mariah, but she was making progress at being respectable.

After visiting Mr. Williams, she would take tea with her new friend, Mrs. Julia Bancroft. Knowing a clever, amusing female near her own age was in some ways even better than the vicar's admiration.

The local midwife, Julia was a young widow who was also the local substitute physician since there were no real doctors for miles around. She treated minor injuries and ailments and knew something of herbs.

They'd met after a church service and immediately struck up a friendship. Granny Rose had taught Mariah a great deal about herbs. Mariah wasn't a natural healer like Julia, so she was pleased to pass on her great-grandmother's knowledge to a woman who appreciated it.

When the snarls were out of her hair, she twisted a neat knot at the back of her head. Sarah approved. The young maid of all work arrived with a tray containing toast and a cup of hot chocolate and helped Mariah dress. Mariah felt like quite a grand lady.

After finishing her light repast, she pulled on her gloves and cloak, collected her straw bonnet, then headed down the stairs, whistling cheerfully. She stopped before reaching the kitchen. She was quite sure that Sarah wouldn't know how to whistle.

"Good morning, miss." The cook, Mrs. Beckett, spoke with a Cumbrian accent so thick that Mariah could barely understand it, but no matter. She was a good plain cook, and she welcomed the new

26

owners because they were living in the house. For years, Mrs. Beckett had been a general house-keeper and sometime cook on the rare occasions when the previous owner had chosen to visit. It was good to have a steady position, she'd confided, but she'd missed having people about.

"Do you need anything from the village shops?" Mariah asked.

The cook shook her head. "No need, the pantry 'tis full. Have a nice walk, miss."

Mariah was fastening her cloak when the maid scuttled into the kitchen, her eyes wide. "Mr. George Burke is calling to see you, miss," she blurted out.

Mariah's cheer fell away. If only her father was here! But she hadn't even received a letter from him in over a week. "I suppose I must see the man," she said reluctantly. "Please ask him to wait in the small salon."

After the maid left, Mariah said, "At this hour, I don't suppose I'm required to serve him refreshments. I wonder what he wants?"

Mrs. Beckett frowned. "I don't know what Mr. Burke will do, and that's a fact. I'd heard tell he was staying at the Bull and Anchor. I hoped the rascal would leave Hartley without calling here. You watch yourself with that one, Miss Mariah."

A good thing Mariah was dressed to go out. That would give her an excuse to keep the meeting short. "Do I look proper?"

"You do indeed, miss."

27

Conjuring Sarah's serene expression, Mariah headed to the small salon. When she arrived, George Burke was contemplating a small, inlaid table. In his early thirties, he was fair-haired and good-looking in a bluff, manly way.

As she entered the salon, she said, "Mr. Burke? I am Mariah Clarke."

"Thank you for receiving me." He ran his fingers over the inlaid wood wistfully. "This table belonged to my grandmother."

It was a pretty table and Mariah liked it, but she and her father had agreed that Burke should be allowed to remove personal belongings and anything with sentimental attachments. "In that case, you should have it, Mr. Burke."

He hadn't looked at her when she entered, but at her words he glanced up. His expression changed. Mariah recognized that look. It was the interest of a man who found a woman attractive and was wondering how beddable she might be. "You are gracious," he said. "I'm sorry we meet under such circumstances."

Then why hadn't he stayed away? Coolly she asked, "You have returned to Hartley for a visit?"

"I'm staying at the inn." He frowned. "This is awkward. I called largely because I wondered if you had heard the news about your father."

Alarm shot up her spine. "What news? If you wish to speak with him, you must wait until he returns from London."

"So you haven't heard. I feared that." Burke glanced away, not meeting her gaze. "Your father was killed by highwaymen just outside of London, in Hertfordshire. I was staying at the local inn when I heard about the stranger who had been murdered, so I stopped to see the body in case I could help identify him. I recognized your father immediately. His face, the scar on the back of his left hand. It was unquestionably him."

She gasped in disbelief. "How do I know you're telling the truth?"

"You insult me, madam!" Burke took a deep breath. "I will make allowances for your grief. If you don't believe me—how long has it been since you received a letter from your father?"

Too long. When he first left, she'd received a letter about every other day. "It . . . it has been over a week." She sank onto a chair, still not quite grasping that her father could be gone. But highways could be dangerous, and she'd been feeling anxious about the lack of letters. Her father had promised to write often, and he never broke his word to her.

"This was taken from your father's body. I wasn't sure he had family, but since I was coming to Hartley, I said I'd try to return it." He pulled a gold ring patterned with a twisting Celtic design from his waistcoat pocket. She accepted it with trembling fingers. The ring was well worn and utterly familiar. Her father wore it always.

Her gloved hand clenched over the ring as she accepted that Burke was telling her the truth. She was alone in the world. Her last letter from her father didn't say that he had called on his long estranged relatives yet, so they wouldn't know of her existence. She didn't have the faintest notion where his family lived, so she couldn't write them and introduce herself. For all practical purposes, they didn't exist.

She was alone. Granny Rose and her father were both gone, and all she had was Hartley. But that was a good deal more than she'd had two months earlier.

Still between shock and disbelief, she asked, "Why didn't you notify me so I could see that he was properly buried?"

"At the time, I didn't know of your existence. But you may rest assured that he was buried decently. Since I'd known him, I gave the local authorities the money to put him in a local church-yard. I also gave them the name and address of your father's lawyer, whom I'd met during the transfer of Hartley's ownership. I expect you'll hear from him."

"Thank you," she said numbly.

"This is very difficult, Miss Clarke, but I must tell you that your father cheated in the game where he took my estate," Burke said tersely. "I was prepared to challenge him legally, but his death complicates the situation. I returned to Hartley to reclaim my property, and learned about you. I decided I'd best call to give you the bad news if you hadn't heard."

His words cut through her numbness. "How dare you make such an accusation! You insult my father, sir!" Despite her words, a small, cold corner of her mind wondered if the claim might be true. Her father was generally an honest gambler. As he had told her more than once, that was just good business. A cheat would soon be barred from play with gentlemen.

But Charles Clarke did know how to cheat. He'd demonstrated various methods of crimping cards and signaling and other techniques so that Mariah would be able to recognize the tricks when she was herself playing. She was a competent card player, and she had found that great ladies might cheat no matter how old and honorable their family names. If necessary, Mariah knew how to cheat back.

But she would not show doubt about her father to Burke. "My father is an honest man. If he were here, he could defend himself from this slander!"

"Since he is no longer with us, I shall speak no more of what he did." Burke studied her face, his pale blue eyes calculating. "Miss Clarke, I know this is not a good time, but a thought has occurred to me. You have been orphaned, and I want my estate returned. I was prepared to go to the law to reclaim that, but the courts are slow and expensive. There is a more convenient solution for both of us."

31

Mariah gazed at him, only half aware of his words. There was no solution that would bring her father back.

"I need a wife, and you are a gentle lady in need of a man to protect you," he continued. "I propose that we marry. There will be no lawsuit and no unpleasantness. Both of us will have a home, income, and standing in the community. It will be a most suitable match." He glanced around the salon approvingly. "I can see that the household runs well under your supervision, which pleases me almost as much as your beauty and grace. Will you do me the honor of becoming my wife, Miss Clarke?"

Her jaw dropped in shock. A complete stranger was asking her to wed because it would be *convenient?* That was the trouble with pretending to be ladylike: obviously she looked like a helpless fool.

His proposal was outrageous, even if she'd liked the man, which she didn't. Granted, he was good-looking and his offer had a treacherous logic to it, but she had no desire to join her life to a gamester's. She had seen what hell such men created for their families. If she wed the man, she would be at his mercy.

The absurdity of Burke's offer pushed her to the edge of hysterical laughter. She put a hand over her mouth in a vain attempt to smother that.

His jaw tightened. "You find the idea laughable? I assure you that my birth is more than adequate, and I should think it would be obvious that marriage is in the best interests of us both. To be blunt, you will benefit more than I, given your rather murky origins. In your position, I would consider an offer of honorable marriage most carefully."

Mrs. Beckett had warned her against Burke, and the expression in his eyes confirmed that he could be a dangerous man to cross. She sobered and gave him her best wide-eyed gaze. "I'm so sorry, Mr. Burke. I was laughing because I am overwhelmed by all that . . . has happened." It was easy to sound confused and grief stricken. But what excuse could she give that would send him off once and for all?

An outrageous thought struck her. She considered it for an instant, rather appalled at her own ability to prevaricate. But this particular lie would serve her purpose well. "I am honored by your offer," she said with her most sincere expression. "But I already have a husband."

Chapter Three

"You're *married?*" Burke's gaze shot to Mariah's left hand.

Mariah resisted the temptation to hide her hands behind her back. Luckily she was wearing gloves, since she'd been about to walk to the village, so he couldn't see her bare third finger. "Indeed I am, Mr. Burke. Though I am honored by your offer of marriage, I obviously can't accept."

"No one in the village said anything about you having a husband," he said suspiciously. "And you are called Clarke, like your father. In fact, you're called *Miss* Clarke by everyone."

"My husband is a distant cousin, also named Clarke." She shrugged. "Since I have been known as both Miss and Mrs. Clarke, I answer to both."

He glanced around the room as if expecting her husband to materialize. "Where is this mysterious spouse?"

"I've only been in Hartley for a few weeks," she pointed out. "He has not had time to join me."

Burke looked even more suspicious. "What kind of a man isn't with his beautiful wife when she moves to a new home?"

Deciding she'd had enough of Burke, she swept to her feet. "The kind who serves his country in the Peninsula rather than gambling away his patrimony in a drunken stupor! It is time you *left,* Mr. Burke! Take your grandmother's table and go."

Instead of losing his own temper, the infuriating man smiled at her. Like all gamesters, he loved a challenge. Loved risk. "Forgive me, Mrs. Clarke. I should not have spoken with you about personal matters when you are still absorbing the news of your father's death." He bowed. "I offer my condolences. I shall return for the table at some later time." He turned and left, closing the door quietly behind him.

She would prefer never to see Burke again, but at

least his presence had been a distraction. Knees weak, she sat again and opened her right hand to reveal her father's gold ring. He was dead. It still didn't seem real. She must contact the London solicitor who had handled the transfer of ownership for Hartley Manor and ask him to investigate further. Perhaps more details would make Charles Clarke's death seem more real. She would also see if his body could be brought to Hartley for reburial. Papa had so looked forward to living here. . . .

Mariah closed her eyes, tears stinging. He had been too young to die! Too *necessary*.

But she had seen sudden death more than once and knew it played no favorites. She must make the best of her life here in Hartley. She gave thanks that she was in so much better a position than she had been two months before. Her father's luck at cards had left her a young woman of means rather than in desperate straits. It was his last gift.

The only thing desperate about her now was the enormous lie she had just told. Years of traveling with her father in sometimes sticky situations had made her very good at prevarication. She could open her big brown eyes and lie with utter conviction when necessary, though she disliked having to do it. But she was a practical female, and when she'd concocted this particular lie, she was ready to say anything that would persuade Burke to go away and leave her alone.

Had she ever told anyone in the village she was unwed? The subject hadn't really come up that she could remember. She was called Miss Clarke and no doubt everyone assumed she was a spinster, but she had never said so.

In public she usually wore gloves, like a proper lady, so the presence or absence of a ring was unlikely to have been noticed except by the manor servants and her friend Julia Bancroft. Mariah must find a ring for her wedding finger, at least until Burke left Hartley for good. How her father would laugh when she told him of this scene. . . .

Her body spasmed at the visceral realization that her father was dead. She began to weep uncontrollably.

Rest in peace, Papa.

The day after Burke's visit, a letter arrived from the London solicitor who had handled the transfer of title to the estate. He confirmed the death of Charles Clarke and offered his sympathies in dry, lawyerly prose.

The letter killed Mariah's despairing hope that Burke had lied about her father's death in the hope of coercing her into marriage. In the following pain-filled days, George Burke called on her regularly. He brought flowers and left his polite best wishes even though she wouldn't receive him at first. The servants and her friend Julia were the only people she could bear to see.

Eventually her social conscience caught up with her and she went downstairs to see Burke when he called. He was so polite and charming that she wondered if she'd misjudged him. That first time they met, both had been upset and less than reasonable.

She suspected that he was trying to decide whether or not she really had a husband. He was attracted to her—she could feel lust radiating from him and perhaps he sensed that she was lying. Whatever his private thoughts, his behavior was beyond reproach. Since he acted like a gentleman, she must be a lady.

As she began coming to terms with her new life, the Sarah side of her began murmuring that perhaps it was worth considering Burke's offer. Though she had been admiring the vicar, that was mere daydreaming. Burke had made her a genuine offer, and being a wife would give her more standing in the community. He would likely spend much of his time in London, leaving his wife free to run the estate. And he was undeniably good-looking. One could do worse for a husband, and many women did.

Besides, she was so lonely knowing that her father would never come home. . . .

At this point in her ponderings, Mariah would tell Sarah that she couldn't possibly be lonely with an imaginary sister living in her head. Burke was a gamester and would make his wife's life hell. He'd probably gamble Hartley Manor right out from underneath Mariah's feet. She had craved stability for too long to place her welfare in unreliable hands. Far better that Burke believe she was married and out of his reach.

Yet Burke persisted in his attention. One night Mariah awoke shaken by a vivid dream that she was marrying him. They were pronounced man and wife, he took her hand—and squeezed it painfully hard, trapping her with him forever. She knew why she'd dreamed that: he'd visited again that afternoon and hinted about lawsuits between his compliments. His noose was tightening around her.

She buried her face in her hands and whispered, "Oh, Granny Rose, what should I do? If Burke keeps coming around, in a moment of weakness I might say yes."

While Sarah was a product of her imagination, Granny Rose was an indelible part of her memories. Dark, calm, and loving, she had raised Mariah, teaching her cooking and riding and laughter. Though Mariah had waited breathlessly for visits from her father, it was Granny Rose who had been the center of her life.

There were some people in their small village of Appleton who had called her grandmother a witch. That was nonsense, of course. Granny Rose made herbal potions, read palms, and gave wise counsel to girls and women of the village. Occasionally she performed rituals to achieve particular ends, though she always said there was no magic involved. Rather, rituals focused the mind on what was desired, and that made goals more likely to be achieved. Like prayer, but with herbs added.

Mariah needed a good ritual. She thought back and decided that a wishing spell would be best since she could ask for whatever would best solve her problems. Her grandmother had always cautioned Mariah against being too explicit with her wishes, because sometimes the best solution was one that she'd never thought of.

She had some lucky incense that she and her grandmother had made together years earlier, and tonight the moon was full, a good time for a ritual. Since she couldn't sleep, she might as well try a ritual. At the least, doing so would strengthen her resolve to keep George Burke at a distance.

She tied a robe over her sleeping shift, slid her feet into slippers, then wrapped a heavy shawl around her shoulders. After collecting a tinderbox and a packet of lucky incense, she descended the stairs and went outside toward the sea. The night was cool and clear, and moonlight silvered the fields and the sea.

The garden included an open gazebo with a stone patio and a sundial. Thinking this a good place for her ritual, she closed her eyes and thought about her lost loved ones until she felt their friendly presences.

She started by setting the incense on the brass top of the sundial. After striking a spark and setting it ablaze, she silently asked for help through this difficult time. Healing, protection, strength, luck . . .

For an instant she imagined a real husband—not Burke but a man who fit her dreams. Ruthlessly she suppressed that image and concentrated on asking for mental and emotional strength.

As the pungent scent of the burning incense faded into the wind, she stepped into the gazebo and sat on one of the stone benches that circled the interior. She leaned back against the wall, feeling peaceful. Her night braid had come undone and her hair was drifting around her shoulders, but she felt too lazy to redo it.

As a child, she'd had few playmates—that's why she'd invented Sarah. But she'd had her grandmother, and they did everything together for many years. She'd nursed her grandmother in the old woman's final illness, and her father had appeared at the end to help. She and Charles had mourned together, and then he had taken her with him on his restless travels around the British Isles.

Now they were gone and she was truly alone for the first time in her life. That was why George Burke was looking treacherously attractive. He did seem to like her, and it was very appealing to be wanted.

But *not* by George Burke. Though she'd like a husband someday, she wanted a reliable, kind man like the local vicar. Whom she had been avoiding since her father's death, because of her complicated situation. She really couldn't be glancing coyly at the vicar under Burke's nose when she was claiming to be married.

Closing her eyes, she rested.

Hold on hold on hold on. . . . In the far corner of his spirit to which he had withdrawn, he was aware that the end was near. He had been clinging to life for an eternity, and soon the sea would claim him. By now, he no longer cared if he lived or died. Almost, he didn't care.

The dream brought Mariah sharply awake. *Go to the shore.* The internal voice sounded like her grandmother, and it was filled with urgency.

Not stopping to question, she pulled her shawl around her shoulders and raced down the lane at a tomboy's speed. The full moon's light was bright but uncanny, and she felt a chill, as if she had entered a world where magic could really happen.

Waves crashed hard on the narrow beach, which was a mix of sand and shingle. She halted, wondering what madness had brought her here in the middle of the night. Then she saw a dark object floating not far offshore, every wave bringing it closer.

Curious, she studied it. Good heavens, was that a head? Perhaps a corpse?

She gagged at the thought, wanting to run away. But if this was a drowned man, it was her Christian duty to bring him ashore so he could be properly buried. The tide would shift soon and she couldn't be sure the . . . object . . . wouldn't be washed out again.

She pulled off her slippers and wrapped her shawl around them. After setting the bundle above the waterline, she waded into the waves. She was almost knocked off her feet, and the water was *cold*. Luckily, she managed to regain her feet before she went under entirely, but by the time she reached the floating object, she was soaked to the skin.

Hoping the sight wasn't too ghastly, she looked closer and saw that it was indeed the body of a man. His arms were locked around a large chunk of wood, perhaps a piece of beam. Wondering if he could possibly be alive, she caught hold of the wood and towed man and beam ashore, fighting rough water all the way.

A last wave helped lift him onto the sand above the tide level. His clothes were tattered to the point of indecency, with shirt and trousers reduced to rags. Shivering, she knelt beside him and cautiously spread her hand across his shirt. To her amazement, there was a faint, slow heartbeat. The man's flesh had a deathly chill from the water and there were lacerations and other marks on his skin, but he *lived!*

His hair and complexion looked dark in the moonlight, so she guessed he was a foreign sailor. Since water lapped around his feet, she took hold under his arms and dragged him onto the coarse sand. As she pulled, he began coughing convulsively.

Hastily she let go and the sailor half rolled onto his side, spewing water. When the violent fit ended, his breathing was rough but he was undeniably alive. Relieved, she wondered what to do. She didn't want to go for help and leave him alone, but the faster she got him indoors and warm, the better.

Hoping he could walk, she leaned over and asked, "Can you understand me?"

After a long moment, he nodded, head bent.

"If I help, do you think you can walk to my house? It's not far."

He nodded again. Though his eyes were closed and he shivered with cold, at least he had some awareness of his situation.

She brushed the sand from her feet and put her slippers back on, then knelt and draped his left arm around her shoulders. "I'll lift as best I can, but I can't manage without your help."

She lifted and he struggled. Between them, he got to his feet, swaying. She used her free hand to wrap her shawl around his shoulders, hoping the heavy wool would dispel some of his chill. "We're on our way. It's not a very long walk."

He didn't reply, but when she started walking, he

followed her lead. Their floundering progress through the sand was excruciating and the breeze sliced through wet clothing.

Matters improved once they reached the path. A pity it was all uphill. But with her under his arm and taking half his weight, the sailor managed to keep moving.

He used a railing to drag himself up the steps into the house while Mariah supported him on the other side. They staggered inside, Mariah wondering what to do next since he surely couldn't manage another flight of stairs to the guest bedrooms. Then she remembered a small chamber at the back of the ground floor. Once it had been used by an elderly housekeeper. The room was shabby and underfurnished, but there was a bed. It would suffice.

She steered the sailor through the darkened house, occasionally banging into furniture. She hoped her charge wasn't acquiring as many bruises as she was. It was a huge relief to enter the small bedroom. Because the aged housekeeper had been infirm, the bed had been built low. With the last of her endurance, she steered him to it. "You can lie down now."

The sailor folded onto the bed in an ungainly sprawl and promptly clutched a pillow the same way he'd hung on to his beam. Mariah swung his legs onto the mattress, then used her tinderbox to light a lamp. Even though the room hadn't been used for years, the capable Mrs. Beckett had oil in the lamp and a fire laid in the tiny fireplace. The bed wasn't made up, but there would be blankets in the small, battered wardrobe.

After she lit the fire, she tugged at the pillow he was crushing. "You're safe now. *Safe.*" His grip eased and she was able to remove the pillow and examine him.

She patted his shivering body dry with a thin towel from the washstand. His clothing was so tattered that she was able to examine him fairly thoroughly without stripping off the ragged remnants. Some of his garments were charred at the edges. Perhaps a ship's fire drove him to jump into the sea.

He was massively bruised and had cuts and scrapes beyond counting. There were also areas of blistered and scorched flesh, which fit with the charred clothing. Mercifully, the burns weren't severe. He must have hit the water quickly.

She found no major wounds on his limbs and torso. Though some of his injuries had bled, his time in the seawater had washed away the actual blood and nothing seemed to be bleeding now.

She pulled blankets from the wardrobe and wrapped him in multiple layers. Luckily the fire was warming the small room rapidly and he was losing his deathly chill.

Taking the lamp, she made a trip to her room for dry clothing, then descended to the kitchen. While tea water and broth heated, she brought a pitcher of water and a glass back to her patient. He was sleeping. In the soft light, his complexion and his unfashionably long hair were dark. She was no expert on male whiskers, but it looked as if he had at least a couple of days' growth. If he had been in the water that long, he had to be as strong as an ox to have survived.

It was hard to guess his age under the facial bruises, but she thought he was somewhere around thirty. Though not broadly built, he had a well-muscled working man's body, with calloused hands.

She frowned when she noticed the way his hair matted on the left side of his head. Setting down the lamp, she explored with her fingertips and discovered a long, deep gash that oozed traces of blood.

She swore under her breath as she swaddled his head with another towel. Everything she had done so far was common sense, but the head injury looked serious and she didn't know what to do. She must summon Julia Bancroft now rather than wait until morning.

Mariah brushed wet hair from the sailor's face, wondering where he came from. Somewhere in the Mediterranean, perhaps. She was pulling the blankets up when his lids rose, and he stared at her with mesmerizing green eyes.

Chapter Four

After an eternity of cold water, numbness, and despair, he was dragged ashore. Emerging from the water had pulled him from the deathlike trance that had allowed him to survive for so long. Dimly he remembered stumbling along with help, sliding into blackness, and then awaking to . . . perfection.

The woman bending over him seemed more dream than reality, yet the warmth radiating from her was palpable. Her eyes were warm brown and a cloud of golden hair floated around her perfect oval face. She shimmered in the lamplight. Wondering if he'd drowned and gone to some other realm, he raised an unsteady hand to stroke those fine spun strands. They were gossamer silk against his fingers.

"You're safe now." She pulled her long hair back and tied the shining mass in a loose knot at her nape. Her every movement was grace. "Do you speak English?"

He had to think to answer her question. English. Language. Understanding. He licked his dry lips and whispered, "Y . . . yes."

"Good. That will make things easier." She slid an arm under his shoulders and raised him enough to drink from a glass that she held to his lips. He swallowed thirstily, thinking it strange how much he craved water when it had almost killed him.

And humiliating that he was so weak that he couldn't even drink without help.

When he'd had enough, she took the glass away and gently laid him down again. She wore a night robe, and though it covered her thoroughly, her dishabille was deliciously tantalizing. "Such green eyes you have," she observed. "They are striking with your dark complexion."

His eyes were green and the rest of him dark? He shifted his gaze to his right hand and examined it. The skin was medium tan, a half dozen shades darker than her ivory complexion. He realized that he had no idea what he looked like, beyond tan and bruised. Or what he ought to look like.

She continued, "Can you tell me your name?"

He searched his mind and came up with . . . nothing. No name, no place, no past, just as he had no sense of his own body. That had to be *wrong*. Panic surged over him, more terrifying than the cold sea that had nearly drowned him. He was nothing, nobody, torn from his past and thrust into an unknown present. The horror of that echoed through every fiber of his being. Struggling to master his fear, he choked out, "I . . . I don't know."

Seeing his fear, she caught his cold hand between her warm palms. "You've endured a considerable ordeal. After you rest and recover, you will surely remember." She frowned uncertainly.

"Can you have forgotten that I'm your wife, Mariah Clarke?"

"My . . . my *wife?*" He stared, incredulous. How could he possibly forget being wed to a woman like this? But even though he didn't remember their marriage, his fears diminished as he compulsively clenched her hand. "Then . . . I am a most fortunate man."

She smiled warmly. "Rest while I go for tea and broth. I've sent for someone who will know how to treat that blow to your head. With luck, she'll be here soon. By tomorrow, you will likely remember everything about yourself."

He raised unsteady fingers to the ragged gash that ran down the left side of his skull. He had so many aches and bruises that he hadn't noticed any in particular, but now that she mentioned it, his head throbbed like the very devil. "Tea would be . . . welcome."

"I'll only be gone a few minutes," she promised as she whisked away.

He stared at the ceiling after she left. He had a *wife*. He hated that he remembered nothing about that vision of loveliness who had saved his life, nor about being married. It was easy to imagine kissing her, and a good deal more. But of actual memories he had none. It seemed damned unfair.

He spent her absence searching his memory and trying not to knot the sheets with nervous fingers. He recognized objects around him. Bed, blanket,

fire. Pinkness in the sky outside. That would be . . .
dawn. Oddly, a second set of words shadowed the
first. *Palang. Kambal. Aag.* He was quite sure the
words meant the same as the English ones that
came to mind, so he probably knew a different language, though he had no idea what it might be.

But he had no personal memories. Again he
fought the rising fear. The emotion was a
screaming, vulnerable awareness that he was alone
and so helpless that he didn't even know what
might threaten him.

Strangely, deep inside he sensed that this was not
the first time he had been torn away from himself.
Perhaps that was why his fear was so great. But he
could remember nothing about that other situation,
whatever it might be.

He had survived that earlier loss. This time he
had a wife who told him he was safe. Surely she
would look out for him until he was strong enough
to look out for her.

For now, he remembered the most basic fact of
all: that he was male and Mariah Clarke was
female.

Mariah clattered down to the kitchen, knowing she
was blushing beet red. Why on earth had she
blurted out such an outrageous claim? To tell the
poor man she was his wife! The words had just
popped out, almost as if Granny Rose had spoken
for her.

But he had looked so stricken to realize he remembered nothing. Terrified, in fact. When she thought about her fears of being alone in the world, she understood. It was bad enough to be alone, with no known kin and few friends, but at least she knew who she was. To have lost one's very identity . . . She shuddered at the idea.

A bizarre thought struck. She had done the wishing ritual, asking for help. Within the hour, this unusual man was delivered to her, a gift from the sea. She'd even heard her grandmother's voice urging her to run to the shore. And she'd swear it was Granny Rose who spoke the words about her being the man's wife.

Mariah had originally told George Burke she had a husband, to discourage him. Could the sailor, a stranger she could claim as her spouse, be the answer to her wish? Was she being guided by Granny Rose, or simply insane?

Her Sarah self was quite clear: she was insane. But she didn't feel mad. Granny Rose had not been a witch or a seer, but she had been very perceptive and she believed in intuition. If something felt wrong, it probably *was* wrong, even if the reasons were so subtle that it was hard to identify them. Mariah had had a bad feeling about her father leaving for London, and she'd been right about that. Every day she reread the letter from the London solicitor, hoping the words would change, but they never did.

Equally true was that if something felt right, it probably was, if one was thinking clearly. Intuition had led her to the sailor, and intuition told her she would be wise to take advantage of this opportunity to acquire a pretend husband to dismiss George Burke once and for all. It had felt right to offer the sailor the reassurance that he was not alone in the world. She had seen from his expression that her words had dispelled much of his fear.

For his sake, it would be best for him to remember his life. But she remembered a thatcher in her grandmother's village who fell from a roof and cracked his head and never could remember a thing that had happened before that day. He had continued to live a fairly normal life and quickly relearned thatching. His wife had confided to Granny Rose that there were some things she was glad the old boy had forgotten. Perhaps the sailor would end in the same condition.

If he didn't regain his memory, she would eventually have to tell him they weren't wed, but for now, she would not deprive him of that comfort. And if he did recall, she would explain that she said she was his wife so he wouldn't feel so alone, or compelled to leave her care. Those were good reasons. Downright noble, in fact.

Her conscience reconciled, she made a pot of tea, adding lots of sugar to sweeten it. The chicken broth was also hot, so she poured some into a mug, then set everything on a tray. When she entered his room, she said cheerily, "Here you are. Which do you prefer first, tea or chicken broth?"

"Tea, please." He had good manners and was well spoken, too. Mariah guessed he'd had some education and he sounded English, despite his foreign appearance. She stacked two pillows behind him, then poured half a cup of the sweet tea.

He swallowed deeply, then gave a sigh of pleasure. "What did we do before tea was discovered?" He drank the rest more slowly.

"We suffered greatly." She refilled the cup. "Mint tea is nice, but not the same."

"Mariah," he said hesitantly, as if studying how the name felt in his mouth, "what is my name?"

She'd thought about this in the kitchen. "Adam," she said promptly. The name of the first man. It seemed suitable for a male born of the sea with no memory of the past. "Adam Clarke."

"Adam!" His expression lightened with recognition. "Of course."

Surprised, she asked, "You remember that is your name?"

"Not exactly remember," he said slowly. "But it feels right."

"Do you remember anything else?" If he regained his memory quickly, she could abandon the pretense they were married. If that happened, she would ask if he would pose as her husband long enough to get rid of Burke. Her Adam seemed an agreeable man, so perhaps he would cooperate from gratitude.

He shook his head, expression darkening. "No, nothing. Though the name Adam feels right, Clarke feels less familiar. Neutral." His mouth twisted. "Everyone around me will know more about my life than I do."

"Actually, no. I've only lived in Hartley for a couple of months and you've just arrived here, so you are unknown in the neighborhood." He was mostly bare under the blankets, so she tried not to notice what a handsome pair of shoulders he had. She had seen very few bare male shoulders in her life, and the sight was remarkably appealing. Struggling for decorum, she continued, "My father won the manor at cards, which is why we came here as strangers to the region."

"Was it your father whom you sent for help?"

She bit her lip. "I wish it was, but he was killed near London several weeks ago."

"I'm so sorry." With quick sympathy, Adam took her hand. His cool grip was comforting. "It is maddening that I can feel your sense of loss, but not picture his face."

"You were not well acquainted with him." Remembering what she had told Burke, she added, "We are distant cousins who were both already named Clarke."

"So upon marriage, you became Mariah Clarke Clarke," he said, with a glimmer of a smile.

"At least I didn't have to remember to change my signature." She smiled, glad to learn he had a sense of humor, and it had survived his situation.

His gaze caught hers, the green eyes compelling. "Tell me more about myself."

She hesitated, thinking how quickly the situation was getting complicated. "I think it better if you remember on your own. There is much I don't know about your background. We were acquainted only briefly before becoming husband and wife." An amazingly brief time—less than an hour. She continued, "I don't want to plant memories that might turn out to be less than correct."

He looked as if he was about to protest, then exhaled roughly. "That is sensible, I suppose. My mind is so empty that I had best take care how I fill it." He still held her hand, and his thumb stroked her palm gently. It felt entirely too good.

She removed her hand and offered him the broth. "How long were you adrift?"

"It seemed like . . . forever. I remember at least two nights, two dawns. Perhaps more. It all runs together in my mind." He sipped the chicken broth cautiously. "I knew the cold water was deadly, so I slowed my breathing and retreated to a quiet corner of my mind to preserve myself."

"Slowed your breathing and retreated in your mind?" she asked, puzzled.

He looked equally puzzled. "This is not something you do? It seemed very natural to me."

"I've never heard of such a thing, but it seems to have worked." Despite his flawless English, she wondered again if he was a foreigner. Retreating into a corner of one's mind to survive dangerous conditions seemed . . . rather foreign. But it must have worked for him to have survived for so long.

He asked, "Why was I at sea?"

Again thinking of the rapid lies she had offered George Burke, she said, "You had been away on the Continent and were on your way to join me here. You must have been shipwrecked near the end of your journey."

She was relieved when they were interrupted before he could ask more questions. Julia Bancroft entered the room, escorted by Tom Hayes, the groom who had brought Julia to the manor. "I came as soon as I could, Mariah. This is the injured man?"

Julia set down her satchel of medicines and approached the bed. Adam's spurt of energy was gone and he now looked utterly exhausted. Mariah said, "Mrs. Bancroft, meet Adam Clarke."

Adam said in a thin, rasping voice, "My apologies for not rising to greet you, Mrs. Bancroft."

Julia smiled as she bent her dark head over him. "There is a time for gallantry, Mr. Clarke. This isn't it." As Mariah held the lamp close, Julia examined his injured head. "This is a nasty gash."

"I'm not so badly injured, ma'am," Adam protested. "My wife has taken good care of me."

Julia's glance shot to Mariah. Mariah shook her head slightly, wanting to defer questions. Understanding, Julia asked, "Could you find Mr. Clarke a clean nightshirt? The warmest one available."

Mariah nodded and left. After learning of her father's death, she had entered his bedroom and touched his belongings, inhaled his scent, which made her think of safety. Then she had left, weeping, unable to dispose of his possessions. Now she was glad, because his garments could be used by Adam, who was of a similar size and build. She collected a heavy flannel nightshirt and a worn but warm wool banyan that would be useful when Adam was able to rise from his bed.

By the time she returned to the sickroom, Adam was asleep, his face gray with exhaustion. Julia rested her hands on his chest, her eyes distant and her expression intent. When Mariah entered, Julia returned her attention to the room. "I was praying," she said simply. "I thought it couldn't hurt."

Mariah nodded, thinking the man from the sea needed all the help he could get. "How is he doing?"

"Fairly well, all considering. Go to the kitchen and make more tea while Mr. Hayes and I get the nightshirt onto your patient," Julia replied. "I'll talk to you there."

Mariah nodded agreement and headed downstairs. The sky was lightening and soon Mrs.

Beckett and the kitchen maid would be rising. Smothering a yawn, Mariah added coal to the fire and hung a kettle to heat. She also found a loaf of bread and sliced several pieces to toast. By the time Julia arrived, there was tea, toast, and marmalade waiting. As Mariah poured for them, she asked, "What happened to Tom Hayes?"

"He decided he would rather have another hour of sleep than an early breakfast." Julia spread marmalade on her toast and bit in with enthusiasm. After swallowing and taking a sip of tea, she continued, "I don't like to talk about patients within earshot, even if they seem to be asleep. They may hear and understand more than we think."

Mariah set her cup down, her heartbeat accelerating. "Is Adam in danger?"

"He's young and strong and I think he'll recover well," Julia assured her. "But I'm no physician, and I've had no experience with serious head wounds."

"Should I send to Carlisle for a surgeon or physician?"

"You could, but to be honest, I don't know if they would be able to do much more than I have. Head injuries are mysterious. All one can do is wait and see how they heal."

Mariah was inclined to agree. Julia had already cleaned the wound and put salve on it. A surgeon would probably do the same, and charge more for the privilege. "I suppose you're wondering why I never mentioned having a husband."

"I must admit I'm curious. But secrets are something of a specialty of mine." She smiled wryly as she took another piece of toast. "I have enough of my own."

In other words, Julia would not gossip about the strange man and his relationship to the heiress of Hartley Manor. Yet Mariah found that she had a powerful urge to unburden herself. "May I tell you the whole story?"

After Julia nodded, Mariah tersely described the pressure she'd been feeling from George Burke, her impulsive claim of a husband, and the fortuitous arrival of the man from the sea. "I hope that he regains his memory quickly. And that when he does, he'll cooperate in helping me get rid of Burke once and for all."

"But he might not regain his memory, and he is already most attached to you," Julia pointed out. "I think his belief that you are his wife is his anchor in a frightening time. What will you do if he doesn't remember his old life, and he wants to claim his marital rights? Men do tend to want to do that."

Marital rights. The toast suddenly tasted like ashes. "I . . . hadn't thought that far ahead." She imagined those green eyes close to hers, that well-muscled body holding her close, and shivered. But not with revulsion. "If we like each other, I'll whisk him off to Gretna Green and make it official. From what I've seen of my man from the sea, I'd rather have him than George Burke!"

"A total stranger, of unknown family and parentage?" Julia's brows arched. "One who might have a wife and children elsewhere?"

Mariah choked on her tea. "I didn't think of that! How awful for them, believing him dead!"

"We don't know that he has a family, any more than we know that he doesn't. But my guess is that somewhere, people are missing him. It's a rare man who can disappear without anyone being concerned." Julia smiled encouragingly. "There's a good chance this situation will resolve itself within a day or two as your Adam recovers from the shock of his injuries and near drowning. I don't think he could speak so sensibly if his brain injuries were severe enough to permanently wipe out his past."

"That makes sense," Mariah said, relieved. "I shall wait for him to return to himself. And if he doesn't, I'll tell him the truth."

"Don't do that too soon." Julia covered a yawn. Outside, birds were chattering a dawn chorus to start their day. "Though I believe he'll recover, head injuries are chancy and he is in a weakened state. It would be a severe shock if he found that he has neither name nor wife and is adrift in an alien world."

Uneasily Mariah recognized the truth of that. She had impulsively thrown the stranger a lifeline to anchor him. She couldn't suddenly decide to release it now.

Chapter Five

"Mr. Burke is here to see you."

Mariah glanced up from her account books. Rescuing the man from the sea had meant no sleep the night before, and her fatigue made her want to deny that she was at home. But she also wanted to dismiss George Burke permanently, and now she had the opportunity. "He is in the drawing room?"

The maid nodded. "Shall I bring refreshments?"

"No need. Mr. Burke will not be staying long."

Mariah rose from her desk, knowing that she looked less than her best after the long night. All the better for driving Burke away.

She took the back stairs to the ground floor, coming out in the narrow passage that separated the drawing room at the front of the house from Adam's room at the back. She hadn't checked on him in the last hour, so she looked inside. He was sleeping peacefully and there was more color in his face. He stirred a little when the door opened but didn't wake. Julia had said to let him sleep, for rest was the best medicine after his ordeal.

Reassured, Mariah turned and opened the opposite door, which led into the back of the drawing room. She entered to find Burke gazing from a window. He was dressed with his usual dandyish elegance. A good-looking man. A pity he wasn't more likable.

She felt a moment of sympathy for him. The fact that Burke had foolishly gambled the estate away wouldn't dim the pain of his loss. Rather, the contrary.

Her sympathy vanished when he turned and gave her a lazy smile while he studied her with insulting frankness. She frowned. She was used to being admired by men, but the polite ones at least started by looking at her face.

"Mariah." His smile implied greater intimacy than they shared. "How lovely you look today."

Given the circles under her eyes, she assumed that he was either blind or a liar. "You flatter me. I look like a woman who needs a good night's sleep."

She was about to explain that she had been kept up late by her "husband's" return when Burke said with dripping solicitude, "You are carrying too great a burden for a woman. I admire your spirit and determination in attempting to run the estate by yourself, but you need a man to take care of these business matters."

"I do not," she retorted. "I am entirely capable of managing Hartley. And if I do need help, I'll have my husband."

He smiled pityingly. "Isn't it time you gave up that pretense? I know you invented a husband to keep me at a distance because I was fool enough to offer marriage when you were still shocked by the news of your father's death. The time has come for honesty between us."

He stepped close and took her hand, his hand-some face earnest. "Marry me, Mariah. We can drive up to Gretna Green and be married in a day." His voice became caressing. "I should like to take you to London before the Season is over. You deserve a London Season, and how better to see the delights of the city than with a devoted husband by your side?"

She was tempted to laugh. Or possibly throw something at him. "I doubt you have it in you to be a devoted husband! Even if you do, just last night my husband returned." She tried unsuccessfully to remove her hand from his clasp. "And I have *not* given you leave to call me by my given name. I am Mrs. Clarke."

After a startled moment, he laughed outright. "You are certainly persistent in your claims! Where is this husband of yours? I should be delighted to meet him."

Exasperated by his arrogance, she managed to jerk her hand free. "You can't see him just now. He is unwell and resting from a difficult journey."

"And I'm the Sheik of Araby." His expression changed, and she saw the first genuine feeling he'd shown today: lust. "I do adore you, Mariah. For your sake, I think I could even become a devoted husband."

Before she could protest, he pulled her into his arms and crushed his mouth into hers. He tasted of brandy. At this hour of the morning! No wonder he was behaving so badly. She wrenched her head to one side and cried, "Let go of me!"

He ignored her protest, saying thickly, "We are both beautiful and a little wicked. We were meant to be together, Mariah!" He forced another kiss on her.

She tried to break away but only managed to pull them both off balance. They tumbled onto his grandmother's small table, which fell over with a crash, but he kept her trapped in his embrace.

Mariah had been kissed by amorous and slightly foxed gentlemen before, but she had never felt real fear because her father had always been close. Now she was unprotected and no match for Burke's strength. There were no male servants in the house, only the housekeeper and two maids, and they were unlikely to be within earshot.

Furious at her helplessness, she kicked him in the ankle, but her soft slipper didn't even make him flinch. Toes hurting, she raised her foot to stamp down.

Before she could, Burke released her with such abruptness that she almost fell. No, he hadn't released her; he was being wrenched away—by Adam.

Her sailor loomed over her, barefoot, head bandaged, and wrapped in her father's worn banyan. As she watched in shock, he twisted and pitched Burke across the room. Her assailant slammed into the sofa and crumpled to the floor, expression incredulous.

Adam caught her elbow and steadied her, his eyes dark with concern. "Are you all right?"

She nodded shakily. "Right enough."

"My poor darling." He wrapped his left arm around her shoulders, then turned to her assailant. Though not as tall as Burke, Adam radiated an authority that could make a man twice his size cower. "Do not ever touch my wife again," he said in a voice like flint. "Do I make myself clear?"

"I . . . I didn't think Mariah was really married," Burke stammered.

"You will not use my wife's given name," Adam said coldly, his arm tightening around her shoulders. "She is *Mrs. Clarke* to you, and you owe her an apology. Not only did you assault her, but you insulted her honesty by refusing to believe the truth."

Mariah winced inwardly. In fact, Burke had read her lies accurately. But that gave him no right to maul her!

Burke struggled to his feet, no longer a confident dandy. "I . . . I thought it was a kind of game she was playing. Everyone in Hartley thought she was single. The first time she mentioned a husband, she seemed to be pulling the idea out of the air. I was sure that after she absorbed the news of her father's death, she would see the advantages of marrying me and accept my offer."

"He wants his property back," Mariah explained. "George Burke is the former owner who lost this estate to my father in a card game. Saints preserve any woman fool enough to entrust her future to him!" She took a deep breath. "But I don't think he intended harm today. He was just . . . thoughtless and carried away."

Burke scowled, his expression a blend of anger and shame. "I apologize for my behavior, Mrs. Clarke. My admiration and hopes led me to misread the situation." He retrieved his hat. "I shall leave Hartley today. There is nothing more for me here."

There was no mention of a lawsuit. Maybe that had always been an empty threat, now dissipated by the presence of a living, breathing husband who was willing to defend Mariah and her rights. Hoping there would be no more strife, Mariah said quietly, "I wish you well in the future, Mr. Burke."

He acknowledged her with a jerky nod of his head, then left. She exhaled roughly. "I feel sorry for the man, but I shan't miss him." She glanced up at Adam, who was looking exhausted now that the crisis was past. "You heard us arguing?"

"Raised voices and crashing furniture have a way of capturing one's attention."

Since he was beginning to sag heavily on her shoulder, she steered him to the sofa. "Sit down. I'm amazed that you had the strength to walk in here, much less save me from George Burke."

Adam smiled at her with a sweet intimacy that made her catch her breath. "I couldn't let that fellow hurt my wife."

"I am very glad you came to investigate." She was ashamed of the quaver in her voice. "How did you manage to toss a great lummox like Burke across the room?"

Adam frowned uneasily. "I . . . just knew. There are ways of using a man's weight and size against him. Not that I thought about that. I just saw you fighting him and acted from instinct."

So whatever his past, he knew how to fight. That went with his workman's hands, but not his cultured speech. He was an enigma. And he believed completely in their marriage. Knowing he had defended her honesty to Burke made her feel wicked. "I'll help you back to your room when you can walk again. You're recovering splendidly, but Julia won't like it if I let you overexert yourself."

"I should like to sit up for a bit." He pulled her down next to him on the sofa and put an arm around her, drawing her close. "I have missed you."

Though she knew it was unwise, she relaxed into him, grateful for his strength and protectiveness. "Do you remember being with me?" she asked warily.

"I'm afraid not." He rested his cheek against the top of her head. "But holding you feels so right that I know I must have been missing you."

Her deception was getting more dangerous by the second, yet she couldn't bring herself to move away from him. She, too, felt right when they were close. "You're feeling better, I gather."

"My head still hurts and right now I'm too weak to swing a cat, but I feel much better than when I was hanging on to wreckage at sea." His warm hand stroked down her arm. "Though it might be best not to talk about my past, what about your father? How did he come to win the estate from the unpleasant Mr. Burke?"

"He supported us by traveling from one house party to the next. He was a charming guest, a good sportsman, never a burden. His card playing was good enough to keep us comfortable," she explained. "Mr. Burke is *not* a good card player."

"Was your father from around here?" Adam halted. "Where am I, anyhow?"

"Cumberland. The extreme northwest of England, just south of Scotland. Does that make sense to you?"

He frowned and with his free index finger began to trace a shape on the fabric of his banyan where it lay across his knee. Mariah saw that it was the rough outline of Britain. "Cumberland is here, yes?" He touched a spot on the northwest coast.

"Exactly. So you remember Britain." She glanced up at him. "Do you know if you're British?"

He frowned again. "In my mind, I hear yes and no at the same time."

"It's such an interesting mixture of things that you know and you don't know," she said thoughtfully. "Surely you will recall everything soon."

And the sooner, the better. It struck her that with Burke leaving Hartley, she could now tell "Adam" the truth—that they were strangers, not spouses.

But she couldn't do that to him. Not when he looked at her as if she was the center of his universe. She could not bear to tell him that he was alone, with no name or friends or family. His help had freed her from Burke. Now she must aid him while he was vulnerable.

"Tell me about yourself," he said. "Where were you born? Where is your family from? Now that your father is gone, do you have relations nearby?"

She smiled ruefully. "I know little more about my family roots than you do. My father and I were close. I knew him better than anyone in my life. Yet he would never talk about his past. I don't know where he was born, who his family was, how he and my mother met, or even how she died."

"So you have had two men of mystery in your life." Adam's mouth quirked up. "Why wouldn't your father talk about his past?"

"I think that he was born into a gentry family, and that he was cut off because of bad behavior," she said candidly. "He was barely twenty when I was born, and he lost my mother when I was about two. I remember nothing about her. After that, I lived with my grandmother in Shropshire. My father would visit several times a year. We had the loveliest Christmas holidays. Then he'd go off and join some hunting party." She sighed, remembering how hard it was to say good-bye whenever he left.

"His family was from Shropshire?"

"Though Granny Rose lived there, I never heard anything to suggest that we were related to anyone in the neighborhood." She didn't intend to say more about her grandmother but changed her mind. The fact that she had told Adam a big lie made it seem essential for her to be truthful in everything else. "Granny Rose was half gypsy. She was my great-grandmother, actually. The village midwife and healer."

Mariah watched to see if Adam was shocked to hear that she had gypsy blood, but he seemed only interested. "I can hear in your voice how special she was to you. Did you get your brown eyes from her?"

Mariah nodded. "She said the gypsy blood made the women in our family irresistible. I think the blood has thinned in me, but Granny Rose was beautiful till the day she died, and her daughter was lovely enough to win the heart of a gentleman."

"The blood has not thinned in you," Adam said firmly.

His gaze was so warm that Mariah blushed and looked away. "I was eighteen when Granny Rose died, and after that I traveled with my father." Her lips thinned. "Burke accused him of cheating to win Hartley, but that's a lie. Papa never cheated. He didn't need to. Burke threatened to sue me to regain the property, using cheating as his grounds. If I'd have him for a husband, no lawsuit."

"Outrageous that he talked so to a married woman! I should have thrown him into another wall before he left."

"You weren't here and I didn't really discuss my situation with anyone." She laughed a little. "Not talking about the past seems to run in my family, so I can understand why he didn't believe me. But it was maddening that he thought I needed a man to take charge of Hartley Manor. Though I don't know much about agriculture, I can learn, and I'm far better with the account books than George Burke ever was."

"When I'm a little stronger, I can take over managing the farm," Adam said.

She stared at him, startled by his calm presumption that he would take over management of *her* estate. But he thought he was her husband, and in English law, a wife's property belonged to her husband. Still another drawback to having him think they were married.

Misunderstanding her expression, Adam said, "I believe that I actually do have farming experience, though I can remember no particulars." He frowned. "It just feels like something I understand."

"More mysteries." She pulled herself together. "I

expect you to remember everything soon, but if not, when you're better I'll show you around Hartley Manor and we can test your understanding."

He stood, swaying with the effort. "I think I can make it back to the bedroom with your help. I promise to revive if you need any other unruly chaps tossed."

She laughed and slid a supportive arm around his waist. She liked touching him, liked the way his arm came easily around her shoulders. They returned to his room and she helped him out of the banyan and into the bed. As she pulled the covers over him, he murmured, "Could I persuade you to lie down with me? Just till I fall asleep."

His suggestion was equally shocking and appealing—and wouldn't have been shocking if they truly were wed. The deciding factor was her fatigue. "That sounds like a lovely idea." Carefully she stretched out on top of the covers on his right side so he wouldn't injure his head if he rolled toward her. She made a mental note to check if the bandage needed changing later.

For now, she rested. Though she was on the out-side of the blankets and he was underneath, it still felt deliciously wicked to cuddle full length against him. She could get fond of this. . . .

Despite his fatigue, Adam was wakeful. He'd had enough sleep, and he would much rather savor the feel of his wife in his arms. She had fallen asleep immediately with her head on his shoulder, tired by her long night and difficult interview with that dolt Burke. Thank God Adam had been able to summon enough energy to protect her.

Most of her luminous blond hair was pinned back demurely, but the strands that had escaped were silky to his touch. The memory of her glowing in the lamplight when he woke the night before was enough to make him wish he was strong enough to be a proper husband.

It would be a great waste if his memory didn't return. He wanted to recall every detail of how they met. Their first kiss. Their wedding night.

He even wanted to remember the pain of having to leave her. For that matter, where had he been and why had he left?

He released his breath in a sigh. All in good time. He bent and kissed the top of her head. If his memory never returned, they would just have to make new memories.

Chapter Six

Glasgow

Randall gazed out the post chaise window as they rattled through the dense and teeming city. "I didn't know Glasgow was so large."

"It's not so big as London, but the city is home to some of the greatest merchants and manufacturers in Britain," Kirkland said. "And busier than a hive of hungry bees."

"Your accent is sliding toward Scottishness," Masterson said with interest.

" 'Tis only natural," Kirkland said with deliberate broadness. "But if you think I sound Scottish, wait till you hear the average Glaswegian. You won't even know they're speaking English."

Randall smiled a little at the byplay between his friends. On the whole, it had been a silent trip up from London. They'd hired the post chaise and set off to Scotland at the fastest speed possible. Though being cooped up in the carriage with minimal halts had been hell on his wounded leg, they'd made good time. But if it hadn't been for the wound, he would be back on the Peninsula now and he would have learned of Ashton's death weeks after the fact.

He had lost friends on campaign, both in battle and to vicious fevers like the one that had brought Will Masterson home to recover. But friends who were back in England were supposed to be safe. They weren't supposed to be getting themselves blown up in bloody bedamned steam-powered ships.

As they rumbled over the Clyde River on a vast, crowded bridge, he thought what a relief it was to finally be here so they could *do* something. "Do we know where Ashton's shipyard is?"

"Somewhere in Port Glasgow, west of the city

proper," Kirkland replied. "It won't be hard to find the right yard. Glasgow has more than its share of engineers, and projects like Ashton's would be discussed at every tavern and coffee-house in the city."

Masterson remarked, "You seem to know Glasgow well."

Kirkland shrugged. "I spent a fair amount of time here as a boy. My unfortunate fondness for my mercantile relations helped get me sentenced to the Westerfield Academy. For which I am eternally grateful."

Masterson chuckled. "I should love to know all the reasons that students ended up in Lady Agnes's hands."

"The ways a boy can deviate from civilized standards are legion," Randall said dryly. "And we discovered most of them. How long until we get to Port Glasgow?"

"At least an hour." Kirkland studied Randall narrowly. "It will be near dinnertime by then. I suggest we book rooms at an inn and get a good night's rest before we start searching for information about Ashton and the *Enterprise*."

Randall nodded. His impatient mind wanted to start investigating immediately, but his abused body needed a rest. The time wouldn't be wasted. If he knew Kirkland, a master of intelligence gathering, by morning they'd know where to start their search.

• • •

Randall's guess was right. When he met his friends in the taproom of the Crown and Sail to break their fast the next morning, Kirkland had the address of the chief engineer of the *Enterprise*. Archibald Mactavish lived in a pleasant house on a quiet street not far from the bustling waterfront. The men were admitted by a shy little maid who took their cards, then whisked off to tell the mistress of the house that a trio of gentlemen were calling.

Mrs. Mactavish was a tired-looking young woman with a toddler in tow, and she was not pleased to have three hulking gentlemen in her sitting room. "I've no time for entertaining," she said bluntly. "Are you here to see my husband?"

"If we can," Kirkland spoke, a Scottish lilt clear in his speech. "We're friends of the Duke of Ashton, and we'd like to learn more about the accident that took his life."

"It wasn't Mactavish's fault!" she said vehemently.

Masterson, ever tactful, said, "We are not looking to cast blame, Mrs. Mactavish, only to understand what happened. We all went to school with Ashton, and he was very dear to us. We'd like to know more, if your husband is well enough to talk."

"Very well," she said reluctantly. "I'll see if he's willing."

She left the room with the child, returning alone several minutes later. "He'll speak with you. But mind you don't tire him. He was lucky to survive."

She led the way upstairs to a bedroom that looked out over the waters of the Clyde. Mactavish was a lean man in early middle age with thinning red hair, a large collection of bruises and bandages, and an expression of deep misery. His wife propped him to a sitting position with pillows, then consulted the visitors' cards. "Your visitors are Kirkland, Masterson, and Randall. I'm not sure which is which."

Kirkland, taking the lead again, said, "I'm Kirkland." He stepped forward to offer his hand, then stopped. Mactavish's right arm ended in a bandaged stump.

The other man's mouth twisted bitterly as he raised the stump. "Aye, 'tis not much of an engineer I am now. What do you want to know?"

"How and where Ashton died," Randall said before the silence could get too awkward. "We're hoping that if we can determine the site of the explosion, we might find his body to take him home for burial."

Mactavish's expression softened. "That's what friends do, though the sea might not cooperate. He was a good man, Ashton. Ye would hardly know he was a duke."

"He will be missed," Masterson said quietly. "Do you know what caused the explosion? Steam engines are tricky brutes, but in his letters, Ashton indicated that the project was going well."

"Aye, it was." Mactavish made a fist of his left hand and struck the bed angrily. "We had a good long run all the way down into the Firth of Clyde. The engine was singing like a nightingale."

"That's quite a distance," Kirkland said, startled.

"It was indeed. With enough fuel, we could have sailed her all the way to Liverpool. We had just turned back when the boiler exploded. It was like being struck by lightning."

"Could that have happened?" Masterson asked. "If there was a storm . . ."

The engineer shook his head. "It was a bit misty, but there were no storms."

"Where was Ashton when the boiler went up?" This time Kirkland asked the question. "Were you with him?"

"I was up on the deck trying to reckon how far we'd come. I had just decided we were near Arran Island when the boiler blew. I was thrown into the water." Mactavish looked at the ugly stump. "I don't even remember how my hand was crushed. Lucky for me, Davy, the pilot, is an ace swimmer. He caught hold and got me to shore on Arran, which wasn't far."

"Did you see Ashton in the water?" Kirkland again.

"Saw not hide nor hair of him," the engineer replied. "Likely he was below decks in the engine room. He spent a good bit of his time there." He touched his bandaged head. "My wits were scrambled and I don't recall seeing anyone but Davy. I was surprised later to learn that two of the others also made it to shore."

Randall geared himself up to ask the hardest question. "Have you heard of any bodies washing ashore in that area?"

"There are so many islands that a body could end up in a thousand places and never be found," Mactavish said. "But my best guess is that Ashton's body was trapped in the wreckage of the ship."

It sounded likely. Randall asked, "How many casualties were there altogether?"

"Four, including Ashton. One body washed ashore near Troon, the mainland opposite Arran." Mactavish sighed heavily. "So far as I know, the others are still lost."

And might never be found. Randall went back to what the engineer said earlier. "Since the *Enterprise* was close to shore, is there any chance of salvaging the wreckage?"

Mactavish looked thoughtful. " 'Tis possible. I'd be right interested to find out why the engine exploded."

"We'd need a salvage ship with a good strong crane and an experienced crew," Masterson said. "Do you know who might be capable of a job like this?"

"Jamie Bogle in Greenock is the man to see. He's got the best salvage equipment in Scotland." A spark came into Mactavish's eyes. "I should like to see the salvage."

"That could be arranged." Kirkland regarded Mactavish narrowly. "If you'll be looking for a new job, my Uncle Dunlop has a shipyard and is looking for engineers with steamship experience."

"You're nephew to George Dunlop?" Mactavish looked startled, and his wife, sitting quietly to one side, sucked in her breath. They must be worrying about money now that Mactavish's job had blown up, leaving him crippled. The engineer glanced at the stump where his right hand used to be. "I . . . I canna be doing the work I did before."

"Hands can be hired. My uncle is interested in a man's mind and experience. I'll let him know that he might hear from you." Kirkland reached inside his coat for a small notebook. "Now, what are the names of the other survivors, and do you know where they're to be found?"

By the time they left, Mrs. Mactavish was happy enough with her visitors to have served them tea and cakes. Back in the carriage, Randall asked, "Is your Uncle Dunlop really looking for engineers with steamboat experience?"

"If he isn't, he will be," Kirkland replied. "He became one of the best shipbuilders in Britain by hiring good men. He'll be happy to have this one."

Randall settled back in his seat. They might not be much closer to finding Ashton, but at least someone had benefited today.

Chapter Seven

He was a boy roughhousing with other boys. "See, this is how you throw someone." He demonstrated on a blond lad, using the methods he'd been taught to toss his opponent onto a bed.

The blond boy was first shocked, then gleeful. "Show me how to do that!" he whooped.

"Me too, me too!" echoed from the others in the room. He had been pleased to demonstrate, knowing that his fighting skills not only were fun and useful, but earned him respect.

A tall, forceful woman entered the room as two of the boys were flying through the air at the hands of two others. Instant silence except for the flopping of small bodies onto mattresses.

She surveyed the scene, and he could have sworn he saw amusement in her eyes. "I see I shall have to set you lads to playing ball games before you kill each other from an excess of energy. You'll have to play with the village boys, though, because there aren't enough of you in the school for a proper game of football or cricket."

A dark-haired boy with darker eyes said, "We'll be better. Blood will tell, my father says."

"Not on an athletic field," the woman said, unimpressed. "It will do you good to be defeated by boys with more skill than breeding." Her stern gaze went to each of them in turn. "Time you got

some sleep, and no breaking of the furniture!"

They all nodded solemnly, then broke into giggles after the woman was safely away. There was no more tossing, though. The broad, cheerful-looking boy with brown hair brought out a tin full of ginger biscuits, which they shared as they sprawled on the beds and talked. Some talked more than others.

He couldn't remember names, or any of the conversation. But he felt the good will and affection that flowed among them.

Friends. He had friends.

Adam awoke early, smiling with pleasure at the lingering remnants of the dream. A cautious stretch confirmed that the bruises and sore muscles hadn't yet healed, but overall, he felt very well. He prodded his memory, wondering if that dream had been a piece of his past, or just a dream, inspired by his confrontation with George Burke.

His earliest real memories were still of being in the water, drifting ever closer to death. He recalled nothing before that, though the events since Mariah pulled him ashore were clear.

Clearest of all was his fear when she was assaulted by her would-be suitor. He still wasn't sure where he'd found the strength to heave Burke across the room. But he knew that if necessary, he would have smashed through locked doors to get to Mariah.

Most vivid of all was the peace he felt when he and his wife lay down to rest after Burke departed. She had left him after an hour or two, with a gentle touch to his hair. Perhaps a kiss? He'd like to think so.

He had slept for most of a day since, with occasional periods of waking, during which he ate, drank, and used the chamber pot. He also hazily remembered a visit from Mrs. Bancroft, who had changed his bandage and pronounced that he was doing well.

Now he was fully awake and no longer felt like an invalid. He swung from the bed and got to his feet. He swayed unsteadily for a moment, then managed to walk to the washstand without incident. He grimaced when he saw his reflection in the small mirror hanging above the basin. He looked like a proper ruffian. His chin was covered with dark stubble, bruises were turning from purple to unpleasant shades of green and yellow, and the bandage around his head had a rakish tilt.

He tested the beard thoughtfully, wondering how many days' growth it was. Impossible to tell without knowing how fast his whiskers grew, but he suspected they were quite vigorous. After washing his face, he searched for a razor, without success. He'd ask Mariah for one.

Without conscious thought, he folded down to sit on the worn carpet on crossed legs. Resting his hands palm up on his knees, he closed his eyes and inhaled deeply. He had already fallen into a rhythm of slow breathing before he really thought about what he was doing.

Clearly, sitting like this was something he did regularly, but he was quite sure that the people around him would think such behavior odd. So what was he doing?

Meditating. The word snapped into his mind. With the ease of long practice, he stilled his thoughts and brought his awareness to the center of his being. Despite the dark curtain across his past, he was alive and well and safe. For now, that was enough.

A few minutes of quietness left him feeling focused and ready for whatever might come. He suspected that he meditated every morning after washing up. The water splashed on his face must have triggered a well-established pattern. As he stood, he wondered what other habit patterns would appear.

In the absence of memory, intuition must be his best guide. Already there had been times when a particular subject had *felt* familiar. He was sure he knew something about agriculture. What else did he know?

Horses. He was quite sure he knew about horses.

Ready to explore, he investigated the small wardrobe and found a variety of clothing, worn but still serviceable. Not his, he thought; he would make different choices of color and fabric. The garments were well cut and well made, but they reflected a sensibility not his own. Mariah must have brought the clothing while he slept.

Unless his tastes had changed along with his memory vanishing. A disquieting thought. He preferred to believe that he was the same man he had always been even if his memories were temporarily unavailable. He needed to believe in something.

He believed that he was a lucky man to have won a wife like Mariah.

Warmed by the thought, he dressed in clothes suitable for the country. The process confirmed that the garments weren't his. He was a little taller, a little leaner in the waist, and the coat and boots had shaped themselves to a different body. But overall, the fit was decent. Much better than the rags he'd been rescued in.

He guessed that the garments were his father-in-law's. He tried to visualize Mariah's father and came up with a male version of her, with blond hair and warm brown eyes. Invention, not memory. Of the real Charles Clarke, he found nothing.

Curious to explore the home he'd never seen, he left his room. Soon the household would be stirring, but all was quiet as he made his way outside. The manor house had a lovely view west to the Irish Sea, with distant islets and perhaps a mainland peninsula. Sunsets must be memorable.

He found a lane that led from the manor to the

shore and walked down to a thin crescent of sand and shingle. This had to be the way they'd come after Mariah had pulled him from the sea. The distance seemed short now. The other night, it had been endless.

He inhaled the salty air, waves lapping within a yard of his feet. Was he a sailor, a man of the sea? He wasn't sure. He knew the sea well, loved being near the water even now, after he'd nearly died in those dark depths. But he didn't have the sense that his life was built around the sea, which would be the case if he was a sea captain.

Now why did he automatically think he'd be a captain? He suspected that he was used to giving orders.

As he climbed the lane back to the house, he found himself breathing hard and his limbs trembling. Though his mind was alert, his body hadn't fully recovered from its ordeal.

Rather than return to the house, he headed to the outbuildings beyond. A small paddock adjacent to the stables contained several horses. One, a bright-eyed blood bay, trotted toward him enthusiastically.

He smiled and quickened his step. Horses were definitely a subject he knew.

On the way downstairs for breakfast, Mariah stopped by Adam's room to see how he was doing. Her heart jumped when she tapped on the door and looked inside to find the room empty. What if he had wandered off during the night and become lost? What if he'd been drawn down to the sea again and been swept away by the tide?

She told herself not to be an idiot. Adam had been quite rational in the intervals when he was awake, so likely he'd risen early and decided he was well enough to leave his bed. A check of the wardrobe proved that some of her father's clothing was missing.

Hoping Adam had gone no farther than the kitchen, she headed there and found Mrs. Beckett baking oatmeal scones flavored with dried currants. Mariah took one, so hot it scorched her fingers. As she buttered it, she said, "Mr. Clarke is up and about. Has he made his way down here?"

"Not yet." The cook eyed her severely. "You never mentioned that you had a husband."

"I'd seen so little of him that I didn't feel very married," Mariah said, her conscience nagging. Horrible how one lie begat a whole swamp of lies. "We're going to have to get acquainted all over again." She bit into her scone. "Delicious!"

She suspected that Mrs. Beckett had questions about this suddenly revealed marriage, but the older woman didn't pursue the matter. "What does Mr. Clarke like to eat? If he's up and about now, he'll be ready for a proper meal."

"Light food would be best today," Mariah said, since she hadn't the faintest idea what Adam's tastes were. "Perhaps a hearty soup and a bit of fish for dinner." She scooped up two more scones. "I'll see if he's outside."

"If you find him, I'll make a nice herb omelet for his breakfast."

"I'd like one of those, too." Mariah kissed the cook's cheek as she headed for the door. "Mrs. Beckett, you are a treasure!"

The older woman chuckled. "I am indeed, and don't you forget it."

Outside, Mariah scanned the slope down to the sea, but didn't see Adam. She turned to the stables, scones in hand. In her experience, it was a rare man who wasn't drawn to the nearest horses, so the stables were her best guess. Hartley Manor had the usual workhorses, plus two excellent riding horses that her father had won at cards.

She was taking another bite from one of the scones when her father rode around the corner of the stable.

She cried out and pressed her hands to her mouth, the scones tumbling to the grass as she almost fainted from shock.

Adam catapulted from the horse and darted toward her, concern in his vivid green eyes. "Mariah, what's wrong?"

Adam. Not her father—Adam. Shaking, she choked out, "I . . . I thought you were my father. You were wearing his clothing, riding his horse, Grand Turk. For a moment, I was sure you were he."

As Grand Turk ate her partial scone from the ground, Adam enveloped her in his arms. There was a faint scent of her father in his garments, but the embrace was definitely Adam.

"My poor darling," he said softly. "You've had a very bad few weeks. I'm sorry that I startled you so."

She burrowed against his chest, painfully grateful for his support. "I . . . I still haven't quite accepted that Papa is gone," she explained. "If I had seen him dead, it would be different, but hearing a report isn't the same."

As Adam stroked her hair, she realized there was something unfamiliar in the way he held her. The embrace wasn't lust, and it was more than the comfort of a friend. It was . . . intimacy? Adam thought of himself as her husband, and he was acting with a protective tenderness that took for granted the fact that he had a right to hold her.

The thought was as disturbing as his touch was pleasant. He moved so naturally into the space of a husband that she had to wonder if he really did have a wife somewhere. A wife who was as desperate to learn his fate as Mariah was desperate to be truly certain what had happened to her father.

Shielding her thoughts, she moved away from him. He scooped up the other scones before Turk could eat them. The scones were still warm as he offered her one. "How did you learn of your father's death? Is there a chance the report was wrong?"

"I heard the news from George Burke." Seeing Adam's expression, she smiled humorlessly. "No, he's not a reliable source, but he had the ring my father wore all the time. It was convincing."

"Having met the man, it wouldn't surprise me to hear that he stole the ring," Adam said before biting into his scone.

"He's probably capable of that, but soon after I received a letter from our London solicitor confirming Papa's death." She bit hard into her scone, chewed thoughtfully, then said, "The most convincing proof is that I haven't heard from my father in so long. He had been writing me several times a week. Then . . . nothing. He simply wouldn't stop writing like that if he were well." She drew a shuddering breath. "I do believe he's dead, yet it seemed perfectly natural that he come riding toward me on Turk."

Adam ate the last of his scone. "I think it's natural to hope against hope that a mistake has been made. That tragedy can't strike *us*."

"Do you know that from experience, or are you just wise?"

He looked thoughtful. "I don't know, but I wouldn't gamble that I possess great natural wisdom."

She chuckled. If Granny Rose had sent a faux husband, she had picked one with a sense of humor. "Do you like Grand Turk? My father said he was the best horse he'd ever owned. He won him at cards, of course."

Adam's face lit up. "He's splendid. Beautiful paces, and spirited without malice. The chestnut mare is also very fine. Another prize at the gaming table?"

"Yes. She's my mount, Hazelnut. Hazel for short." Mariah studied Adam, who looked like a proper country gentleman in her father's clothing, but his face was drawn. "I didn't expect to find you on horseback. Riding wasn't too much for you?"

"My strength is not yet back to normal," he admitted, "but I really wanted to be on a horse again. Perhaps we can take that ride over the estate today?"

"Later, if you think you're ready, but now Mrs. Beckett would like to feed us both breakfast. Are you ready for an omelet?"

"Definitely!"

He took her arm and they turned to the house. He liked to touch. Again she wondered if he was demonstrating the ease of a married man who was used to having a woman of his own to touch whenever he wanted.

The sooner her gift from the sea recovered his memory, the better for them all.

After an excellent breakfast, Adam withdrew to his bedroom to rest again. In early afternoon, Mariah tiptoed into his bedroom and found him sprawled across the bed on his back. He'd peeled off his boots and coat but still wore his shirt and breeches. He was a fine figure of a man who fulfilled the gentlemanly ideal of fit, well-proportioned elegance. Was he a gentleman by birth? She wasn't sure, but he had become one.

Thinking she'd let him sleep if he didn't wake easily, she whispered, "Adam? How are you feeling?"

He woke and gave her a smile that made her feel like the most special woman in the world. "I could manage a ride around the estate."

She studied him, his visible bruises reminding her of all the ones that weren't visible. He had taken quite a beating. "Let's wait till tomorrow for the tour. Better not push yourself too hard."

"Then I need to find a different physical activity." He caught her hand and tugged her down so that she was alongside him on the bed. Gaze intense, he said, "I wish I remembered our first kiss. I shall have to start all over."

Before she had fully grasped his intent, he drew her down and kissed her. His mouth was firm and warm, his tongue gentle as it parted her lips.

Sensation flooded through her, scrambling her wits and judgment. She had been kissed by earnest young men, and more than once had fought off drunks like Burke, but she'd never experienced a kiss like this. She felt his wonder and delight, as if they were new lovers, yet she also sensed commitment and his belief that they had a history. That they belonged to each other.

She gasped as his caressing hands moved down her back, honoring every curve and hollow. Where their bodies touched, she burned. She wanted to melt into him, kiss until they were both senseless.

His right hand slid under her gown and moved up her bare thigh, as shocking as it was seductive. She jerked away from his embrace, her heart pounding. Somewhere inside, her Sarah self was saying, "This is your own fault."

Mariah couldn't deny it. If they continued on this path, she would lose her virginity and possibly entice Adam into adultery. She should run screaming from this impossible situation.

He stared up at her flushed face, puzzled and a little hurt. "What's wrong, Mariah?"

Briefly she thought of confessing, but she couldn't bear the thought of cutting him loose from what little certainty he had. She struggled for an answer that would put more distance between them while also having some honesty.

"I'm sorry, Adam." She sat up on the edge of the bed, unable to think clearly in his arms. "This is too . . . too sudden for me. We've had so little time together, and now I am a stranger to you."

"A beloved stranger," he said quietly. "And surely I'm not a stranger to you. Or have I changed greatly?"

She shivered, wondering if his feelings were for his real wife and Mariah was merely a convenient substitute. Remembering what she'd said to Mrs. Beckett, she said, "It's not that you have changed, but that the situation itself is so strange. Will you court me as if we just met? We can discover each other anew." She took his hand. "Your memory could return at any time, of course, and that will simplify everything. But until that happens, can we begin again?"

He hesitated, and she guessed that he would prefer to get to know her in a more biblical way. But then he smiled and raised their joined hands, kissing her fingertips. "What a wise idea. Miss Clarke, you are the loveliest creature I have ever met. Will you join me for a walk in the garden?"

"I should like that very much, Mr. Clarke," she said with relief. "We can admire the daffodils and each other."

He laughed and swung his legs to the floor. He reached for his boots. "I hope you are enthralled by bruises and whiskers. I'm not sure myself what I look like."

"You are altogether lovely," she said firmly. And that was most certainly the truth.

Chapter Eight

By the time Adam had pulled on his boots and coat to go outside, Mariah reappeared with a delightfully frivolous bonnet decorated with silk flowers, and a shabby blue shawl. He offered her his arm. "You look enchanting, Miss Clarke."

She batted her eyelashes outrageously as she took his arm. "How kind of you, sir. If you're very, very good, I may eventually allow you to use my proper name."

He grinned as he held the door open for her to leave the house. "If it wouldn't make you feel fast, you may call me Adam."

"I would never do anything fast, Mr. Clarke," she said firmly. "I am a most properly brought up young lady, I'll have you know."

"No one could possibly think otherwise," he assured her. He'd been disappointed—*very* disappointed—that she had been unwilling to let him make love to her, but now he realized that she was right. They needed courting time to become reacquainted, to rebuild a foundation of affection and companionship. Desire was a fine thing in marriage, but there needed to be more, especially for a woman confronted by a husband who didn't remember her.

Not only were they reacquainting themselves, but the make-believe was a delicious game, better than a real game, because the end, their marriage bed, was foreordained. He wished he could remember how her elegantly curved form looked uncluttered by clothing. It was maddening to know that they had been lovers, yet not be able to summon exact memories of her body. Or the taste and feel of her.

Outside the house, she guided him to the left, the opposite side of the manor house from the stables and other farm buildings. He savored the light warmth of her hand resting on his arm, the sweetly astringent tang of lavender that wafted from her clothing. "I know nothing of fashion, but your delightful bonnet looks like it ought to be fashionable."

"Thank you, sir." She dropped her exaggerated demureness and chuckled. "I've redone this straw bonnet over and over again, so it's not particularly fashionable. There was seldom money to spare, so I became very good at refreshing gowns and hats with lace or ribbons or flowers."

Were all genteel young ladies willing to admit a shortage of funds, or was her directness because they were married? Whatever the reason, her bluntness was refreshing. "Your shawl seems less likely to be accused of being fashionable."

She pulled the worn blue garment closer. "Granny Rose knit this for me one Christmas. Whenever I wear it, I can feel her arms around me, so I wear it a great deal."

Though her tone was light, he heard the loneliness underneath the words. She'd led an unusual life that had little in common with most well-brought-up young ladies. "Was it hard to be always traveling from one place to another, with no real roots? How did you amuse yourself? I suspect that in some households, the women resented having a girl as pretty as you around."

She made a face. "Clever of you to realize that. Everyone enjoyed my father's presence, since he was such good company. But women often thought I was looking to marry their sons, and a penniless bride would never do."

He voiced a thought that had been troubling him. "So you chose a penniless husband? Was I unable to provide a decent home for you?"

She frowned and looked away, as if unsure how to answer. "You had intelligence and prospects. I was not concerned for our future. You had to leave shortly after we married so it made sense that I stay with my father until you returned." She made a gesture that included the manor. "Then Hartley happened."

"How long were we separated?"

"It seemed like forever."

"Why did I have to leave you? What was my occupation?"

"You were involved in rather secretive work for the government. You never spoke of it to me. I thought you preferred I not ask." Changing the subject, she said ruefully, "This stroll would be more romantic if the gardens were attractive, but they've run wild and I haven't had time to consider what to do. Burke never spent a penny on the estate if he could avoid it. Mrs. Beckettt, the cook, says there used to be an old gardener but he died and wasn't replaced. Now the gardens are the next thing to a jungle."

She exaggerated, but only slightly. The overgrown parterre more nearly resembled a maze, trees were shaggy and unpruned, and flower beds and borders were ragged. Even in spring the gardens looked neglected. By high summer, some areas would be impenetrable.

"A great deal of work is needed," he agreed as they headed down a rough brick path. "But the basic design is good and the plants are certainly vigorous." He held back a branch so that Mariah could walk by. "Would you object if I tried my hand at sorting out the gardens?"

She gave him a quick glance. "Gardening is something else familiar to you?"

"It seems to be." He flexed his fingers unconsciously. "I have a strong desire to work with my hands. To grab hold of something and make it better."

"Then this is the place to start. Anything you do will be an improvement. I can hire some people from the village to help you if you like."

"That will be good after I decide what needs to be

done." He raised his hand and interlinked his fingers with hers. She caught her breath, for she wore no gloves and bare skin touched bare skin. As they resumed their walk, he remarked, "I see the gardens differently now that I'm plotting their fate."

She laughed. "The shrubs have been yearning for attention. There are sections of the gardens I've never even seen. There's always too much else to do."

"Then we shall explore every inch. Where does this path go?"

"I have no idea. But I'd like to find out." She moved closer as the path narrowed between encroaching hedges.

"Pruning is definitely called for." He looked at his hands, itching to get to work, and questions of rank and class floated into his mind. "Am I not quite a gentleman?"

"You have always been one to me." She traced a line down the middle of his right palm. His response to her touch shot right through him, tingling and erotic.

He reminded himself that they were courting and he really could not lay her down in the lush grass and rediscover that lovely soft body. He took a deep breath to control the more unruly parts of his anatomy, then resumed walking. The path swung to the right and ended in an enclosed garden. Two gently weathered stone walls met at a right angle set into the slope of a hill. The other two sides were defined by dense shrubbery. Daffodils were on the verge of blooming, and an espaliered fruit tree spread over the south-facing wall. The other wall was covered with vine that would turn brilliant red in autumn, while a graceful tree offered shade.

He stopped and caught his breath. "This seems . . . familiar."

She glanced up sharply. "Have you been here before?"

"No," he said slowly as he tried to analyze the swift image that had flickered across his mind before vanishing. "Rather, the atmosphere is familiar."

"In what ways?" she asked encouragingly.

"The fact that it's enclosed and feels . . . safe. Protected. Peaceful." He closed his eyes and tried to recall that other garden. "I have a vague memory of a similar place, though with many more flowers. Brilliant flowers. In one corner was a fountain with . . . an elephant in the middle? I think it was an elephant."

"That garden might not have been in England."

"It wasn't," he said with certainty. "But I have no idea where it was."

He opened his eyes and studied the garden. The foliage of the shrubs was a pleasing mixture of colors and shapes. Brick paths were set in herringbone patterns, and large rocks seemed intended for sitting. "But I think both places were designed to encourage thought or prayer or serenity."

"Speaking of peaceful, there's Mrs. Beckett's kitchen cat, Annabelle." The cat was snoozing in a patch of sunshine below the espaliered fruit tree. Feline eyes opened as Mariah approached, and she didn't object to being scooped up and cooed over.

Mariah should carry the cat with her everywhere, Adam decided. She was irresistible with a lock of blond hair spilling over her shoulder and the black and white cat purring in her arms. Her tender affection made her even more beautiful.

"Living in the kitchen must explain Annabelle's generous contours."

"That's politely put," Mariah said with a chuckle. "She's a sweet moggy. Some nights she even condescends to sleep on my bed."

Adam turned around slowly, thinking of that other garden. He saw it more clearly now. The water in the fountain sprayed not from the trunk of an elephant, but an elephant-headed man. Very un-English. The air had been burningly hot, and a woman sat in the shade of a great tree. He could not see her clearly, but he knew she was dark haired and beautiful. . . .

Mariah perched on the largest rock with the cat. "I can see where surroundings like these would be good for calming one's nerves."

"I'll clean this up and turn it into a true meditation garden as my first project." He sat on the rock beside her and stroked Annabelle's silky fur, his fingers provocatively close to Mariah's breast. "If

I were courting you, Miss Clarke, I'd use this privacy to steal a kiss."

He leaned forward and pressed his lips to hers as gently as if it were their first time. She made a small sound in her throat and her lips clung to his. A kiss that started in innocence rapidly became more. He leaned closer, his hand moving to cup her breast. The cat gave a squawk of protest and kicked away from Mariah's lap.

Annabelle's action made Mariah gasp and pull back. "I would allow you to steal a kiss, but no more. Because I'm a v . . . very proper young lady."

His hands clenched. Though his body cried out for her familiar warmth, he had agreed to move slowly. She deserved no less. "As a not quite proper gentleman, I would apologize for my ill-bred behavior while secretly hoping to repeat it as soon as possible."

She laughed a little unevenly as she stood and brushed down her skirts. "I think you are more honest than an ordinary suitor would be."

"This is not an ordinary courtship." He stood, feeling a little light-headed. Offering his arm, he said, "Shall we return to our explorations?"

"As long as we avoid any more gardens that are too private. The kitchen gardens should do nicely. All those vegetables are most unromantic."

Her smile was a little hesitant as she took his arm. He reminded himself again that she needed this time to accept how he had changed. He wasn't the man he had been before, and the fact that they were wed didn't automatically mean she would invite him to share her bed again.

Uneasily he wondered if amnesia was grounds for annulment. He hoped not.

Chapter Nine

Greenock and Arran Island, Scotland

Will Masterson caught the ship's railing as the *Annie* bobbed at anchor on a cool, rainy afternoon. Beside him, Randall asked, "What's that thing on the back deck?"

"A diving bell," Will replied. "Like a church bell, it's open on the bottom. Because of the weight, it stays upright when lowered into the water and air is trapped underneath. Divers can ride down inside the bell and swim over to where they work, then reenter the bell when they need to catch a breath."

"Ingenious," Kirkland remarked. "What will they think of next?"

"Aristotle wrote about an early diving bell, so it's not the newest invention around," Will said. "But they've improved greatly in recent years. This one has a window to look out under the sea and compressed air so it can stay down longer."

Randall frowned. "I hope it can do the job."

"It's likely Ash was in the engine room. If so, we

should be able to recover his body." Will's voice was calm, though his emotions weren't. As long as there was no body, he could hang on to the faint hope that Ash was still alive.

With shouts and creaking timbers the *Annie* set off on the first leg of the journey. Archie Mactavish had been right: Jamie Bogle of Greenock had a first-rate salvage operation, with all the latest equipment. The diving bell even had a compressed-air line. Bogle also had something more: a personal motive for helping to find the *Enterprise*. His cousin Donald was one of the men missing and presumed dead.

"Donald liked working for your duke," Bogle had told Will gruffly when they'd met to see if Bogle could take on the job. "Said it was the best position he'd ever had."

"Then maybe we can bring his body home," Will had replied.

"The family 'ould like that," Bogle had said. "Can you sail on the afternoon tide?"

They could. The salvage ship *Annie* and a barge sailed south with Will, Randall, and Kirkland, plus two other passengers: Archibald Mactavish and Davy Collins, two of the four survivors of the *Enterprise*. With their recollections of landmarks on Arran Island, it took less than a day to locate the steamship's wreckage. The waters were shallow, which meant the salvage operation should be straightforward.

Under a damp and threatening sky, the diving bell submerged with two divers, one of them Bogle's son, Duncan. The time the men were below seemed interminable, though it couldn't have been too long. The chain of the crane rattled and became taut as it was attached to a piece of wreckage.

The divers returned to the surface. As they wrapped themselves in heavy wool blankets, Duncan reported, "We found the aft section of the ship, including the engine room. Lucky the *Enterprise* wasn't a great thumpin' sailing ship. I think we can raise her with a bit of care."

His father nodded and ordered his crew to start lifting. Chain squealing, the load was raised, water pouring from every crack and crevice when the massive piece of wreckage cleared the surface.

Will's fingers bit into the ship's railing as he wondered if Ash was inside. He had trouble believing that Ash, with his quiet wit and absolute loyalty, was really gone. Which was why recovering a body was so important.

The crane was swinging the wreckage toward the barge when the chain supporting the load snapped, whipping toward Duncan Bogle. Quick as a cat, Randall tried to yank the young diver out of its vicious path. He was only partially successful. The end of the chain hit Duncan with brutal force.

The young man cried out and fell to the deck. A tidal wave of water exploded in all directions as the massive chunk of wreckage plunged back into the sea, rocking the *Annie*.

Swearing, the captain bent over his son, who gasped with pain from the impact of the violently recoiling chain. "Are you all right, lad?"

"Right . . . enough," the young man managed. "If that Sassenach hadn't dragged me back, the bloody chain would have cut me in half, I think."

"It came close even so." Randall, who had experience tending wounded men in the battle-field, knelt by Duncan and examined his chest and shoulder. "A broken shoulder and maybe a cracked rib, I think. With binding, he should heal well."

"But he won't be diving for a while." Bogle frowned. "I can replace the chains, but diving is a two-man job and Wee Geordie can't do it alone. We'll have to return to Greenock for another diver."

"I can dive," Will said. "I lived in the West Indies as a boy and learned to swim as soon as I could walk."

"Are you sure?" the captain said doubtfully. "It's hard, dangerous work even for men experienced with a diving bell."

"I had experience with a bell when I worked on a salvage ship looking for Spanish treasure in the Indies," Will replied.

Kirkland, who had joined them, said, "I didn't know that."

Will smiled. "We all have our secrets. How long until you can send the bell down again, Captain?"

Bogle assessed the sky and the surface of the sea. "There's weather moving in, so we'd best do it soon as possible. Maybe half an hour."

An amazing amount of cursing was required to replace the chain. Will wished he understood the Glaswegian dialect: the blistering oaths were downright poetic.

As the bell was readied Will changed into the crude leather suit used to ward off the cold. This was Duncan's suit, so it was clammy wet and not really large enough, but he'd be glad for the protection when he went under.

Wee Geordie was a muscular young man as large as Will himself. It was damned chilly in the bell as they sank beneath the surface. As he perched on the cold metal bench that ran around the inside of the bell, Will thought wistfully of the clear, turquoise waters of the West Indies.

During the descent, the water level slowly rose to his feet, then his ankles. His ears began to hurt. He'd forgotten about that part. "Lucky the wreck is only a few fathoms deep," Wee Geordie said. "Else our ears would feel stabbed by needles." He frowned. "Are ye sure ye know what ye're doing?"

"I think so, but you're the expert here." Will guessed the Scot couldn't believe an English lord would be good for anything useful. He had a point, but Will hadn't always been an English lord. "You've already studied the site."

"It shouldn't be hard to recover the aft end of the ship," Wee Geordie said. "The chains went down with it, so it's just a matter of attaching them again. We'll be back up ta the surface before ye know it."

Will peered through the heavy glass window set into the wall of the bell. Those dark shapes that loomed through the water must be the broken bones of the *Enterprise*.

When they were in position, Wee Geordie inhaled deeply several times over. Will did the same. "Don't try to spend too long out of the bell," the diver said. "The captain paid a right fortune for the compressed-air equipment, and he likes it to be used." He leaned forward, then slid through the watery floor feet first.

Will followed a few seconds later. The water was *cold!* Once more he thought regretfully of the Indies. Even with the protection of the leather diving suit, they'd have to work fast, or risk becoming dangerously chilled. With smooth, powerful movements, he swam after Wee Geordie.

As the younger man had predicted, the recovery operation was straight forward. The hooks on the ends of the chains had to be secured again, then the crane hook attached where the three lifting chains came together. Multiple returns to the bell were required, Will more often than Wee Geordie. His wind wasn't as good as when he swam regularly.

When the chains were solidly in place and they were ready to return to the surface, Will asked, "Did you and Duncan check the rest of the wreckage for bodies?"

Wee Geordie nodded soberly. "Aye, we did. Most of the wreckage is open and any bodies would have been washed away. The aft section is closed enough that we might find someone in there."

They settled into the bell and signaled to be pulled up. When they reached the surface, they were immediately swaddled in blankets and offered mugs of steaming tea augmented with sugar and whisky. Will gulped his drink and asked for a refill. After his bones thawed, he went below to change into dry clothing. He kept the blanket.

When he climbed on deck again, the aft section of the *Enterprise* was being positioned on the barge. Kirkland helped Archie Mactavish cross between the vessels, for the engineer was grimly determined to see what had gone wrong.

Two of Bogle's crewmen used sledges and crowbars to open up the wreckage enough to allow them to enter. Everyone else waited in silence as the wind increased and rain began to fall. Will braced himself when one of the men called, "There's a body in here."

The two workers brought the dead man out and laid him on the floor of the barge, their movements respectful. Randall knelt by the body. After a tense moment, he said, "It's not Ashton."

"Aye," the captain said heavily. " 'Tis my cousin Donald." He took off his hat and held it over his heart. "At least now we know."

Will released his breath roughly, glad not to have proof of Ash's death and sorry to be left with uncertainty. "With that mystery settled, let's look at the engine."

A crewman lit lanterns and Will, Mactavish, and the captain entered into the wreckage. Mactavish studied the engine with painstaking thoroughness while the other two men held the lanterns. When he finished scrutinizing the front and sides of the engine, he said, "I see nothing that could have caused the explosion."

"Come around to the back," Will suggested. "The engine ripped free of most of its mountings, so you can see this side."

Mactavish wriggled by him in the tight, dark space and looked at the back of the boiler. After a moment, he swore viciously. "Look at that." He pointed the stump of his right arm at a ragged hole in the curving side of the boiler.

Will frowned at the hole. "Obviously the engine blew from there, but why? A weakness in the boiler casing?"

"Look more closely," Mactavish growled.

Will bent close and saw that the edges of hole showed glints of brighter solder. "A weak spot in the boiler was patched here and the repair didn't hold?"

"The boiler was perfect. This hole had to have been cut in and patched badly so it would blow after it was in use for a while."

Captain Bogle said incredulously, "So that means . . ."

Will finished the sentence, his voice savage. "The explosion wasn't an accident."

Chapter Ten

The massive door was opened by a hard-faced man in livery. Seeing who was on the doorstep, the footman tried to slam the door. Adam promptly shoved his foot in the gap, glad he'd worn his heaviest boots. "I will see him," Adam said grimly. "Will you tell me where he is, or will we have to search the house?"

"This is an outrage!" the footman snarled as he tried to kick Adam's foot from the opening. Raising his voice, he said, "Help! The house is being invaded!"

Ignoring the servant, Adam and his three companions forced the door open. "We should stay together," Adam snapped. "He's probably upstairs."

As screaming maids and shouting footmen rushed about, Adam and his companions charged up the staircase. In one bedroom, they disrupted an illicit tryst between a squealing maid and a male servant, but they didn't find the man they sought.

When they turned from the last room, Adam said, "The attics."

The stairs were painfully narrow, and on this hot day the heat was suffocating. Most of the attic rooms clearly belonged to female servants, and were empty.

They found their man in the smallest, meanest room in the attic, the ceiling slanted and the floor covered with dust and dead flies. There were no furnishings except for a pallet on the floor. The stench of infection and unwashed body was nauseating.

Adam gasped at the sight of the skeletal, unmoving figure, fearing his friend was dead. His face was lifeless and his blond hair dull and filthy. But his eyes flickered open when Adam knelt beside the pallet. "I . . . wondered when you'd get here," the man said with a travesty of a smile.

"Sorry I didn't arrive sooner. I was out of town." Adam scanned the damaged body, hoping they would be able to remove him without causing further injury. Raising his voice, he said, "Someone get water and a blanket from one of the other rooms."

It took only a few moments to provide him with a chipped pitcher of tepid water and a heavy, cracked tumbler. "Would you like a drink?" he asked as he poured water into the tumbler.

"God, yes!"

Adam raised his friend's head enough to allow

him to sip. The cords in the man's throat showed as he swallowed convulsively.

"That's enough for now," Adam said as he removed the tumbler. "Too much might make you ill."

The blond man looked as if he would argue, then changed his mind. "Pour the rest of the water over my head."

Adam complied, and the blond man gave a long sigh of relief. "Coolest I've been since God knows when."

Adam stood. "Let's get him wrapped in the blanket and out of here."

Two of his companions spread the blanket on the floor, then lifted the blond man from the filthy pallet and set him in the middle of the coarse fabric. The injured man gave one sharp gasp of pain, but that was the only sound he made, even when he was being carried down the narrow staircase with his head and feet bumping the walls, despite the best efforts of the two men carrying him.

The next set of stairs was wider. They had made it down to the entrance hall when a furious old man burst from the drawing room to block their exit. His expensive garments proclaimed wealth, but his eyes were mad and his gnarled hands held a shotgun. "Damn you for an arrogant piece of filth!" he howled, the weapon aimed squarely at Adam's chest. "You have no right to take him from my house!"

Adam drew a slow breath, wondering how large a hole the shotgun would blast in him at this range. "And you have no right to let him die of neglect."

"He deserves to die!" The shotgun swung toward the man wrapped in the blanket, then back to Adam.

"Shoot if you will," Adam said. "But if you want to avoid scandal, murder is not the way to do it."

The shotgun wavered, then lowered. "Damn you!" the old man swore again, his eyes wild. "Damn you and all your evil, lawless friends!"

"No doubt damnation will arrive in its own good time. But not today." Adam swung the door open and gestured the others to leave before the old man could change his mind. He half expected the shotgun to be fired, but they loaded the injured man into the carriage without incident.

As Adam studied the slack face of the man they'd rescued, he wondered if his friend's life could be saved, or if it was too late.

He was closing the carriage door when a shot rang out.

Adam jerked awake, heart pounding. He heard another sharp sound. Not gunfire, but an ax chopping wood. He and Mariah had discussed removing a tree that was dying, and likely that was being done this morning. An efficient woman, his wife.

He rose and crossed to the washstand, now supplied with a razor, so he could temporarily tame his whiskers. As he washed and shaved, he wondered about the dream. Was it pure invention, or memory of something that had happened? It had felt very real.

As he settled into his meditation, he wondered what the dream had to say about his life if it reflected a real incident. Who was the blond man, and what had driven Adam to invade a grand house?

Some of the answers could be deduced. The blond man was clearly hated by the angry old fellow and was being left to die of neglect after a serious injury. Adam had learned what was going on and rescued his friend. The old man hated him as well. Very likely he hated everyone.

Had any names been used? He couldn't recall any. It would have been convenient if the old man had been more specific in his insults.

What else did the dream suggest? That Adam moved among people of high status, though his own status was unclear. That he was indeed used to giving orders.

And that he had friends.

By the time Mariah stopped by Adam's room for a quick check, again he was gone. He seemed to be an early riser. Also healthy enough that she probably needn't hover over him regularly.

She found him in the breakfast room attacking a

plateful of eggs, ham, and toasted bread. "You look well this morning." She signaled the maid to bring her own breakfast.

After pouring a cup of tea, she settled opposite him. "Are you feeling any strain from all you did yesterday?"

He shook his head. "Some sore muscles and other aches." He touched the bandage on his head. "But I feel well enough to ride over the estate today."

"Very well, I'll order the horses after breakfast." She sipped her tea, thinking how much she enjoyed watching him. There was a smooth efficiency in his movements, an air of being comfortable in his own skin even though he didn't remember his past.

She wondered if he would be as relaxed if he didn't have the false identity of Adam Clarke to hold on to. Her life would be so much easier if she could confess the truth! The longer she maintained the lies, the more infuriated he would be when he discovered them. The fact that she found him attractive made everything more complicated. She asked hopefully, "Any new memories today?"

He frowned. "I had a dream so vivid it seemed like a memory, but even so, it didn't really tell me anything about myself. No names or places were mentioned, though I think the location was London."

Disappointed, Mariah said, "So that wasn't any

help." The maid set a plate of eggs and toast in front of her. As she turned her attention to her breakfast, she said, "I look forward to discovering how much you know about farming."

He grinned. "So do I."

Three hours later they pulled up their horses on a hill that gave a dramatic view of the estate, the sea, and the steep hills. She now had her answer. Adam rode with unthinking skill and he could talk agriculture like a duke's land steward. "You're a man of parts, Adam," she said, choosing her words carefully. "I never heard you discuss agriculture before today, yet you obviously know a great deal about the subject."

"I didn't realize I had so many opinions about livestock and crops. Which breed of pigs fattens most quickly, which cows give the best milk." He sighed. "It's maddening to remember cattle and pigs, but nothing of my life."

"That will come."

"I hope so." He started his horse down the hill. "You were dead right that Burke neglected this place shamefully. The estate has quite a bit of arable land for this part of England, but a seed drill and harvester are required, along with better seed. With investment and good management, the estate's income could double in five years."

"That would certainly be welcome." She would need to hire a good steward to manage the property. Adam would be wonderful, but it was unlikely he would be here for very long. She gave him a sidelong glance, admiring his seat on the horse. Though if he never regained his memory . . .

Her vague dream ran jarringly into the knowledge that he might have a wife waiting with increasing fear for her husband to come home. If Adam were Mariah's husband, she would certainly start searching if he disappeared. Horrors, what if he had a wife who did exactly that, and showed up at Hartley Manor to demand her husband back?

Mariah shuddered, thinking she had entirely too much imagination. She was glad when Adam pointed at the church tower just visible over the top of a hill. "Is that the village? Can we visit?"

She bit her lip uneasily. She would much prefer not having to introduce Adam to the village as her "husband." But it must happen sooner or later. "I suppose we can, if you're feeling strong enough. Are you sure you wouldn't rather return home and rest?"

He gave her a bright and probably lying smile. "I'm sure."

He most likely wanted to push himself as hard as possible to rebuild his strength. Male to the bone. "Very well, the village it is. The road forks soon. If we take the lane on the right, it will take us down to the high street."

They reached the fork a few minutes later and turned into the lane, which was sunken so deeply from generations of use that it was almost a tunnel. Adam said, "When it rains, the water must rush through here like a tidal wave."

Mariah studied the steeply slanted sides, thinking she wouldn't like to have to climb out of the lane if there was a heavy storm. "I suspect you're right, but I haven't seen that. I don't usually travel this route."

They were nearing the village when they heard the frantic barking of a dog. Frowning, Adam urged his horse into a trot, Mariah doing the same. They rounded a curve and saw three boys throwing rocks at a half-grown dog. In its attempts to escape, the small creature was racing toward Mariah and Adam, but a bad limp slowed it down and the sides of the lane were too steep for it to scramble up and away.

As she watched, horrified, a stone thrown by the largest boy struck the dog. The dog yipped while the younger boys howled with delight. Adam kicked his horse into a gallop and thundered down on the boys. "Halt!"

He swung from his horse and snapped, "How dare you abuse a helpless creature! Where are your parents?"

"Tha' dog don't belong to nobody!" the oldest boy protested. "My da said to get it away from the house."

"So you decided to torture the poor beast," Adam said in a voice that bit to the bone. "Life is precious and never to be ended casually. Your behavior is a disgrace. How would you like to be stoned to death when you were only trying to escape?"

The boys looked as if they wanted to run, but they couldn't escape easily any more than the dog had been able to. "We didn't want to kill the ugly critter, just make it go away," one of the smaller boys protested.

Mariah dismounted and scooped the panting pup into her arms. Under blood and filth were floppy ears and brown and black patches mixed with white. She guessed some hound ancestry mixed with heaven knew what else.

The dog struggled at first, but she held tight, stroking it as she said soothingly, "You poor pup. Don't worry, you're safe now." Too tired to run anymore, it settled in her arms.

She had missed part of Adam's dressing down of the boys, but when she glanced up, the culprits looked near tears. Adam ended, "Do I have your word of honor that you won't act with such cruelty again?"

They all nodded mutely, then turned and raced away when he released them, saying, "See that you live up to that."

As the boys vanished around a bend, Mariah said, "Do you think they'll behave better in the future?"

"One lecture won't reform them entirely, but per- haps they'll think twice before casually tormenting other creatures." He turned and gently took the dog from her. Beginning to recover, the dog reared up and began licking Adam's chin. He laughed. "She has a remarkably forgiving disposition. Shall we keep her?"

Mariah had always loved animals, but her wandering life hadn't allowed for pets. Now that she had a real home, it was high time she acquired some animal companions. "If no one in the village claims her, we might as well since she doesn't look fit for anything but charming susceptible humans." She scratched the puppy's head. It lolled happily into her hand. "What shall we call her?"

"Bhanu," Adam said promptly.

She frowned. "I've never heard that before. What does it mean?"

He looked blank. "I have no idea. But in my mind, it's definitely a dog's name."

"Another piece of the past arrived without explanations," Mariah said wryly, thinking how attractive it made a man to be kind to animals. "Bhanu she is. Look at the size of those feet. She's going to be big."

"She's an armful already. I'll carry her back home. I hope that leg isn't broken."

Adam set Bhanu down and helped Mariah into her saddle. Then he handed her the dog, mounted his own horse, and took Bhanu back. The dog settled down happily across his lap.

At a walking pace, they continued down the lane

and into the village. After a detour to look at the small waterfront, home to several fishing boats, they rode down the high street. Adam said thoughtfully, "Hartley looks familiar. Not that I've been here, but it seems like any number of other English villages."

"It may be typical, but it's very pretty," Mariah said a touch defensively.

"Very pretty indeed," he said, smiling at her.

She colored and turned from his gaze. She was not surprised to see exactly what she'd feared: people peering out of windows and some even finding reasons to suddenly emerge from their cottages. As the owner of the largest property in the area, her activities were of great interest in Hartley. Especially the acquisition of an unexpected husband.

First to intercept them was Mrs. Glessing, whom Mariah had met in church. The woman was the village gossip, eager to be the first with the news on any subject. "Mrs. Clarke, how lovely to see you!" She stepped into the road so that they must stop to greet her. "And this handsome fellow must be your husband? I heard he'd arrived up at the manor, and quite a tale it was about him being rescued from the sea!"

Mariah had known the story was too good not to spread through the village instantly. "Indeed he is," Mariah said, keeping the introductions as brief as possible.

Mrs. Glessing frowned when she saw the dog. "Did that creature trouble you? It's been skulking around the village."

"If she has no owner, we're taking her home." Adam was polite but he showed a cool reserve Mariah hadn't seen before. He also proved to be a master at avoiding answers as Mrs. Glessing probed for information about his origins. When they took their leave, Mrs. Glessing knew no more than when she intercepted them.

Luckily, no one else was bold enough to stop them in the street, though a number of people Mariah had met in church or the shops waved at her. She smiled and nodded back but didn't stop. As they rode past the inn, the Bull and Anchor, she wondered if George Burke had left town. She certainly hoped so.

"Isn't the church handsome?" she said as they approached. "And look, there's Julia Bancroft coming out with the vicar, Mr. Williams. She lives nearby and helps out at the church regularly."

Mariah's brows drew together as she watched her friend and the vicar together. She had admired Mr. Williams since she met him. He was kind and scholarly and devoted to his church and parishioners, and rather handsome as well. She'd thought he regarded her with special warmth, and even daydreamed sometimes about what it would be like to be a vicar's wife.

But he was not for her. He was the sort of gentleman who belonged with a woman like her imaginary sister, Sarah. Or Julia, who was laughing at something the vicar said. Mariah wondered if a quiet romantic relationship was growing between the two. Certainly Julia would make an exemplary vicar's wife.

With a mild pang, Mariah released her dreams of Mr. Williams. Though he was an admirable person, a good part of her interest had been because he was the most eligible and attractive man in the area. She much preferred Adam even though she knew nothing of his past. He may or may not be a gentleman, but it didn't matter. He was the one she dreamed about now.

Adam, who might have a wife waiting anxiously for his return.

Julia glanced up and saw them. "Mariah, how good to see you. Mr. Clarke, you shouldn't be riding yet." But she spoke with the wry amusement of a woman who accepted that patients didn't always behave.

Mariah was grateful that Julia performed the introductions, because that spared her having to lie to the vicar. Mr. Williams smiled warmly and offered his hand to Adam. "I heard of your rescue, Mr. Clarke. Surely it was the hand of providence that spared your life and brought you home to your wife."

"I am very aware of that." Adam shook the vicar's hand. "I would dismount, but that would disturb the dog and she's already had a difficult day."

Williams laughed and scratched Bhanu's floppy ears. "She's a stray who has been wandering around the village. Probably she was driven off one of the farms. She seems happy now."

Mariah said, "Julia, could you do a quick examination of Bhanu's left rear leg? Some boys were throwing stones at her and she was limping when Adam rescued her."

"Poor beast." Julia gently probed the dog's leg. Bhanu yipped and drew her leg back but didn't struggle.

"I don't think the leg is broken," Julia said after her examination. "Just bruised. She was most fortunate." Julia pulled out a handkerchief and wiped her hands. "And I'd suggest a bath as soon as you get her home!"

"Yes, ma'am," Adam said with a grin. "Mr. Williams, it's a pleasure to meet you. We shall see you in church this Sunday."

As they collected their mounts and headed home, Mariah thought that she and Adam were becoming positively domestic. She wasn't sure if that was good or bad.

Chapter Eleven

He stood in a vast, echoing chamber, the air perfumed with tangy scents that were exotic yet hauntingly familiar.

The darkness was choking, so thick he felt he

could hold it in his hands. Then brass lamps slowly ignited around the edges of the hall. The flickering oil lights hinted at a richly decorated ceiling and walls.

He turned, trying to orient himself, and was startled to find a great golden goddess towering over him. She wore an expression of remote benevolence as she studied him. Her four graceful arms seemed entirely natural. After a long glance, she turned away, as if he were a creature of no importance. Desperate to regain her attention, he ran after her, but she dissolved into the darkness.

A flash of light caught his eye and he turned to see another huge golden figure. This time a god danced in a circle of flames, his many-armed movements a timeless balance of power and serenity. Adam tried to approach, but the god raised his arms and was consumed by blazing fire.

Adam was so small compared to these beings, a mouse among giants. As the thought formed, he saw another great golden god. This one had a human body topped by the head of an elephant with wise and ancient eyes. He had seen this being before, though he could not remember where.

Heart pounding frantically at the strangeness of it all, he fell to his knees to honor the god. But the shining golden presence also disappeared, leaving emptiness.

He climbed to his feet, aching with loss and half suffocated by the incense-laden air. Another

*movement caught his eye. He turned and saw a
real woman who was of normal size and had
normal limbs. She knelt before a cluster of lamps
and mounds of brilliant flowers, but when he
caught his breath, she rose and faced him. Her
garments were flowing veils of vivid color and gilt
embroidery that enhanced her dark-haired beauty.
Seeing him, she smiled radiantly and offered her
hands.*

*His heart bursting with happiness, he ran toward
her, knowing she would fill the emptiness of his
heart. But just before he reached her, he was seized
in a powerful grip and dragged away. Frantically
he kicked and twisted and bit to escape his captor,
but he was helpless.*

*Helpless. The golden gods had vanished, the
rich, spicy scents faded to dust, . . . and the dark-
haired woman was gone forever.*

Adam awoke, racked with anguish. When a raspy
tongue licked his cheek, he wrapped one arm
around Bhanu, grateful to have a warm, loving
body in his bed. The dog must have sensed his distress.

Why had this dream made him feel such despair?
Maybe because the other dreams seemed to reflect
real experience, but this one came from the world
of visions and hallucinations. He tried to visualize
those great golden figures, their slow, sinuous
movements attuned to a different rhythm of life,

but the details eluded him. They were familiar, yet he couldn't remember why.

He had seen the elephant-headed being before, when he remembered a long-ago garden. And the beautiful dark-haired woman was the one in the garden and real, he was sure of it. But what was her relationship to him? She was his age or a little younger. And she was forever gone. Perhaps that was why the dream burned with a sense of loss so profound that it had shaped his very soul.

Could his amnesia be a way of concealing that loss from himself because remembering would be unbearable? Mariah was an anchor in high winds, but she knew surprisingly little about his life. She said that was because they hadn't been together long enough to learn much of each other, but he suspected that the real problem was that he had told her very little.

Had he committed a great crime? Or suffered unspeakable tragedy? If so, a blow on the head might have given him a blessed release from an unendurable past.

Feeling ill, he pushed himself up in the bed. It was deep, dark night, but he doubted he would fall asleep again. Though he closed his eyes and reached for peace, his mind was too chaotic for meditation.

He gave up trying when Bhanu lurched across his lap making whuffling noises. He scratched the dog's head. Though no more handsome than she'd been when he found her, she was now considerably cleaner. "Who said you could sleep on the bed? I believe we have discussed your sleeping arrangements and decided on the carpet in front of the fireplace."

Bhanu gazed up worshipfully, ignoring his nonsense. The faint light from the window made her black and white face look clownish. He couldn't help smiling. While he would prefer the company of his warm and beautiful wife, the dog was much better than nothing. "Do you want to come to the library?" Bhanu's ears perked up.

"You're thinking a walk and food. It's not much of a walk, but afterward, I'll find you something to eat." He slid from the bed and donned the warm banyan and oversized slippers, then lit a lamp and headed to the manor's library. Perhaps he could find a book that would tell him what he needed to know.

In keeping with the rest of the estate, the library showed little care or thought. There were only a few shelves of books, and those probably bought used to make a show of learning. Half were bound volumes of sermons or collections of old and uninteresting magazines. But the sheer randomness of the selection meant that possibly there might be a volume that would help him unlock the secrets of his mind. He turned up the lamp and began studying the books.

• • •

Mariah was on her way to the kitchen to find a late-night meal when she heard a sound in the small room that was rather grandly called the library. Wondering if Bhanu was exploring the house or yearning to be let out, she detoured there and found Adam methodically scanning the shelves by lamplight.

Raising her own lamp, she said, "Adam? Are you looking for something in particular?"

Seeing her, Bhanu bounced over and jumped up in joyful greeting. Adam merely turned, his face drawn. "I had another dream, this one of strange beings and symbols. They were familiar, as if they're part of my past, yet I can't remember." His expression changed. "*I can't remember!* I tell myself that soon I will, that the pieces will start falling into place. By day, I can believe that. By night, it's . . . harder. What if I never recall my past? What if I am condemned to be always alone in my own mind?"

Until now, he'd seemed so composed about his situation that it was shocking to see the raw pain in his face. Except for a few fading bruises, he no longer looked injured. Even the head bandage was gone, because the wound was healing well. But his spirit was heartbreakingly vulnerable.

She set her lamp on the table and crossed the room to take his hands. "You might never remember," she said gravely, "but that doesn't

130

mean you have to be alone. Look at the memories we've created in just the last few days."

His expression eased. "I don't know what I'd do without you, Mariah. It's frightening to imagine what it would have been like if I'd washed ashore in a place of strangers with no one to tell me my name and care if I lived or died."

His words were both knife and chain. Though her distaste for her masquerade worsened daily, she couldn't tell him that he had indeed come ashore among strangers. He needed to believe in her.

What if he never remembered his true identity? If he didn't, and he wanted her, then, by God, she would be his wife. If he had a wife elsewhere, eventually that woman would accept widowhood and perhaps find another husband.

If Adam was doomed to be a man without a past, he was *hers*. She had met more than her share of men both eligible and ineligible, and Adam was the only one she wanted for herself. He was kind and funny and intelligent—just what she wanted in a husband. If he never recalled his identity . . . well, he could find a new one here.

Together they could run Hartley Manor in peace and prosperity—though she would arrange for a proper marriage ceremony. She would tell Adam that since he was in some ways a new man, they needed to renew their vows.

Embarrassed once more by the deftness of her

lying, she said, "The past shapes us, but what matters is the present and the future. You still have those, and they will be what you make of them."

"You are as wise as you are beautiful." His gaze holding hers, he cupped her face in his hands and kissed her, his lips yearning. She responded intensely, the near darkness making it easier to express her feelings. Her man from the sea was so dear, so kind and fascinating and male. She usually thought of him as average sized, but he seemed very large and very strong as he embraced her.

Dizzily she realized that her back was pressed into the bookshelves as his hands explored her without restraint. After untying the sash of her robe, he curved his palms around her breasts. Without the armor of stays, the intimacy was as shocking as it was exciting.

Her mouth opened under his, their tongues mating. She pressed her hips against him. The hard heat of his body was alarming, yet as alluring as a siren's song.

Daring, she slid her hands inside the banyan. His body heat burned through his nightshirt as she stroked his beautifully muscled back. She had been kissed more than once, and sometimes welcomed it, but desire had never threatened to burn out of control. Until now. She wanted to draw him into herself, meld into one flesh.

"I want you so much, my exquisite wife," he whispered before pressing his mouth to her throat.

She moaned, her nails digging into him. When his hand slipped under her nightgown and moved up her thigh, she almost melted on the spot. A man's embrace had never affected her like this, never like this.

If he were to draw her down to the cold and dusty carpet, she would welcome him gladly. But before that could happen, Bhanu reared up against them both, whining for attention. Mariah gasped and pulled away as she remembered all the reasons they shouldn't become intimate. Not least of which would be explaining why she was a virgin. "I . . . I'm sorry," she whispered. "I can't do this. Not now."

Adam reached to embrace her again, then stepped back, his hands clenching. "Are you afraid of me, Mariah? Or is it that you don't want me?"

She gave a choke of hysterical laughter. "You can't believe that I don't want you, not after that! How can I be afraid when you have been all that is kind and understanding? But . . . to me, it still seems too soon. Perhaps when you know me better, you won't want *me*."

"Impossible." He touched her hair, then trailed his hand down her body, leaving a swath of fire in its wake. "I feel that I know you deep in my soul. But . . . not so well here and now." His hand dropped and he gave her a crooked smile. "When my blood cools, I will certainly agree that you're right. But it is hard to be reasonable just now."

He wasn't the only one having trouble with heated blood! She retied her robe. "Food would be good. I'm sure that's what Bhanu wants, and I was heading to the kitchen when I heard you in here. Shall we see what we can find in the pantry? Mrs. Beckett keeps it well stocked."

He laughed and wrapped an arm around her shoulders. "A splendid idea. If one appetite can't be satisfied, feeding another is a good cure."

She blushed but enjoyed the weight of his arm around her as they headed down to the kitchen, Bhanu scampering ahead. "What were you looking for in the library?"

"I hoped there might be a book with images of the beings I saw in my dreams." He sighed. "It was a long shot, but I thought worth trying since I couldn't sleep."

"I haven't found the library useful for anything except pressing flowers," she said. "Hot soup from the pot kept simmering on the hob will help you sleep."

"That sounds good." He gave her a slanting glance. "It would help even more if you'd share my bed."

She stopped, wary. "I thought we agreed that now was not the time."

"I don't mean to be together as lovers," he said softly. "But I would like nothing better than to rest with you in my arms."

She thought of being enfolded by his warm, hard body and smiled. Sweet sister Sarah would have said no. But Mariah simply wasn't that virtuous. "I'd like that, too."

She would like it a *lot*.

Chapter Twelve

Laughing over bread, soup, and cheese with Mariah didn't precisely cool Adam's blood, but the heat was reduced to a simmer. Later, they climbed the stairs to her rooms, which he'd not seen before. As in the rest of the house, decoration and furniture were uneven in quality and condition, but her bedchamber was welcoming, rich with color and scented with bright lavender.

Shyly she took off her robe, then climbed into the bed. He recognized that he was still something of a stranger to her. But she was not a stranger to him. Odd, considering that he was the one who'd lost his memory.

He climbed into the opposite side of the bed, trying not to look alarming. Mariah leaned forward to press a light kiss to his cheek. "Good night, and sleep well." She lay down and turned onto her side with her back to him. Not the most welcoming position.

That was easily corrected. He rolled onto his side behind her and drew her against him spoon style. There was a familiar rightness in the way she fit into his arms. "You feel like heaven," he murmured.

She tensed when his arm came around her waist, but his words relaxed her. "So do you."

He loved the feel of her hair against his cheek. Someday soon he wanted to see the full golden glory of that hair spread wantonly over the bed as she lay under him, her lovely face flushed with desire. For now, it was almost enough to have her tucked against his chest. To not be alone.

He stroked down her body. Her nightgown was old, worn cotton, as deliciously soft as she was. As his hand moved over her stomach, she said breathlessly, "You had better return to your own bed. What you are doing is far too tempting, and I'm not sure my willpower is capable of resisting you."

His hand stilled on the gentle curve of her abdomen. She was serious about not reconsummating their marriage, and in the part of his mind that was still rational, he understood and agreed. But he couldn't bear the idea of leaving her and sleeping alone.

"If I give you my word of honor that I will not join with you tonight, will you allow me to remind you of the pleasures we have shared in the past?"

She caught her breath. "You remember us being lovers?"

"No," he said with regret. "But I know what I must have done, and I want to do it again. Both for the pleasure of touching you, and in the selfish hope that soon you will decide you are ready to truly be my wife." His hand moved up to her breast and he gently thumbed the nipple. It hardened instantly.

"Oh, my . . ." She exhaled slowly. "Your word of honor that you will not lose control of yourself?"

"I swear it, and I would not break my word to you because you would never trust me again," he said frankly. He licked the pale, delicate skin below her ears, reveling in her sigh of pleasure. "And rightly so. But it will be my delight to remind you of what a man and his wife can do short of the ultimate act. Will you allow me to demonstrate?"

Her laugh was unsteady. "If I were a better and more sensible woman, I'd say no and go to sleep elsewhere to remove myself from temptation. But I am neither good nor sensible, so proceed in your demonstration. Just remember your promise."

"You are truly good, Mariah, and in this, perhaps neither of us is being sensible." He moved his hips against her lovely round bottom so that they were molded together. "But sometimes sense is not true wisdom."

She tensed at the evidence of his arousal but did not draw away. He decided to stay in this position because he would be less likely to forget his promise. He could still reach all the sweetest places on her elegantly curved body.

Her breasts, ah, her breasts . . . lovely and round

and fitting his palm perfectly. Just the right size. Not too large, not too small. Though he suspected whatever size they were, he would think them perfect.

Now that she was no longer worried about where they would end this lovemaking, she was wonderfully responsive to his gentle kisses on her ear and throat and his slow, thorough exploration of her breasts. She didn't object when his hand moved down to her waist, though she tensed again when his fingers reached the juncture of her thighs.

As he rhythmically stroked that hidden heat, her hips began pulsing against him. He guessed that she was unaware how much her body was revealing.

"No!" she gasped when he tugged up the hem of her nightgown so he could touch her tender, intimate flesh. "You promised!"

"I have not forgotten," he said, his voice soothing even if his mind was half crazed with longing. Concentrating on her helped keep his control from splintering. Though it was a near run thing. "I will stop now if you wish."

"I . . . I don't want you to stop."

Her trust was too sweet, too precious, to betray. He slid his fingers between the moist, delicate folds. Her body remembered this even if her mind was wary.

He began stroking the silky warmth, moving faster and faster as he sensed her excitement.

Suddenly she gave a suffocated cry and her body convulsed, her hips thrashing against him fiercely. To his shock, her culmination triggered his own violent release. He clutched her to him as mutual fire raged through them, blending them together body and soul.

For an endless time they lay locked together, their breathing ragged. When he realized he was holding her with rib crushing force, he relaxed his embrace. He lifted her hair and kissed the nape of her neck. "When I chose you," he whispered, "I chose even better than I knew."

"That was . . . more of a demonstration than I expected," she said faintly.

"And more than I intended," he said with a shaky laugh. He swung from the bed and padded across the cold floor to collect two towels from her washstand.

His footsteps triggered a hopeful whine and scratching on the outside of the door. Thinking they could use some distraction, he let Bhanu in. The dog bounded through the door, panting happily. He scratched her ears and returned to bed, handing one of the towels to Mariah. As he cleaned up, he said, "We may have company soon. It depends on whether Bhanu can manage the jump onto the bed."

Claws scrabbled on the walnut chest that sat across the foot of the four-poster. The mattress sagged as Bhanu jumped onto it. She circled several times, then settled between their feet, adding canine warmth. Mariah chuckled. "Clever Bhanu. Lucky that the bed is large enough for three."

"All the lonely creatures are drawn to you for comfort," he said seriously.

She settled back against him. "I don't think Bhanu is too discriminating. Any bed with a warm body will do."

"But that wouldn't do for me." He kissed the side of her neck. "Only you will do. Only my wife."

She caught her breath and squeezed his hand where it rested on her ribs, but she said no more. Soon she was breathing with the slow regularity of sleep.

Earlier, after that nightmarish dream of loss, he'd thought that he wouldn't sleep again this night. Now he wanted to stay awake so he could savor the wonder of Mariah in his arms. Remember her rapturous response to his touch.

Yet, to his surprise, he yawned and soon drifted toward the world of dreams. Surely not nightmares, not this time . . .

The weather was filthy, with sleet and freezing rain blowing sideways across the road. Much too rough for a carriage, which would have bogged down in no time. So he rode, using his sturdiest, most reliable horse.

Ordinarily the ride out of the city wouldn't have taken much more than an hour, but the storm slowed him to a walking pace. More than once, he feared he had wandered from the road. As his body numbed, he wondered if he should have brought someone with him. But he hadn't wanted company, not on a journey like this.

Eventually he reached the handsome house that overlooked the Thames. He rode directly to the stables, man and horse equally grateful to be out of the bitter wind. There was no groom because this household's groom had ridden into London with the message. He had wanted to return, but Adam had flatly forbade it because the man looked half dead already from the journey into town.

So Adam tended his mount himself, brushing the tired gelding down and giving him feed and water despite his impatience to go inside. Another blast of ice and rain struck him like a blow as he crossed to the house and banged on the door.

Too long a wait in the vile weather before a servant opened the door. The footman gasped. "Sir! Thank God you're here. I didn't think you would be able to make the journey till the storm passed."

"It was not the sort of message one ignores." He stripped off his coat, which was so saturated that it felt as if the pockets were stuffed with rocks. "Where is he?"

"Upstairs in their room. He . . . he won't leave her."

Adam handed over his dripping coat and hat, then headed up the staircase. He'd visited the *house often in happier times. Now grief saturated the very air.*

He found his friend in the chamber he'd shared with his young wife. The room was illuminated only by the fire flickering in the hearth. On the bed, a slender body barely made a mound in the blanket that covered it.

His friend, a tall man with wide shoulders and powerful limbs, sat in a chair beside the bed, head buried in his hands. He glanced when the door opened, unsurprised to see his visitor. "She's gone." In the firelight, his ravaged face was very young.

"I know." Adam crossed the room and dropped a hand onto his friend's shoulder. "And the baby?"

"He was . . . too small to survive." The man laid his hand over Adam's as he drew a shuddering breath. "How will I go on without her?"

"You will endure," Adam said quietly. "You will grieve, and the scars will stay on your soul forever. But eventually you will carry on. She would have wanted nothing less for you."

"I suppose you're right," the broad man said flatly. "But it's damnable."

"Damnable indeed." Seeing a brandy decanter on a side table, he poured two glasses. They both needed the blaze of brandy, though for different reasons.

His friend gulped half the fiery spirits, choked, then drank the rest. When he had his breath again, he said, "I don't know what I'll do with myself now."

"You need a new home and a new occupation. Something that will keep you busy." Adam sipped his brandy slowly. "You thought to enter the army before you married. Perhaps that is a path that would suit you now."

The other man turned his empty glass absently. "Perhaps. Serve my country, and maybe find a bullet on some foreign field. Both decent prospects."

"Don't you dare go off and get yourself killed," Adam snapped. "I forbid it."

His friend's response was almost a laugh before the dream shifted to another scene entirely. . . .

Mariah was in the happiest dream she'd ever known—warm and safe and cherished. Until she realized it wasn't a dream but reality. Alarm spiked through her as she remembered what had passed between her and Adam the night before. She'd been mad to permit him to touch her that way! Yet she could not wish that she hadn't experienced such pleasure. She was a wanton, just as Sarah had told her.

Warily she opened her eyes to find that she was lying on her back with Adam's arm across her and his green eyes watching with cherishing warmth. He really was most amazingly handsome, with a touch of the exotic in the structure of his bones. A purist might say his hair needed cutting, but she liked it long. She lifted her hand and stroked the glossy dark locks. "Good morning."

"Good morning," he replied. "Did you sleep well?"

His smile dispelled her worry about just how a woman woke up in bed with a man for the first time. This was marriage, she realized—a circle of intimacy that bound just the two of them in their own private paradise. Dangerously alluring.

Her pleasure faded when she wondered what other woman might have known him like this. A woman who was not a casual lover, but who had been a beloved wife.

Mariah's stomach tightened into a knot. For the first time, she hoped that Adam would never regain his memory. That he would stay here and be her husband till death did them part.

Horrified at the selfish wrongness of that hope, she sat up and managed a smile. "Wonderfully well. And you?"

He looked thoughtful. "I didn't expect to sleep, but I did. And I dreamed, though it wasn't like the nightmare I had earlier."

Bhanu popped her head up at the foot of the bed, then came up and flopped between them. Good. The more separated they were, the better. She stroked the dog's flopping ears and was rewarded with a sigh of canine bliss. "What was the dream?"

"There were several. One was riding to be with a

friend who had just lost his wife. It was very sad, but not a nightmare. Then I dreamed about playing with two other children, a boy and a girl. He was about my age and she was younger, I think. They both had green eyes. I wonder, did I have a brother and sister?"

Avoiding more lies, she said, "If you did, I never heard you speak of them."

"I wonder if they died. I felt a sense of loss in the dream." Shaking his head, he swung from the bed. "I feel as if I have a handful of pieces from a puzzle so large that I'll never see the whole."

"Give it time," she said. "Julia Bancroft says the mind is the most complicated part of the body." As Mariah watched Adam don his robe and slippers, she decided that the best possible outcome was for him to regain his memory, be unmarried, and willing to forgive her deception. Then they might have a future—but the odds seemed hopelessly against that.

She might as well enjoy what time they had together. "Would you like to go for a ride this morning?"

"I'd like that very much." He grinned. "Then, my lady, I shall start to build you a garden."

Chapter Thirteen

Greenock, Scotland

After another long day of pursuing separate investigations, the three men met for dinner in the private parlor of the inn that had become their headquarters. Kirkland dumped his damp coat over a chair and set the long leather protective tube on the table.

His friends had already arrived. Randall tossed a scoop of coal onto the fire. "More damned cold Scottish weather," he said gloomily as he limped back to a chair by the fire. The search had been hard on his damaged leg.

Kirkland grinned. "It's bracing. Only thin-blooded Sassenachs would complain. Has anyone ordered dinner?"

"It's on its way," Will replied. "Have you learned anything?"

"A possibility. Faint. What about you two?" Kirkland accepted a glass of claret from Will and subsided on a chair by the fire, stretching his legs out wearily.

Will said, "The other engineers I called in to examine the steam engine agreed with Mactavish. The patched hole in the boiler was meant to destroy the ship. No real engineer would repair a boiler that way because it was guaranteed to fail.

But none of us found any evidence to suggest who might have done such a wicked thing."

"It had to be a man with engineering experience," Kirkland said. "And he had to do his damage at the right time, so it wouldn't be discovered."

Will nodded. "Our best guess is that he came aboard one night when the boiler had been set in place but not yet bolted down. Since a project like this is talked about in half the taverns along the Clyde, a clever man could easily learn when to make his move. If the patch was discovered, the accident would have been prevented but the vandal who did the damage wasn't likely to be caught, so there was little risk in trying. Randall, have you learned anything about the men who worked on building the *Enterprise*?"

"I've interviewed most of them. They're well-respected locals with solid reputations and no reason to destroy another man's ship," Randall replied. "You know Ash—he never minded paying good money to hire the best. His employees are the sort who believe that everyone who works on Clydeside benefits by engineering innovations."

"Most?" Kirkland refilled his glass with claret. "Did you find some men who might be less upstanding?"

"One of the men lost when the ship sank was new to the area. His name was Shipley," Randall replied. "He was variously considered to be either Irish or a Londoner, but he was the silent sort. No one knew much about him except that he was bad company but a capable engineering assistant. With tattoos."

"Was his body found?"

Randall shook his head. "Not yet."

"If he died in the explosion, he probably didn't cause it," Kirkland said. "Of course, he could have set his trap and abandoned ship before the explosion. But if he did, his absence would have been noted, I think, and none of the survivors have mentioned such a thing."

"I've written Lady Agnes about what we've learned, and also to ask if she knows anyone who might want Ash dead," Will said quietly.

There was a brief, heavy silence. "We can't be sure that damaging the ship was aimed at Ash," Kirkland said finally.

"No. But that's the most likely explanation. No one else aboard seems a likely target of a murder plot, and there are enough other steamships under development that it's unlikely that anyone would have singled out the *Enterprise* for destruction," Will said bluntly. "Whereas Ash was a duke, and a man who in some quarters was resented merely for existing."

"If someone wanted Ash dead, it wouldn't have been difficult to kill him with a knife or a pistol ball," Randall said. "If the explosion was an assassination attempt aimed at him, considerable effort went into making his death look accidental."

"An accident is a chancy way to kill a man," Will said. "He might easily have survived. Half the men on the *Enterprise* did."

"If he'd survived, another attempt could have been made," Kirkland pointed out. "We were lucky to find the wreck and salvage the engine so quickly. If the ship had gone down in deeper waters, it might not have been recovered and we'd never have become suspicious."

"Now that we've reported in, have you found anything, Kirkland?" Will glanced at the leather tube on the table.

Kirkland opened the tube and pulled out a rolled map. "After our salvage operation, three men were still missing. Ashton, Shipley, and a sailor named O'Reilly. This morning, I learned that a body washed ashore well down the coast."

Randall stiffened. "Ash?"

"O'Reilly. He was wearing one of those Irish sweaters with the elaborate patterns that can be used to identify the bodies of drowned men. So Ashton and Shipley are the only ones still missing." Kirkland spread the map on the table, weighting the corners so the others could see the coastal area from a little north of Glasgow all the way down to Lancashire. "I spent the afternoon in a fishermen's pub buying drinks and asking about water currents. Specifically, how far a body might be carried if lost by Arran Island, and where it might end up."

"Assuming it's ever found," Randall said grimly. He came to stand by Kirkland so he could study the map. "Where did O'Reilly end up?"

Kirkland tapped the map. "Near this village, Southerness."

Randall whistled softly. "That far? It's just across Solway Firth from England."

"There are so many factors of wind and weather and tide. We should make inquiries over in Ireland—that's actually closer to Arran than Southerness." Kirkland sighed. "No one carried that far could have survived, not in such cold water. If Ashton had made it safely ashore, he would have returned to Glasgow by now, or at least sent a message to his people there."

"He might have been injured so severely that he couldn't do that," Will said stubbornly.

Kirkland recognized that Will couldn't bear to let go of hope, no matter how slim. "It's possible," he agreed. "But not very likely. Too much time has passed since the accident. An injury that severe . . . probably wouldn't have been survivable."

Randall tapped places along the coastline where crosses had been drawn. "What do these marks mean?"

"Most likely spots for a body to turn up, based on the usual currents. I think we should split up and visit other areas around Southerness to see if drowned men have been found," Kirkland said. "In some villages or farmsteads, the locals would just say a prayer and bury a body that had no identification."

"How shall we divide the territory?" Will asked.

They quickly split up the likely sections of coast so they wouldn't overlap. With that decided, Randall said somberly, "This is the only thing left we can do. After, we shall all have to return to our normal lives."

Will sighed. "I'm not looking forward to telling Lady Agnes we failed."

"Her prime concern was always that we do our best," Kirkland said. "Success was valued but not essential."

Two serving maids entered with trays of meat, bread, and potatoes. Kirkland realized he was famished and it was time to end the discussion. He glanced at the map for the southernmost cross. "When we're done, let's meet at this little town on the English side of Solway Firth, since it's more or less opposite Southerness and looks large enough to have an inn." He tapped his finger on the spot. "Hartley."

Chapter Fourteen

Mariah soon found that Adam had not been joking about building her a garden. In the days that followed, he hired half a dozen men from the village to start clearing the neglected beds and plantings. The spring growing season was just beginning, so bringing order to the gardens now was imperative.

That was by day. By night, they were now sharing a bed, though they kept to the physical limits Mariah had set. Once, Adam had risen, swearing under his breath, and returned to his own room before he lost control.

She was glad for his restraint, and sorry to see him go. She loved having him near, loved the pleasure she was learning from him. And she was tentatively learning to pleasure him as well, so after that night, he hadn't had to leave.

Where would it all end? With him remembering and leaving her, or with them becoming lovers? Or both, though not necessarily in that order.

She had grown fatalistic. She would enjoy him as long as she could—and try to avoid doing anything that would ruin her future.

Adam's team of laborers tackled the larger gardens, but he worked on the enclosed garden personally. His goal was to create a true meditation garden that would produce serenity in all who entered. Chopping vines and clearing overgrowth gave him a deep sense of satisfaction, though by the end of the day his mud-splotched appearance pretty well settled the question of whether or not he was a gentleman. He wasn't.

Mariah was impatient to see the meditation garden, but he wouldn't allow her before he was ready. Once a day, she would leave her office for some fresh air and try to slip into his garden. He would stop her. It was a game they both enjoyed.

He had just finished cleaning the weathered stone fountain he'd found embedded in the wall when he heard Bhanu approaching, which meant that Mariah was, too. He hastily rose and wiped his hands on a battered old towel, then went to intercept her before she reached the garden entrance.

Mariah gave him a wickedly coaxing smile. In her plain blue morning gown, she was enchanting. "Are you finished yet? I am perishing of curiosity!"

He shook his head, eyes dancing. "Not yet. Of course a garden is never really finished, but I want this one to be in reasonable shape when you see it."

"Forbidding entrance is the best way to make me want desperately to visit." She made a quick move to circle around him, but he caught her, laughing.

"Some things are worth waiting for." He bent and kissed her, only their lips touching because he didn't want to muddy her dress. Her mouth was a feast, and he would always hunger for her.

"You're just trying to distract me," she said breathlessly when the kiss ended.

"Is it working?"

"I'm afraid so." She gave him a look of exaggerated confusion. "Why was I wandering down this path?"

He cupped her chin in one hand, his touch

caressing. "You wanted to ask me when the garden would be ready for you to view, and you were offering to have Mrs. Beckett pack a picnic luncheon for us to eat here on that day."

She chuckled. "That was my mission? Very well, when will the viewing be?"

"Two days from now, if the fine weather holds." He glanced at the sky. "Which is never certain in this part of the world."

"I shall hope for the best. Mrs. Beckett will be delighted to cooperate. She adores your hearty appetite." She quietly tried to slip around him.

He got a firm grip on the slippery wench and kissed her again. "I shall see you later at dinner and we can trade news of our accomplishments."

"Very well." She glanced down at Bhanu, who was happily investigating interesting scents. "Bhanu, will you come with me or stay with Adam?"

The dog glanced at her, then returned to sniffing. "I think you and the garden have won her allegiance for the moment."

"She is a fickle beast and will be looking for you soon enough." He studied the dog. "How is it possible for a creature to be simultaneously so lovable and so ugly?"

"She's an exceptionally talented dog." With a last winsome glance, Mariah turned and headed back to the house.

Adam felt as if his heart followed her down the

path. What a lucky man he was. Apart from his chancy dreams, he still had no memory of his past, but Mariah had been right when she said the present and future mattered more. As long as he had her, perhaps the past didn't really matter.

The fine weather held, for which Mariah was grateful. She envied Adam for working outside. She spent much of her time in her study developing plans to improve the estate with the rather modest funds at her disposal. Adam had been a great help. Even better, the vicar had introduced her to Horace Cochrane.

Mr. Cochrane had been steward to an earl in Northumberland. Since he was getting on in years, he had recently retired and come back to his home town of Hartley. A month of leisure had persuaded him that he preferred working, but at a less strenuous pace. In just a few days at Hartley, he was already making a difference.

On the day she was to visit Adam's garden, Mariah found it difficult to concentrate on her accounts. It was a relief when midday arrived and she could set her work aside. Adam had announced at breakfast that he wanted to blindfold her so she could enter the garden and be surprised. That had given her the idea of surprising him in turn. Eyes dancing with amusement, she descended to the kitchen to collect the picnic basket Mrs. Beckett had prepared.

As always, he heard her approach on the winding path and came to meet her. His outside work suited him wonderfully. The bruises had faded away, and he was fit and healthy. He was hatless, his dark hair tousled and the vivid color of his eyes enhanced by all the greenery around him. In his white shirt and dark blue trousers, he looked positively dashing.

She greeted him with a smile. "The fine, sunny spring day you ordered has turned up right on schedule."

"I'm most pleased about that. Orders for perfect weather so often go astray." He kissed her, making her toes curl with pleasure. The last days had been so perfect that she felt as if they were on their honeymoon.

Taking the heavy basket, he said, "Am I to use one of these large floppy bows as your blindfold?"

She nodded. "I thought tying scarves on the handle made the basket look festive. This is a special occasion, after all."

He glanced down the path. "Where is Bhanu?"

"She considered joining me but didn't want to leave the kitchen—Mrs. Beckett is roasting a joint for dinner." Mariah grinned. "Plus, Bhanu and Annabelle are getting quite friendly. I saw them curled up around each other by the hearth."

"Faithless pup." He set the basket down and untied the blue scarf, carefully chosen to go with her gown. As he wrapped the cloth around her head so that her eyes were completely covered, she remarked, "This is very foolish, you know. I'm sure I'll love what you've done even if there's no surprise involved."

"I hope so." He tucked her hand into the crook of his arm, then picked up the basket. "But the real reason for blindfolding you is so that you will first experience the garden with other senses. Sight is so powerful that it overwhelms everything else."

"That's an interesting thought." After a dozen steps, she said, "You're right, I'm more aware of how the stones feel under my feet. Small irregularities, the tufts of grass between the stones, when one stone is raised or depressed." She tightened her grip on his arm as she stepped on a particularly low stone. "Strange to have to depend on another person for something as simple as walking."

"I won't lead you astray." His voice was low and compelling.

Intensely aware of the rich tones, she asked, "Did you blindfold me as a . . . a metaphor for the way I've been guiding you since you can't see your past?"

Voice startled, he said, "I hadn't thought of it that way, but it's true." He kissed her forehead. "You haven't led me astray."

The trust in his voice made her cringe inwardly. After a few more steps, she said, "Did we just pass through the archway that leads into the garden? The air felt . . . more compressed for a moment."

"You're very perceptive." He led her forward another dozen steps and stopped, removing her hand from his arm. "We're here. Tell what you sense."

"To begin with, I just heard you set down the basket. The bricks I'm standing on feel different from the flagstones of the path that led here. Softer but more even." She turned in a slow circle. "The air is very still—the walls protect us from the breeze. They also collect the sun. Your garden is noticeably warmer than outside."

"What do you hear?"

She caught her breath. "Running water! The overall sound is made up of several smaller sounds that are like different notes, high and low. Did you install a fountain?"

"I restored an existing fountain that had been concealed under the vine," he replied. "What else?"

"Birdsong. Songbirds are everywhere in the country, but I usually don't notice them so much. There are pipits right here inside your garden, aren't there? And I hear . . . warblers and sparrows, I think. Farther away. Layers and layers of lovely sounds. And the scents! Daffodils are in full bloom, I think. I can smell them. They always make me think of butter. But there are other scents, too. Different plant smells. And I think that espaliered fruit tree is starting to blossom. Apples?"

He chuckled. "You're doing very well with this. You've used scent and sound and touch. Everything but taste. Would you like to nibble on a flower?"

"I can do better than that." Using his voice as a guide, she moved to him and caught his arms, then stretched up to kiss his throat. "Mmm, salty. Very pleasant." She squeezed his arms. "Strong but a little yielding. A nice, solid feeling."

He laughed and drew her into a hug. She was very aware of how the length of her body pressed against his. The stimulating pressure of her breasts against his chest, the throb of blood through her most private places because of their closeness.

Abruptly vision returned when he pulled the scarf from her eyes. She was almost sorry to be pulled from the world of her senses, though glad to see his darkly handsome face so close to hers. "You've graduated with flying colors," he said. "I was brought blindfolded into a garden as a child, I think. Again, I don't really remember, but it feels as if I experienced this myself, long ago. That's why I wanted you to try this."

"Was that visit to the other garden you remembered?" she asked as she stepped from his embrace.

He frowned, then shook his head. "Perhaps, but I really don't know."

Wanting to take the dark expression from his face, she surveyed the garden. It had been lovely in its wild state, but Adam's careful work had created a deep sense of harmony. An old wooden bench had been set invitingly under the tree, and what had been a ragged patch of greenery had been turned into a pleasant swath of grass.

Best of all was the fountain. She crossed the garden to look more closely. "I love the way the water flows from the lion's mouth on top, then spills into those different-sized basins, to create different sounds. You said the fountain was here when you cut back on the vine?" She touched the lichened gray stone of the lion's head, then trailed her fingers in the clear water of the basin below.

"It was completely covered. I'd planned on installing a fountain, so it was great luck to discover this one. The pipe and basins needed to be cleared, but that was all."

She drifted around the garden, examining and touching. "You've done a marvelous job here. Even breathing the air is relaxing."

"I'm glad you like it." He looked around with satisfaction. "Much remains to be done, but I'm pleased that it is becoming what I wanted."

"It's time to celebrate your creation." She lifted the lid of the basket just enough to pull out a somewhat ragged lap rug. After spreading it on the grass, she set the basket in the middle of the rug and settled gracefully beside it. At least, she hoped she looked graceful. "You had a surprise for me. Now I have one for you." She gave him a wicked smile. "We're going to have a dark luncheon."

Chapter Fifteen

At Mariah's words, Adam glanced up at the sunny sky, which contained only a few puffy white clouds. "I hope that doesn't mean I must wait until nightfall to eat."

"We'll eat now, but blindfolded," she explained. "My father once attended a gaming house in Paris that served a *souper noir*—a black supper. The dining chamber was completely lightless and the servants were blind men skilled at working in darkness. A variety of foods were served. My father said it was interesting, if rather disconcerting." She grinned. "He also said the dinner was essentially the prelude to an orgy."

"Your father said such a thing to his young daughter?" Adam said, scandalized.

"He used rather more delicate language, but yes, that was the general idea." For a moment she felt again the suffocating pain of loss. But it was not so bad since Adam had arrived. She had, almost, given up hoping that a cheerful, news-filled letter would arrive from her father apologizing for not having written in so long.

Forcing herself to continue, she said, "He thought I should know the ways of the world since I accompanied him to all those country-house parties. The black-supper story was just for amusement, since it happened so many years ago. He was a lad on the Grand Tour, I believe."

"He made the Grand Tour? He was fortunate to have the opportunity." Adam folded down onto the blanket. "Since the French Revolution, young English gentlemen have been deprived of the chance to make fools of themselves in the great capitals of Europe. Was your father from a wealthy family?"

She made a face. "He never talked about such things. I had the impression that he was traveling companion to the heir of some grand lord. An alarming thought, that my father might have been considered the responsible one!"

Adam chuckled. "Whatever his faults, he raised an excellent daughter."

She untied the second scarf from the handle of the basket. "I have no more idea what is here than you do. I explained about the dark luncheon to Mrs. Beckett and told her to use her imagination. She looked quite keen on the idea, so be prepared!"

She rose on her knees and wrapped the scarf around his head. "Can you see anything?"

"The faintest hint of light comes through the cloth, but I see nothing. It's an odd sensation," he said thoughtfully. "Different from nighttime dark. More . . . vulnerable. Now for you. Can you blindfold yourself? Mustn't have any cheating!"

"That would take the fun away. I'll do the wrapping, but it would help if you could tie the scarf." She wrapped the length around her head, covering her eyes as thoroughly as she'd done with Adam. "I'm going to bend over the basket so you can fasten the scarf."

She heard the slight sounds of a man shifting position. Then his seeking fingers touched the nape of her neck. She caught her breath as erotic sensations shot through her. Her voice was less than steady when she said, "That's my neck. The scarf is a few inches closer to you."

"Sorry." His hands moved to where she was holding the ends of the scarf behind her head. As he deftly tied the scarf, she marveled how every touch between them seemed more intimate in their blindfolded state. Even the brush of his fingertips on her hair was riveting.

Once the scarf was tied on, she flipped back the lid of the basket. "Now to discover what we have. Ah, four napkins so we can cover our laps and have a spare for cleaning up spills. Here—I'm holding yours above the middle of the basket."

"She's a wise woman. Mess is inevitable. But amusing, I think." His seeking hand located his two napkins.

"This will probably be easiest if we eat one dish at a time, since anything set down might get lost." Mariah spread a napkin across her lap, then dug into the basket again. "Let's start with our drinks. Mrs. Beckett said she's put in two bottles of something suitable, but she didn't say what. Here's yours."

Several moments passed before his hand touched the bottom of the bottle, then moved up over her fingers, his palm caressing. She licked her lips, wanting to lean forward and nibble on him.

She was startlingly aware of his presence, in some ways more so than if she could see him. Body heat. Motion in the air when he reached toward her. The faint sounds made even when a person was sitting still. His individual scent, which she hadn't noticed consciously. His was . . . intriguing. Male. She wanted to rub her face against him.

She blushed as she realized that consciousness could not be sharper if they were sitting on the blanket naked. Thank heaven he couldn't see how she was reacting!

His fingers closed on the bottle, brushing the side of her hand. "I have it now, so you can let go. A cork, I see, not shoved in too deeply." There was a pop, followed by fizzing sounds. "Champagne! Mrs. Beckett certainly entered into the spirit of the occasion. Let's see if the other bottle is the same."

He opened it. More fizzing. "Champagne for each of us. Here's yours."

She took her bottle and tilted it up to sip. The wine bubbled down her throat, making her feel equally bubbly. "Delicious! The pride of Burke's cellar, I suspect."

"Lovely stuff," he agreed. "What next?"

His bottle gurgled as he tipped it to drink. She imagined his lips closing over the glass lip and shivered at the suggestive thought. To keep her bottle safely upright and easy to find, she set it between her knees, again grateful that he couldn't see her unladylike behavior. "You choose."

Soft sounds as he explored the basket's contents. "There are all sorts of interesting shapes. I'll take a look at this round object wrapped in cheese-cloth." He gave a rueful chuckle. "Sorry, looking and seeing are so much a part of the language that it's hard not to use the words."

She smiled with him. "What does your prize feel and smell like?"

A rustle of wispy fabric in motion. Then he sniffed. "The package contains two spheres about three inches across. They're warm and yielding. Crisp and rather greasy. Some sort of fried meat, I believe." He paused. "There are places where certain . . . essential parts of a bull's reproductive equipment are eaten as a special delicacy. You don't suppose . . . ?"

"Surely Mrs. Beckett wouldn't do that to us, even assuming the ingredients were available!" She also paused, disconcerted. "Or would she? Which of us will taste first?"

"I will, because I'm a brave husband who protects his wife from unpleasantness." His bite sounded cautious. "There is meat, but inside it's smooth and slippery. I don't think it's what we were discussing. Here's the second one. Maybe you can identify it."

After an enjoyable tangling of fingers, she took the warm sphere from him. A bite confirmed her guess. "A Scotch egg! I should have realized, but I've always identified them by sight." She washed the bite down with a generous swig of champagne. She was starting to feel a gentle, happy buzz from the alcohol. If they were at a ball, she would dance all night. "A hard-boiled egg is covered with ground sausage, rolled in egg and bread crumbs, then fried. Quite tasty when one knows what it is."

"This tastes much better now that I know." There was a grin in his voice. After they finished their Scotch eggs, he said, "Your turn."

She felt around inside the basket. "I've found two short, broad jars with corked tops. Warm." She lifted one and tilted it. "Soup, I suspect. Mrs. Beckett makes marvelous soups. Would you like some?"

He took the warm pottery jar and removed the cork stopper. An exotic, spicy aroma was released. "Good God, curry!" he exclaimed.

She opened her own jar and inhaled. "It's very distinctive, isn't it? I've had curried food occasionally. Obviously you have, too."

"The scent is very evocative," he said slowly. "I think I've had it often, but I don't remember any actual occasions."

"Perhaps eating the soup will refresh your memory. There should be spoons in the basket. Ah, here's yours."

They had developed some skill at passing items back and forth by using the same area over the basket. When his hand touched hers, his fingers stroked down her wrist, trailing across her pulse. "Hmm, soft," he said. "Not a spoon."

Her fingers clenched involuntarily on the metal implement. It was an effort to say calmly, "Your spoon, sir."

He accepted it, and she sampled the soup. "Creamy. I think there are chopped onions and carrots, but I'm not sure what the bits of meat are. Chicken, maybe?"

"That or rabbit. It's hard to say since neither of those are particularly distinctive. It's good, though."

After they finished and Mariah set the empty jars back in the basket, he said, "The curry flavor is tantalizing, but no memories surfaced."

Hearing the frustration in his voice, she said, "I shall ask Mrs. Beckett to make curried dishes until the memories take shape. Now it's your turn to choose."

Adam dug in again. "Here's another soft item wrapped in cheesecloth. Let's see . . . two slices of a squishy substance with pastry around the rim. Here's your slice."

Her portion had an intense aroma, familiar but maddeningly elusive. "Not cheese. Something meaty." She nipped off a bit and let it dissolve in her mouth so she could taste the flavors completely. "Paté."

"With mushrooms," he agreed. "Mrs. Beckett has an impressive range."

She ate the rest of her slice and washed it down. Everything tasted better when followed by champagne. "I'm getting rather full, but the basket is not yet empty. I'll see if I can find a sweet ending to the meal."

Her probing hand found an oval bowl with a lid, the earthenware warm to the touch. "Here's a shallow crock that might hold a baked pudding. Let's see. . . ." She lifted the lid and poked in a tentative finger. She jerked it out quickly. "Oooh, that's disgusting! It feels like chopped worms."

"Surely not." His fingers touched hers as he felt for the bowl. He gave her a little caress before reaching into the bowl. "Definitely . . . odd," he agreed. "But it smells good and I have faith in Mrs. Beckett. I'll try some."

She heard him taste and swallow. "Macaroni cheese," he announced. "And a very good version. I never realized just how alarming macaroni cheese feels if one can't identify it by sight."

It was a dish Mariah liked, so she said, "We'll have to share since there's only one bowl. Have a fork. We can hold the bowl between us and both eat from it."

The dish was so tasty that soon they were laughing as their forks clashed. "I'll have to use fingers to find if there's any left. Ah, here's some. You get to eat it since you braved the chopped worms. Can you take this last bit from my fingers?"

"To prove that you have me eating out of your hand?" he said with a smile in his voice. "Most willingly."

She shivered with pleasure when he found the tidbit and nibbled it away with warm lips. He lingered, sucking gently on her fingertips.

She inhaled sharply as her whole body tingled with awareness. "Fingers are . . . not on the menu."

"No?" He trailed his tongue over the exquisitely sensitive center of her palm. She gave a choked moan.

Adam caught his breath and pressed his cheek into her palm for a moment. "You are sweeter than the finest dish ever created," he whispered. Shoving the basket aside, he pulled her down onto the blanket. His mouth found hers and their tongues mated with fierce sensuality.

Dizzy with champagne and erotic play, Mariah yearned for his touch in every fiber of her being. Their mutual exploration in the last nights had taught her something of passion's delights. Now she wanted him—all of him. The blindfolds removed them from the normal world to a realm of pure pleasure. Her senses were on fire. She loved his taste, his scent, his voice.

Most of all, she loved the feel of his hands and lips as he tugged up her skirts and caressed the smooth skin of her belly. She gasped as his hand slid between her thighs, his fingers as intimate as his wickedly skilled mouth. "Beautiful," he breathed. "Every aspect of body and soul, you are beautiful."

Giddy with desire and champagne, she didn't care about morals or the future or possible consequences. Passion had been building since the night they first met, and nothing mattered but to join in the most primal of ways.

She moaned into his throat when his fingers slid deep inside her. She was all heat and moisture and hot need. The moments when he paused to unbutton the fall of his trousers and free himself were too long. She bit his shoulder, wanting to consume him.

"I don't think I can make this last," he said raggedly as he pressed against her.

"I don't care!" She wrapped her arms around his chest and pulled him hard against her body.

They joined together with a swiftness that left no room for second thoughts. He was inside her, hot and hard, amazing and shocking and *necessary.* The brief spike of pain didn't dim her desire, only intensified her need to become one flesh. She rocked against him, feeling every movement in his lean, powerful body.

They swiftly found a rhythm that intensified the searing pleasure with every thrust. She was a coiled spring, winding unbearably tighter until he slid his fingers between them and touched her with expert skill.

She shattered, no longer aware of boundaries between them. Only intimacy and unholy pleasure beyond anything she'd ever dreamed. *Dear God, dear God, dear God . . .*

As her nails bit into his back, he gave a choked cry and went rigid. She wrapped her arms and legs around him, holding him safe as he spilled into her.

With passion burned out, normal awareness returned. She drew a ragged breath as she recognized that they were locked together on a scratchy blanket, the birds singing as if the two humans below hadn't just performed an act that changed their relationship irrevocably. Her head spun with champagne and shock.

"Mariah, my love." Adam rolled onto his side but kept her close. She heard the rustle as he removed his blindfold. Then he tugged hers off. As she blinked from the light, he kissed the corner of her eye with aching tenderness. He was so honest, so true. And she was not.

"I give thanks for the day you became my wife. But . . ." he hesitated, his voice uncertain. "Perhaps I'm wrong, but . . . did we not consummate our marriage after our wedding?"

Even now he trusted her, giving her the benefit of the doubt when the facts didn't agree with what she had told him. Guilt over her cascading lies ripped through her. She scrambled to her feet, tears of anguish and self-loathing brimming in her eyes. "I'm sorry," she gasped. "So sorry."

Wanting to escape before she broke down entirely, she spun around and tried to bolt from the garden, but he was too quick. He caught her from behind, drawing her back against his body with arms around her waist. "I'm sorry, Mariah," he said, confusion in his voice. "I thought you wanted to lie with me."

"I did," she replied, her voice choked.

"Did I hurt you? That's the last thing I would ever want to do." Keeping her secure with one arm around her waist, he used his other hand to stroke her shoulder and arm as if she were a nervous pony.

"Nothing to signify," she whispered.

"Then what's wrong, Mariah? I love you and I want to be a good husband. Am I so different from what I was before?"

Much as she wanted to disappear into the ground, she must tell him the truth. She took a deep breath and broke free from his embrace, turning to face him. "I don't know what you were like before," she said bleakly. "We are not husband and wife. I never saw you in my life before the night I pulled you from the sea."

Chapter Sixteen

Adam's breath vanished as if a giant had slammed him in the belly. Mariah's shimmering blond hair spilled around her shoulders, loose and sensual, as he had longed to see it. He ached to take her into his arms—and she was saying that they didn't belong together. "We're not married?" he said numbly, unable to believe that she wasn't his. "You're not my wife?"

She used a scarf to blot away her tears. Even with swollen eyes and red nose, she was lovely. "No. I'm so sorry. I lied, and it . . . it just got out of hand."

"Why did you say we were married?"

She balled up the damp scarf. "I was so lonely, and George Burke was courting me," she said haltingly. "I knew in my bones it would be a terrible mistake to marry him, but usually he was charming and reasonable. I could feel myself drifting toward saying yes. That way I'd be spared a lawsuit, I'd have a husband with roots in Hartley—everything would be so much easier. In a weak moment, I might have accepted him. S . . . so I told him that I had a husband who was away in the Peninsula."

"Fighting the French?" Images of soldiers and high hot plains and bloody combat flickered through his mind. Had he experienced that? Perhaps he had only read of battle in the newspapers, since the images lacked the clarity of his dreams. "Then I appeared and didn't know who I was. Convenient material for a husband who didn't exist."

"There's more." She folded down on the far end of the bench. "I learned different little rituals from Granny Rose. Simple ways of concentrating on what one wants or needs. I woke up one night desperate, so I decided to perform a wish ritual, asking for a solution to my problem with Burke." She smiled wryly. "Granny Rose used to say her rituals were like prayers with herbs added."

"So you wished for a husband."

"I didn't mean to be that specific. But as I burned the incense out in the gazebo, I found myself yearning for the . . . the husband of my dreams. Someone not like Burke. After the ritual, I felt at peace and dozed a little, and then I woke up hearing an urgent voice in my head that sounded just like Granny Rose. She said I must go down to the shore." She glanced up at him. "That is when I found you."

"I have trouble believing I looked like anyone's dream husband then." He sat on the opposite end of the bench, as far from Mariah as he could get. His sense of identity had shattered into hopeless confusion. *He wasn't Adam Clarke. He was nobody.*

He'd assumed he loved Mariah because she was his wife, so of course he loved her. Belief had been easy, given her beauty and kindness. But everything between them was based on a lie. They were strangers, and he no longer knew how he felt about her.

She continued, "I didn't connect you to the wish ritual at first. I just wanted to get you ashore and safe." She fell silent for a dozen heartbeats. "When

I asked if you remembered that I was your wife, it was almost like Granny Rose was speaking through me. But I can't blame her. I said the words, and I didn't withdraw them later."

In a weird way, he understood how circumstances could make something seem right and logical even if it wasn't. But—she had lied about a critical fact that had become his anchor. Now that anchor was gone. "My appearance must have seemed fated. But why didn't you reveal the truth after Burke left?"

"I wanted to, but you seemed very happy to think me your wife." She looked down at the balled-up scarf. "I worried how you would react if you realized that you were alone, with no memory of who you are."

She had been right to worry, but he thought it would have been easier to accept that they didn't know one another at the beginning. From the moment he woke up, still damp around the edges, he had embraced her statement that they were married. Soon he came to feel that he needed to know nothing else.

Now much that was mysterious made sense. No wonder she was so ignorant about his past, his family, and his occupation. Perhaps it was the blow on his head that made him so accepting of her explanations. Looking back, he was amazed that he hadn't questioned her harder. "Why did you call me Adam?"

"He was the first man, and you seemed comfortable with it." She sighed. "I kept hoping your memory would return and I could confess. If it had been only a day or so, it wouldn't have mattered so much that I had lied. I could have come up with a reason that would have seemed somewhat plausible. But the longer my pretense went on, the harder it was to tell the truth."

So he was a nameless stranger living on the charity of a woman who had needed protection from a rascal. He looked at his calloused hands. Not the hands of a gentleman. Knowing he might be a gardener or sailor didn't upset him unduly. Not knowing who he was did. "I'll leave tomorrow, though I'll have to borrow clothes since I have nothing." He gave a harsh bark of laughter. He had nothing, knew nothing, *was* nothing.

"No!" She stared at him, horrified. "I would be happy to supply you with clothes and money, but where would you go? What would you do?"

"I have no idea. But I'll be damned if I'll stay on as a beggar at your table," he said bleakly.

"You're no beggar!" she exclaimed. "You're my . . . my friend. You are welcome here always."

"Your *friend*." The numbness that had started in his middle was spreading, dissolving the strength and happiness he had known with Mariah. "I had thought I was so much more. But now I understand why you avoided my bed."

"I . . . I was trying to be wise," she whispered.

He studied her face. "Why did you change your mind today? It was careless of you to give away your virginity to a stranger."

"You are no longer a stranger." She flushed scarlet. "And today I wanted you so much that I didn't care about the consequences."

Her remark was flattering, but it still chilled him. "And if the consequences include a baby?"

The blood drained from her face. "I . . . I wasn't thinking of anything beyond how much I wanted you."

"Babies are a standard consequence of intimacy. In fact, they're rather the point." He looked across his garden, which was no longer his. "If you're with child and I've gone away, you can tell the neighbors I'm dead. That would make you a respectable widow. I promise I won't return to complicate your life."

"I don't want you to leave!!" Tears glinted in her eyes.

He studied her face again. Perhaps he should be outraged at her lies, but mostly he felt deeply sad. He could see how she'd started with one small, expedient lie that had spun out of control. Now her anguished face was transparent with honesty. Certainly her passion had seemed real. Yet he had trusted her without question before, and that simple trust was no longer possible.

But he still desired her. He clasped her left hand. Her cold fingers clutched hard. "If you want me to stay, we could turn your lie into truth. It's not far to Gretna Green."

She bit her lip. "I would like nothing better, but what if you already have a wife?"

Adam felt as if he'd been struck a mortal blow. He might be married to another woman? "I . . . I haven't had time to think of that."

"You settled into the role of husband so naturally that I wondered if you're married." Her mouth twisted. "That is more likely than you being single. You are too handsome and kind not to have had girls setting their caps for you. If you're married to a small blond like me, I might even have seemed familiar to you."

More flattery, but he couldn't get beyond the realization that in practical terms, he hadn't a penny to his name, or a shirt to cover his back. He rubbed his throbbing temples. The blood vessels felt on the verge of bursting. "The thought of another wife is more than I can grasp."

Mariah crushed the scarf in her free hand. "I keep imagining a wife waiting for you, despairing of your return. And perhaps children. How could I marry you knowing that another woman might be breaking her heart over your absence? Not only would it be bigamy, it would be *wrong*."

He felt almost ill. Children were another subject he hadn't considered. Yet it wasn't unreasonable that he might have a young family. "If I have children, of course I could not knowingly abandon them. But what if I never remember who I am? Must I live my life alone?"

"I've thought about this rather a lot." She smiled unsteadily. "It hasn't been that long since your accident. The fact that you've been having dreams that might be memories implies that soon you might remember who you are."

He thought of those dreams. Somewhere in his mind, the truth of his identity must still exist. All he had to do was find it. "How long should I wait before it would be safe to move forward with my life?"

"I think a man must be missing for seven years before he's presumed dead," she said hesitantly. "If at the end of that time you still don't know who you are or where you came from, it should be safe to assume your new life is the only one you will have."

"Seven years," he said flatly. "That's a very long time. Much can happen in seven years."

"Do you think you could ever learn to trust me again?" she whispered. "Or if not trust . . . at least forgive."

"I hope so." He studied her delicate features and her sensual, perfectly proportioned figure, wishing he could have seen her unclothed. He supposed it didn't mean much for an amnesiac man to think she was the most beautiful woman he'd ever seen, but more than beautiful, she was . . . very dear. Trust and desire didn't have much to do with each other. "But it's too soon."

She nodded, unsurprised. "I wish there was something I could do to help you remember. You've already helped me so much by getting rid of George Burke. Now that he thinks I have a man to protect me, he hasn't bothered with a lawsuit."

"It would have been better if you'd done less. But I'm glad that Burke has ceased troubling you." He sighed as he gazed at the water spilling from the fountain. "If you're with child, I think you'll have to marry me. Then if I wake up one morning and remember that I have a family elsewhere, I shall leave and you can mourn my untimely death. At least the child will not bear the public stigma of illegitimacy."

"That seems . . . reasonable," she said in a choked voice.

Though he couldn't trust her, he couldn't bear to see her misery. He slid across the bench and crushed her in a hard embrace, thinking how quickly he had gone from passionate joy to equally passionate sorrow.

She clung to him, shaking at first, but gradually she relaxed. He stroked her shimmering hair, sliding his fingers into the golden mass. He wanted to pull her down on the soft grass and make love to her again. This time should be slow and sensual, with all garments removed so they could lie flesh to flesh.

But now that he knew they were not married, passion no longer had the upper hand. If they hadn't made a child today, they must not risk it happening when so much was uncertain.

He buried his face in her hair, and wondered what would happen to them.

That night they each slept alone. Or perhaps didn't sleep.

Chapter Seventeen

Hartley, Northern England

The days were getting longer as spring advanced toward summer. Will Masterson was glad for that, or he would have been riding in the dark. Not wise when traveling on strange roads in wild places.

He rode into the courtyard of the Bull and Anchor, Hartley's only inn, as the light began to fade over the Irish Sea. The place was small, but it looked well kept. He hoped they had a room for him, but given his present level of fatigue, he'd willingly accept straw in the stables if it was reasonably clean.

He was in luck. Three of the inn's five rooms were available, so if Randall and Kirkland showed up the next day as planned, there should be space.

For tonight, Will was glad to be alone. The taproom had decent boiled beef and beer. He considered asking the landlord if any bodies had washed ashore in the previous weeks but decided to wait until his friends joined him. He didn't need more bad news. So he ate in silence, knowing that Hartley was the end of their quest.

After finishing his dinner, he took advantage of the long northern dusk to walk down to the town's little waterfront. Half a dozen fishing boats were tied to the small docks. The splash of waves and the mournful cries of gulls were soothing.

Though his friends thought him an incurable optimist, he had known there wasn't much chance of finding Ashton alive. Still, he'd hoped they would find a body that could be taken home. Ash deserved the dignity of a proper burial. Though he had enemies because of his position, he had far more friends because of the man he was.

The chances of that proper burial were now slim. After this much time, the sea was unlikely to give up her dead. As Will gazed at the after sunset sky, he made his peace with that knowledge. Ash had loved the sea, and it was not a bad resting place for a man's bones.

But that still left the matter of how Ashton had died. Will had lost friends to battle and disease and accidents, and one damned fool who couldn't keep his breeches buttoned had been shot by a jealous Spanish husband.

But he'd never lost a friend to cold-blooded murder. The search for Ashton's body was over. The search for his killer would never end until the bastard was found.

• • •

The next morning, Will was pleased to learn that the inn served quite a decent breakfast. The landlord's pretty young daughter, Ellie, arrived with a large tray that held a steaming mug, a basket of fresh-baked bread, and a plate piled high with sausage and eggs, fried potatoes and onions.

As Ellie set the food down, she asked, "Is there anything else you'd like, Mr. Masterson?"

"This should do nicely." After a swallow of tea, Will decided it was time to ask the question. "A friend of mine was lost when his ship sank north of here. I and two other friends have been searching to see if his body has turned up anywhere along the coast. Do you know if any drowned men have been found in this area in the last two or three weeks?"

She shook her head. "There was Mrs. Clarke's husband who washed up here while on his way to her, but he's alive. No bodies, Lord be thanked."

Startled, Will asked, "This Mr. Clarke. He's well-known locally, I presume. He had a boating accident?"

"You're right about the accident, but he's new to Hartley," Ellie replied. "His wife just inherited Hartley Manor and Mr. Clarke was coming to join her when his ship went down or some such." She frowned. "No one in town here knows exactly what happened." Clearly the lack of information irritated her.

"Have you seen Mr. Clarke?" Will asked, suddenly having trouble breathing. When the girl nodded, he continued, "What does he look like?"

"Oh, he's a handsome fellow, and ever so much a gentleman," she said warmly. "I've seen him ride through Hartley several times. Not over tall, but a fine figure of a man. Dark coloring, except that his eyes are a rare shade of green. A blessing that he didn't drown."

Will swore under his breath and leaped from his chair. Almost before Ellie had finished speaking, he was on his way to the stables.

Chapter Eighteen

Mariah spent a restless night wondering if Adam's shocked numbness would turn into anger. The misery in his face when she'd confessed had made her feel ill. And despite her guilt, she missed having him in her bed. Though they had slept together for only a few nights and made love only once, his absence ached like an amputated limb. She could hardly bear the thought that they might never be physically close again.

There was some comfort in waking to find Annabelle standing on her chest, the furry black and white face earnest in the faint light. The cat usually stayed in the kitchen by the fire, but perhaps she sensed Mariah's distress. Whatever the reason, she was glad to have the sleek black and white body settle next to her.

Mariah was nervous when she got up and went downstairs. Adam wasn't in the breakfast room when she arrived. Her imagination immediately produced an image of him packing up in the middle of the night and fleeing on horseback to get away from her lying, untrustworthy self. Sister Sarah would *not* have found herself in such a situation.

He appeared when she was pouring tea and gave a faint smile as he accepted the cup she poured for him. "Did you sleep well?"

"Honestly? No." She smiled ruefully. "Annabelle kept me company."

"And Bhanu joined me." He buttered a piece of toast. "It was . . . not an improvement on what I had come to expect."

They shared a wry glance. She almost melted with relief. It might be impossible for them to be together in the future, but it mattered tremendously that he didn't hate her.

Feeling a dangerous desire to kiss him, she reminded herself sharply that at any moment, Adam might recall a life that had no place for her. "Try some of the blackberry preserves. Mrs. Beckett's daughter made them."

"Thank you." He scooped out a heaping spoonful. "I think it best if we continue to act as we have in the past. Up to a point."

And she knew exactly where that point was. He hadn't touched her since that last, desperate

185

embrace in the garden. He was a wise man. Wiser than she. "I agree. I much prefer being on friendly terms with you."

"And I with you," he said softly.

They were chatting amiably, almost like they had before her confession, when the downstairs maid entered the breakfast room, her eyes round with excitement. "There is a gentleman here to see Mr. Clarke. A Mr. Masterson. He's waiting in the drawing room."

Granny Rose had sometimes had flashes of certainty that she said were like being splashed with ice water. For the first time, Mariah experienced that chilling sensation.

Adam rose and said, "Likely it's someone from the village looking for employment. He should have gone to Cochrane, but he might not know we've hired a steward. I'll talk to him. I like to get the measure of men we . . ." Adam hesitated, then continued, "Men you might employ."

Heart pounding, Mariah also rose. "I'll go with you. Perhaps I'll recognize him from church." As she walked beside Adam, she wished she could grab his hand and run away, but she knew in her bones that whatever fate awaited could not be avoided.

They entered the drawing room, and she immediately understood why the maid had said "gentleman." The tall stranger, Masterson, stood by the window, his broadly built body tight with tension.

Brown haired and gray eyed, he wore power and authority as easily as his well-tailored clothing. He was around Adam's age, and while not as handsome, his wide-cheekboned face looked designed for laughter.

As soon as they entered, he stared at Adam, riveted. "Ash!" he breathed.

Pain stabbed through Mariah. Disaster had arrived.

Masterson rushed over and grabbed Adam's right hand with both of his. He didn't even see Mariah. "My God, you're alive! We were all sure you had drowned!"

Mariah felt shock blaze through Adam. Shock, but also eagerness. He asked, "You know me?"

"Anytime these last twenty years." Masterson's brow furrowed and he released Adam's hand as he realized something wasn't right. "Don't you recognize me?"

"I'm afraid not." Adam closed the door. "We must talk. Why did you think I was dead?" He took Mariah's hand and led her to the sofa, his clasp numbingly tight.

Masterson took a chair opposite. "Your steamship exploded on a test run out of Glasgow. You were missing and presumed dead. After Randall, Kirkland, and I heard the news, we traveled to Glasgow and we've been looking for you or your body ever since. How did you end up this far south?" He studied Adam's impassive face.

"I had a head injury that scrambled my wits." Adam absently touched the healing scar on his head. "I don't remember the accident, but I vaguely recall clinging to a piece of wreckage for a long time. Days. Eventually I came ashore here with no memory of my name or past." He frowned at Masterson. "Yet . . . I've seen your face in a dream. An icy night near London, and a woman's death."

Masterson's face paled. "There was such a night. Do you remember nothing else from before you were in the water?"

"Only dreams that might be true dreams." His voice became intent. "How do I know you?"

"Six of us met as the first class at the Westerfield Academy when we were around ten or eleven years old. We've been fast friends ever since." He smiled a little. "It was a school for problem boys. I'm Will Masterson. My problem was acute stubbornness." For the first time, he seemed to notice Mariah, and his gaze was uncomfortably sharp. "Will you introduce me to this lady?"

"She is Miss Mariah Clarke. The woman who saved my life by pulling me out of the water and taking me in." Adam's grip on her hand tightened. "My fiancée."

Mariah was almost as startled as Masterson, whose jaw dropped. Apparently Adam wished to maintain the illusion that they were a couple. If they could be. Afraid of hearing the worst, Mariah asked, "He isn't married already, is he?"

"No." Masterson collected himself. "Forgive my rudeness. I am merely surprised by the suddenness. It's a pleasure to meet you, Miss Clarke. Especially since you saved Ash's life."

Mariah almost dissolved with relief. Thank heaven that the devoted wife and loving children of her imagination didn't exist! She wasn't sure why Adam claimed her as his fiancée, but guessed that she was his shield against this new uncertainty.

"I'm glad I haven't forgotten a family," Adam said. "But you have not yet told me who I am."

Masterson smiled apologetically. "Sorry, I'm not thinking clearly. I'm still stunned by the miracle of your recovery. Your name is Adam Darshan Lawford."

"Adam?" He glanced at Mariah, startled.

"I picked the name at random!" she said under her breath.

"This explains why it felt comfortable." To Masterson, he said, "So my name is Adam Lawford. Where do I live? What is my occupation? Do I even have one?"

"You have several homes. One in London, of course," Masterson said, as if a London house was the most natural thing in the world. "While you own a number of other properties, your principal seat is Ralston Abbey in Wiltshire."

As Mariah bit her lip at the thought of so much wealth, Adam said warily, "I sound . . . prosperous."

"Rather more than prosperous," Masterson replied with amusement. "And you're kept rather busy as well. You're the seventh Duke of Ashton."

Mariah's relief at Adam's single status vanished. "Adam is a *duke?*"

He was as far away from her as ever. Perhaps even farther.

Adam heard Mariah gasp. Her shock echoed his. He was getting devilish tired of shocks. "A duke. If I recall correctly, that's a very high rank, is it not?"

"The highest, outside the royal family," Masterson replied.

A duke. Adam hated the idea. Just thinking about it made him feel strangled. "It seems improbable that I should be a duke."

"Improbable, but true," Masterson said patiently. It must be strange for him to be talking with an old friend who didn't recognize him. Though not as strange as it was being the old friend.

Adam flashed back to the dream he'd had in which a younger Masterson had just lost a beloved wife. The friendship between him and Masterson had been palpable. Yet he had no true memory of the thousand small interactions that had built into that friendship. He did, however, retain an under-lying trust. He had no doubt that Will Masterson was telling the truth.

Adam had expected to be delighted to rediscover his past, but he had assumed his memories would come back on their own. Having his life explained to him was profoundly strange. "I'm glad no wife and children have been mourning me." He squeezed Mariah's hand again. Despite the awkwardness of their situation, she was familiar. "Do I have other family? A mother, brothers, sisters?"

"You haven't many close relations." Masterson frowned. "I'd best start at the beginning. You were born in India. Your father served as the British Resident at a Hindu royal court; I'm not sure which one. He was a cousin to the Duke of Ashton, but not closely in line to inherit. I believe there were four or five nearer heirs. So when he fell in love with a lovely, high-born Hindu girl, there seemed no reason not to marry. Many other British officers serving in India have done the same."

Adam stared down at the hand that wasn't holding on to Mariah's. So this was the source of his dark, un-English coloring. He thought of the familiar taste of curry on his tongue, and the exotic flowered garden. Most of all, he thought of the beautiful dark-haired woman. "I presume the other heirs died, then my father, so the Ashton inheritance went to an un-English half blood."

"Exactly so. I believe your father had just been informed that he was the sixth duke and he was making plans to return to England when he was struck with a fever and died." Masterson's voice turned dry. "Naturally the authorities stepped in and sent you back to London with a British family that was returning home so you could be raised as a proper English gentleman."

How casually "the authorities" had ripped him away from everything he had known. "What of my mother? Do I have any younger brothers or sisters?" He thought of the dream where he had played with a boy and a girl with green eyes.

Masterson started to reply, then halted. "Now that I think of it, I don't know the circumstances of your mother's death. You've never talked much about your past. Perhaps she died before your father inherited. There were no younger children, or they would have been brought home, too."

"What crime landed me in a school for problem boys? Being foreign?" Adam's voice was edged.

Masterson looked embarrassed. "I think that was much of the reason. You were being difficult and your trustees just didn't know what to do with you.

"But being sent to the Westerfield Academy was for the best. Lady Agnes Westerfield is the founder and headmistress of the academy, and she's the most amazing woman. She has traveled the world, visiting wild and dangerous places. She used to tell us tales of her adventures if we were good. She started the school to keep herself busy. In fact, you were the first student. She actually likes boys, which made the academy a fine place to be." More quietly, he said, "She became the mother none of us had."

Adam looked at his dark hands again, with their

calluses. He couldn't have been anyone's idea of a duke. "I have no other family?"

"You spent summers and holidays in the household of your father's first cousin. He and his family were away from England when you first returned, or you might have been sent to them instead of Westerfield. You called them Uncle Henry and Aunt Georgiana. He died a while back, but she and her two children, Hal and Janey, survive."

Glad he wasn't entirely devoid of relations, Adam asked, "Do my cousins have green eyes?"

Masterson thought about it. "As a matter of fact, yes. Their eyes are very like yours. As far as I know, you get on well with both of them. Hal is a good fellow, and Janey is a real charmer."

A thought struck Adam. "This cousin Hal. He would be my heir, I think. He may not rejoice to learn I'm alive."

"I suppose that's true." Masterson's expression changed, as if an unpleasant thought had just struck. "He may be somewhat disappointed that he won't be the eighth duke—that's only human. But he'll be more happy than sorry to see you alive, I think."

Masterson's statement seemed rather tentative. Even a fond cousin was apt to feel disappointed when a great prize he thought he had inherited was taken away. A pity that Adam hadn't been left in India so this cousin would have been the duke. He surely would have enjoyed the rank more.

He glanced down at Mariah, who was sitting silent and unhappy, her fingers locked in his. With her blond loveliness and grave expression, she looked like a wounded Madonna. If he had never left India, he never would have met her, so he must be grateful for his inheritance, despite his confused feelings about her.

"What more do you want to know?" Masterson spread his hands. "I'm not sure where to start. You are well respected and have many friends. You like working with your hands, whether it's building a steam engine or digging in your garden." His gaze strayed to Mariah. "And you have been considered one of the greatest catches on the Marriage Mart since you first entered society."

Adam winced. "I think I'd rather not have known that." His head was throbbing with the worst pain he'd experienced since Mariah had pulled him from the sea. Now, despite everything, he wanted to be alone with her. "I think I've heard all I can absorb for now."

Taking the hint, Masterson got to his feet. "Kirkland and Randall should be arriving in Hartley today, barring the unforeseen. They'll want to see for themselves that you're alive. When would be a good time to call?"

As Adam and Mariah stood, she said, "You can all join us for dinner tonight if that's all right with you, Adam."

That would give him the rest of the day to collect

himself. He nodded. "We shall see you later then, Mr. Masterson."

"You've always called me Will. Everyone does." Masterson paused in front of Adam on his way to the door. "I'll let myself out. And . . . I thank God you're alive." He exited hastily, as if embarrassed at showing such naked emotion.

As soon as Masterson left the room, Adam turned and engulfed Mariah in his arms. "I thought I'd be glad to know who I am," he said tightly. "Now I wish Masterson had never found me."

She buried her face against his shoulder, her grip as tight as his. "It's better to know, I think. But this knowledge is . . . huge."

"Too huge," he said bleakly. Ending the embrace, he said, "Let's go outside. I am in need of peace."

Side by side, they went outside into the patchy sunshine and headed toward the meditation garden. "I had a dream of great golden beings with many arms," he said. "I didn't understand then, but I think they were Hindu gods."

"You must have seen statues in India when you were a child." She glanced up at him. "The garden that you remembered—was that also in India?"

"I think it must have been. The flowers and forms were not European." He conjured up the garden again. "Several times, I've dreamed of a beautiful dark-haired woman in flowing silk garments. My mother, I think."

She squeezed his hand. "How sad that you lost her so young."

"At least I had her long enough for some memories. You do not even have that, I think." It was a melancholy bond between them. They finished the walk to the meditation garden in silence.

His tension eased as they entered the enclosed space. Gently flowing water was immensely soothing. They sat down on the bench, so close they were almost touching. "I'm wondering if I ever enjoyed being a duke. The idea certainly doesn't appeal to me now. It seems like . . . like a cage with golden bars."

"I'm not fond of the thought, either." She sighed. "I realize now that I had retained a faint hope that perhaps we might someday be together, but that's gone. You are too far above me."

"Don't say that!" he said sharply.

"But it's true," she said quietly. "A man of great wealth and power has many responsibilities and claims on his attention. Generally he marries a woman of similar background so that she can run his households, be a hostess to his guests, and give credit to his name. He doesn't marry the daughter of a barely respectable gambler."

"Masterson doesn't know who your father was," Adam pointed out.

"No, he merely suspects that I'm an opportunist who scooped you up while you were vulnerable and confused." She laughed a little. "But you are welcome to claim me as your fiancée as long as you need a shield from ambitious maidens and their mothers. When you feel secure in your position, I shall politely end the betrothal, and no scandal will attach to either of us. You have my word on it."

Her expression changed as she realized that he had reason to doubt her word. "I swear on the grave of Granny Rose that I will not hold you to an unwanted engagement."

He believed that oath. He always believed her. That was the trouble. "I accept your promise. I'll admit that I'm glad to have a reason to keep you near me while I rediscover who I am the hard way."

"Claiming me as your fiancée may end up causing more problems than it solves," she warned. "I have always lived on the fringes of society, and the well bred can be cruel to those who are judged inferior. Even Masterson, who seems an easygoing fellow, was not pleased when you said we were betrothed."

Adam lifted her hand and kissed her palm. Mariah shivered at the touch of his lips.

Interlacing his fingers with hers, he said, "I hadn't realized how simple life was before Masterson arrived. All I had to worry about then was having no memory. Now I feel like I'm standing on the edge of an abyss."

"I can only imagine how disturbing your situation is." Her fingers squeezed his. "I'm so sorry for my part in making it all worse."

"You said we were friends, Mariah. Just . . . continue to be my friend. I like Masterson, but at the moment, I know you much better than I know anyone else." Knew her intimately. Knew the sweetness of her body, the joy of her laughter . . . Sharply he reined in his imagination before he gave in to desire and did something to make the current situation even more disastrous.

"Whatever you wish, I will try to give you," she said simply. "I owe you that."

He exhaled roughly. "If I were a stronger man, I'd reject aid based on obligation, but for now, I need you near me."

"You are strong, Adam. Most men would be gibbering lunatics after all you've endured." She stopped. "Should I call you Ashton? Or your grace?"

He winced. "Adam will do. Dukeliness is a great deal to absorb."

"Actually, I have no trouble seeing you as a duke," she said rather surprisingly. "You are knowledgeable about so many things. You have a composure that says you are at home anywhere, even if you are somewhat unsettled now. And you have an air of authority, as if you're used to being heard and obeyed."

"I'd thought of that last myself. But I was thinking more along the lines of being a ship captain." He had a long way to go before he would see himself as a duke.

Chapter Nineteen

Troubled, Will spent several hours riding through the rugged countryside before returning to Hartley. It was after noon when he rode into the courtyard of the Bull and Anchor. Kirkland's and Randall's horses were in the stables, so all three of them would be able to dine at Hartley Manor.

After tending his own mount, he proceeded directly to the private parlor. As expected, his friends were enjoying a luncheon of cold meats and cheeses.

Kirkland poured ale from a pitcher and offered it to Will. "I expect you'll want something to eat. The landlord said you'd arrived last night, then gone off somewhere."

Randall added, "If you're wondering if we have news to report, the answer is no."

"Unlike you, I do have news." Will took a swig of ale and settled into one of the chairs. "Mostly, but not entirely, good."

Kirkland caught his breath. "Ash's body was found near here?"

"Better than that. I found him alive and generally healthy, but he received a head injury and doesn't remember anything before the *Enterprise* sank." Will swallowed more ale. "And that includes us. I was a stranger to him."

"My God!" Randall stood so fast his chair fell

over. "Where is he? Why didn't you bring him here?"

Kirkland's face lit up. "I hadn't believed it possible that he could be alive. But amnesia . . ." He hesitated, then said, "You're absolutely sure it's him?"

"It is unquestionably Ash, right down to the scar on his hand that he got when he separated two fighting dogs. As to why I didn't bring him . . ." Will frowned. "He has taken up with a local female. The landlord's daughter who told me that Ash had been found on the shore said that he is called Mr. Clarke and is married to the woman, Mariah Clarke. Ash says she's his fiancée. She has a firm hold on him, and she's not letting go."

Randall sank back into his chair. "So a fortune-hunting harpy has sunk her claws into Ash. We can fix that. The important thing is that he's alive."

"I don't think she's a fortune hunter. She seemed shocked to learn he's a duke."

"Perhaps she's just a good actress," Randall said cynically. "Maybe she saw him in London once and recognized him when he turned up here, help-less and confused."

"Perhaps, but not likely." Will sliced himself two pieces of bread. "Ash was also shocked when I told him who he was, and not at all pleased."

"He's probably the most conscientious duke in England," Kirkland observed. "But his real pleasure lies in steamships and gardening and his other pursuits."

"Maybe he enjoys not being a duke." Will spread a thick layer of chutney on a slice of bread, then stacked slices of ham and cheese to make a sandwich. "Not knowing one's identity must be devilish unnerving, but there's a certain freedom to it. Miss Clarke saved Ash's life, she's a real beauty, and she owns Hartley Manor. The circumstances might be strange, but she's no penniless social climber."

"No wonder he's grateful to her," Kirkland said. "But gratitude doesn't require marriage."

"Ashton is obviously in no condition to choose a wife, not after a head injury so severe," Randall added.

"Maybe they felt love at first sight and this is a great romance." Will had felt that when he first met Ellen. He bit hard into his sandwich. "She seems pleasant, and to be honest, I'm glad to see Ash so besotted. I've sometimes wondered if he even liked women. He's a master at keeping them at a distance."

"He keeps everyone at a distance," Kirkland observed. "Even us. He has been the most steadfast of friends. But how often does he reveal himself, or ask for help? We grew up with him, but in many ways he's a mystery."

Randall said slowly, "I've sometimes wondered if there is a part of him that's too foreign to know."

"I've had similar thoughts," Will admitted. "But I'm inclined to think that his reserve is his defense against a society that hasn't always been welcoming." Whatever her character, Mariah Clarke seemed to have penetrated Ash's reserve. Or perhaps not knowing who he was had enabled him to reveal himself to her in ways he couldn't as the Duke of Ashton. An interesting thought.

Randall asked, "Is he well enough to return to London? We could leave in the morning. There's certainly no reason to linger here at the end of the world."

"He may prefer to stay here." Will made another sandwich, this time with sliced beef. "We really can't just kidnap him."

Randall shrugged. "I'm willing to do what's necessary to get him out of the clutches of this wench. Since he has been injured, we have the right to act for his own good."

" 'For his own good' is a very insalubrious phrase," Kirkland murmured. "The sort of thing they said about all of us when we were children and didn't do what the adults thought best."

Randall winced. "Point to the Scotsman."

"Lady Agnes never told us she was acting for our own good. She asked us what we wanted, made sure we understood what success would cost, and then helped us achieve it if we still wanted it," Will said. "Speaking of Lady Agnes, I must write her and Hal Lawford to tell them we've found Ash."

There was a thoughtful silence before Randall said, "It's going to be a shock for Hal. He and Ash have always been friendly, but if we're looking for someone who had a motive to kill—well, Hal certainly benefits the most."

Kirkland shook his head. "I know Hal fairly well, and this doesn't seem like something he would do. He would enjoy being Duke of Ashton, but murder? I don't think so."

"How much does anyone ever know about another man's heart?" Will asked softly.

Randall shrugged. "Not being a philosophical sort, I shall consider Lawford a suspect. I also want to meet the wench who has attached herself to Ashton."

"You'll have your chance soon." Will poured more ale. "The wench has invited us all to dine with them tonight at Hartley Manor."

Chapter Twenty

Mariah dressed carefully for her unexpected dinner party. None of her gowns were new. In her travels with her father, she'd sometimes been given clothing by the lady of the house. Altering those garments had taught her to be a very good seamstress. Her best evening gown had been a gift from a jolly female who was definitely not a lady, but who had provided Mariah with valuable information on worldly matters.

Tonight, Mariah wore a simple but elegant blue gown with a demure blond lace fichu that made her look innocent and young. Not like the fortune hunter Adam's friends must think her.

Her approach to the meal itself was equally pragmatic. Mrs. Beckett was no French chef, but she was a fine English country cook. In Mariah's experience, most men were happy if there was a well-cooked joint and plenty of it, and Hartley Manor could provide that. Nor would the guests find fault with fish fresh caught that afternoon and lapped with a delicate wine sauce. For Adam's sake, Mariah added curried chicken. With a good selection of side dishes, no one would have reason to complain.

Somewhere the Duke of Ashton must have wardrobes full of impeccably cut clothing, but tonight Adam had to make do with her father's best coat and pantaloons. Mariah spent several hours altering the coat. Adam protested, "You needn't go to such trouble. From what Masterson said, I've known all these men for twenty years, so there is no need to impress them."

"You don't have to impress, but I do," she retorted. "Even though we're not really betrothed, I want them to think that at least I take good care of you."

"I will vouch for that." The warmth in his eyes made her look down with a blush, but he didn't protest further.

As they waited for their guests, they sat on the sofa and held hands, not speaking, though Mariah studied Adam from the corner of her eye. He looked particularly handsome tonight, his regular features calm and reserved. He'd been very quiet since Masterson's visit. His nerves must be as tight as bowstrings at the prospect of meeting three men who knew a great deal about him, while he knew virtually nothing about them. Though naturally he wouldn't admit to such a thing.

Mariah almost jumped from her skin when the heavy door knocker was wielded, the boom resonating through the front hall and adjacent rooms. Adam smiled as he stood. "Come, my lady. It should be an educational evening."

"You are a master of understatement." She steeled herself, grateful for the touch of his hand at the small of her back. Facing these strangers drew them together.

The maid ushered in their guests, her eyes round as she announced, "Lord Masterson, Lord Kirkland, and Major Randall." Then she vanished back to the kitchen, where she would help serve the meal.

Oh, heavens, Masterson and Kirkland were also lords? At least Masterson gave her a smile, probably because they'd met already.

The other two went for Adam in a controlled rush. Randall was blond, taut, and dangerous looking. He walked with an officer's posture and a noticeable limp.

The dark-haired Kirkland was more contained.

He would usually be a hard man to read, she guessed. But for the moment, he and Randall were joyful.

"My God, Ash!" Kirkland caught Adam's right hand in both of his. "I half thought Masterson had lost his wits, but sure enough, you're you."

Randall punched Adam in the shoulder with considerable force. "Don't you ever get yourself killed like that again! The weeks while we searched for your drowned carcass have meant far too much bad Scottish cooking for my taste."

Adam shook hands with Randall. Mariah wondered if the others recognized that he was uncomfortable with such effusive greetings from men who were strangers to him. He said, "Masterson told you about my amnesia?"

Kirkland nodded. "It must be a devilish odd feeling. I'm hoping that by the time we finish telling you about yourself, you'll remember everything on your own. Like priming a pump."

Adam frowned at Randall. "I had a dream about Masterson, and also about you. You were ill, and I . . . forcibly removed you from where you were living."

Randall grimaced. "Of all the damned things to remember." Remembering his manners, he turned to Mariah. "Excuse my language, Miss Clarke, and my failure to greet you properly."

She recognized hostility in his gaze. Masterson was easygoing and inclined to give her the benefit of the doubt for Adam's sake. Though Kirkland was withholding judgment, he would be fair, she guessed. But Randall viewed her as a menace to his old friend, and he would not accept her easily, if at all.

"Of course. You are excited to see your lost friend," she said mildly. "If I lost Adam, I would certainly be glad to find him again. Would you gentlemen like sherry?"

They all said yes, so she took on the task of pouring. Adam said to Kirkland, "I don't seem to have dreamed of you. Except . . . perhaps when we were boys. I dreamed I was in a room with several beds and bouncing little hellions. A woman came in to hush us up. She said she'd put us to playing sports with the locals to use up our energy."

"Lady Agnes!" Kirkland said with a grin. "She had to quiet us rather often."

Sherry in hand, Adam led Mariah to the sofa. "Tell me more about this school."

The visitors were happy to oblige, distributing themselves around the drawing room with their drinks. As they described the Westerfield Academy, Mariah realized Masterson hadn't been joking when he'd said that none of the students had had a decent mother.

Instead, they had had the magnificently eccentric Lady Agnes, a duke's daughter with a kind heart and the ability to handle small, angry boys. Her assistant, Miss Emily, the general, the idyllic green

Kent countryside—all emerged vividly from the descriptions.

But though Adam listened with interest, no memories emerged. As they moved into the dining room he said, "It sounds like an excellent, if rather strange, school. How long was I there?"

"Eight years, until you entered Oxford. You took double firsts. Holidays you usually stayed with your cousins," Kirkland replied. "You remember nothing of this?"

"No, yet what you describe sounds . . . not unfamiliar." Adam's gaze moved from one man to the other. "The four of us were the first class?"

As they took places at the table, Kirkland replied. "There were two others. Ballard has been mostly in Portugal since leaving school, running his family's port company. He gets home for a visit every year or two. Wyndham—we aren't sure. He may be alive . . . or not. He was in France when the Peace of Amiens ended and the French interned every British male in the country. We haven't heard from him since."

"Occasionally internees manage to get letters out of France to England," Masterson added. "Wyndham's name has never been mentioned, but that doesn't mean he isn't still alive." He raised his wine glass to Adam. "After all, you have returned from the dead."

The other men joined in the informal toast. Mariah took a thoughtful sip of her wine. So these friends had already lived with the uncertainty of not knowing if one of their number was dead or alive. That might explain the intensity of their search for Adam.

Masterson glanced at Mariah. "I'm sorry that we are boring on about our school days, Miss Clarke. Tell us more about yourself. At the inn, they said that you had recently inherited the estate?"

She had already decided that she wouldn't pretend to be anything other than what she was. "My father won the estate from the previous owner, George Burke. We arrived here early in the spring. A few weeks later, my father traveled to London, and . . . and was killed by highwaymen. So I own Hartley Manor now." She made a mental note to write the lawyer again. She had yet to receive a reply from him, though there must be formalities connected to her inheritance. Perhaps he was delaying a letter until he knew more about her father's death.

"I'm sorry for your loss," Masterson murmured.

Less polite, Randall said in an edged voice, "Was your father Charles Clarke?"

"He was." She braced herself. "Did you know him?"

"Not personally, but I've heard of him. He had a reputation as a Captain Sharp whose play was none too honest."

"Your information is wrong," she said coolly. "He was a very skilled card player. He never

209

needed to cheat. His opponents, who were usually drunk or incompetent and probably both, often impugned his honesty rather than admit their lack of skill."

"You said your father won this estate," he snapped. "Fleecing a young man out of his inheritance is not the mark of a gentleman."

Her hand tightened around her fork as she reminded herself that Sarah would never attack a guest at her table.

To hell with Sarah. "You will not speak of my father in such a way in my house," she said flatly. "Apologize, or I must ask you to leave."

She heard a thump that suggested Masterson had just kicked Randall's ankle. "I'm sorry," the blond man said in a stiff voice. "My remarks were out of line, especially given that I have never met your father."

"I accept your apology." Their gazes caught. Neither of them felt very forgiving. Thank heaven for manners to buffer a difficult situation.

Trying to ease the atmosphere, Masterson said, "Your cook is excellent, Miss Clarke. Do you think she might be willing to part with her recipe for mushroom fricassee? It's the best I've ever had."

"I'll ask her. I think Mrs. Beckett could be persuaded. She likes having her food appreciated." And if large quantities consumed meant appreciation, Adam's friends were being very complimentary.

The meal was nearing its end when Kirkland said, "I assume you'll be wanting to return to London, Ash. We can travel back together."

Adam tensed. "I don't know that I want to go to London."

His friends showed varying degrees of dismay. Mariah wondered if any of them realized how difficult—even frightening—it would be for Adam to return to a complicated world where he was at such a disadvantage. People would make demands, expect him to be the same. He wouldn't know whom to trust. Men in Adam's position were always magnets for the untrustworthy.

"You have many responsibilities," Kirkland said. "You can't ignore them forever. At the least, you need to sort out the confusion caused by your reported death."

"Given that I don't remember any of those responsibilities, I doubt I can fulfill them," Adam said dryly. "Didn't I employ competent people to oversee my property in my absence? Surely they can manage."

"You have excellent employees," Masterson agreed. "But even if you can't work in your usual way, being in familiar surroundings might stimulate your memory."

Adam's brows drew together. "You could be right. While it's good that you have found and identified me, it would be far better for me to remember who I am."

Heart sinking, Mariah accepted that she was going to lose him. Once he returned to his regular life, she would fade to a fond, ambivalent memory. She clenched her hands together under the table. That was surely for the best, since she doubted she could fit into his world even if he wanted her. But she hadn't expected to lose him so soon.

He looked at her, his green eyes intent. "If I go to London, Mariah must come with me."

There was a rustle of unease from his friends. Relieved that he wanted her but doubtful, Mariah said, "Even as your fiancée, I can't travel with you and three other men. Someone in your position is watched carefully. My presence would be a scandal."

"Then we can marry before we leave. Gretna Green isn't far."

Mariah inhaled sharply, her heart constricted. "Much as I want to marry you, it's too soon. You need time to rediscover your life."

Mariah's protest was echoed by the other men. Masterson said, "A Gretna marriage would be scandalous and reflect badly on Miss Clarke. It would be assumed that she had seduced you into pledging marriage to her when you were in a weakened state."

Randall's ironic lift of his brows said that the latter was exactly what had happened, but he didn't speak.

Adam frowned. "I don't want to damage

Mariah's reputation in any way, but I won't go to London without her."

"There would be no scandal if Miss Clarke is chaperoned," Kirkland said. "Do you have a friend who could join our party, Miss Clarke? If not, I could ride to Glasgow for an aunt or a cousin, though I can't guarantee finding one who is good company."

Adam looked thoughtful. "Do you think Mrs. Bancroft would come, Mariah? She's a widow and sensible, as well as your friend."

Mariah thought about it. She wanted desperately to be with Adam, and with almost equal intensity, she wanted to go to London to find out more about her father's death. "I don't know if Julia will agree, but I can ask. Even if she's willing to chaperone me, I doubt she would go out into London society. She would hate that."

"There will be no shortage of respectable chaperones in London, starting with Ash's Aunt Georgiana and cousin Janey," Masterson assured her. "What is needed is a companion to make the trip scandal free."

"Do we have a plan acceptable to everyone?" Adam asked. After murmurs of agreement, he said, "Then London it will be."

He sounded unenthusiastic, but there was no help for it. He couldn't avoid London for long, and clearly he needed the security of Mariah's presence.

Two maids came in to clear the table. At their heels trotted Bhanu, who had escaped from the kitchen. Adam snapped his fingers and the dog bounced over to him, ears flopping. Randall said with a rare smile, "You've a talent for finding ugly dogs, Ashton."

For the first time that evening, Adam laughed. "Bhanu isn't ugly. She's just beautiful in a way you haven't seen before."

Masterson caught his breath. "You had a dog in school named Bhanu. Amazingly ugly, and a great favorite of everyone. He was indirectly responsible for you ending up at the Westerfield Academy. Lady Agnes told us the story."

"Indeed?" Adam scratched the dog's head. "What does Bhanu mean?"

"The sun," Kirkland said. "It's Hindustani."

Adam smiled. "Clearly both Bhanus were beautiful in a Hindu way."

The men all laughed, but in that moment, Mariah became sure that Adam would recover his memories. Small things, like the dog's name and Adam's dreams, proved that the past was close, just waiting to emerge into the present.

Then he would need her no more.

Chapter Twenty-One

A maid brought in a decanter of port and four goblets. Adam wasn't surprised to see Mariah rise to her feet with unseemly swiftness. "I will leave you gentlemen to your port," she said brightly.

As Adam poured a glass, Kirkland asked her, "Is it Ballard port? That would be from the firm run by the other old school friend we spoke of earlier. Very good it is, too."

"I really don't know." Mariah edged toward the door. "Someone else filled the decanter."

"I'm sure we'll manage." Adam slid the decanter to Kirkland. "We shall see you later in the drawing room." He glanced at Mariah, trying to convey that he fully understood her desire to escape her guests for a while.

Unfortunately, Masterson also got to his feet. "The light lingers so long this far north. I'd like to see the grounds if you're willing to guide me, Miss Clarke."

She did not look enthralled but was too polite to refuse. "I would be happy to show you some of the property," she said. "Just let me get a shawl."

She returned wrapped in her grandmother's shawl despite its shabbiness. She must have felt that she needed Granny Rose's support. Masterson opened the door for her and they departed, Bhanu at their heels.

Adam hoped that Masterson was as benevolent as he seemed. Mariah had enough to endure with these strangers invading her house. He wasn't sure how he felt about them himself. They were all honorable, intelligent men, even Randall, apart from his obvious suspicions of Mariah. But Adam didn't feel any particular bond. He rubbed his aching temple, thinking that his old life was a source of regular headaches. After the door closed, he said, "In Hartley, people think Mariah and I are married. It seemed a way to remove the scandal from my living under her roof. I would ask that you maintain the pretense as long as you're here."

"Very well. That has the virtue of simplicity." Kirkland frowned. "There is something we must discuss with you, Ash, and I'd rather not do it in front of Miss Clarke."

"I do hope you aren't going to try to convince me that she is not suitable to be my wife," Adam replied, his voice edged. He might not be sure he could trust her, but he'd be damned if he'd see her criticized by men who had barely met her.

"Nothing like that. She is an attractive, intelligent young woman and you seem to care about each other, which is a good foundation for marriage. This is quite a different matter." Kirkland exchanged a glance with Randall. "Do you remember anything at all about the accident that left you injured and lost at sea?"

Adam's brows drew together as he thought back

to his earliest, dimmest memories. "I vaguely recall hanging on to a beam and floating in cold water for what seemed to be forever. But I have no memory of the accident. Why would it matter?"

"Because we started looking for you by salvaging the wreckage of your ship, the *Enterprise*," Randall replied. "We found that the boiler had been deliberately damaged and sloppily repaired in a way that guaranteed an explosion. Apparently someone was trying to murder you."

Stunned, Adam exclaimed, "Murder? What have I done to earn such an enemy?"

"Nothing," Kirkland replied. "But there are some who disapprove of a half-Hindu English duke. You've been the target of scurrilous cartoons and satirical pieces. Though it has nothing to do with you personally, there are people who dislike you on principle."

"I can understand being despised for my blood," Adam said slowly, "but would such anger be great enough to blow up a Scottish ship with a number of British crew members? It seems a complicated way to kill when a bullet in the heart would do. Could the villain have been trying to wreck the ship itself? Perhaps some rival steamship builder wanted to destroy the competition."

Kirkland made a rueful face. "Anything is possible. We have no evidence. But there is no history of murderous rivalry between Scottish engineers and shipbuilders."

"If I was the quarry, there might be another attempt." Adam tried to grasp the fact that someone might be trying to kill him. "If I take Mariah to London, she might be hurt if someone is after me."

Though Randall looked as if this would be a good excuse to leave her behind, Kirkland said, "I would hope you'd be safe with us, and you are more than formidable in your own right. But you need to be aware that someone might wish you ill."

"I'm formidable?" Adam asked, bemused. "I had no idea."

Randall's eyes glinted. "On a good day, you can shoot as well as I can."

"And on any day, you can defeat Masterson, Randall, or me in hand-to-hand fighting," Kirkland added. "You learned some unholy fighting techniques as a boy in India, and because you needed sparring partners, you taught your classmates. None of us was ever quite as good, though."

"I always suspected that you didn't teach some of your best moves, and you were too quick for me to figure them out." Randall's gaze was distant. "But I still learned enough to save my life more than once in battle."

"So I'm a duke and a master of deadly arts," Adam said dryly. "I hadn't noticed. But I know that it would be altogether simpler if you hadn't found me."

"Would you have preferred that?" Kirkland asked quietly.

Adam rubbed his aching head again, wondering. The life he'd left behind sounded overwhelming and not particularly attractive. Cumberland was much more peaceful, and he would have time to come to terms with his complicated feelings about Mariah. But as long as his memory was gone, he would always wonder what he had lost. "I suppose . . . it's better to know the truth."

Yet despite his words, he wasn't sure.

As Mariah left the house with her guest, she said, "Adam has been working on restoring the gardens, Lord Masterson. We can walk there, or we could go down to the seaside where I found him. It's not far."

"Call me Will. Everyone does. I'd like to see where you found Ash." Masterson fell into step beside her. "Perhaps tomorrow he can show us the gardens. He has always been interested in landscaping. The grounds of Ralston Abbey are some of the finest in England. The garden of Ashton House is much smaller, of course, but very lovely. When you walk there, you will have trouble believing you're in the heart of London."

In a fortnight, Mariah would be in London as the guest of a duke. The visit would be very different from previous visits with her father, when they stayed in rented lodgings that were modest at best. She ached for the days when her father was alive and they were constant companions, but there was no going back. And as long as she and Adam were together, there was a chance for a future, no matter how slim.

They strolled down the lane down to the small beach. She was glad Masterson didn't seem disposed to chat. He was right about the long days this far north. Even though it was well after dinner, the sun was still above the horizon. When high summer arrived, there wouldn't be much night.

The shore was windy, with choppy waves slapping hard on the sand and shingle. Bhanu trotted to the water's edge, giving a yip when a wave splashed her nose. Masterson asked, "Was the water this rough when you rescued him?"

"Worse. It was late, near midnight." She gestured to the place where she had first seen Adam. "There was enough moonlight that I could see something dark floating. I thought it was a drowned man." She made a face. "I was tempted to run and hide, but the tide was starting to turn. I thought the body might be swept out to sea again, so I waded in and found Adam. Not quite dead, though close. I don't think he would have lasted much longer."

"What brought you to the shore in the middle of the night?" he asked curiously.

If she told him the truth about Granny Rose's ritual, she would definitely be too strange for a duke. "I was restless and couldn't sleep. Burke, the former owner of the manor, was trying to persuade me to marry him and I was afraid that in a weak moment I'd agree, then regret it for the rest of my life. So I decided to take a walk and tire myself out."

He nodded as if that sounded perfectly reasonable. Gazing out at the water, he said, "I'm amazed that Ash was carried this far south, and that he survived the cold water. His ship went down near Arran Island, not Glasgow, but even so, he must have been adrift for days. It's a miracle he's alive."

"Not quite a miracle." Mariah tried to remember Adam's exact words. "One of the first things he told me was that he slowed his breathing and retreated into a corner of his mind to preserve himself. I'd never heard of such a thing, but perhaps that kept him alive."

Masterson looked interested. "That sounds like one of his bits of Hindu magic."

"Magic?" she asked warily. Not that she would deny magic existed. Granny Rose had made her aware that there was much humankind didn't understand.

"Not magic precisely, but as you probably know, Ash maintains some Hindu disciplines. Like his daily meditation."

Mariah felt foolish. "I didn't know that he did that."

Masterson frowned. "Perhaps he has forgotten. He would meditate quietly in his room after washing up in the morning. If he still does, you wouldn't necessarily know. He is very private. During his life in England, he has been subject to contempt and insult because of his mixed blood. His response has been to be a perfect English gentleman, concealing his Indian heritage."

"He rose from a sickbed and threw George Burke across the drawing room when the man was being difficult," she said thoughtfully. "I wondered how he did it. His movements weren't like boxing at all. More Hindu practices?"

Masterson nodded. "It's called *Kalarippayattu* and it's a fighting skill of Kerala, in southern India. Adam is from the north, and he learned *Kalarippayattu* with the sons of the royal court, who were trained in all warrior arts. He in turn taught us, usually late at night." Masterson smiled reminiscently. "Small boys can be monsters. Ash earned a great deal of respect because of his fighting skills."

"Why are you telling me such things?" she observed. "This is not casual conversation."

He smiled ruefully. "I thought you'd notice that. I'm explaining Ash's background because you're important to him, and for now, the person who is closest to him. The more fully you understand him, the better for both of you."

Her brows arched. "So you don't disapprove of Adam's fiancée being a gambler's daughter?"

"Are you a gamester yourself?" he asked.

"Not at all. I dislike the uncertainty of it." She smiled a little. "For me, money is something to be cherished and used carefully, not flung away."

"A wise attitude. Do you have any different vices?"

She laughed. "Are you interviewing me for the position of Adam's wife?"

He laughed with her. "Perhaps. When people meet in society, they usually know each other's backgrounds, or can quickly learn. That isn't the case here. But you seem to be kind and level-headed, and you care for Ashton. I think you might suit very well."

She turned to look out across the water, thinking how unlikely it was she would become the Duchess of Ashton. She didn't want to explain that Adam distrusted her and why, but she could give a partial truth. "To be honest, I expect that when Adam returns to his old life and regains his memory, our betrothal will end. When he remembers his friends, he won't need me as he does now."

"I very much hope he does remember his friends." Masterson looked somber for a moment before glancing at her askance. "You're remark-ably calm about the prospect of losing him. I thought you were . . . quite attached."

She sighed. Tactful of him not to ask outright if she was in love with Adam. It was not something she wished to discuss. "I have always had to be practical. Romantic delusions too often end in misery." She pulled her shawl tighter, wanting to feel Granny Rose close. "Though Adam isn't mar-ried, I have wondered if he might have a sweetheart whom he has been quietly courting. If there is such a female, surely she will come rushing forward when she learns he's alive."

"I know of no such woman," Masterson said, startled.

Bhanu bounced over and put her muddy feet on Mariah's best gown. She bent to ruffle the dog's long ears. "Can you be sure there isn't one?"

"No," he admitted. "As I said, Ash is very private, and I haven't been much in London in recent years. But if there isn't such a woman and he still wants to marry you, will you do so? Or are you only acting the part of fiancée because he has been so alone?"

Masterson was remarkably perceptive for a man. "I would marry him gladly, if that's what he wants. But I doubt he will know what he wants for some time to come. If ultimately he doesn't want me"— she shrugged as if it was a matter of no great importance—"I won't hold him against his will, and I won't miss being a duchess. Such a rank would mean being always watched and measured and judged, I think."

"Particularly a beautiful young duchess," he agreed. "But you can choose how public a life to live. Ashton goes out in society regularly, but he is by no means addicted to the social round. He would probably be glad to have reasons to stay home with you."

That didn't sound so bad. "You asked about my

vices, Will. I have too much imagination and sometimes that gets me into trouble." She thought of the very proper and mythical Sarah. "But I try to keep it under control."

"There are worse things than imagination." The sun was setting in streaks of gold and crimson and indigo as he turned from the sea. "It's getting cool. Time to return to the house."

She tugged her shawl closer and fell into step as Bhanu scampered back and forth across their path, feet and floppy ears dripping wet. She liked this friend of Adam's very much. It was good to have an ally.

After Mariah and Masterson returned to the house, tea was served in the drawing room. The party broke up shortly thereafter. Adam's friends had already done most of the planning required for the trip south. He had accepted their ideas willingly since he had no better ideas himself.

He and Mariah escorted their guests to the door, both of them sighing with relief when the men were gone. As they wearily turned from the front door, he yearned to draw her into an embrace, but he controlled the impulse. It would be too easy to slip back into intimacy, which wouldn't be fair to either of them when he was so unsure of his feelings.

Mariah said, "That went about as well as could be hoped for. Did any memories return when you talked to your friends?"

Adam rubbed his head. "No, though I can see why we became friends. I feel comfortable with them all even though I don't really remember them."

She frowned at his gesture. "Do you have a headache?"

He dropped his hand. "A bit of one. They kept looking at me hopefully, waiting for me to cry out, 'Now I remember everything!'" He sighed. "I wish I could oblige. The way my head aches . . . it almost feels as if the information is locked in my mind just waiting to burst out. But it hasn't happened yet."

"It will," she said comfortingly. "When you are back in your own home, you'll probably wake up one morning and everything will have returned."

"Perhaps." He'd rather wake up the next morning and find Mariah beside him. He clenched his hands to prevent himself from touching her. "Good night. Thank you for entertaining my old friends so well."

She hesitated, as if waiting for a good-night kiss, or at least a touch. Her face smoothed out as she accepted that he wouldn't act. "Sleep well, Adam."

He watched as she walked away, her steps graceful and her hips swaying. Desire, yes. It was a fire in his blood. But he was less certain of what lay beyond desire.

Adam slept badly, his dreams haunted by angry gods and murderous strangers. If these were memories, he wanted no part of them.

Chapter Twenty-Two

Mariah walked into town to visit Julia Bancroft the next morning. Her friend answered the door with a smile. "How nice to see you! We haven't really spoken since Adam recovered enough not to need my services. Join me for tea?"

"Has it been that long? I suppose it has." Mariah removed her hat and followed her friend to the kitchen, in the back of the cottage. "Sorry. I've been distracted."

Julia poured tea for Mariah, then offered a plate with slices of ginger cake. "Wild rumors have been flying around since those three very impressive gentlemen arrived at the Bull and Anchor. I hear they dined at the manor last night."

Mariah sighed. "Indeed they did."

"I have been hoping to hear the truth from you." Julia chuckled. "And if that isn't a heavy enough hint, I shall have to learn to live with my curiosity."

Mariah nibbled the ginger cake, wondering where to begin. "The gentlemen are friends of Adam, whose given name actually is Adam, amazingly. They had been looking for him, or rather, his body, since the steamboat he was on sank off of Arran Island. Now they have found him, but so far, Adam hasn't regained any memories."

"Given how well dressed his friends are, I

assume Adam wasn't a deckhand. Is he a ship owner?"

"Much, much worse." Mariah's mouth twisted. "He's the Duke of Ashton."

"Good God," Julia said blankly. "He's a duke?"

"Either that or his friends are all liars." Mariah began tearing the slice of cake into crumbs. "They want to take him home to London. He and I . . . we care a great deal for each other, but I think I've lost him, Julia. Before his friends arrived, I told him that I'd lied about us being married. He was upset, of course, and now he isn't sure what he thinks of me. He doesn't hate me, but he doesn't trust me, either. I think that as he returns to his old life, there will be no place for me."

"I'm so sorry," Julia said quietly. "Circumstances have conspired to bring you together very quickly. I understand why you claimed to be married, but I also understand why he is now upset. Perhaps in time he'll forgive your lack of truth."

"Perhaps, though I'm not confident." Mariah's mouth twisted humorlessly. "But he does want me to go to London with him. I think he wants a familiar face nearby. That will pass when he becomes comfortable with his old life again. Still, I do want to go, if for no other reason than to talk to the lawyer about my father's death."

"You've still heard nothing? Perhaps the lawyer is ill himself."

"Either that, or he doesn't feel the need to exert himself on behalf of a female client. If that's the case, I might have to find a new lawyer." Mariah was not looking forward to dealing with a dilatory lawyer, but she would have to learn to do so. Perhaps Masterson would help her find a better man if that was required.

"If you go to London with a group of handsome young men, you'll need a maid," Julia said. "Better yet, a chaperone."

"That's one of the reasons I'm calling today." She smiled coaxingly. "Would you like a trip to London with all expenses paid?"

"You want me to come?" Julia lowered her teacup with a clink. "I can't possibly do that. What about my patients?"

Mariah had known her friend would resist. Julia was not a native of Cumberland. Her accent placed her as educated, perhaps the daughter of a doctor or a vicar. Mariah suspected that her friend had come to this remote corner of England to get away from her past. But there was yearning in her face at the thought of London. "You said that your apprentice is becoming very skilled. If there is a real emergency, Jenny or the patient can call in another midwife."

Julia was tempted, but not yet convinced. "I haven't the right clothes. Even if transportation and lodgings are covered, I would need pin money." She smiled. "Much of my income is barter, and I don't think I could use a chicken as currency in London."

Mariah laughed. "I suppose not. But we're near the same size, so we could share some clothing. My wardrobe isn't up to London standards, but I've received some nice things from ladies I've met along the way. I'm also quite a good seamstress. We could buy some used garments and I'll alter them." Changing her approach, she added, "Wouldn't it be nice to get away for a bit? We could see the sights of London together."

"I really can't," Julia said. But her eyes were longing.

"You needn't go into society," Mariah said. "Not if you don't want to."

Julia smiled ruefully. "How did you know that I wish to avoid society?"

"Just a guess." Mariah made a face. "I'm not keen on the idea myself, but I must find if I can swim in those waters if there is any chance that Adam and I might wed. My father and I never moved in high circles, but I had to continually adapt to new situations, so I should be able to manage."

Julia's uncertain expression firmed. "I know I shouldn't, but . . . yes, I'll go with you. I, too, have some business in London." She got to her feet. "As to the clothing, wait here a moment."

The moments stretched out enough that Julia's tabby jumped onto Mariah's lap and made herself at home. Another cup of tea and slice of cake had been consumed by the time Julia returned with an armful of gowns. All were fine-quality day dresses, not the very latest in fashion but made with good fabric and rich colors. Mariah caught her breath, startling the cat from her lap. "Where . . . ?"

"Don't ask," Julia said as she laid the garments over a chair. "Please."

Mariah nodded, guessing that the clothing came from Julia's former marriage. She must have been very young when her husband died, because she wasn't much older than Mariah and she'd lived in Hartley for years.

Turning up the hem of the top garment, Mariah studied the stitchery. "Very well made. A little out of date, but they can be altered to be more fashionable."

"I don't want fashionable," Julia said firmly. "Simple and unobtrusive will do."

That would suit Julia's style now, but the clothing confirmed Mariah's suspicion that her friend had a more glamorous past. "Whatever you wish. It won't take long to do the alterations. Changing trimmings and perhaps adding fichus to the gowns with low necklines."

Julia pulled a rose-colored gown from the bottom. "I'd like you to have this. This color suits you much better than me."

Mariah stroked the sleeve with pleasure. "You're sure? This satin is lovely. The gown could be cut apart and joined with colors that would suit your dark hair."

"I'd rather you have it." A furrow appeared between Julia's brows, as if the dress carried bad memories.

Mariah pulled out a handsome green walking dress. "Put this on and we'll decide what needs to be done."

Julia's usually serious face lit up. "I'm going to enjoy this enormously, Mariah. As long as I avoid society, I'll have a wonderful time!"

Mariah had already eaten and left the house by the time Adam rose the next morning, tired from a night of bad dreams and poor sleep. He was halfway through a quiet breakfast when Randall breezed in ahead of the maid who had admitted him. "Good morning, Ash. I thought I'd take you out for some shooting practice."

Adam blinked. "I'm supposed to murder defenseless creatures even before finishing breakfast?"

Randall grinned. "That's the most convincing proof yet that you're still you. Mind if I have some ham?" Not waiting for a reply, he helped himself to ham and toast from the sideboard, then poured tea and sat opposite Adam. "I've never known you to actually hunt game, but as I said last night, you're a crack shot. I thought we should do some target shooting. See if you're still any good."

"An interesting question: does shooting skill reside in the mind or in the body?" Adam said thoughtfully. "I wouldn't know where to begin handling a gun."

"Good! If getting knocked on the head ruined your marksmanship, I should be able to outshoot you today." Randall helped himself to another piece of toast.

"Are you and the others taking turns spending time with me to see what memories you can shake loose?" Adam asked a little dryly.

"That didn't take you long to deduce." Randall swallowed a bite of ham. "Miss Clarke's cook really is excellent. No wonder you don't want to leave."

"Is there a competition to see which of you can best stimulate me to remembering?"

"Not yet, but it's a thought." Randall polished off his food and glanced at Adam's empty plate. "Ready to test your marksmanship?"

"I don't appear to have a choice. I trust you will provide the weapon?" Adam stood, privately admitting that he was curious about whether he'd retained his skill.

"Weapons are a specialty of mine." As they headed into the front hall, Randall scooped up a long leather gun case that he'd tucked into a corner.

The early morning drizzle had cleared into pale spring sunshine. Adam wondered where Mariah was. He was happier when he knew she was close. Likely she had gone to the village to visit Julia Bancroft. "Beyond the gardens is an area that should make a good range. A few trees without much undergrowth and a hill behind, so stray balls will go into earth rather than traveling on."

"So you do remember something, even if you don't know you're remembering," Randall said thoughtfully.

"Perhaps. Or maybe it's just common sense." Adam studied the other man. Tall, blond, and rangy in build, Randall was the image of an Englishman, though his coiled tension was less typical. "You're much more cheerful than last night. Then you looked ready to bite. Which mood is more usual?"

"Biting, I think. Today I'm in a good mood because it has finally sunk in that you really are alive. I haven't so many friends that I can spare any. Losing army friends is expected, but not men who are lolling around England in the lap of luxury."

"Sorry that I nearly failed you." Adam realized that they were sliding into the sort of teasing banter one would expect of old friends. Interesting. "The dream I had, where I took you from a house in London when you were very ill. That really happened?"

Randall's expression tightened. "I'm the nephew of a man who doesn't like me very much. He couldn't kill me outright, but when I returned wounded from the Peninsula, he was willing to let me die of neglect."

Adam winced. "I'm glad I acted. Were there any legal repercussions?"

The other man shook his head. "He could hardly bring charges without admitting what he was doing, so the matter was dropped. I recovered very nicely in Ashton House. That happened last summer. You saved my life. It's a considerable debt."

"Given my amnesia, I'd say there is no point in worrying about debts." They left the formal gardens behind and emerged into a clearing set against a hill. "Here's the spot where I thought we could practice."

"Perfect." There was a table-sized rocky outcropping to the right, so Randall laid the gun case down and opened it. Inside were two sleek rifles and a pair of pistols, as well as powder and shot.

Adam studied the weapons. "Do you always travel armed like this?"

"On a long cross-country trip, I'll certainly have both a rifle and a handgun. And a knife, of course."

"Of course," Adam said dryly. "A gentleman and an arsenal."

Randall grinned as he tapped one of the rifles. "This one is mine, the other Masterson's. Kirkland contributed one of the pistols. Do you want to see how much you remember?"

Acting quickly so he couldn't think too much, Adam lifted Masterson's rifle and weighed it for balance. A nice weapon. He checked for cleanliness and was unsurprised to find it immaculate. In a handful of efficient movements, he loaded powder, patch, and ball, then looked for a target. "Let's see how accurate this rifle is. The blossom at the top of that gorse bush."

Still using instinct, he raised the rifle and fired. The yellow blossom exploded into fragments. "Quite accurate, though I think it throws a hair to the left." He lowered the weapon. "I found that I remembered how to ride, too. Apparently muscles have memories that are separate from those of the mind."

"So it would seem. Certainly you haven't lost any of your shooting skill," Randall observed. "I'm not sure whether I should be glad or disappointed."

"Be glad. Smiling makes us feel better," Adam said. "If I recall last night's conversation, you should be able to match that. Show me."

Randall loaded his weapon. A crow flew by and he raised his rifle. "A moving target is more of a challenge."

Adam lifted his hand. "Don't. That creature has done you no harm."

Randall lowered the gun, wonder on his face. "You really haven't changed, not inside. Very well, I'll try for the blossom on the left side of the same bush." He sighted swiftly and shot.

As the flower disintegrated, Adam said, "We need to use another bush. This one has sacrificed enough to our cause."

Randall laughed. "That also is characteristic of you. Welcome home, Adam. Now shall we try the pistols?"

Chapter Twenty-Three

In the three days before their party left for London, Mariah barely saw Adam. He was frequently busy with his friends, while she spent most of her time at Julia's as they worked on their wardrobes. It was more restful to be with her friend than with Adam.

They saw each other long enough to exchange messages: Yes, Julia was willing to accompany Mariah. Yes, Kirkland had hired two post chaises in Carlisle, and they would collect everyone on Tuesday morning. No, there would be no problems with Cochrane running the estate while Mariah was gone, and he knew to write her at Ashton House while she was away if anything vital required her attention. The steward had been most impressed at learning she was to be the guest of a duke.

She presumed that Adam would have told her if there had been any breakthroughs on the memory front, but he said nothing. Though his friends were teaching him about his life, so far that had triggered no flood of recollections.

She spent her last evening in the library, which she used as an office and workroom. She was sewing trim on a sleeve when a light knock sounded on the door. Adam entered looking calm and reserved, and damnably handsome.

"Sorry to interrupt you." He stood in the doorway as if wary of getting too close. "I wanted to check that all was in order for leaving in the morning. Is there anything you would like me to do?"

"No, I'm ready as soon as this gown is finished and packed. Julia is also prepared. She's quite looking forward to the trip." Mariah knotted a thread and bit it off.

"Good." He rubbed at his head. His hair was long enough to cover the healing scar, but the wound obviously still bothered him. "I never even asked you if you were willing to come with me to London. I wanted you there so I wouldn't feel so alone. But if you'd rather not make the trip, it's not too late to change your mind."

He'd left this very late indeed. She threaded her needle again. "No matter what happens between us, I do want to go to London. I need to talk to my lawyer, Mr. Granger, and learn why he hasn't answered my queries. Perhaps he has no more information about my father's death, but I should have heard about my inheritance."

"Of course. Perhaps I can be of aid there. It sounds like the sort of situation where being a duke might help." Adam shifted from one foot to the other, restless but obviously not ready to leave. Desire radiated off him in waves. And God help her, she felt desire, too.

There was a reason why unmarried males and females were kept apart. With only two of them here, impious thoughts were all too easy. She wondered how he would react if she crossed the room, wrapped herself around his lean, muscular body, and kissed him.

Her guess was that he would forget all his doubts and take her right on the carpeted library floor with her full cooperation. She closed her eyes for a moment, overwhelmed by sensual memories of when they had made love.

No!

Reminded of the news she must tell him, she said, "You may rest easy on at least one score. I found out today that I am not with child."

"Thank God," he breathed, his expression relieved.

How glad he was to be free of her. She jabbed her needle into her hem with such force that she stabbed her finger. "There is really no need to take me to London. Your friends will look out for you, and by this time you know them well that you won't feel alone. I will travel to London on my own."

"Nonsense. You'll be much safer in our group. More comfortable, too." He gave her a wry smile that melted her irritation. "And I really would like to have you close. At the least, I owe you some hospitality, and at the most . . . a good deal more."

"Very well. I'll save a good deal of money by traveling with you."

"I hate being dependent on my friends. First you, and now the others. Kirkland is paying for the post chaises, and Randall and Masterson are discussing how to split lodging and food. I intend to pay everyone back, but at the moment, I don't even have the clothes on my back."

"I have the impression that you've done much for your friends in the past, and they are very happy to help you now." She took another minute stitch. "Accepting graciously will be good for your soul."

He grinned, more relaxed. "Excellent advice. I'll do my best."

She took another stitch. "Do you wish us to maintain the illusion of betrothal?"

"Yes." He sighed. "Please be patient with me, Mariah. I haven't stopped caring for you. Not even a little bit. But—I need to understand the life I will be inhabiting before I know what I can change and what I must accept."

She wondered if any of his friends would be as willing to admit vulnerability. Masterson possibly. Kirkland . . . she wasn't sure. Randall would probably rather be torn apart by wild horses than admit weakness. "You're right to proceed cautiously. I try to imagine what it would be like to deal with all that has been thrown at you, but I can only guess." She smiled at him. "You're doing admirably, you know."

His brows arched. "I feel clumsy and incompetent. I'm glad you don't think so."

Mariah rested her hands on the fabric in her lap. "Loss of memory is as much a gift as it is a disaster. You have the opportunity to be the person you are meant to be, without the constraints of how you were raised or what other people expect of you. Do your friends find you different from before?"

"Masterson made such a comment today," Adam said with surprise. "He said that I seemed somewhat less reserved. Less . . . less dukely."

"Probably not a bad thing, given that dukeliness was forced on you at such a young age." Her brows furrowed. "I wonder what I would have thought of you if we'd met before your accident? I have had little to do with the beau monde. I probably would have found you too grand to speak to. Now you're very approachable."

He laughed. "Approachable is all very well, but like most men, I would prefer to have a beautiful woman think of me as dashing or handsome or intriguing."

"All of those as well," she said softly.

His hand locked on the doorknob as their gazes caught. Dear heaven, she wanted to go to him! He said tautly, "I will leave now before we do something we'll both regret." He pivoted into the hall and shut the door behind him, hard.

Mariah bit the knuckles of her right hand from sheer, raging frustration. In a few minutes of talk, her blood had been raised to boiling point. A real lady wouldn't feel such . . . such *lust!* Sarah wouldn't. Mariah was more like a wanton dairymaid.

The only consolation was that Adam had felt exactly the same.

Adam realized that it had been a mistake to talk to Mariah before going to bed; seeing her had left him aroused and yearning. She looked so guileless and honest, as well as entrancingly lovely. But she had looked honest from the first time he'd opened his eyes and found her leaning over his bed. His judgment was flawed. Perhaps he could trust her. What was clearer was that he couldn't trust himself.

When he finally dozed off, his dreams were the most upsetting yet, starting with him as a small, shrieking boy being dragged from his home. The setting was clearly India and the sentiment understandable. That was a memory he would have been happier not to recover.

That was followed by a disturbing dream of a lovely young woman in his arms. He spoke to her, and she raised her face, radiant. She was fair and green eyed and English, not his mother. Though he had no wife, might he have a sweetheart? Mariah had wondered if she resembled another woman in his life, and she might be right.

Worst of all was his dream of walking into a ballroom filled with beautiful, exquisitely dressed people—and discovering that he was naked, every inch of his too dark skin exposed. He woke up sweating, both head and heart pounding.

Inhale, exhale. Inhale, exhale. He managed to find wry amusement in the situation after he calmed down. He was quite sure no such incident had ever happened. The dream must have been about his fears of entering London society when he felt so unprepared. He would feel naked and vulnerable no matter what he was wearing.

Thank heaven for his friends. Though his lack of recollection frustrated them, they showed no signs of abandoning him. He would be well defended.

He must also give thanks for Mariah. Her lying about their marriage was a deep ache that he didn't want to contemplate, but she was still his favorite person. More than anyone, she saw him as he was now. He felt better when they were together.

Unfortunately, he couldn't even talk to her without having his brain clouded by desire, and the less he saw of her, the more intense his yearning. That was another reason for his difficulty in sleeping.

At least he had figured out how to alleviate

unruly lust, though doing so was less satisfying than being with Mariah. As he touched himself, he wondered if such behavior was forbidden in English society. That was one piece of information he didn't need.

After three days of busyness, Mariah found it a relief to let Adam hand her into the "yellow bounder," as post chaises were called. The bright yellow body made the hired carriages unmistakable. This one had room for four passengers and was drawn by four horses. The chaise that was collecting Adam's friends in Hartley would be the same.

By changing horses several times a day, they should be in London in a week or so. A mail coach was faster, but the chaise would be quicker than most other methods of traveling. She and her father had usually traveled by regular coach, which was slower and less comfortable, so a post chaise was luxury.

She relaxed back into the leather seat and smothered a yawn. She'd slept little the night before, worrying about whether she'd packed all she would need as well as brooding about Adam. Annabelle had jumped off her bed this morning, given her an injured glance, then stalked off to the kitchen. Mariah hoped the cat would forgive her absence when she returned to Hartley. But cat and estate would be in good hands with Mrs. Beckett and Mr. Cochrane.

Adam was about to join her in the carriage when Bhanu leaped inside enthusiastically. She seemed prepared to settle down and travel to London. Mariah leaned forward and scratched the dog's head. "I'm sorry, but you'll have to stay here. Think how Annabelle would miss you."

Adam scooped the dog into his arms. "I think she'll have to be locked inside or she'll follow. I'll take her to the kitchen and she won't notice we're gone."

A short time passed as he took Bhanu inside. Then he returned and the driver set the chaise in motion. Adam's gaze rested on the house as they pulled away.

"Are you thinking you might never return?" she asked, keeping her voice even.

Looking uncomfortable, he replied, "I certainly hope to come back, but . . . I just don't know." The carriage turned into the lane that led to the road, ending his view of the house. He gazed at Mariah. "So much has happened here."

"I've wondered if something will happen to bring back memories of your early life, and this time since the accident will disappear," she said reflectively. "I once met a physician who had dealt with many head injuries, and apparently anything can happen."

"I cannot imagine forgetting you." His gaze was intense.

She shifted restlessly under his gaze at the same

time the chaise hit a rut. Her knee brushed his. He caught his breath. "I think I should ride in the other chaise most of the time. Not a rejection of you. Rather . . . the contrary."

"Very wise," she agreed. "Of course, Julia will ride with me, but if she didn't, there would always be the danger of *this* happening." She slid forward and caught his shoulders, then offered a kiss that tried to say everything that she couldn't put into words. That she loved him, desired him, was sorry for lying . . .

If she hadn't claimed they were husband and wife, would they have become so close? No point in wondering now.

He gasped and circled his arms around her waist as he kissed her back, his mouth devouring. "This is dangerous," he said huskily.

"There isn't room for misbehavior in a carriage," she said with a choked laugh.

"You think not?" He tightened his hands around her waist and lifted her toward him, pulling her onto his lap with her legs straddling him.

She was shocked at how intimately they were pressed together. Shocked, and aroused. As his hands caressed her back, she melted into him, her hips moving in an involuntary rhythm. "It would be *easy* . . ." she gasped. The rocking of the carriage added to the intoxicating motion. Her hand slid down between them.

"Easy, but not wise." His breathing ragged, he

caught her hand before it could descend farther. "Luckily, it's a short ride into Hartley."

"Oh, heavens!" She tried to break away as reason returned.

He held her on his lap, his hands again caressing. "We still have a few minutes."

But only a few. She wondered if this would be their last kiss. There would be few opportunities to be alone together during this journey, and once they reached London, circumstances would rapidly come between them. She rested her head on his shoulder as she thought about the days ahead. "Are you ready for London?"

"As ready as I can be." He wrapped his arm around her shoulders. "I've asked the others not to discuss my amnesia. My close friends and family will need to know, but I'd rather not have my weakness tittered about by everyone in London society."

"It's not a weakness; it's an injury."

"It feels like a weakness when everyone knows more about my life than I do."

"You're a duke," she said. "Sneer them all down."

He gave a surprised laugh. "You're a mischievous minx." His arms tightened around her. "How can something wrong feel so right?"

"Because you're weighing on two different scales." She stroked her hand down his chest. "Feeling is . . . feeling. Taste, touch, emotion, excitement—matters of the heart. Right and wrong are quite a different matter. They involve morality, wisdom, justice—matters of the mind." She sighed. "So often they don't agree."

"Wisdom is something you have a great deal of. In London, I hope to slay the dragons of my mind. Then—we shall see what comes next." He caressed her cheek tenderly with the back of his hand, then lifted her from his lap—not easy since he was sitting—and set her back on her seat. "You look misleadingly demure."

"It's my specialty." She locked her gloved hands together. Demurely.

A few minutes later they pulled up in front of the Bull and Anchor. The other chaise awaited with Adam's friends lingering in the open air as long as they could. The men climbed in and followed to Julia's cottage, which was on the way out of town.

Mariah climbed out of the coach and walked to the cottage, Adam beside her. Julia opened the door, bonneted and ready to go. Like Mariah's, her luggage consisted of a small trunk and a bandbox. Adam scooped up the trunk. "I'll take this for you."

Julia gave him a bemused glance. "I didn't know dukes carried baggage."

"I'm sure I will grow in arrogance as I approach London," he said solemnly. "But for now I prefer to be useful." He turned and headed to the chaises.

Mariah waited as Julia locked the door. "Are you having second thoughts?"

"Second, third, fourth, and fifth," Julia said wryly as they walked to the chaises. "But—I'm glad to be going. There is someone I must see before it's too late."

"We shall have each other for support. We'll need it, too, I suspect."

When they reached the chaises, Adam introduced Julia to his friends, who had climbed out to meet her. Masterson was his usual affable self and Kirkland was impeccably polite, but Randall frowned and gave Julia a stare that would freeze the whiskers off a badger. "A pleasure to meet you, Mrs. Bancroft," he said icily.

"The pleasure is mutual," Julia said, not raising an eyebrow. She allowed Adam to help her into the chaise and Mariah followed. For Mariah, Adam had a special hand squeeze, but he then turned away and told his friends that he would not selfishly keep two beautiful ladies to himself and asked who would like the first chance to ride with them.

"What was that about?" Mariah inquired in a whisper as the men discussed seating arrangements. "Do you know Randall?"

Julia shook her head. "We've never met. He obviously took an instant dislike to me."

Mariah gave a ladylike snort. "Randall doesn't think highly of females. He's convinced I'm a fortune hunter, trapping Adam into marriage."

"But you had no idea who Adam was when you found him."

"Randall is not a man to let facts interfere with a good snarl."

They shared a smile. Masterson opened the door and joined them in the carriage. "I'm the lucky man who has won the company of two lovely ladies."

Mariah laughed. "We should have let Bhanu come to balance out the loveliness. Though, to be honest, I find her beautiful."

"If you can love an ugly dog enough to find beauty, you shouldn't waste yourself marrying a handsome man like Ash," Masterson said promptly. "Better you should ally yourself with a man like me who needs your gift of ignoring reality."

For an instant she saw something in his gaze that made her think he was at least half serious, but the moment passed. "By the time we reach London, we shall all be heartily tired of the sight of each other," she said.

"And bruised and stiff and weary of traveling," Julia added.

"But at least we'll be uncomfortable at a high rate of speed rather than a slow one," Masterson pointed out.

They all laughed. It was a good start to a long journey.

Chapter Twenty-Four

Adam had assumed that Ashton House would be a substantial town house. Not a freestanding Mayfair mansion surrounded by gardens and a high stone wall topped with formidable spikes. "Good Lord," he said as they pulled up to the high iron gates. "This is rather more than I expected."

Kirkland, sitting on the opposite side of the chaise, said, "Didn't any of us mention that it's the largest private house in London? It's quite nice, actually. There's plenty of room for your friends, so it often seems like a particularly fine hotel."

"I always stay at Ashton House when I'm in London. You've given me my own rooms, actually," Randall said. "Is that still acceptable?"

"Of course." Adam studied the sprawling mansion. "The place is so large I could go days without seeing you."

The journey had gone as smoothly as one could hope, with endless changing of horses and only one instance of being bogged down in mud during a drenching rainstorm. They had stayed at good inns, usually opting for three rooms, with the women sharing one and the men the others. But days in a carriage allowed too much time to think.

No doubt he could deal with London and its demands, though the likelihood that someone had tried to kill him added a little too much excitement.

While the subject was never mentioned, he was very aware that his friends kept a sharp eye on their surroundings. Since Masterson had written ahead to tell the Ashton household and cousins that he was returning, it wasn't impossible that a determined assassin might be able to deduce their route. It was another good reason not to ride in the same chaise with Mariah. If he was shot, at least she should be safe.

But that meant they'd almost never seen each other. Her absence had ached like a missing tooth. The only times he saw her was when all six of the group had dined together in the private parlors of various inns. No matter how long the day, Mariah had been calm and unruffled and uncomplaining.

Julia Bancroft had been an equally good traveler. Though she was quiet, her presence had been soothing. Everyone liked her but Randall, who stiffened whenever she was around. He'd never shared the women's chaise. With Masterson and Kirkland to carry the conversation, their dinners had been pleasant.

After dining, the ladies had withdrawn to their shared rooms. Adam hadn't been alone with Mariah since the carriage ride from Hartley Manor to the village. Surely this great sprawling barracks of a house would allow them some privacy. Not that he wanted to ravish her—well, he did, actually, but he wouldn't—but he would love to sit and drink tea and perhaps hold her hand. To relax with her as he couldn't with anyone else.

A liveried gatekeeper, elderly but sharp eyed, emerged from the gatehouse to inspect the two muddy yellow bounders. The driver of Adam's carriage announced grandly, "The Duke of Ashton and friends."

The gatekeeper must have been informed of Adam's survival, but his face still worked for a moment as he glanced into the chaise to confirm Adam's identity. "Welcome home, your grace." He bowed deeply, then opened the gate.

As they drove up the sweeping arc of driveway, Randall said, "We're back to the land of fussing servants and social obligations."

"Complain if you like," Kirkland retorted, "but I for one will be glad to have fresh clothing and my valet to dress me." He glanced down at his dark green coat and buff pantaloons, which looked well lived in. "I shall tell Jones to burn what I'm wearing. But traveling rough does make one appreciate the comforts of civilization."

"Traveling rough is the retreat to Corunna," Randall said dryly. "A journey to Scotland is merely tiring. Though I'll admit that sharing quarters with you and Masterson for weeks was punishing in its own way."

As Adam and Kirkland laughed, the chaise pulled up under a wide porte cochere. A young footman with powdered hair rushed outside, his face beaming with excitement. As he opened the carriage and pulled down the steps, Adam said, "I wonder how large the welcoming committee will be."

Randall grimaced. "Large. Though no one knew the exact time of arrival, by the end of the afternoon, all of fashionable London will know and half of 'em will be calling to see with their own eyes that you're alive."

"And that's not counting the staff waiting inside," Kirkland added.

The second chaise halted behind theirs and the footman assisted Julia and Mariah out, followed by Masterson. Adam offered his arm to Mariah. "Shall we enter the lion's den?"

Her eyes smiled reassurance as her hand curved under his elbow. "Lead on, your grace." It was the first time they had touched since Hartley. The effect was . . . energizing.

Despite his trepidation on the journey, he found he was now eager to immerse himself in his life. Surely here he would reclaim what he had lost.

His party entered the vast, echoing spaces of a three-story-high entry hall. It was full of servants. Dozens of them.

When he and Mariah appeared, there was a tidal wave of movement as the females curtsied and the males bowed. Everywhere he looked were beaming smiles. These people he didn't recognize were genuinely glad to see him alive. He noticed several pretty housemaids and hoped he'd been gentleman enough not to have molested them.

Three senior servants approached. The middle-aged woman had to be the housekeeper, immaculately dressed and radiating confidence. The man to her right was an equally immaculate butler. Adam's friends had briefed him on the senior staff, so he knew that the couple were Mr. and Mrs. Holmes. Strange how he remembered how a large household was run, but not his own life.

The other man was . . . very different. Though well dressed, he had the burly build and scarred face of a street fighter. Randall murmured, "The fellow on the right is Wharf, your valet. I should have told you more about him."

Too late. The trio reached him and said, "Welcome home, your grace," in near perfect unison. He wondered if they had practiced.

"It's good to be here," he said. "You know most of my friends, I believe, but you haven't met Miss Clarke and Mrs. Bancroft. They will be staying at Ashton House. Take very good care of them."

"Of course, your grace." Mrs. Holmes looked thoughtful. "The blue suite has two bedrooms connected by a sitting room. Would that be satisfactory?"

"Of course," Mariah murmured. Julia nodded agreement. Both of them wore expressions of calm acceptance, as if they stayed in ducal residences regularly. He was amused, but didn't like the reminder of what a good actress Mariah was.

"Mr. Randall, your usual rooms are ready." The housekeeper's gaze returned to Adam. "If it suits your grace, luncheon will be served in an hour, so there will be time for you and your guests to freshen up."

Since breakfast had been at dawn, Adam was hungry and he assumed his friends were, too. Masterson and Kirkland planned to go on to their London homes, but at the least, he owed them a meal now that he had resources again. "That would be very good, Mrs. Holmes. Masterson, Kirkland, will you stay?"

"I should be happy to spend the next hour in your library with a pile of newspapers and a glass of sherry," Kirkland said. "Not moving!"

Masterson laughed. "I'll join you there."

The ranks of servants dispersed, Adam's friends being led off in different directions. Turning to his valet, Adam said, "I'm in need of a change of clothing myself. If you would guide me to my rooms?"

"Of course, sir."

So far, so good. As he followed Wharf upstairs, Adam wondered what the afternoon would bring.

Mariah left a maid unpacking her garments and opened the connecting door to the sitting room. Julia was already there, having left another maid unpacking behind her. Closing the door so they were private, Mariah exclaimed, "Have you ever seen such a place, Julia? One assumes that dukes have wealth, but this place would put Carlton House to shame!"

"Carlton House is more grand, but less welcoming, at least from what I've seen." Julia drifted across the room and looked out a window at the gardens.

Mariah stared. "You've been in Carlton House?"

"Many years ago. But it's not a rare privilege," Julia said with a smile. "For every aristocrat who is an invited guest of the Prince Regent, there are dozens of servants and workmen and laundresses."

Mariah doubted that Julia had visited the royal residence as a laundress, but she didn't pursue the subject. "I'm looking forward to seeing the sights with you. But first I must locate my lawyer and pay a call."

Julia settled in one of the silk-covered chairs. "We both have tasks to accomplish, but I'm sure there will be time for touring as well."

Seeing Julia's strained face, Mariah said softly, "Judging by your expression, your business will be difficult. I will gladly accompany you if that would help."

Julia shook her head, but her expression eased. "No need. I'm sad, but this is a very common sort of grief. I'm going to visit my grandmother. She is old and frail, and this visit might be my last chance to see her. She has lived life long and well, which makes it easier to accept that soon she will be gone. But I want to see her, and that wouldn't have happened if you hadn't persuaded me to come to London. Thank you."

"The benefit is mutual." Mariah sat on the elegant sofa opposite Julia and contemplated the elaborate crown moldings and the handsome paintings. This sitting room and her bedroom were the loveliest places she'd ever stayed.

Seeing Ashton House made her realize just how wide the gap was between her and Adam.

Unbridgeably wide.

Chapter Twenty-Five

As Wharf opened the door to the ducal suite, Adam said, "You were told that the head injury I suffered has damaged my memory?" After the valet nodded, Adam continued, "I remember very little of my previous life. That includes you." His eyes glinted with amusement. "This would be an ideal time for you to tell me that I had promised you an increase in wages."

"No, sir!" Wharf looked shocked as he closed the door to the corridor. They entered a spacious sitting room with several doors opening from it. "I'm already paid most generously."

And the man was too honest to be amused by the idea that he might take advantage of his owner's disability. That spoke well for him. "I hope that in time my memories will return, but for now, I'd prefer that stories of my weakness not circulate. It will be impossible to keep such a thing entirely secret, but the less said the better. Since you would be a primary source of such information, I must hope you're discreet."

Wharf looked even more shocked. "I never, ever talk about your grace's personal business. And most certainly not now."

Better and better. "You don't fit the usual image of a valet. How did you come into my employment? What is your history?"

Wharf's expression became wary. "I was born in the East End. My da was a stevedore. Died when a hogshead of sherry fell on him. My mother was a washerwoman and couldn't support us all, so I enlisted in the army soon as I looked old enough. I gave my mum the bounty to help care for the young ones."

The London accent was now explained. Adam crossed the sitting room and opened a door to a bedroom containing a massive canopied bed draped with heavy blue and silver brocade hangings. "How old were you in truth?"

"Thirteen, but big for my age. Some who join up are scrawny, so I looked well enough grown to pass."

Adam walked across the bedroom, Wharf trailing behind. Another door opened to a huge dressing room full of shirts, breeches, and coats hanging on specially designed fixtures. Boots, hats, and other male paraphernalia were neatly laid out on shelves. "Good God, I actually wear all these garments?"

"Your grace is known for impeccably fine dress, neither too flamboyant nor too conservative," the valet said rather pompously.

"I presume I owe much of my reputation to you." Adam fingered a fine cotton shirt, one of many that hung on individual wooden frames the width of a man's shoulders. A door on the far side of the room led to Wharf's own neat bedroom, which had a separate exit to the corridor. "How did you come to be my valet?"

"I was invalided out of the army after being wounded and coming down with a putrid fever. My mate, Reg, and I were both sent home to recover if we could," Wharf explained. "Back in London, we were attacked by a gang of drunken cutthroats. Both of us were beat up pretty bad before Major Randall came along and drove them off."

"By himself?" Adam asked. "How many were there?"

"Reg and me took down four, but there were four still left." Wharf looked wistful. "If we'd been in fighting trim, Reg and I could have handled them, but not the way we were then. Still, it was a rare treat to see the major in action.

"He thought ex-soldiers shouldn't starve on the streets, so he brought the two of us to you and asked if you could give us work. I would have been happy to scrub the kitchen floor like a scullery maid as long as I was fed and back in England, but you did better. You put Reg in the stables since he's good with horses. You told me you needed a new valet, and would I be interested in learning the trade. When I said yes, you hired a valet from an agency to teach me the tricks of maintaining a gentleman's wardrobe."

Maybe Adam at that earlier time had sensed that it was good to value loyalty over credentials. "I must have liked you to have you trained for the job."

"That, plus even though I was half starving and built like a prizefighter, my clothes always looked good," Wharf said wryly. "I'm not built to be fashionable, so it's been a rare treat to valet you." His gaze flicked over Adam's clothing. "What you're wearing isn't bad, but not up to our usual standards."

Adam turned to look his valet in the eye. "What sort of relationship did we have? I didn't take you to Scotland with me. Why not?"

Wharf's face tightened. "My mother was dying and you told me to stay in London with her. She passed just before the news of your accident reached us."

"My condolences on your loss," Adam said quietly. "I would have been a brute to demand you leave under such circumstances."

"Most lords wouldn't have thought beyond their own convenience," Wharf said bluntly. "I was grateful at the time that you didn't insist I go, but maybe if I'd been with you on the *Enterprise*, you wouldn't have been hurt so bad."

"Or maybe you would have died. There is no point fretting over the past." Adam studied the valet's scarred face. "We appear to have had a relationship that is . . . less formal than is usual between a gentleman and his valet."

"I've always known my place, sir," Wharf said, choosing his words carefully. "And I hope I've never been encroaching. You're the finest gentleman in London, and I don't say that just because I work for you. But—you and I, we're both a little different from the rest. I think maybe that affects how we deal with each other."

"I presume my difference is in my Hindu blood." Adam examined the rack of beautifully tailored coats, the colors a rich, dark rainbow. "What is your difference? The fact that you were not bred to service?"

Wharf flushed a deep, unhappy crimson. "There's that, but also . . . I . . . I should tell you first, before someone else pulls you aside and accuses me 'n' Reg of having a . . . an unnatural relationship."

An unnatural relationship? That must mean sexual. From somewhere in the depths of his mind, Adam recalled that such a connection was a capital crime. No wonder Wharf looked so upset about mentioning the matter. "Do you?"

"Yes, sir." Wharf's voice was a bare whisper. "We can leave if you don't like it."

Having an "unnatural relationship" might explain why Wharf and his mate were attacked by a gang of angry men. Adam wondered exactly what two men might do together, but this was not the time to ask. "Did I know about this before?"

The valet nodded.

"I presume the knowledge didn't bother me?"

Wharf shook his head.

"Then I don't know why it should bother me now." He turned back to the clothing. "Will you choose an appropriate luncheon outfit? I am overwhelmed by choices." He glanced down at himself. "My present outfit was borrowed. It must be cleaned and repaired for return."

"Very good, your grace." Wharf's voice vibrated with relief.

Adam left the dressing room and tried another door. This one was locked. He frowned. "Why can't I enter here?"

"The room is a . . . a private study of yours. That's why you lock it."

"Do you know where the key is?"

The valet nodded. "I clean the room now and then because you don't want the maids going in." He crossed to an elegant and complicated desk, pulled out one of the drawers, and removed a key from the underside. "This is where the key is kept."

Adam examined the carefully constructed secret compartment. "Apparently I am serious about no one else entering."

"Very serious indeed." Wharf handed him the key. "I'll prepare a change of clothing for the luncheon while you go inside."

Glad the valet gave him privacy, Adam unlocked the door, wondering what his old self was so secretive about. He entered the room—and found himself in a Hindu shrine. The air was scented with incense, and light came from high windows that illuminated altars supporting exquisitely carved and painted statues of deities. Richly colored fabrics swept from the center of the ceiling and draped down the walls, making the room feel like an exotic tent. The brass oil lamps matched those of his dreams.

Opposite the door was the elephant-headed god again. *Ganesha.* He remembered the names easily now, and their attributes. Ganesha was a popular fellow, the remover of obstacles and lord of beginnings. The patron of arts and sciences and wisdom. On his altar lay a nosegay of flowers so dried out that the variety couldn't be identified.

Adam lifted the bouquet, petals drifting to the floor. If Wharf came here only to clean, Adam must have left these flowers as an offering before traveling to Scotland. What had he prayed for?

Success for his steamship, or something less obvious?

This space was deeply calm, like a meditation garden but more so. He turned to his right and recognized Lakshmi, the consort of Vishnu and goddess of beauty, love, and prosperity. Rather like Aphrodite or Venus. Lakshmi was the essence of femininity who was celebrated during Diwali, a festival of lights. Mariah looked nothing like this dark-haired deity, yet she possessed that same profoundly female essence.

There were also altars to Shiva the Destroyer, the dancing god of annihilation and rebirth, and Vishnu, the supreme being who stood above all others. The gods of his dreams. Feeling a sense of homecoming more powerful than when he had entered Ashton House, Adam turned in a circle, the thick carpet muffling his steps.

This room represented the secret, Hindu part of himself. When he was forcibly removed from his mother and taken to England to be trained for his inheritance, he had instinctively realized that to stay sane, he must seem English. He couldn't eliminate his dark skin, but he could talk like a lord, dress like a lord, perform the activities of a lord. Hence those handsome garments hanging in the next room.

Had anyone seen this private shrine except Wharf? No. Adam knew immediately that even the friends who had dropped everything and traveled to Scotland in search of his drowned body were unaware of this hidden sanctuary. He had trusted no one with this part of himself except the valet, who had reasons of his own to hold his tongue.

Struggling with thoughts he couldn't quite clarify, he skimmed his fingertips along the bronze wheel of fire that contained the dancing Shiva. There was a deep, complicated connection between his amnesia and the way he had hidden so much of his inner nature. But he wasn't sure how he could make himself whole again.

He remembered how he had attended church with Mariah in Hartley, and how the services had felt natural and uplifting, rather like this room. He walked out of the shrine, locking the door behind him. Wharf was in the dressing room brushing a dark blue coat that didn't need the attention. "Wharf, did I consider myself a Christian?"

The valet gave him a straight look. "You told me once that you were Christian and Hindu both, but that you didn't think most people would understand."

That surprised a laugh from Adam. "Probably not. I had best continue to keep that to myself. You are the only person who knows about my . . . my private temple?"

"I believe so, sir."

Their gazes touched for a moment before Adam looked away. They each had their secrets and respected those of the other man. "I gather that coat is what I shall wear when I join my guests again?"

"Yes, sir. Your other garments are also laid out. I thought morning wear, since your friends have not had the opportunity to change from their travel clothing."

In a few minutes, Adam was dressed as the Duke of Ashton, with flawlessly cut coat, waistcoat, and breeches. He had to admit that the effect of superb tailoring was impressive. His top boots gleamed and he'd found that his fingers remembered how to tie a cravat fashionably. Feeling that he knew himself better than when he'd arrived, he asked, "How do I find my guests?"

"I'll show you the way, sir. The house takes some learning."

With Wharf's guidance, Adam reached the small dining room at the same time as his other guests. Mariah was laughing at something Julia said, and she looked so lovely and lovable that his heart constricted as if squeezed by a fist.

He had been upset by her false claim they were married, but his hidden Hindu shrine was proof that he'd been less than truthful in his own life. It was still too early to make a final commitment—he had too many pieces of himself to rediscover. But he was ready to accept that he wanted to be with her always. Giving her a private smile, he took her arm. "Shall we see what the kitchens of Ashton House have provided?"

"Surely it will be very fine," she murmured, eyes alight as she saw his expression.

"The food will be better than fine. You have the best chef in London, Ash." Kirkland offered his arm to Julia. "Our reward for all those dinners along the road."

The butler, Holmes, caught Adam's gaze, then flicked his glance toward one end of the table to show Adam where to sit. He pulled out the chair to his right for Mariah, saying softly, "We must talk later. There's something I want to show you."

He would reveal his hidden shrine, because if they were to have a future, she must understand and accept the part of himself that he'd buried. But he didn't anticipate a problem. Mariah was as tolerant as she was beautiful. Their gazes met for a moment, and from her smile, she recognized what he couldn't put into words in public.

Adam was about to seat himself when three people swept into the dining room. One was the Ashton footman who had admitted Adam earlier. At his heels were a well-dressed, fair-haired man around Adam's age and a handsome woman of middle years. Adam stared at the young man's green eyes. Not as dark as his own, but definitely green. Could this be . . . ?

"Mrs. Lawford and Mr. Lawford," the footman announced breathlessly.

Adam's cousin and aunt—the closest relations he

had. The young man's face broke into a smile. "Ashton, it really *is* you!"

He rushed forward and caught Adam's hand. Under his breath, he said, "I'm your cousin Hal, you know."

Just as quietly, Adam said, "I wasn't sure. Thank you for confirming that." He shook Hal's hand, thinking that his cousin seemed genuinely happy to see him alive.

Of course, Hal had already received the news, so there was time to prepare his response. If he lied about being glad, he was a good actor. Experimentally, Adam said, "You aren't angry about not inheriting?"

Hal made a rueful face. "I'd like the title, of course, but this is much too soon. I'd prefer several carefree decades before inheriting because you have only daughters. Much more pleasant." His grip was hard.

Hal's mother was tall and well dressed, with a touch of silver in her fair hair. "My dear boy! I can't tell you what a wonderful surprise it was to learn that you were alive." She presented her cheek for a kiss, though her pale blue eyes showed little warmth. "Hal insisted we come over the instant we heard that you were home again."

Glad he'd been told her name, he said, "It's good to be home, Aunt Georgiana. I hope you will both join us for our luncheon." At her assent, he instructed the footman to set two more places at the table.

When the servant was gone and only family and friends were present, he added, "You have heard that I am suffering from memory problems. I had not recollected how beautiful my aunt is."

Her gaze softened at the flattery. "I'm glad to see you looking so well after such an ordeal. We owe your friends a considerable debt for finding you."

"They have gone far beyond the call of duty." He placed his hand on Mariah's shoulder. "Allow me to present my new friends, Mrs. Bancroft"—he indicated Julia with a nod—"and Miss Clarke, who traveled down with us from the north." His hand tightened on Mariah's shoulder. "Miss Clarke and I are betrothed."

Georgiana's jaw dropped in shock. "Ashton, that's impossible! You are betrothed to my daughter, Janey!"

Chapter Twenty-Six

Betrothed to Janey. Adam's fingers bit into Mariah's shoulder as the words hammered her heart. The warmth in Adam's expression when they met outside the dining room had given her hope that they could work out their problems. Now that hope was gone.

Adam and Janey had grown up together. She knew him in ways Mariah never would. They had decided to wed, and a gentleman did not break a betrothal. Not ever.

"Why has no one else mentioned this?" Adam exclaimed, his voice tight.

Startled but not surprised, Hal arched his brows. "I've half expected a betrothal for years, though my naughty sister should have told me when it happened. You two have always been thick as thieves. I thought you'd wait for Janey's twenty-first birthday and ask her then. It's only a few weeks now." He grinned. "Congratulations! I couldn't wish for a better brother-in-law."

"Originally you did mean to wait, Ashton," Georgiana said. "But when you came to me to ask my blessing, you said that since you were heading off to Scotland, you wanted to offer for Janey before you left." She smiled fondly. "You didn't want her to fall in love with someone else during the Season."

"I . . . see," Adam said slowly. Mariah saw how he was struggling to accept that he was betrothed to a woman he couldn't remember. "Where is Janey now? Why didn't she come with you today?"

"She was in alt after you offered," Georgiana explained. "Having had two Seasons already, she had no taste for this one without you, so she decided to visit my sister in Lincolnshire until you returned. I was planning to hold a grand ball to celebrate Janey's birthday and announce the

271

betrothal, until we heard the terrible news about your accident." Georgiana's expression turned grave. "She was devastated when I wrote her about your apparent death. She chose to stay in Lincolnshire and mourn there privately, rather than return to London."

"Does she know I survived?" Adam asked.

"I wrote her as soon as we received Masterson's letter, so she must know by now. She'll want to rush back here to greet you, but she has been ill, so she'll be delayed."

"Nothing serious, I hope." Adam's words were wooden.

"She came down with the ague, a combination of grief and the dampness of the fens, I think." Georgiana frowned. "I worried about the damp when she decided to make the visit, but she wanted to see her aunt and cousins. My sister won't let her return to London until she's well enough to travel, so it might be several weeks."

"I wish her a speedy recovery," Masterson said.

Georgiana glanced at Mariah, her gaze cold. She was glad that her daughter was going to be a duchess, and her expression made it clear that a nobody from the country was not going to interfere with this perfect family arrangement. "As you see, Miss Clarke, it's quite impossible for you to be betrothed to Ashton."

Trying to hold on to what dignity she could, Mariah said, "Of course Ashton and I were both aware that there might be an existing relationship that had not yet become public. You know you have my best wishes, Ash." She thought she managed to sound calm, though Masterson and Julia watched her with worried expressions.

"Thank you." His voice was a whisper as his hand dropped from her shoulder.

The congealed silence broke when servants entered with two new place settings. The guests seated themselves and the first course appeared in an abundance of platters and bowls. Masterson and Kirkland carried much of the conversation, with help from Hal Lawford. The women were uniformly silent, and Randall frowned into his plate. Adam looked numb. Though the food was undoubtedly delicious, it sat in Mariah's stomach like gravel.

The luncheon dragged on for what seemed like forever. As soon as was polite, Mariah excused herself, saying she was tired from the journey and wished to rest. Adam's wounded gaze followed her as she left. If she were more selfish, she might be glad that he was as unhappy as she.

She was very proud of herself. She managed to control her tears until she was safely back in her room.

The luncheon party broke up quickly after Mariah left. In the bustle as guests prepared to leave, Adam took Will Masterson aside. "This betrothal to Janey Lawford—is it plausible that I asked her to marry me?"

"You never gave a hint that you might ask her, but yes, it does make sense," Will replied, his brow furrowed. "You've always been very fond of Janey. I thought you regarded her more as a younger sister, but feelings change, and she's grown from a tomboy to a beautiful young woman."

Adam thought of the dream he'd had of embracing a green-eyed young beauty. Was he remembering when he and Janey had become engaged? "No one seemed surprised to hear of the betrothal."

"You were more relaxed with Janey than any other woman in the ton, but as her legal guardian, you would have considered it inappropriate to declare your feelings before she came of age." Will looked thoughtful. "If you were quietly waiting for her to turn twenty-one, it would explain why you showed no interest in courting anyone else."

Adam felt the prison bars clanging shut. He was betrothed to a woman whom he couldn't remember. Afraid he knew the answer, he asked, "If I recall correctly, it is unacceptable for a man to cry off a betrothal."

"Quite. It simply isn't done by any man of honor." Masterson's expression was sympathetic. "When you meet Janey again, you will remember why you wish to marry her. She is a warm, charming, intelligent young woman." He hesitated. "If you had met Miss Clarke before offering for Janey, it might have been different. Miss Clarke has equal warmth and intelligence, plus a maturity and seasoning that Janey hasn't had the opportunity to develop. But you met Miss Clarke too late."

Too late. Damn, but he should have insisted Mariah run off to Gretna with him!

Before Adam could say more, a soberly dressed gentleman of middle years approached him. "Your grace, I'm George Formby, your secretary. If you have time this afternoon, there are urgent matters of business that require your attention."

So much for going after Mariah. Duty called, and apparently the Duke of Ashton always did his duty.

The well-organized Formby had a mountain of documents for Adam's consideration. Adam signed the ones that were simple, urgent, and easy to decide. More complex issues he set aside for later. The secretary patiently explained everything. There was a vague sense of familiarity to all these business matters, but without Formby, Adam would have been lost.

It was an exhausting session for both of them. The afternoon was well advanced when Adam said, "I've absorbed all that I can for one day. Are there any other matters that must be addressed instantly?"

Formby reached for some papers, then stopped.

"Nothing is so urgent that it can't wait. You've done well for your first day home." He collected the papers that Adam had signed. "On behalf of the entire household, your grace, we're glad you survived."

Adam rubbed his aching temple. "Thank you, Formby. And thank you for your patience with my shortcomings."

The secretary inclined his head and withdrew. Adam sat wearily at his desk. This ground-floor study was a handsome room with dark wainscoting, lavish Oriental carpets, and plenty of books and comfortable furniture. It made a good cave for him to hide in.

He hadn't the vaguest idea what to do next. During his journey he'd hoped that returning to his real life would bring back memory and a sense of belonging. Instead, he felt more like a stranger visiting this life on sufferance.

When a tap sounded at the door, he called out permission to enter. His heart somersaulted when Mariah entered. He rose and gazed at her hungrily. Her expression looked almost normal, though she stood with her back against the closed door, as if prepared to bolt.

"I came to ask permission to borrow a footman to escort me to my lawyer's office in the morning," she said in a voice of exquisite neutrality. "I want to take care of my business promptly so I can return home."

"There is no need to rush away from London," he said, his throat tight. "You are always welcome in my home."

"There is every need to leave," she said softly. "I have no place here."

She was wise. Wiser than he, because he wanted nothing more than to keep her close. But saying so would be wrong and would make the situation worse.

Forcing his voice to evenness, he said, "Of course you can have the services of a footman, but why not start by sending a note? That way you can set a time rather than go to his office and perhaps find him away." He smiled. "Use Ashton House stationery. That will catch his attention."

She made a face. "I hate to rely on your name, but that would be convenient. Mr. Granger has been neglectful. He hasn't answered a single one of my letters. Though perhaps he is ill and can't."

"It's generous of you to give him the benefit of the doubt, but it's more likely that he's incompetent," Adam said. "A capable man would have a clerk to carry on the business if he's ill. Would you like me to come with you? It would be my pleasure."

She considered, then nodded. "A lone female may not be taken seriously. After I meet the man, I'll know if I need to find another lawyer."

"I will be happy to help you, and Mrs. Bancroft

as well." His smile was wry. "I might as well get some use out of my exalted station."

Her answering smile was equally wry. "If there is one thing I've learned in my irregular life, it's to be practical. I'm sure you'll alarm the lawyer, and if George Burke ever returns to threaten a lawsuit, I will be happy to watch you terrify him. Thank you, your grace."

He drew in a painful breath. "Please don't call me that. I prefer Adam, or Ash, or Ashton, but 'your grace' is just too absurd from you."

"Very well, Ash." She turned and reached for the doorknob.

He wished she would call him Adam, but that was too intimate. Needing to speak of their situation, he said haltingly, "When you speculated that perhaps I had made a commitment to a woman I didn't remember, I really didn't think it likely, but you were right. I'm . . . very sorry indeed."

Mariah looked wistful but shook her head. "So am I, but when your aunt revealed the betrothal, I realized we had been wise to wait before doing anything rash."

They'd been rash that afternoon in the garden, and he wasn't sorry. "You are a better person than I. My first thought was regret that we hadn't gone to Gretna. Nothing could have been done if we had come to London married."

"You say that now because you don't remember Janey, but think of how that would have been for her. She's known you most of her life, and probably loved you all that time. She would be devastated if you returned with a bride." Mariah's expression turned brittle. "And she may well be a better wife for you. She was raised in your circle; she knows your friends and how to be a duchess."

Adam sighed. "You may be right, but it's hard to feel for a stranger. You're the one whom I know and want."

Her eyes narrowed. "When we met outside the dining room, you looked at me differently."

"While in my quarters, I realized I'd been less than honest in my own life, and decided I had made too much of the one lie you told," he said. "I was about to ask you to forgive me in the hope that we could resume where we left off."

"There is nothing to forgive." She looked away, no longer able to meet his gaze. "I am glad that we met, even if I never see you again after I leave London."

Her words were searing, but irrefutable. If he was bound to another woman, it would be foolish and unfair to see Mariah again.

But even if he couldn't spend his life with Mariah, he wanted her to know the hidden part of him. "Will you come up to my rooms? There is something there I'd like you to see." He smiled wryly. "I know it's not respectable to take you there, but my motives are not dishonorable, and I think you'll find it . . . interesting."

"My curiosity always has been stronger than my judgment," she said with an answering smile that almost made him forget his honorable intentions. "Lead on, your grace—Ash."

As they left his study and climbed the stairs, he asked, "Is your room comfortable?"

"It's the best I've ever had, and I speak as someone who has been a guest in far too many country houses." She glanced at him curiously. "How do you feel about this house? It is familiar?"

"A little. But I had hoped that returning to my home would bring back my past." At the top of the stairs, he directed her to the right. "Instead, it's more teasing frustration. There is only one place so far that really speaks to me. That's where I'm taking you."

He opened the door to his suite, then crossed to the writing desk and removed the key from its hiding place. He made no attempt to hide the location. This was only a small act of trust compared to revealing his inner self.

"Enter my secret retreat." He opened the door and gestured her inside.

Her eyes widened and she turned in a slow circle, her fascinated gaze studying the statues. "This is prayer, not art, I think."

He nodded. "You said it better than I could."

She touched the dried flowers in front of Lakshmi. "You have kept your childhood faith in your heart."

"Are you appalled by my heathen habits? I'm not a proper English Christian gentleman."

"You knew the Anglican prayers and responses as well as I did," she said thoughtfully. "I think you have become more than a usual Englishman, not less."

He gave a sigh of relief. "I wasn't sure how you would feel about this. Perhaps I shouldn't care what you think of my Hindu nature, but . . . I do care. I don't want you to be repulsed."

"Granny Rose said that long, long ago, the Rom—the Gypsies—came from India. Perhaps we are far distant cousins." She gestured at Lakshmi. "You were not appalled when I told you of my Gypsy blood. We can share tolerance."

"Thank you for your acceptance," he said quietly. "Would you like to know more about the different gods?"

She gave him a quick smile. "Please."

Talking about the different deities helped him control his simmering lust. As they left the room, she said, "You remember a great deal about the gods. This part of your memory is working, I think."

"So it is," he said, surprised. "I hope that's a good sign. I think that acknowledging the Hindu side of my nature is critical to my regaining my past." He locked the door. "I wonder if Janey will accept this part of me, or if she'll be appalled."

"I don't think you would have offered for her if

you didn't have faith in her acceptance," Mariah said. "In fact, perhaps you've already brought her here."

"Interesting thought. You're always one step ahead of me." He frowned as he tried to visualize himself and Janey in his sanctuary. "It doesn't feel like that happened, but I can't trust myself on that when I barely remember what she looks like."

"Do you remember her at all?"

"I think so," he said reluctantly. "I have an image of her throwing her arms around me while she smiled radiantly. Perhaps it was when I offered for her."

"Very likely." All the animation left Mariah's face as she glided to the door that led to the corridor. "Thank you for sharing such an important part of yourself."

Her expression was a blade in his heart. She was walking away, and soon she would be gone from his life entirely. The thought was unbearable.

He caught up with her before she opened the door. "Mariah . . ."

She turned, her face anguished. They came together like a firestorm, kissing and touching frantically. He buried his fingers in her sunshine hair. Her mouth intoxicated like wine, and her warm body molded perfectly to his. He forgot the barriers between them as he caressed and tasted and inhaled her essence. Mariah, his savior and delight, the center of his life. He wanted to protect her forever, and make love to her for just as long.

"I'm trying to do the right thing, Adam," she whispered brokenly, "but it's so hard to want you this much when I can't have you."

They pressed against the door, hips pulsing in an instinctive desire to join. Burning with tenderness and desire, he kissed her throat. "How can this not be right?"

She gasped, her fingers digging into his back. Then she wrenched away, panting as she struggled for control. "What we are doing is dishonorable. We mustn't continue, no matter how compelling lust is."

He wanted to take her in his arms again. Even more, he wanted to carry her to his bed. But the corner of his mind still capable of reason knew she was right. "What I feel for you is far more than lust. But . . . honor matters."

"We can't be alone again." She smiled shakily as she brushed her hair back. When had the golden waves tumbled loose? "Neither of us have the willpower for that."

"We can't be alone in private, but surely we can be together in public for what little time we have left." He needed to store memories for the dark years when she would be gone. "Will you ride with me in the morning? On horses and in a park with a groom behind, surely we can control temptation."

She gave a rueful sigh. "If I had any sense, I'd say no, but I've proved I have little sense. Very well, tomorrow morning we go riding. But tonight, I will take dinner in my room. I don't think I could manage sharing a table with you after this moment."

With a ride to look forward to, he could let her go now with some semblance of calm. "Let me check the corridor. It's better you not be seen leaving my rooms."

She smoothed her hair back and rearranged her expression to calm detachment. "By all means, let us maintain appearances since it's far too late for good behavior."

He opened the door and glanced out. No one in sight. Stepping back, he gestured her through.

But as she left, he touched her shining hair and locked his hand around the gossamer memory.

Chapter Twenty-Seven

As soon as Mariah reached her room, she folded onto the bed, shaking. Would it have been better if Adam hadn't forgiven her lie? It was agonizing to know that he wanted her now but that unbreakable social custom stood between them.

She had the wicked, un-Sarahish thought that she might be able to seduce him into marriage; his amnesia meant that his grasp of a gentleman's code of honor was weaker than it would be otherwise. The thought was tempting, so tempting. But Adam's life was still too volatile, too full of changes. She'd be a fool to manipulate him into doing something he might regret forever.

But the idea was still . . . painfully tempting.

Mariah shared tea and toast with Julia in their sitting room early the next morning. Then Julia helped her friend don a dark brown habit with silver trim that Adam had not seen her wear.

After Julia left, Mariah examined her reflection. She would not disgrace a duke. Even though the habit had been given to her by an older woman several years before, Mariah's skillful alterations had removed the worn fabric and made the outfit look new and fashionable.

Ruthlessly she reminded herself of the habit's origins to underline the distance between her and Adam. He was a duke, and she was barely respectable and wore hand-me-down clothes. And he was betrothed. They lived in different worlds.

Carefully she tucked an unruly strand of hair under her shako-styled hat. Her appearance was perfectly under control. She could manage a ride in a park with a man she couldn't have.

She left her room and headed down the grand staircase to the front hall. Adam was waiting for her, his expression admiring as he greeted her.

She froze for a moment, realizing that she could control her appearance but not her eyes. She prayed that her eyes didn't give away as much as Adam's did.

She resumed her descent. "A lovely morning for a ride."

"Indeed it is, and I like the looks of the mounts the head groom has chosen for us," he replied, as consciously casual as Mariah.

They continued to exchange commonplaces as they left the house and walked to the stables. And they didn't look at each other.

The horses were indeed beautiful. Mariah used a mounting block to swing into the sidesaddle on the chestnut chosen for her. Better not to let Adam assist her. Her intense consciousness of him made her realize that she would have been wiser to refuse this invitation. But she longed for a good gallop to burn off her restless energy almost as much as she wanted to be in Adam's company.

Led by Murphy, a lean, tough-looking Irishman, they rode to the park through the Mayfair streets, which took attention even this early in the day. She began to relax when they reached Hyde Park. During the fashionable late-afternoon hours, Rotten Row would be crowded with carriages, but now it was almost empty. "Race you to the end of Rotten Row!" she called to Adam.

Not waiting for his response, she took off down the broad, sandy road. It was glorious to feel the wind in her face, as if she could run away from her problems. She heard Adam's laughter as he matched her pace. Side by side, they galloped the length of Rotten Row.

As they neared the end, she slowed her horse to a walk. Adam did the same. When they turned back, Mariah patted the chestnut's neck. "Your stable is truly excellent, Ash."

"I'm impressed with my ability to judge horses, though probably it's Murphy I should thank." His admiring glance ran over her. "You look particularly fine in that riding habit. Not all blondes can wear dark brown well."

Ignoring the admiration, she said, "It sounds like your memory of fashion is returning. Are you recalling other things?"

"I seem to remember things more than people." He sighed. "I've been hoping that something will trigger my memories in one great flood and I'll recall everything at once, but that seems increasingly unlikely."

"Perhaps when Janey returns, everything will fall into place," Mariah said, her voice carefully neutral.

He shrugged. "Perhaps. By the time we return to Ashton House, the footman should have returned with word from your lawyer. I assume that you inherit everything as your father's only heir even if he didn't leave a formal will."

"Very likely, but a will would make the process go more smoothly. I know he intended to have one drawn up, but I don't know if he had time before . . . before his death." She wondered when she would be able to refer to his death without flinching.

"Nothing can replace a lost parent, but at least he left you well situated," Adam said quietly.

"The purest luck," she said, her smile restored. "And I am suitably grateful. I am Miss Clarke of Hartley, and that does wonders for my confidence."

Their pace back along Rotten Row was slow, as if neither of them wanted the ride to end. Murphy followed several discreet lengths behind. Adam was right: having a groom near did help control unruly impulses. Even so, she was intensely aware that Adam was only a few feet from her, and that time was running out.

There were more riders now. A military gentleman cantered toward them on a handsome bay, and in the distance several men were trotting at a leisurely pace. It was hard to believe the park was in the heart of London. Trees on the right screened them from city streets, and on the left ducks squabbled on the calm water of the Serpentine.

Suddenly Murphy shouted, "Sir, there's a rifleman in the trees! Get away!"

Mariah whipped her head to the right and saw the glint of sunlight on a long barrel aimed in their direction. Adam spurred his horse forward between Mariah and the rifleman, slashing his whip over her mount's hindquarters. "Go!"

Her chestnut took off like a startled fox as the crack of a firearm shattered the morning peace. As Mariah struggled to maintain her seat, Adam's horse sprang forward alongside hers.

She regained her balance swiftly, then glanced over her shoulder to see Murphy galloping furiously toward the grove, a pistol in his hand. The military-looking gentleman was also charging the thicket.

A second shot exploded. Mariah sensed that it passed near her and Adam as they bent over the necks of their speeding horses. They galloped half the length of Rotten Row before Adam slowed his mount to a walk. "We're out of range now."

From his frown, she guessed that he didn't like running while other men chased the rifleman. He had put her safety over his desire for pursuit. "What kind of madman would shoot strangers in a park?"

"I don't know." He touched his right shoulder, and his fingers came away scarlet.

Mariah gasped as she saw a stain spreading across his white shirt. "Adam, you're bleeding!"

He looked at his bloody fingers, puzzled. "I didn't notice until you spoke. My shoulder stings. But I don't feel shot."

Terrified that he was badly wounded and in shock, she swung from her mount. "Get off your horse so I can examine you."

He obeyed, wincing. She helped him peel his coat off his right arm. There was a hole in the shirt across the top of his right shoulder, and a lot more blood. She ripped the fabric open and saw that a rifle ball had grazed him. "It's probably not dangerous, if you don't take an infection. With cleaning and some basilicum powder, you should heal quickly."

"Messy, though." He regarded his shoulder. "I'm not fond of seeing my own blood."

"I can't say that I like the sight of your blood, either." She folded her handkerchief into a pad, then untied and unwound his cravat. "A good thing cravats are long enough to act as bandages."

"Who knew fashion could be practical?" His tone was light, but he flinched when she pressed the pad over the wound. "Wharf is not going to be pleased about the ruination of this coat."

She knotted the cravat in front of his chest, then helped ease the coat back on so the wound and blood were less obvious. "He will be too glad you're alive to care. A few inches lower and you'd be dead."

Murphy and the military man joined them. "We couldn't catch the devil, sir," the groom said as he dismounted. "He chose his spot near the edge of the park so he could vanish into the streets right quickly." His expression darkened when he saw the bandage. "You were hurt, sir?"

"Just a graze, Murphy. My thanks for going after the villain."

"Wharf told me to look after you, sir," the groom said.

Adam nodded, as if the words confirmed a thought. "You're his friend who served with him in the army."

Looking a bit wary, Murphy said, "Aye, sir."

"I'm grateful that you're both looking out for my welfare."

The military man, a straight-backed fellow with gray hair, said, "The weapon was a Baker rifle. I recognized the sound."

Murphy nodded agreement. "An infantry weapon, and the bastard was a damned good shot. You were lucky, sir." Remembering Mariah's presence, he tugged his hat. "Begging pardon for my language, miss."

"I couldn't agree more with your assessment." Mariah looked in the direction the rifleman had concealed himself. "I think it's time to go back to Ashton House to call a surgeon."

"Agreed." Adam slid his arm back into his coat, almost controlling his wince. He turned to the military stranger. "I'm Ashton and this is Miss Clarke. Thank you for driving the villain off before he could do more damage."

The other man studied Adam intensely, his shrewd gray eyes set in a sun-weathered face. "Would that be the Duke of Ashton? I'm lately returned to England after serving in India. I had heard of you, but when we reached London, it was said that you had recently died in a steamship accident in Scotland."

"I was injured, but survived. I've only just returned to London yesterday."

"I'm pleased to see you alive," the older man said, his expression unreadable. "I'm John Stillwell."

Murphy exclaimed, "Is that General Stillwell of Mysore, sir?"

Stillwell nodded. "I've been called that. I've retired from the army."

His modest words concealed the fact that he was a military hero, from what Mariah had read in the newspapers over the years. No wonder he'd gone charging off after a dangerous rifleman.

Interesting as this was, she said firmly, "It's good you were both here, but now it's time to leave. Murphy, can you help me mount my horse?"

He stepped forward and linked his fingers to provide her a step up onto the chestnut, which had stayed close. Adam mounted on his own, concealing any pain he felt. "General Stillwell, I would appreciate it if you'd keep this incident private. I've no desire to become an object of more gossip. Returning from the dead is dramatic enough."

"Of course." Stillwell swung onto his own horse. "With your permission, might I call on you? I knew your father in India."

Adam smiled. "You would be very welcome, sir. Do you know the location of Ashton House?"

"Doesn't everyone?" the general said with a glint of humor. "I look forward to seeing you again,

Ashton." Expression thoughtful, he turned his horse toward the far end of Rotten Row and resumed his ride.

Mariah suggested, "Let's take a different route back to the house. Just in case."

Murphy gave an approving nod.

Adam and Murphy were far too unsurprised by an attack that could have been lethal.

Something was wrong—and she intended to find out what.

As Adam returned to Ashton House with Mariah and Murphy, he noted how the groom continually scanned their surroundings for possible danger. Like a soldier, or a bodyguard. If Murphy hadn't been alert, the rifleman might have succeeded in his mission.

The idea that a secret enemy had engineered the explosion of his ship had been a little remote, but the burn in his shoulder was vividly real. His enemy must be located and stopped, because Adam was damned if he'd spend the rest of his life hiding indoors.

Mariah had fixed his appearance well enough that a crowd of worried servants didn't descend as soon as they entered the house, but when they reached the front hall, she said quietly, "Adam, no one was surprised enough that you were shot in the middle of London. Is there something you aren't telling me?"

Mariah had a right to know. "My friends think someone wants to kill me," he replied. "I wasn't sure about that before, but after today, I'm inclined to think they're right."

She paled. "Why would anyone want to kill you?"

"An interesting question. I wish I could answer it. Perhaps because my heathen blood is a disgrace to the British aristocracy. No one has a better theory." He turned to the butler, who was bearing down on them. "Holmes, could you call a surgeon? I had a small accident in the park."

Holmes's eyes widened as he saw the blood-stains that weren't fully concealed by Adam's coat. "I shall do so immediately, your grace."

After the butler rushed off, Adam said, "Given that I might be a target, the sooner you return north, the better. You could have been shot today." The thought chilled him. "If that happened, I couldn't bear it."

"I'm not sure I can bear going home and waiting to hear that the Duke of Ashton has been murdered," she said tautly, her eyes huge.

"That won't happen," he said, with more assurance than he felt. "Now that it's confirmed I have an enemy, I will focus my ducal powers on finding the villain." Not wanting to explain just how he would do that since he didn't have an answer, he glanced at several letters and messages waiting on the polished sideboard. He pulled one out. "Here's the response from your lawyer." He handed the note to Mariah.

She broke the seal and scanned the half-dozen lines. "This is from his clerk. Apparently Mr. Granger is out of town, but he is expected home sometime today, and the clerk has set an appointment for tomorrow morning. I suppose Mr. Granger's absence from London explains his lack of response until now."

"I look forward to what he has to say when we call on him." When she glanced up with a frown, he said, "We shall travel in a plain carriage without a crest when we leave the premises. I won't be an easy target again."

"That will have to do," she said, her expression still troubled.

He didn't blame her. He was troubled himself. But he'd not spend the rest of his life in hiding.

He glanced at the letters again and saw one written in a hand that looked very familiar. He broke the wax seal and opened the letter to find it was from Lady Agnes Westerfield.

My Dearest Adam,

There are no words to describe the joy I felt at receiving Masterson's message that you had survived. There are never enough good men in the world that one can be spared.

He said that the injuries you received have affected your memory. I have tried to imagine

*how strange it must feel not to recognize your
own life, with little success. It must be disquieting in the extreme.*

*I talked to Mr. Richards, the surgeon who has
patched up so many of my students, including
you. He has had some experience with head
injuries, and he said that it is impossible to say
whether or not memory will return, which is a
sobering thought.*

*If you never remember your early years, then
you are starting a new life, and that is not
entirely a bad thing. There are few of us who
do not have experiences we would prefer to
forget. Though you are not starting out as an
infant with parents to raise and protect you,
you have many friends who will do anything
for you. You may count me among them.*

*Though I was sorely tempted to come up to
town to see you, one of my new lads is going
through a difficult time, and I really shouldn't
leave him. But I shall be in London as soon as
possible. You may take that as either promise
or threat.*

*As a boy you endured great changes in your
life and adapted magnificently. You will again.*
With fondest wishes,
Lady Agnes Westerfield

He heard a warm female voice in his head as he
read, and images began pulsing through his mind.

First was a clear memory of looking down at a tall, handsome woman who acted as if it was perfectly natural to talk to a boy perched in a tree and clinging to a grubby mongrel. Mentally he regarded the dog and saw that his friends were right: the original Bhanu was possibly the ugliest dog on the face of the earth, but also the most loving. Lady Agnes had understood that.

Other memories of her began spinning through his mind. Teaching, disciplining, comforting. He could feel her arms around him when he wept after receiving a letter from the Ashton lawyers telling him that his mother was dead. Lady Agnes had given him the warmth he desperately needed, and without revealing to anyone that he had been so weak as to cry. The memories jostled painfully.

Mariah grasped his arm firmly and guided him toward a nearby door. "Let us wait for the surgeon in the small salon." When they were in private, she drew him down onto the sofa beside her, expression concerned. "What's wrong? You looked like someone had struck you after you read that letter."

He realized he was rubbing his aching head and dropped his hand. "It was a very kind letter from Lady Agnes Westerfield, and it has triggered a number of memories of my school days. A blow of sorts, but in a good way."

"How wonderful!" She took his hand, her clasp comforting. "Do you remember other things, like going to Scotland to test your steamship?"

He thought, then shook his head.

"What about your childhood in India?"

He tried reaching back to that time but found nothing new. Her questions helped him focus on the memories he had just retrieved, though. "Mostly I'm recalling school and my friends. How we met, how our friendships developed."

"Can you recollect your school days in a fairly orderly fashion?"

"Let's see. . . ." His brows knit as he sorted through the jumble of memories. "I remember meeting Lady Agnes, traveling to her house in Kent, and meeting the other boys as they arrived. Learning. Getting into mischief. Summers and holidays with my cousins." He had sharp recollections of Janey now, and she was truly an adorable child. Feeling disloyal for the thought, he continued, "The memories that have returned seem to be just of those school years, but they feel reasonably complete."

He smiled as he remembered how each friendship had been built up over time as mosaics of shared enjoyment, worry, and occasional conflict. He'd been amazed that Masterson, Randall, and Kirkland had come all the way to Scotland to look for his body. Now he saw that he would have done exactly the same for one of them. They were nearer to being brothers than friends.

He vividly recalled tossing Randall across the room during one of the *Kalarippayattu* lessons he gave the other boys. Randall's arm had broken. He'd laughed through pain and demanded that Adam teach him the trick of that throw later. The local surgeon, Richards, an imperturbable man of middle years, had bound up the injury. There were countless such stories, such moments, attached to each of his friends—and Adam remembered them all, including what he'd experienced with Wyndham and Ballard, his other classmates.

"This sounds very promising," she said thoughtfully. "Since you've just regained a large chunk of memory all at once, other pieces may fall into place with equal completeness."

"Maybe it's a matter of finding the right keys," he said. "Lady Agnes was the key to my school days."

Mariah's expression turned neutral. "Janey may be the key to your more recent years."

Wharf entered the room looking worried. "Your grace, you were hurt?"

Mariah stood, her fingers slipping irrevocably from Adam's clasp. "I leave you to your valet's care. The surgeon will be here soon. You've had an eventful day."

A murder attempt and a restoration of a large chunk of memory—yes, eventful. It was exciting to have so much of his life back. Perhaps he might recall a clue to who was trying to kill him.

The hard part was watching Mariah walk away.

Chapter Twenty-Eight

Mariah was getting better at leaving Adam without looking back. Perhaps when she left for the last time, she'd have the knack of it. She didn't even collapse on her bed. Instead, rather blindly, she made her way to the sitting room she shared with Julia and folded down into a wing chair. Her friend was out, so there was blessed silence.

Were women the keys to Adam's past? Lady Agnes had unlocked a large door, and Mariah suspected that Janey Lawford would do the same when she returned to London. Adam had found more of his past in the private shrine connected to his bedroom. Soon he would have most of his life back again.

He wouldn't need her, and that was as it should be. It hadn't been long since they'd first met, only a few weeks. She would return home and build a life as Miss Clarke of Hartley. When she was old and gray, the time she had known Adam would be the merest ripple in the lake of her life.

But she would not forget him. Oh, no, she would not forget.

Her numbness lasted until Julia swept into the room, her face glowing. "Mariah, I'm so glad to see you! I had the most wonderful visit with my grandmother. The more we talked, the stronger she seemed. I'm so glad I made this journey."

Mariah pulled herself out of her reverie, which was drifting dangerously close to self-pity. "You look five years younger yourself," she said warmly. "Tell me about your grandmother."

Julia's expression became guarded. "She's wise and kind and has always approved of me, even when no one else in the family did. I don't know how I would have managed without her."

"That is exactly what grandmothers are for," Mariah said nostalgically. "My Granny Rose felt the same about me, even when I was at my most mischievous."

Julia settled in the opposite chair with a flurry of skirts. "Did you enjoy your ride with Ashton?"

"Right up until the point when someone shot him," Mariah said wryly. "He wasn't hurt badly, but it wasn't a good start to the day." When Julia gasped, Mariah explained what happened in the park.

"For a pleasant man, he seems to have acquired some dangerous enemies," Julia observed. "And you could have been hurt, too. Or killed."

Mariah sighed. "I'll be safe when I leave London, and that's only a few days away. I just hope that Ash stays safe, too."

"He will. He is powerful and intelligent, and he has good friends."

"I hope that's enough." It tore at Mariah's heart to think of Adam's warm, passionate body lying cold and dead. She realized her hands were clenched and carefully relaxed them. She had an idea so wicked she shouldn't say it aloud, but once more the virtuous Sarah side of her nature went down in defeat. "Julia—do you know how a woman can prevent herself from becoming *enceinte*?"

Julia blinked but showed no other sign of shock. "I know a method or two. They're not guaranteed, but usually they work." She gave a glimmer of a smile. "It's the most common reason that women come to me. Especially wives who have too many children. Having babies or not has always been female business."

"What is the best way to prevent one?" Mariah stared at her hands, which were clenched again. If Julia asked why she wanted to know, she would dissolve with embarrassment.

But Julia didn't have to ask. "A vinegar-soaked sponge is usually effective." In calm, nonjudgmental words, she described how the sponge was used. "I have a couple of sponges with me, actually. One never knows when one will meet a woman in need. Shall I get you one?"

"Please." Mariah's voice was barely a whisper.

Julia rose to go to her bedroom for the sponge. As she reached Mariah, she laid a gentle hand on her shoulder. "Are you sure you know what you're doing?"

"I might not do it." Mariah's nails were digging semicircles into her palms. "But . . . I might have regrets forever if I don't."

"Fair enough."

As Julia turned to head to her room, Mariah asked, "Do you have any romantic interest in the Reverend Mr. Williams?"

"Good heavens, no!" Julia exclaimed, her brows rising. "I've had one husband and I certainly don't want another. You have my permission to flirt with him as much as you like when you return to Hartley."

Mariah managed a crooked smile. "Perhaps I will. He's pleasant and attractive, and after I go home and embark on a life of blameless virtue, he may be the only eligible man I'll ever meet."

Julia laughed. "If you go out in London society at all, you will have men clustering about you like honeybees."

Mariah made a face. "I am not looking to be stung."

Julia became serious. "Have you wished that Ashton had washed up on someone else's shore?"

"Never," Mariah said instantly. "Nor am I sorry I fell in love with him." There, she had said it out loud. "My heart may be dented, but I shall survive. And I quite like Mr. Williams, you know. Perhaps someday I will feel more."

As Julia left, Mariah wondered if she would have the courage to use the sponge and seduce Adam. And if she tried, whether she would succeed. If he had a clear memory of his betrothal, he would be honor bound not to betray his future wife. But if

Janey remained a misty obligation . . . well, that would be a different matter.

Janey would have him always. Mariah would settle for one single night.

Mariah's meeting with her lawyer was mid-morning, so after breakfasting in her room, she went to the stable yard behind the house. Adam was standing next to a small, rather shabby closed carriage and conferring with Murphy.

Bemused, she asked, "Was this vehicle already in the Ashton mews, or was it conjured up overnight?"

Adam smiled. "Conjured up. I talked to Murphy yesterday and told him what was required, and, lo, a miracle."

She chuckled. "Well done, Murphy. This vehicle will disappear into the London streets very easily."

"Particularly since there is a rear exit to Ashton House," Adam said. "We must hope that the villain doesn't have colleagues to watch all the exits."

"This carriage was driven through the gates this morning and looks like it might belong to a tradesman," Murphy said. "It won't be obvious that the duke is leaving in it."

Murphy was clearly a talented protector, but as he helped Mariah into the carriage, she wished such skills weren't needed. She settled on the seat that faced backward so that she and Adam wouldn't be sitting next to each other. The more distance, the better—and there wasn't a lot of distance in this small vehicle, even if both passengers were doing their best not to touch.

Murphy himself drove the carriage, dressed in neat but nondescript clothing. As they rolled by the back gardens toward the rear exit, Mariah noticed several soberly dressed men walking inside the walls. "You have guards now?"

"Former soldiers," Adam replied. "My secretary, among others, insisted on it. The number of guards will increase after dark."

Mariah tried to relax against the lumpy seat. "This is not a good way to live."

"It won't be for long, I hope." Adam sighed. "I wanted to refuse the guards, but there are many people in the household, including you. It would be unforgivable if anyone was hurt due to negligence on my part." He gazed out the window at streets that became increasingly crowded as they drove east toward the City, which was the ancient business and financial district of London. "Precautions make sense, but I don't think it's possible to fully protect oneself from a determined assassin."

"Luckily, guns often misfire, and if you're attacked directly, you're very capable of defending yourself," she said pragmatically. "I still cherish the memory of you throwing George Burke across the drawing room."

Adam's grin made her want to lean forward and

kiss him. She didn't, but it occurred to her that she hadn't seen him smile much lately. "You said your friends first suggested that you were in danger. Why was that?"

His smile disappeared and he tersely described what they had learned about the explosion on the *Enterprise*. When he was done, she said, "So someone wants to kill you, and there is no obvious motive except perhaps resentment of your Indian blood."

"Maybe I grievously offended someone and don't remember it. I may have had a debauched secret life that friends and family didn't know about, and made enemies galore." He shrugged. "I'm less interested in the reason than in stopping the fellow."

"Agreed." Mariah's lips curved into a smile. "I'm having trouble imagining you with a debauched secret life."

"So am I," he admitted. "I don't remember enough about debauchery to know what I might have done."

They looked at each other and burst into laughter. She covered her mouth with her hand and gazed out the window, thinking how intimate shared laughter was.

She hoped that he and Janey would be able to laugh together.

Mr. Granger's chambers were in a middling area, neither rich nor poor, Mariah saw as she descended from the carriage. That made sense. Her father wanted competence but would have looked for it at a reasonable price.

Murphy waited with the carriage as Adam ushered her inside. The office was well kept, though the young clerk had files overflowing his desk. He got to his feet with a smile. "You must be Miss Clarke?"

"Yes, and this is my friend, the Duke of Ashton," she said, willing to get every iota of benefit out of Adam's lordly presence.

The clerk's eyes widened. "I shall tell Mr. Granger you are here."

He disappeared and returned in less than a minute, a voice behind him calling, "And make a pot of tea for our visitors!"

Mariah wondered if mere Miss Clarke would have rated tea. When she entered the office, Adam a step behind her, Mr. Granger came forward and greeted her warmly. He was a solid man with graying hair, and while he gave Adam a shrewd glance, he didn't seem inclined to toady.

"Please sit down," he said, indicating two chairs in front of his massive desk. "I'm delighted to meet you at last, Miss Clarke. Your father always speaks so highly of you and your business abilities. Is he also in London?"

Mariah froze. "You didn't know he is dead?"

"Good heavens, no!" Granger said, shocked. "It just happened?"

She swallowed hard, feeling much as she had when she first received the news. Seeing her distress, Adam said, "It's been some weeks. Mr. Clarke was on a journey to London when he was attacked and killed by highwaymen. We were told he was buried in a local church in Hertfordshire."

"Mr. Clarke visited me perhaps two months ago," the lawyer said slowly. "He told me he was considering changing his will and he intended to return soon, but I haven't seen him since. It never occurred to me that such ill fortune had befallen him."

"Did he say why he wanted to make changes?" Mariah asked, puzzled. "I'm his only heir. Does this affect my inheritance?"

"He didn't say why," the lawyer replied, "but since the previous will is unchanged, you inherit all his worldly goods."

"Having recently acquired Hartley Manor, perhaps he wanted to make provision for longtime servants," Adam suggested.

"Perhaps, though he hadn't mentioned that to me. Maybe he'd just thought of doing that. He was often impulsive." Mariah's mind began working again. "I received a letter from you confirming his death, Mr. Granger."

"That's not possible," he said flatly. "Today is the first I've heard that your father is dead."

"The letter was on your printed letterhead."

The lawyer's expression stiffened. "I am not a liar, Miss Clarke."

Adam intervened. "A letterhead can be stolen or forged. Do you have that letter with you?"

Mariah shook her head. "I didn't think I would need it. I assumed that I would dismiss Mr. Granger because I'd written him four times and he'd never replied."

Granger's brow furrowed. "I never received any letters, Miss Clarke. I would have attended to them immediately. I know that Hartley Manor is in one of the most remote parts of England, but surely the Royal Mail operates there."

"It does indeed." Adam gazed at Mariah. "The Royal Mail runs to Hartley, but in most villages, the post office is in a shop. If that's the case in Hartley, might George Burke have bribed the shop owner to intercept letters addressed to you?"

"That would be highly illegal!" Granger exclaimed.

"But not impossible," Adam replied. "It seems like something Burke might do."

Mariah gasped as she thought of another possibility. "If that's the case, letters from my father could have been intercepted as well. He might be alive!"

Adam's eyes were compassionate. "Perhaps. But he has still been gone from Hartley far longer than you expected."

He was right, she realized. There was also her

father's gold ring that Burke had given her. That suggested that her father really was dead. She rose unsteadily from her chair. "Please excuse me, Mr. Granger. I have much to think about."

He and Adam both stood. "Of course, Miss Clarke," the lawyer said. "Let me know if there is anything I can do to help you solve this puzzle." He hesitated. "If there is no clear proof of your father's death, you won't have legal title to Hartley Manor for seven years."

"I understand," she said numbly.

Adam took her arm, saying, "If you learn anything useful, Mr. Granger, send a note to me or Miss Clarke at Ashton House."

Mariah managed to control herself until they were in the carriage and heading back to Ashton House. She began to shake, then turned to Adam, who held her in his arms.

Hope hurt.

Chapter Twenty-Nine

Adam held Mariah until she stopped trembling, wishing there was something more he could do to diminish her pain. They were halfway back to Ashton House before she withdrew from Adam's embrace. Her expression was stark but her eyes were dry. "I had come to accept my father's death. Now . . . I don't know what to think."

"I think it likely that Burke forged the letter from

Granger. He might have learned who your father's lawyer was while they were discussing transfer of title for the estate. I also think it possible that he might have a confederate at the Hartley post office who has stopped your letters from going to London." Wishing he could be more optimistic, he continued, "If so, the confederate could also just as easily block letters from being sent up to you at the manor. But that doesn't explain why your father hasn't returned in person."

Mariah sighed. "I know you're surely right. But what if he was injured or ill and couldn't travel? He could easily be delayed this long. He . . . he could be driving into Hartley now and surprised I'm not there." Her voice broke. "It's hard not to know."

Adam took her hand. "Tragedy is simpler than uncertainty. Not easier, but simpler."

She nodded. "I think you're right. But what can I do now? How does one find a man who is missing and may be dead?"

"I will set people to looking for your father," Adam said firmly. "We know that he reached London because he called on Granger. Write down everything you know about his schedule: when he left Hartley, when he thought he'd return, how he would have traveled. Mail coach, regular stage—what you know, and your best guesses. Also write a description of your father's appearance and habits. Are there places or people he would be likely to visit while in the London area?"

Her expression turned thoughtful at the prospect of positive action. "I shall have the information ready for you this afternoon. Also, when I see Julia, I shall ask her what she thinks of the couple who run the Hartley post office."

"There is a great deal of information out there." He squeezed her hand a last time, then released it. "We will find the truth about your father."

"Finding Burke might tell us what we want to know."

"Believe me, tracking the villain down is high on my list of priorities."

Satisfied, she transferred from his seat to the facing one. For the first time, Adam found himself glad that he was an obscenely wealthy man. He would spend whatever was necessary to give Mariah peace of mind.

Mariah was calm by the time Adam escorted her into Ashton House. Selfishly, he hoped that the mystery about her father would keep her in London a few days longer. Once Janey Lawford returned from Lincolnshire, the situation would become untenable for Mariah, but for now, there was more pleasure than pain in having her under his roof.

The butler approached when they entered. "You have visitors, your grace." Holmes handed over an engraved card. "A General Stillwell and his wife and daughter are waiting in the small salon."

The general hadn't wasted any time in calling. Adam wondered rather cynically what Stillwell wanted—social favor for a marriageable daughter, perhaps. But the man had showed courage in going after the rifleman, and if he hoped to use a duke's influence, he had earned the right to ask. Adam had to discuss with Formby just how much influence he had, and how he'd used it in the past. He glanced at Mariah. "Would you like to see Stillwell?"

She smiled. "I didn't properly thank him before, so this is a good opportunity."

Adam followed Mariah into the salon—then stopped, unable to breathe. Dimly he was aware of Stillwell's tall figure and a young girl by the window, but most of his attention was riveted on the woman who rose and regarded him with uncertain hope. She was the black-haired, beautiful woman of his dreams, and she wore a graceful, embroidered scarlet sari. Impossible. *Impossible!*

She smiled as if uncertain of her welcome. "Darshan?"

She was the only one who had ever called him by his middle name. Memories began ricocheting through his mind, as when he'd read Lady Agnes's letter, but this was a thousand times more intense. He remembered his childhood, his father, the long journey to England.

And not only his early years, but his time in England after he left school. He'd hoped for a great rush of returning memories—and now he was in danger of being eaten alive by them.

Mariah touched his arm, anchoring him to the present. "Adam, are you all right?"

He collected himself enough to give her an uneven smile. What a very strange day he and Mariah were having, both of them learning lost parents were perhaps not so lost. Part of him wanted to retreat from the lacerating pain, but he couldn't, not when a miracle stood before him. He extended his hands, afraid she couldn't be real. "Mother?"

She caught his hands, beaming. Her clasp was warm and firm. He drew her into his arms, thinking of all the nights he'd wept for her. Now she wept for him, her face buried against his shoulder. She was much smaller than in his dreams, but he would have known her anywhere by her perfume, a spicy, exotic scent unknown in England. She was even more beautiful than he remembered.

This close he could see fine lines around her eyes and the expression of a woman who had seen her share of life. Yet she looked very young to have a son his age. He realized that she must have been not much more than a child when she had married his father. Voice choked, he said, "I was told you were dead."

General Stillwell snorted. "Having ripped you

from your mother's arms, naturally the authorities would say she was dead to sever you from your Indian ties. For your own good, of course."

For your own good. Adam could imagine his trustees saying that, smug in the belief that they knew what was best for an underage duke with distressingly mixed blood.

His mother stepped back, blinking tears from her eyes. "I'm sorry for being such a watering pot," she said in fluent, charmingly accented English.

"I think the occasion merits tears," Mariah said softly. "Perhaps we should all sit down. I'll ring for tea."

As Adam's mother drew him down beside her on the sofa, Mariah took a seat to one side, watching him with calm eyes in case he needed her. He thanked heaven Mariah was here to support him in the maelstrom of emotion and memory. Then a thought cut through the painful clamor of his mind. He glanced at the general. "You're my stepfather?"

Stillwell nodded. "As I said in the park, your father and I were friends. Lakshmi wrote asking for help when the authorities took you away, but I was on campaign. By the time I returned, you were already on your way to England. They would tell her nothing except to say that you would be raised as befitted your station."

"Bah, as if strangers would know best how to raise my son!" Lakshmi said, her hand locked around Adam's. Her eyes were gray green, striking against her dark complexion. "I have always dreamed of this day, but thought it would never come. When we arrived in London and heard that you had died . . ." She shivered.

"Sometimes I think Lakshmi married me so I would bring her to England to find you," Stillwell said affectionately.

The warm glance she gave her husband belied his teasing words. "I have been most fortunate in my husbands. Your sister has done well with them also."

"My sister?" he said blankly. Though his head was exploding with memories, a sister was not among them.

His mother gestured to the young woman by the window who watched the scene with intense interest. "This is your sister, Lady Kiri Lawford. I was pregnant when your father died. I didn't tell the authorities for fear they would take her, too."

"Kiri. That's a lovely name," he said, wondering if he could bear any more shocks. His new sister looked . . . like Adam. Dark hair, green eyes, taller than her mother. She was dressed in European style and would fit into any English drawing room despite a subtle air that suggested exotic distant places. Like her mother, she was beautiful.

"I've always wanted a sister." He rose and crossed the room to her. "But I don't suppose you wanted an older brother. I understand they can be dreadful creatures."

She grinned at him, her eyes dancing. "Luckily, my brother, you weren't around to torment me when I was little."

"I wish I had been, Kiri," he said quietly.

Her smile vanished. "I wish that, too," she whispered.

Her words resonated within him, blood calling to blood. He took her hand. "Then we shall have to start being brother and sister now, Lady Kiri."

As she squeezed his hand, the general said, "You also have a half sister and a half brother. Thomas and Lucia Stillwell."

Adam was shaken to discover that he now had a whole family of relatives. "Are they here in London?"

Stillwell nodded. "Yes, but we didn't want to overwhelm you."

"Besides," Kiri said dispassionately, "they're rather wicked young creatures. They might have caused you to reconsider accepting us."

"Kiri!" her mother said sternly.

Adam smiled. "I look forward to meeting them."

But not today. He rubbed at the scar on his head. "I do feel rather overwhelmed."

Mariah said, "Ashton suffered a head injury in the explosion that almost killed him, and his memory is somewhat damaged."

"Plus, he was shot yesterday." Stillwell stood. "We won't stay for tea, but we needed to know that you would acknowledge your mother and sister."

Adam said, appalled, "You thought I wouldn't?"

"It was possible," Stillwell said bluntly. "Depending on how thoroughly the lawyers and trustees convinced you to be ashamed of your heritage."

"They failed. Will you dine with me tomorrow evening? All the family, including Lucia and Thomas." By then, he should have recovered enough to greet them with the joy this situation deserved. "I hope you are staying in London for some time?"

"Forever, perhaps." His mother shrugged. "All of my children are half English. They have a right to know their heritage." She cocked her head to one side. "Do you miss India? Or are you glad you were brought to England?"

He had never thought to ask himself that, and the answer took thought. "Both. I miss India, but I cherish the friends I've made here." His gaze went to Mariah.

Concern in her eyes, she stood. "Ash is too much a gentleman to ask you to leave, so I will do so instead. He has not fully recovered from his injuries."

"Of course." His mother stood and touched his cheek with a shining smile. "You do not look well. Rest now. It is enough to know that I will see you tomorrow."

He managed to hold himself together while he made his good-byes, but after Mariah left to escort his guests—his *family*—to the front door, he folded down onto the sofa, elbows on his knees and his face buried in his hands. So many good things had happened today. Why did he hurt so much?

Chapter Thirty

As the Stillwells waited for their carriage, Adam's mother gave Mariah an enchanting smile. No wonder she had captivated two husbands already. "I am so sorry, miss, we were never introduced."

"So much was happening," Mariah said, wondering how little she could say about her status in Adam's life. "I'm Mariah Clarke. Ashton was washed ashore on my property, and I took him in. He didn't remember who he was at first, but he's recovering. His school friends found him and offered to escort my friend Mrs. Bancroft and me to London. Ashton graciously invited us to stay here during his visit."

Lakshmi's eyes sparkled. "Are you his betrothed?"

The hopeful question hurt. "No, he is betrothed to his cousin, Jane Lawford. I'm sure you'll meet her soon."

The general accepted that, but the two women looked quizzical. Mariah was grateful that the Stillwell carriage drew up then so the conversation could go no further.

After saying farewell, she pivoted and headed back to Adam. His newly discovered family looked like fine people, and surely they would bring him much joy. But he had seemed on the verge of shattering, and it hadn't been from happiness.

When she entered the salon, he was bent as if in pain and his breathing was harsh. She sat next to him and rested her hand on his back. "You look like a man in hell," she said quietly.

His mouth twisted in bleak humor. "An apt description."

"Do you feel physical pain? Mental? Both?"

He drew a long, shuddering breath as he considered his answer. "Both. The scar on my head hurts abominably, but the mental pain is worse. Many, perhaps all, of my memories have returned, and they are all hammering for space in my mind. The end result will be good. The process is . . . difficult."

No wonder he was stretched to the breaking point. "Can you make it upstairs to your bedroom?"

He drew another deep breath, this one steadier, and got to his feet. "Yes. There is nothing physically wrong with me. I'm merely drowning in too much happiness."

"Your whole world has changed, and change hurts." Taking his arm, she guided him from the salon and up the stairs. When they entered his rooms, she retrieved the hidden key from his desk and opened the door to his private shrine.

He released his breath in a long sigh. "How did you know? You're right—I need peace and meditation. Will you join me?"

Grateful that he wanted her company, she walked into his sanctuary. As tranquility eased through her, she realized that she needed this as much as he.

She hadn't noticed the large cushions tucked behind a pedestal until he pulled two out. They made sitting a good deal easier when she folded herself onto the cushion, her knees tucked to one side. Adam sat next to her, bending with ease from long practice, and also possibly because of the custom-tailored clothing he wore.

He took her hand and closed his eyes and began deep, slow breathing. She followed his lead and found that her own tumbled emotions steadied down. Adam would help her find the truth about her father, and she would live with it, no matter what.

After a long, peaceful interval, he squeezed her hand. "My head still hurts, but order is beginning to emerge from chaos. Thank you."

She opened her eyes and saw that while his expression was drained, he looked himself again. "I cannot imagine how you must feel to learn that your mother is alive and you have a whole family you didn't know about."

"That part is wonderful." He grimaced. "Today I received a miracle, while you have been given uncertainty. It seems unfair."

"Even if my father doesn't miraculously return from the dead, I had him for all of those years growing up. You haven't had your mother for over twenty years. The situations balance, perhaps."

"I had Lady Agnes, who was a decent substitute." His brow furrowed. "Just reading Lady Agnes's letter restored one set of memories, and meeting my mother brought back a larger set, which are jangling madly around in my head. It has been intensely disquieting. Like trying to walk through an earthquake where even the ground beneath my feet can't be trusted."

She asked, "Do you think you have all your memories?" Which was more neutral than asking if he remembered falling in love with Janey Lawford and asking her to marry him.

"It's hard to remember what I don't remember," he said wryly. "But after I had found calm in my meditation, I tried to organize my recollections, and they seem fairly complete. At least until the last months. I remember working on my steamship plans and getting ready to go to Scotland, but there's a gap from the autumn until I rolled ashore in Hartley."

She gave up the struggle for detachment. "You don't recall your betrothal?"

He shook his head. "All I have is the earlier

dream image of Janey in my arms." He glanced away. "I do remember that I have always been . . . very fond of her."

Even though his words were as understated as possible, they still stabbed. She had the dismal feeling that there would be no miracles from that direction. Janey was his dear friend of many years, the young woman he had pledged to marry. Lucky that Mariah was getting better at hiding her reaction to the situation. "Do you remember anything that might give clues as to who is trying to kill you?"

"Nary a trace of murderous enemies or a debauched secret life." He gestured to the Hindu statues with his free hand, since the other was still locked around hers. "This seems to be the only secret life I have."

What else would be useful to know? "Since Hal Lawford would benefit most from your death, do you remember anything that might implicate him?"

"As I remember him, he's a terrible liar and doesn't have a devious bone in his body," Adam replied. "It's hard to imagine him trying to kill me."

"But people can surprise us." And what better disguise than seeming honest and straightforward, as Hal did? "Perhaps as your mind settles from all this turmoil, you'll remember more."

"Perhaps." He stood and helped her to her feet,

then ushered her from the shrine room. "It's strange and rather wonderful to search my mind and find something other than empty, echoing corridors. But Lady Agnes was right when she wrote me that we all have things we would prefer to forget."

"Bad things that happened to you, or bad things you did?"

"What happened to me is part of what I am. But things that I did—those are harder to face." He hesitated before continuing. "Some years ago, I was at a large reception at the palace. There was an Indian gentleman there, a diplomat, perhaps. He was being ignored by all the Englishmen present. I should have gone up to him and talked. Instead, I turned away. I didn't want people to see me speaking to the man and remember my tainted Indian blood."

She winced. "In one way, a small event. Looked at from another direction, it was a betrayal of courtesy and of what you are."

"Exactly so." He rubbed at the scar, looking ready to shatter. "I should think you must find it vastly tedious to be always caring for me. For what it's worth, I remember quite clearly that until the ship explosion, I was always appallingly healthy."

She thought of his lean, powerful body and had no trouble believing that. "You will be again. A year from now you will look back at this time as a much too interesting dream." Assuming he wasn't murdered before then. "Do you want me to stay with you?"

He shook his head. "For now, I'll rest and hope that will help my mind sort itself out neatly. Though that may be too much to ask."

"I've never had amnesia, and my mind isn't neat at all," she said lightly. "May I tell Formby that you wish him to start an investigation into what happened to my father? I'd like to get that started as soon as possible."

He started to nod, then stopped. "Talk to Randall instead—he'll be better able to arrange an investigation. And I can't tell you how good it is that now I can remember such a thing!"

"Having seen how you have struggled," she said softly, "I will never take my mind and memory for granted again."

"Nor will I." He caught her hand and raised it to brush his lips over her knuckles in a feather kiss that produced shivers. "You are a treasure, Mariah. I thank all the gods I know for the fate that brought me to you."

"Fate or chance, we have both benefited." It would be so easy to move into his arms. Instead she gently pulled her hand free. "Perhaps Wharf might have a remedy to help your aching head."

Adam looked thoughtful. "Actually, he does have an excellent treatment for aches and pains. I shall ask for it." Lean and dark and unbearably handsome, he pulled the rope to summon his valet.

It was hard to believe that someone wanted to kill him, except that she'd seen the proof.

"Until later," she said. "If you sleep through dinner, I shan't be offended." She slipped from the room and headed across the sprawling house to her own quarters.

After ringing for tea to calm her frayed nerves, she settled down at the dainty writing desk in the sitting room she shared with Julia. The more detailed her descriptions of her father, his habits, and his journey to London, the more useful they would be.

She was finishing her notes when Julia joined her, smiling from another visit with her grandmother. While Julia drank tea and ate several of the accompanying ginger cakes, Mariah described the visit to the lawyer. She ended by saying, "Do you think that the couple who run the Hartley post office could have been bribed to steal my mail?"

Julia looked thoughtful. "Mr. Watkins would be shocked by the very suggestion. He's extremely meticulous and very proud of his responsibilities. But his wife, Annie . . ." Julia shook her head. "She has an eye for a handsome man. Perhaps I'm wrong, but I can imagine George Burke persuading her to steal mail for him. Did you get any letters while you were in Hartley?"

"Almost none. I was so busy organizing the estate and the household that I had little time for correspondence. With no family but my father, and having moved around so much for years, I wasn't surprised to receive so little."

"When you didn't get any from your father, it supported Burke's claim that he'd been killed. No letters from the lawyer suggested merely that he was a bad lawyer."

"Exactly." Mariah rubbed damp palms on her skirt. "I keep telling myself that my father is dead or he would have returned to Hartley, but it's impossible not to hope."

"The fact that George Burke is not a good man doesn't mean he was lying about your father's death," Julia said softly.

Her mind knew that. Her heart was more stubborn.

She wondered if she should share the news of Adam's new family and decided that she could. Their reunion would soon be public knowledge, and better his friends learn about it privately.

By the time she described the visit from the Stillwells, and how more of Adam's memory had returned, Julia was shaking her head in bemusement. "I shouldn't leave Ashton House. So much happens when I'm gone!"

"At least today's news is better than Ash getting shot yesterday." Mariah neatly folded her notes and stood. "I'll take these down and leave them for Randall."

She was almost down the stairs when Randall and Will Masterson were admitted by a footman, shaking raindrops from their hats and looking worried. Will exclaimed, "Mariah, am I glad to see you! What has been happening? Ash was shot?"

"Only grazed," she assured them. "But it has been an eventful two days. Join me in the small salon and I'll bring you up to date." As she entered the room with both men right behind her, she thought wryly that this salon was now as familiar as the drawing room at Hartley. She started by describing the incident in the park, assuring them again that Adam had not been seriously hurt.

From there, she moved to his family and his restored memory. When she finished, Will shook his head, much as Julia had done. "This is beyond wonderful. You say he remembers almost every-thing now?"

"Yes, up until the last few months before trav-eling to Scotland."

Randall muttered an oath under his breath. "I hope Ash regains his memories of that period soon. That might help us catch the villain."

"Adam said you were the one to talk to about an investigation," Mariah said to Randall. "I assume that you've already started the process?"

Randall nodded. "I know a Bow Street Runner who can solve any mystery. Rob has been at work since the day we arrived back in London."

"We have one possibility," Will added. "A man named Shipley was supposedly killed in the explosion of the *Enterprise*, but his body hasn't been found. He was experienced with steam engines and from London. Kirkland has had people investigating Shipley in Glasgow and just this morning received information. If Shipley is alive and has returned to London . . . well, it will be very interesting to talk to him."

Adam's friends had been busy. "Your Bow Street Runner," Mariah said. "Can he investigate more than one mystery at a time? I have some urgent questions."

"Tell me." Randall's expression was so encouraging that he must have forgotten how suspicious he'd been of Mariah at first.

Once again she described the visit to Mr. Granger's office, ending with, "I want to find out what happened to my father. If he is really dead—so be it. But if he's alive—where has he been? What happened?" She handed her notes to Randall. "This is everything useful I could think of."

He leafed through the papers. "Excellent. I'll give these to Rob. He might wish to speak to you directly. Would you be willing?"

"Of course," she said, surprised. "Why wouldn't I?"

"There are ladies who would think a Bow Street Runner too coarse for their delicate sensibilities," he said dryly.

She grinned. "I've progressed to being a lady in

your estimation? I'm shocked, but most sincerely flattered."

Will laughed while Randall glanced down, embarrassed. "You have been a better lady than I have a gentleman. I hope you'll forgive my initial rudeness."

"You were protective of a friend. How can I blame you for that?"

"Many people would." He tucked the papers inside his coat. "Besides information about your father, do you also want George Burke located?"

"My father is more important. But perhaps finding Burke would help in that." Her mouth tightened. "If he deliberately lied about my father being killed, he is beneath contempt."

"Shall I kill him for you?" Randall asked politely.

"Don't tempt me!" she exclaimed, not sure he was joking.

"Very well. I shall only damage him a little."

From the glint in Randall's eyes, Mariah was quite sure that was not a joke. "As long as you don't damage him too much," she said rather half-heartedly.

Wryly she accepted that if she truly was a lady, like her imaginary sister, she would be shocked at Randall's suggestion. But the last weeks had persuaded her that she would never be a model of decorum, and it was better to give up trying.

Because Adam was resting, his friends left and

Mariah went in search of Mr. Formby. The secretary had a spacious office in the back of the house, and he was happy to supply her with the Lincolnshire address where Janey Lawford was staying. He even provided a franked piece of paper so the letter could be sent without paying postage. Before going to Scotland, Adam had signed a number of sheets for use by the household, and Formby still had half a drawer full.

Upstairs at the writing desk again, Mariah thought carefully about what she wanted to say before applying pen to paper. There must be no suggestion that she and Adam had a romantic relationship. Better if Mariah sounded more like a concerned aunt.

My dear Miss Lawford . . . She started by apologizing for writing when they hadn't been introduced and summarized how she had met Adam. Then she got to the meat of the letter.

Naturally your mother is concerned for your health, but please, if you have recovered from the ague sufficiently to travel, return to London as soon as you can. Ashton is too considerate to ask you to leave Lincolnshire just for his sake, but as a concerned friend, I felt you should know that your betrothed needs you at his side.

Very Truly Yours,
Miss Mariah Clarke

With a sigh, she sealed the letter so it could be sent out in the morning. She might not be a real lady, but she was trying to do what was best for Adam.

She hoped that somewhere up in heaven, she was getting credit for being noble.

Chapter Thirty-One

Adam awoke slowly, grateful that his head no longer hurt. In fact, his thoughts had a clarity he hadn't known for . . . a very long time.

Eyes closed, he explored his mind. The jagged, unruly pieces of himself seemed to have settled down into a peaceful whole. Some of the seams might be rough, but no longer did he feel fragmented, as he had earlier.

Now he clearly remembered his life as a duke. Managing his properties, a huge task even with the able assistance of Formby and others. Sitting in the House of Lords, hearing debates, the give and take of negotiating votes. Having people seek out his influence and favor for themselves or their children.

In Cumberland, he'd had trouble accepting his rank, yet now he realized that in his real life he had become comfortable with being a duke. He had worked conscientiously to use his power and money well, and he'd been successful.

Methodically he looked back on his life, starting

with his childhood in India. Though he'd dreamed of his mother, now he also remembered his father: green eyed, good-natured, and reveling in the richness of life in India. Ten years had been long enough for him to know Andrew Lawford well, and miss him forever.

Vivid memories swirled through him. Perhaps the earliest was riding an elephant in a swaying howdah with Andrew's arms around him. His father had pointed out the brilliant flowers and flashing birds in the forest, naming each so Adam could learn. In his mind, he saw the colors, heard the birdsongs, and smelled the rich, mingled scents.

After his father was notified of his shocking inheritance, the new sixth duke had prepared to travel back to England. Adam had a clear sense that his father hadn't wanted to go. Within a fortnight, Andrew was struck with a fever that killed him in less than forty-eight hours. Adam had not been allowed to visit the sickroom for fear of becoming infected.

Looking back, he wondered if his father had been so reluctant to return that he'd been ripe for catching a disease. Now his bones rested in his beloved India forever.

As Adam sorted through that period of his life, he realized that he also had a few memories of the young John Stillwell. Highborn Hindu women usually lived secluded lives, but Lakshmi had moved out of seclusion after her marriage. Had she married an Englishman because she yearned for more freedom? He must ask her that, he thought. Knowing that he could ask sent warmth flooding through him.

Stillwell had been a regular visitor to the Lawford household. His gaze sometimes followed Lakshmi with quiet, resigned longing. Though it had never occurred to Adam that his mother might have remarried and had more children, he was glad she had found someone who loved and cherished her.

He swung his legs over the edge of the bed and stood. His earlier fatigue had vanished. Night had fallen, which meant he'd slept through dinner and well beyond. Quietly he padded out to his sitting room, which was lit by a single small lamp.

After retrieving the hidden key, he carried the lamp into his sanctuary and studied the divine images. The statues seemed almost alive in the faintly flickering light, watching him with ancient wisdom.

His gaze lingered on Lakshmi, his mother's namesake. As a strange silver lining to his head injury and near death, he had fully accepted his vital Indian nature.

But he was equally English, equally a Christian. He had an English gentleman's education, and an English gentleman's brand of honor. The two parts of him had needed to blend together. Now, at last, they were. And he'd be damned if he'd ever again hide what he was.

He left the shrine and checked the time on the mantel clock. Not yet midnight. Perhaps Randall would be awake. He considered putting on shoes, but this was his house. If he wanted to wander shoeless and in shirtsleeves, he would.

Ashton House was silent as he left his suite. During the day there was a continual hum of activity because of the staff required to maintain such a great pile. Far too much house for one man. But he was betrothed, and God willing, someday there would be children to fill up the empty spaces.

He looked to his right. Mariah's rooms were at the far end of this corridor. Only a short walk away. He wished he remembered more about his betrothal. He had retrieved a few memories of the months before his accident, though nothing very useful.

He recalled laughing in delight on the deck of the *Enterprise* as the steamship roared down the Firth of Clyde. They'd all worked with crazy intensity, and success was sweet. As he'd glanced around, he'd seen the same pleasure on the faces of his engineers and crew. He'd meant to reward them with a bonus, and now some of them were dead, probably because they'd worked for him. Rest in peace.

He also remembered Janey's glowing face, but there was a frustrating lack of detail. Had he fallen in love with her during the lost months? Certainly he loved her. She was his sister in a way Kiri could never be because he and Janey had been children together. But had he loved Janey as he loved Mariah? That seemed impossible.

Looking back, he realized that he'd long assumed he would never marry because he hadn't wanted to pass the burdens of a mixed heritage on to his children. Though he yearned for a companion and a family, he'd rigorously concealed the Hindu side of his nature. On some deep, irrational level, he had believed that revealing himself would be fatal, and for that reason, he'd kept everyone at a certain distance, even his closest friends. It would be even harder to conceal himself from a wife.

Was that why he'd offered for Janey? She'd known him for many years and was used to his eccentricities, so perhaps she had seemed safe.

Mariah knew him better than anyone, and accepted him. Indeed, she seemed to like what made him uncomfortably different.

With stark clarity, he accepted that even if he couldn't love Janey as he loved Mariah, he couldn't break their betrothal, and not only because he was now acutely aware of his English code of honor. Janey loved him, and to reject her when she'd accepted him so joyfully was . . . unthinkable.

He pivoted and walked left toward Randall's

rooms. A light showed under the door, so he knocked.

After a scraping of chair legs, Randall opened the door. Beyond him, Masterson and Kirkland were sitting around a table in their shirtsleeves, bottles of claret in front of them and glasses in hand. "I see you three are plotting again," Adam said dryly. "It's time I joined you."

Kirkland's brows arched. "The duke is back."

"I've been back several days now," Adam observed as he entered the room, accepted a glass of wine from Randall, then settled into the one empty chair. The suite was almost as large as his own. Since Randall's estrangement from his family meant he had no other quarters in London, Adam had given him these rooms to call home for as long as his friend wanted them.

"Not back like this," Kirkland said. "Mariah told us about the visit from your mother and how you regained most of your memory. The change is visible."

Adam frowned. "How do I seem different?"

After a thoughtful silence, Will said, "More edges. Your essential nature was the same even when the amnesia was at its worst, but now you've added the sum total of your experiences." He took a swallow of wine. "If that makes sense."

Adam realized that ever since Mariah had found him, he'd shielded himself with the reserve he'd cultivated since boyhood. He was wary, even with these friends. Is that what he wanted?

He stood. "Come with me."

Bemused but willing, his friends followed him down the hall to his rooms. Adam lit a larger lamp, then opened his sanctuary and waved them inside with mocking formality. "Behold my secret life."

His friends' chatter faded as they looked around. "It's a Hindu temple, isn't it?" Randall said, his expression uncertain.

"The carving of these statues is magnificent." Kirkland circled the room, studying each deity. "I gather this is a personal chapel, as many great houses have."

"Only without any crosses on the wall." Will gave Adam a penetrating glance. "This isn't exactly a surprise, Ash. You never made a secret of your Indian heritage."

"No," he admitted. "But I've always hidden how much it mattered to me."

"Give us some credit," Will said, amused. "We knew, but since you never discussed the subject, neither did we."

"Will might have known." Kirkland halted in front of the dancing Shiva, fascinated. "I can't say I was so insightful. But this changes nothing." He gestured at the statues. "You were what you were. You are what you are. I wouldn't want you different."

Adam felt a stinging in his eyes. Smoke from the

lamp, no doubt. "I'm not sure why I felt it necessary to conceal much of my nature, but I did. Quite strongly."

"With justice," Will said soberly. "Though we may not be shocked, strangers might be appalled if they knew you had heathen images that weren't an art collection. Your trustees hammered in that you had to be more English than a full-blooded Englishman to be worthy of an English dukedom."

"Thank heaven for Lady Agnes's subversive teaching methods," Kirkland murmured. "Or we would have all been warped beyond salvation."

True enough. It was Lady Agnes who had allowed Adam to hold on to his Hindu heritage. Doing so had helped him maintain his sanity at a time when too much in his life was changing.

Randall turned away from the shrine. "Don't forget that the man who is trying to kill you might have no reason beyond hatred of your mixed blood."

His words were a sharp reminder of reality. Friends who had known Adam for years would be more accepting than sharp-tongued, condemning strangers. He would keep his inner beliefs private. But no longer secret.

How would Janey react? Would she accept, or condemn? If the latter, perhaps she would end the betrothal. He felt an unruly stab of hope at the thought. But in fairness to Janey, though her first reaction might be shock, she would probably accept his mixed nature, as his other friends just had.

"Speaking of the man trying to kill me, has any more information turned up?" He waved to the chairs in the sitting room. "We might as well talk here. I have more space and a better wine supply."

"You underestimate the quality of the bottles I've coaxed out of your butler." Randall settled into the sofa, his long legs stretched out across the Oriental carpet. "I think we have several bottles' worth of discussion ahead of us."

Wharf entered the sitting room silently. Probably he'd been woken by their voices. After a quick glance, he asked, "Do you need anything, your grace?"

Adam realized that he was ravenous, having missed dinner. "A cold platter would be good. Meats and cheeses, nothing complicated."

He extricated a bottle of claret from his liquor cabinet and opened it as Wharf bowed and headed down to the kitchen. There was heady satisfaction in remembering exactly where to find the wine he wanted. He could just as easily have pulled out brandy, hock, or sherry. Power was being familiar with one's environment.

He topped up his friends' glasses as they made themselves comfortable. "Now—any information?"

"Ned Shipley was a Londoner who worked on the *Enterprise*," Kirkland said. "According to my source in Glasgow, he was recommended to you for this project because of his experience with steam engines. He kept to himself and didn't talk much, but he knew what he was doing and worked hard. Since the explosion, he's been missing and presumed dead. But with no body found, he might not be dead enough."

Adam frowned. Shipley. "I have a vague memory of the name. He could be a victim of the explosion—or perhaps a man who knew how to engineer an explosion."

"We're looking for him here in London. He may have used a false name in Scotland." Kirkland sipped on his wine. "But I have a detailed description of him. He had a tattooed anchor on the back of his left hand, and a skull on the back of the right one."

Adam could easily visualize those tattooed hands, but he wasn't sure if they were memory or imagination. "You said that he was recommended to me. By whom?"

His friends exchanged troubled glances. "That's not entirely clear," Kirkland replied. "But . . . it might have been Hal Lawford."

Adam stared sightlessly at his claret. Though it wasn't certain, he would have to accept that perhaps Hal—Lord, his future brother-in-law as well as his cousin!—might be trying to have him murdered. The Ashton title and fortune were a rich enough prize to unbalance many men. "Is there any way of being sure short of asking Shipley or Hal?"

Kirkland sighed. "Probably not. Apparently you mentioned to someone that you were glad your cousin recommended Shipley, but it was vague. It would be very useful if you could remember this last chunk of your life."

Would that he could do that. "Randall, have you set Rob looking for the assassin from this end?"

"Yes, but so far, he hasn't had much to work with," Randall replied. "He has his informants looking for Shipley. Also for George Burke, at Mariah's request."

Adam narrowed his eyes. "Any luck?

"If Burke has returned to London, it shouldn't be hard to locate him since he probably won't be trying to hide. If he's out of town, it will take somewhat longer."

Adam thought of Mariah's grief when she was told her father was dead. If Burke had lied about that . . . "When he is located, I will speak with him."

Randall frowned. "It's dangerous for you to go about London. If yesterday's rifleman had been a better shot, you'd be dead."

"Yes, but I won't live like a caged animal. I'll take reasonable precautions." Adam shrugged. "I might need to be out and about to lure the assassin from hiding."

Randall and Kirkland looked appalled, but

Masterson said, "That's sensible. Would either of you accept staying trapped inside? No, I didn't think so."

"I'll use the closed carriage and arrange for more bodyguards." Adam finished his claret in a single swallow. "I shall also hold a dinner party here. I'll invite Hal and his mother, my mother and her family, you three, and Mariah and Julia. Look threatening then, Randall. Perhaps Hal will be persuaded to confess."

He poured himself more wine. Hal might prove to be innocent. But it seemed too much to hope.

Chapter Thirty-Two

Given the high drama of the previous days, Mariah decided the next morning to do what any sensible woman would: go shopping with her best friend. They started at the bargain shops, working their way up to Bond Street, which was pricey but had goods unavailable elsewhere. By midday, both were laden with parcels and Mariah hadn't thought about attempted murder or missing parents for hours.

At the last draper's shop on their itinerary, Julia examined two lengths of fabric, one a figured muslin in soft rose, the other a subtle leafy green poplin. "Which should I buy? I can't really afford both."

"Buy both anyhow," Mariah said. "Each will

look very fine on you, and you won't find their equal in Carlisle. Since we're leaving London in a few days, we should take advantage of the shops now. Heaven knows when either of us will be back again, and in the future, we'll have to pay travel expenses. So buy both fabrics from what you saved in travel costs."

Julia grinned. "I wouldn't have made this trip if it wasn't essentially free, but you've just provided me with a good excuse to be extravagant." She signaled the sales clerk that she was ready to make her purchase.

As they later stepped outside, Mariah paused on the shop's doorstep and glanced down the narrow, bustling precinct of Bond Street. "I love the country and I'm looking forward to returning to Hartley," she said wistfully, "but I love London, too. My father and I used to stay here fairly regularly when there was no convenient country estate to visit." She grinned. "Naturally, our quarters were much more modest than those on this trip."

"At least we've had a lovely day of hunting," Julia said. "We can't buy any more because we've run out of hands and carrying bags. Shall we find a tea shop to refresh ourselves before we return to Ashton House?" A parcel slid out of her carrying bag and she bent to pick it up. "I'm now wishing that we'd accepted Holmes's offer of a carriage and footman. My feet are aching from so much walking."

"I don't want to get used to Ashton luxury,"

Mariah said firmly. A carriage and footman would have been still another reminder of the social distance between her and Ashton, and she needed no more reminders.

A woman gasped nearby. Mariah looked up to see a fashionable matron staring at Julia. To her companion, she said, "Surely that's . . . ?"

"Impossible," an equally well-dressed woman said blankly. "She's dead."

Julia turned white. Acting on instinct, Mariah took her arm and pivoted, then walked them away briskly, turning at the next corner. When they had put some distance behind them, she said, "That tea will definitely taste good."

Julia drew a deep, slow breath. "Aren't you going to ask me about that woman?"

"Not unless you wish to discuss the matter."

"Thank you." Julia took an unsteady breath. "Perhaps I will someday. It might be good to speak of the past."

They were interrupted by a friendly male voice saying, "Miss Clarke! Mrs. Bancroft! What a pleasure to see you again."

Mariah turned and saw Hal Lawford step down from a carriage. His smile was hard to resist, yet she couldn't help thinking that he might be behind the attempts to kill Adam. The two disparate thoughts temporarily froze her tongue.

Julia was more articulate. "Good day, Mr. Lawford. The pleasure is mutual."

"I see that you've been taking advantage of the London shops." He cast an assessing eye on their purchases. "May I offer my carriage to hold your parcels, then treat you ladies to a luncheon? There's an excellent tea room around the corner."

Mariah and Julia exchanged glances. "I'm all in favor of being spoiled by luxury," Julia said.

And probably Julia needed that just now. "Thank you, Mr. Lawford. We accept both your offers gratefully," Mariah replied.

"Please call me Hal." He signaled his footman to collect the parcels and store them in his vehicle. "As anyone will tell you, I am nowhere near dignified enough to be called mister on a regular basis."

He was a hard man to dislike, Mariah admitted privately. But she couldn't shake the feeling that there was more to him than his affable surface.

As they were finishing an excellent luncheon, Hal said in a serious tone, "Has anything been learned about the man who attempted to shoot Ashton? I find it very disturbing to think that the villain might try again."

"As do I." Mariah's eyes narrowed. "If one was to make a list of suspects who might want him dead, you would be at the top."

Instead of looking conveniently guilty, Hal said wryly, "A fact of which I'm painfully aware. The irony is that I genuinely don't want to be duke; I'd do a beastly job of it. Adam is first rate—born to take responsibility. His father was a high British official in India, and Adam inherited the blood of Hindu princes through his mother. He reads and understands proposed legislation that I would fall asleep over. He once offered to put me up for a seat in the House of Commons controlled by the Ashton estate. Very prestigious, but I turned it down because I would have been bored senseless."

Julia cocked her head to one side. "What does interest you, Hal? Gambling? Dazzling the ladies?"

"I enjoy both, but my true passion is breeding horses. Ash's mother was of royal blood. My mother is Irish, from a family who has bred fine horses for generations." He grinned. "And despite my boredom with legislation, I keep ridiculously detailed breeding records of every horse I've ever owned. That's never boring."

As the women laughed, Mariah looked into the green eyes that were so like Adam's and couldn't decide if Hal Lawford was an honest man, or the most dangerous liar in London.

Adam was different. Mariah saw that as soon as he entered the drawing room before dinner. She hadn't seen him all day because of their shopping expedition.

But as she watched him cross the room, dark and aloof, she knew beyond doubt that it was time to leave London. The battered, amnesiac man she had pulled from the sea was finally and fully the Duke of Ashton. He wore power and authority as naturally as he wore his flawlessly cut coat. He'd gradually been moving away from her ever since his friends had showed up at Hartley to claim him. Now that he had settled back into his life, there was no room for her.

She swallowed against the tightness of her throat. She couldn't wish for him to live without his past forever. But for a brief time, when he had been merely Adam and the world was a long way off, they had been happy.

He moved to the drinks cabinet and looked over at her and Julia. "Would you like sherry?" His gaze lingered on Mariah, and from its warmth, she guessed that he hadn't entirely put Hartley behind him.

Before she could comment, the door opened and Holmes announced that the Stillwell family had arrived. Close behind were Lakshmi and General Stillwell, Kiri, and two younger people. Adam crossed the room to greet them, kissing his mother lightly on the cheek. "So I didn't dream you yesterday, Mother."

Lakshmi slipped her hand beneath his elbow, as if she had to touch her long-lost son. "I feared that I would never have my four beautiful children in one place." She gestured. "Kiri you have met. Here are Lucia and Thomas. Are they not splendid?"

Lucia blushed, but Adam laughed as he greeted

his half brother and half sister, catching their hands in turn. "I have become rich in family."

All four of Lakshmi's offspring began talking animatedly, their words tumbling over each other. They were indeed beautiful, with a strong resemblance that made it easy to see they were siblings. Adam was obviously going to love being a big brother.

Though Mariah again felt the sadness of not having a place beside Adam, it was impossible to begrudge Adam and his newfound family their joy. Lucia was perhaps seventeen and well on her way to being as striking as Kiri, though her eyes were gray-green, like her mother's. Thomas was a year or two older and a handsome young man, with blue-gray eyes similar to his father's. All four of them had complexions lighter than Lakshmi's, but darker than the average English person's.

As Holmes quietly poured sherry for the guests, General Stillwell drifted over to join Mariah and Julia. "They're a handsome set, aren't they?" he said with pride.

"Indeed," Julia agreed. "They seem to have inherited the best of both English and Hindu blood."

Curious, Mariah asked, "General Stillwell, do you worry that your children will face intolerance here?"

"Of course I worry. Parents are born to worry." His wry smile encompassed both Mariah and Julia.

"You'll find out in your time. But they would have found intolerance in India, too, and they all needed to discover the English half of their heritage. I raised Kiri and she's like one of my own, but she's a duke's daughter, and that counts for a great deal in England. She deserves to benefit by that. And to be blunt, her rank will benefit her younger brother and sister as well."

No wonder the general had been concerned about whether or not Adam would accept his younger half siblings. Being sponsored by the Duke of Ashton would help them all. Kiri was in an even better position. Even if her father hadn't had the opportunity to write a proper will, Adam would surely give her a marriage portion appropriate to her station.

The butler announced that dinner was ready to be served. As people moved toward the dining room, Adam fell into step with Mariah. "My mother, two sisters, and a brother! It's a miracle."

"Indeed." She let her smile show how happy she was for him. "More than that, they are lovely people, not a bunch of dirty dishes, as relations so often are."

He grinned as he took her arm. "I'd welcome even the dirty dishes, but this is so much better."

Since there was no one close, she lowered her voice and said, "I talked to Julia, and she was able to rather easily imagine that Annie Watkins, who runs the Hartley post office with her husband, might have been seduced, bribed, or both to intercept letters to and from Hartley Manor."

Adam's gaze sharpened. "Not hard evidence, but very interesting. If Burke has returned to London, he should be relatively easy to find. He might be the best route to tracing what has happened to your father."

"Then let us hope he turns up quickly." She drew a slow breath. "Julia and I intend to return home in three days. May I ask Holmes to discover the coach schedules for us?"

Adam's hand tightened on her arm and he looked stricken. Softly she said, "It's time, Adam. Any information you discover about my father can be mailed to me, because I assure you I will deal with Annie Watkins. She will intercept no more mail."

"I know you're right." He was silent for half a dozen steps. "I will send you in one of my coaches. I don't want you and Julia to have to travel on the public stage."

She had to laugh. "I have many times before and taken no ill effect from it."

"Let me do this for you, Mariah." His gaze was stark.

It was unnerving to see in his eyes how much he cared—but also gratifying to know that what was between them was real. "If you're sure. I'd be a fool to turn down a free, comfortable ride right to my doorstep. And even if I wanted to, Julia is no

351

fool and wouldn't allow me to decline," she said lightly.

"Will you stay an extra day? I'm having a dinner party so both halves of my family can meet, and I would like to have you there." He smiled a little. "You and Julia would be calming presences, I think."

"I'm sure Julia won't object." And Mariah would have one more day near Adam.

Chapter Thirty-Three

It took only a day and a half to locate George Burke. Adam was in his study, poring over the endless paperwork that went with his property and wondering if he really needed to have an opinion about renewing tenant leases on an estate in Yorkshire. Since the estate steward recommended renewal, he signed an agreement.

The next document concerned subjects being debated in the House of Lords. He really should start attending now that he could recognize people again. There were some interesting issues being considered this session.

He set the documents aside with relief when Kirkland and Randall showed up at his door. "Have you brought me an excuse to escape from my responsibilities?"

"That we have," Kirkland replied. "Burke is staying at an inn near Covent Garden. As of an hour ago, he was in his room. Care to call on him?"

Adam shoved his chair back with alacrity. "The sooner, the better."

They took the old closed carriage again. As they left by the rear exit, Adam wondered if his house was being watched by a man with murder in his heart. Hard to believe on such a bright spring day, but the bandaged shoulder under his fashionable shirt and coat was a reminder that he must be careful.

Burke's inn was shabby and had seen better days. Adam wondered what the man was using for money now that he'd gambled away his estate. The inn didn't suggest that he was prospering.

Their driver pulled up at the inn's front entrance. As the three men climbed out, a lean, brown-haired fellow emerged from the shadows. Adam recognized him as the Bow Street Runner, Rob Carmichael.

Carmichael jerked a thumb upward. "Burke is still here. Top room on the right."

"Thank you for finding him." Adam gazed up at the window. "Have you had any luck locating the mysterious Ned Shipley?"

"I heard on the waterfront that he's been seen around lately, but the information isn't confirmed." Though Carmichael was dressed like a working man, his accent was cultured. Not surprising since he'd been educated at the Westerfield Academy. "Do you want me to go up with you?"

"That could be useful if more investigation is required." Adam entered the inn, the other three men behind him. The innkeeper stuck his head out of a back room, saw that the new arrivals were expensively dressed and determined, and prudently withdrew.

A quick walk up the narrow stairwell and a turn to the right brought them to the door of the corner room. Adam knocked with great restraint, considering that he wanted to bash the panels in with his fists.

"Who's there?" a familiar voice called.

Adam remembered pulling Burke off of Mariah and his hands clenched. "I brought the money with me." Which made no sense, but he thought that any mention of money would attract Burke's interest.

It did. There was a scrape as the latch was lifted, and then Burke opened the door. He was in his shirtsleeves and wore no cravat, and his eyes were bloodshot. He frowned. "We've met but damned if I remember where. Did you lose to me at cards?"

"It was in the drawing room of Hartley Manor." Adam stepped forward, shoving the door back before Burke could slam it shut. "You were forcing your attentions on Mariah Clarke."

Whatever was in Adam's face caused Burke to back nervously across the bedchamber. "No need to bring your friends to give me a beating. My intentions were honorable. Damnation, I asked the girl to marry me!"

"If you recall our first meeting, you should remember that I need no help if I want to kill you with my bare hands. My friends are here to prevent me from doing that." Adam smiled with cold threat. "And you weren't offering honorable marriage. You were trying to bully Mariah into putting herself and her inheritance into your worthless hands. But that is not the worst thing you did to her."

"I left Hartley after I learned that she was wed," Burke said defensively. "I've not harmed her."

"Except by telling her the despicable lie that her father was dead." Adam slowly peeled off his gloves, as if preparing to do violence. "Did you murder him yourself, Mr. Burke? Old Testament law demands a life for a life."

"No!" Burke exclaimed, looking panicky. "I haven't seen the bastard since we went to his lawyer's office to transfer ownership of Hartley after I lost it to him."

"And while you were there, you stole some of Granger's stationery so you could write Mariah and announce her father's death."

Burke flinched, confirming Adam's guess. "I told you, I wanted to marry her! If she felt alone in the world, naturally she'd want a man to look after her, and who better than me? I know the estate and the village. The chit is a beauty and we'd both benefit. I meant no harm. When her father returned, she'd be happy to see him and we'd all have a good laugh together."

"But Charles Clarke has not returned," Adam said softly. "Which leads to the logical conclusion that you murdered him to improve your chances with Miss Clarke. You also seduced and bribed Annie Watkins, the Hartley postmistress, to interfere with Miss Clarke's mail."

"How did you know . . . ?" Distracted, Burke returned to the main point. "I didn't kill him! Several weeks after losing the estate, I stopped to dine at an inn outside London. The local magistrate was there. A troop of soldiers had just captured a pair of highwaymen who'd been terrorizing the area. They'd killed a couple of men in the previous months and robbed plenty of others. The magistrate had a box full of jewelry that had been recovered.

"I was curious and asked to see it, claiming I was one of those who had been robbed by the highwaymen. I spotted Clarke's ring. The design is unusual and I remembered it. I said the ring was mine and the magistrate let me take it."

"Because you were a gentleman?" Randall said incredulously. "You may have scruples, Ash, but I don't. Let me have him."

Randall's words made Burke's face turn white. Adam asked, "Was Clarke one of the men killed by the highwaymen?"

"I don't know. The names weren't mentioned. If Clarke never returned to Hartley, maybe he was one of the victims. Or maybe he got himself killed some other way. He deserved it," Burke said sullenly. "Once I had the ring, I came up with the plan of telling Mariah that her father was dead so she'd accept my offer. I didn't think it would take long to persuade her. I swear on my mother's grave that if her father is dead, it wasn't because of me!"

"Do you know if your accomplice at the post office intercepted any letters from Charles Clarke that might prove he's alive?"

Burke shrugged. "No idea. I haven't seen Annie Watkins since I left Hartley."

So Julia was right in her guess about who had been tampering with Mariah's letters. "Are you quite sure you know nothing about whether Charles Clarke is alive or dead?" Adam dropped a hand on Burke's shoulder and neck. The movement looked casual, but his fingers bit hard into carefully chosen blood vessels.

Burke gasped and fell dizzily back against the wall, clawing weakly at Adam's wrist. "I don't know! For God's sake, let me go!"

"Rob, you've had the most experience with thieves and liars," Adam asked, easing the pressure so Burke wouldn't pass out. "Do you think he's telling the truth?"

Rob deliberated. "I think so. But if you like, I'll light a cigar and apply it a few places. That's always a good way to get straight answers."

Burke whimpered with fear. Disgusted, Adam

released his hold on the other man's shoulder. "What shall we do with this swine?"

"Hand him over to a press gang," Kirkland said helpfully. "Being a deckhand on a man-of-war would do wonders for his manners."

Burke gasped, his gaze flicking nervously to the men behind Adam.

"He might be able to talk his way out of that," Adam said. "We could lay charges against him for fraud and tampering with the Royal Mail. Is that a capital offense?"

"Probably," Rob drawled. "So many crimes are."

As Burke cringed, Adam said, "The courts take so long. I have a better solution."

Misinterpreting Adam's expression, Burke gasped, "You can't just murder me out of hand! You'll be hanged!

Adam smiled angelically. "But I *can* murder you if I choose. I'm a peer of the realm, Burke. I sit in the House of Lords. Behind me are three well-born gentlemen of impeccable reputation who will swear that it was self-defense if I kill you. What are the odds that I will be prosecuted?"

Burke's desperate face showed his recognition that Adam could walk away without consequences. Abruptly, Adam tired of the game. Terrifying Burke wouldn't ease the grief Mariah had suffered because of this man's greed and malice. "I agree Mr. Burke would benefit by a long sea voyage. Kirk, do you have any thoughts?"

"You're in luck," Kirkland said. "One of my company's ships will be departing on the evening tide, heading for the Cape Colony and India. Space can surely be found for Burke, though perhaps not a very comfortable space."

"That will do." Adam had come prepared for this, so he pulled an envelope from his pocket. "Here are two hundred pounds, Burke. It's more than you deserve, but it will give you a chance to start a new life wherever you end up. Or you can gamble it away in a single night and starve if you prefer." His eyes narrowed. "If you ever return to England, count the days carefully, because you won't have very many of them."

Burke's eyes flicked to one side as he considered, probably realizing he would get no better choice. "I must pack and write some letters. Tell people that I'm leaving England."

"Kirk, how much time does he have before he must be taken to the ship?"

"About two hours," Kirkland replied. "Rob and I can stay here with him while he makes his preparations, then put him on the ship."

Adam nodded acceptance. "If Rob is willing, I'll be most grateful. I'll leave the carriage for you."

"My pleasure, Ash," Carmichael replied, looking well entertained. "It's worth the time to see you in action."

"There has been very little action. Just the elimination of vermin." Adam turned on his heel and headed from the room, nodding thanks to his friends. He was still tight with fury as he descended and left the inn, Randall behind him.

Adam gave instructions to the driver of the carriage to wait for Kirkland, Carmichael, and Burke, then headed west toward home at a fast walk. Randall fell into step beside him. "You were stretching a point when you said you had three men of impeccable reputation at your back," he remarked.

Adam's tight lips eased into a genuine smile. "It sounded good." He glanced at Randall. "Are you staying with me as a bodyguard?"

His friend grinned. "Only if one is required. Otherwise, this is just a walk."

Adam wondered how long it would be before his life would become normal, and a walk would be only a walk.

Too long.

Chapter Thirty-Four

Mariah brushed loose her hair, knowing that time was running out. The next night, Adam would hold his dinner party to introduce his two families to each other. The morning after, Mariah and Julia would head north to home. Tonight was stormy, with steadily beating rain and distant thunder. A night for doing secret, shameful things, like seducing a man who didn't belong to her.

She had wavered back and forth for days, wanting to be with Adam so much that it hurt, while knowing that it was wrong and might end up hurting her more. Tonight was her last chance, so she could delay no longer.

She smiled ruefully at the mirror. Her decision was made: she would take action and risk regret rather than be conservative and safe and even more regretful. Her Sarah conscience had given up and wasn't even speaking to her.

The hour was late enough that the house was quiet and she probably wouldn't be seen on the way to Adam's rooms. After soaking the sponge Julia gave her in vinegar and placing it in position, she donned her best nightgown and robe, a shimmery set of sea green silk garments that had been given to her by a rather too dashing widow after a country house party.

She tied her hair loosely at the nape of her neck with a matching green ribbon. Then she took a lamp shielded to cast a narrow light for walking and slipped from her room. It wouldn't kill her if he rejected her. He would do that kindly, she was sure.

But if she didn't at least try, she surely would die inside.

Now that he was home and in possession of most of his memory, Adam had returned to his morning meditations. Sometimes he also meditated at night, for clearing his mind helped him sleep.

But no amount of meditation could make him forget that in a matter of days, Mariah would leave his life forever.

After finishing in his sanctuary, he locked its door and put out all the lights in his sitting room, leaving only the lamp by his bed in the adjoining room to provide light. A storm was rolling over the city, so he opened a set of curtains and gazed out over lightning-splashed London. He liked storms.

A gentle tap sounded on his door. The sound was almost drowned by a distant roll of thunder. Curious, he opened the door—and found Mariah standing there, inches away. She looked up at him, tense and small and misleadingly fragile. "Can I come in?" she asked softly.

"Of course." He stepped aside, wondering why she was here. Surely not to . . .

She glided into the room, graceful and compelling in a gossamer garment that surely was designed for seduction. Turning to face him with enormous brown eyes, she said in a less than steady voice, "There is no subtle way to say this. Will you lie with me, Adam? I've taken measures to prevent any awkward consequences." Her gaze slid away from his. "I know this is wrong, but Janey will have you forever. I will be grateful if we can have one night where we come together freely, with passion and affection. If . . . if you want me?"

Of all the shocks he'd experienced lately, none

was greater than this. "If I want you? I've never wanted anything or anyone more." He clenched his hands, fighting the temptation to touch her. "I shouldn't. Yet . . . I don't feel betrothed to Janey. She is very dear to me, but being with you doesn't seem like betrayal of her. It feels . . . right."

"Then for tonight, let us be together." She smiled wistfully. "We can create memories that will live in our hearts forever."

Amnesia had taught him how much memory defined a man, and how the loss of memory shattered his sense of self. The memory of their love-making in the prayer garden was a spark of light that warmed him. He hungered for more such memories.

He took the lamp from her and set it on his desk, then cupped her face in his hands, marveling at the silky texture of her skin. She gazed up with brave, vulnerable eyes, her yearning as intense as his.

They had kissed before, but never with such aching tenderness as now, when time was running out with terrible swiftness. Her mouth was honey sweet as they explored each other without haste. He untied the ribbon that held back her glorious hair, freeing the thick tresses to run through his fingers like a river of gold. "I've wanted so much to see you," he breathed. "All of you."

She laughed a little. "That desire goes both ways. At our first meeting, I was looking for injuries and bruises and didn't fully appreciate you." She slid her hand between the overlapping panels of his banyan, her palm warm against his chest.

Sweetness blazed into white heat. He yanked her sash open and stripped the robe away. In the faint light of the two lamps, her figure was alluringly visible through her nightgown.

"Mariah . . ." Unable to think of any words powerful enough to express her beauty, he skimmed his hands over the graceful curves of her back. She was perfect in her proportions, a petite goddess who melted his wits away. He bent and kissed her breast through the gossamer fabric, feeling her nipple harden under his tongue.

She exhaled sharply as she untied his banyan. It fell open, revealing his nakedness and the hard evidence of his desire. He groaned when she touched him. "Best slow down, my darling, or this will be over too soon."

"By all means, let us use the whole night." She tugged the banyan from his shoulders, her fingertips tracing lines of fire down his arms.

He let the garment slide to the floor. He didn't feel the coolness of the night air because the world was all heat and flame. It took only a moment to divest her gown. "This is lovely, but you're lovelier."

"As are you," she said as he scooped her up and carried her into his bedroom to lay her on the bed. The lamplight revealed Mariah in all her sensual splendor. Thunder rolled over the house, shaking the furniture, or perhaps that was the pounding of his heart as he joined her on the bed.

"I want to kiss every inch of you." He pressed his lips to her throat, feeling her rapid pulse as he cupped her breasts.

"There are a lot of inches, but by all means, try," she murmured as she buried her fingers in his hair and massaged his head. "I can't believe we're really here, together. I was so afraid you'd be wise."

"With you, my heart is stronger than my reason." They'd made love before in an unplanned tumble of bodies and emotions. This time they were conscious of their goal, and every caress, every kiss, every soft breath built anticipation. When he touched her intimately, she shivered with pleasure. He started slowly, matching his movements to her arousal until she was gasping and frantic with need. She gave a choked cry when she climaxed, her nails biting into his shoulders.

When her dazed eyes opened, she said, "Now it's time to come together."

Despite his desperation, he managed to keep control long enough to enter her gently, since this was only her second time. The ecstasy made it almost impossible to hold still while her body adjusted to his presence. Then she exhaled roughly with pleasure and began moving against him.

They swiftly found a rhythm together, as if they had been mates forever, but they also shared the intoxicated wonder of new lovers. She was the mate he had yearned for in years of loneliness, the woman who completed him. He shattered, and she saved him, her spirit encompassing all that he was. "I love you," he gasped. "For always."

"And I love you," she whispered as tears filled her eyes. He rolled on his side and drew her close, his arms sheltering against the storm that pounded on London.

The sky itself wept because they loved each other, and it wasn't enough.

As Mariah lay peacefully in Adam's arms, content to be in the moment, he dozed, his face relaxed as it seldom had been since his friends found him in Hartley. She tried to remember how she had seen him at the beginning. Mostly she'd seen bruises and lacerations and foreignness.

She recalled thinking that he might be handsome under the bruises. That had turned out to be an underestimation of major proportions. Adam Darshan Lawford was beautiful, with strong features that blended his mixed heritage into a face that was unique and intriguing. His body also was lovely, graceful and lithe with muscle. Though he'd probably be embarrassed if she told him that.

She liked his darker skin, so much more interesting than her English pallor. She brushed her hand lightly down his side, thinking how intensely real his presence was. It was hard to believe that they would never be together like this again. She didn't want to believe it.

She caressed his cheek, feeling the faint prickle of whiskers. He opened his eyes with a smile. "Are you cold?"

"A little," she admitted. The rainy night was cool and they lay on top of the covers in their bare skin. She compensated by pressing closer to him. She would not have believed how natural it would feel to lie beside him naked. A lifetime of modesty had vanished in an hour. Would she ever know this closeness with anyone again?

"You look sad." He brushed her hair back, his hand lingering. "Are you sorry you came here?"

"No." She tried to smile. "Only sorry this night will end."

His face tightened, and she saw the grief in his eyes. "A pity we can't make time stop." A light blanket was folded across the foot of the bed, so he reached down and shook it out over her. "But at least we can be comfortable."

"Thank you," she said. "Though you're better than any blanket."

He grinned as he slid under the cover with her. "We don't want to waste the rest of the night in sleep, do we?"

"I'd rather make more memories."

He rolled onto his back and pulled her on top of him. His eyes laughed at her. "I'm sure you can figure out how to ravish me."

And she did, finding sweet new variations on lovemaking. Both of them were damp with sweat when she collapsed on him after they had journeyed to madness and returned. "I didn't know passion could be like this," she gasped. "Or is it just that you're really good at making love, as you're good at so many things?"

He caressed her hips. "I've not known this kind of lovemaking before, either. It comes from both of us. And if that was an oblique question, I haven't had as much experience as you might think." He smiled wryly. "I was as interested as any young man, but it's always been hard for me to let down the shields. Except with you."

She crossed her hands on his chest and pillowed her chin on them. "I think I was very lucky to find you when you didn't know who you were. I got to meet the man you were meant to be."

"I'm trying to be that person more often now." He rearranged her so that they were lying on their sides, her back tucked into his front and his arm around her waist. They fitted together perfectly.

She tried to stay awake so as not to miss a priceless moment. Adam's regular breathing said that he was asleep. Time was running out. . . .

The lamp was burning low when they wakened again. Wordlessly they kissed. This time desire was a slow burn, fueled by the knowledge that this might be the last time, for surely dawn was approaching. When Adam sank into her, Mariah sighed as waves of pleasure radiated through her. Their bodies knew each other by now, and they melded together effortlessly. "I love you," he whispered. "Never doubt that."

"I will never forget you." She opened her eyes, wanting to watch his beloved face—and saw the dark figure of a man looming over Adam with a knife. "Adam!" She kicked wildly at the man with her right foot, managing a glancing blow to his crotch.

"Bitch!" The man fell back, dropping the hand that held the knife. He had a skull tattooed on the back of his hand. "For that, *you* die, too!"

He was lunging forward again when Adam grabbed her around the waist and rolled them both across the bed, away from the attacker. The world jolted as they tumbled off the bed, the blanket falling with them.

Adam twisted so that he fell on the bottom to cushion the impact for her. She landed on top of him, the breath knocked out of her. While she dizzily tried to collect herself, Adam pushed away and sprang to his feet. "Mariah, get back!"

He moved between her and the assassin, crouching defensively as the man circled the bed swearing, lamplight glinting from his blade. Tall, burly, and dressed all in black, the intruder was a nightmare come to life. Adam, naked and unarmed, looked terrifyingly vulnerable by comparison. But he was unafraid as he waited for his opponent to make the first move.

Mariah scrambled to her feet, wondering frantically what she could do. She'd be useless at tackling an armed man.

A blast of cold air revealed an open window. Lord only knew how the intruder had managed that, or how he knew exactly which bedroom to enter. But as she glanced at the window, she saw the bell rope on the far side of the bed. She dove across the bed and yanked the rope over and over, trying to wake every servant in the house.

"She's a good-looking slut. I'll take her after I kill you." The man sprang forward, slashing the knife with dangerous expertise.

Moving with effortless grace, Adam slid aside and caught his assailant's arm. Pivoting, he hurled the intruder headfirst into the wall.

"Jesus!" the man swore as he staggered to his feet. "You filthy heathen! I'm going to cut you into such small pieces your own mother wouldn't recognize them!"

"What a limited mind you have," Adam replied, circling. "Do you try to kill mixed-blood dukes for amusement, or are you paid?"

"Both," the man spat. "Business and pleasure together." He sprang at Adam, sweeping the knife upward in a disemboweling blow.

Adam wasn't there. Once more he'd slipped away like a shadow, the light playing over his bare skin as if he were a Greek statue in motion. He chopped his hand at the other man's neck. The assassin dodged, but Adam still landed a partial blow.

The door to the dressing room and Wharf's quarters was thrown open with a crash. Wharf and Reg Murphy, the head groom, charged through, both of them carrying pistols. Instantly sizing up the situation, Wharf swore, "Bastard!"

He and Murphy fired so close together that it sounded like one shot.

The intruder clapped a hand to his ribs. His fingers came away bloody. Outnumbered but not seriously injured, he leaped out the window. Mariah saw the dim length of a rope hanging outside in the rain. The man grabbed it and vanished from sight.

Feeling very naked, Mariah retreated and scooped up the blanket from the floor. As she wrapped it around her, pounding feet sounded in the corridor. Adam grabbed her shoulders and pushed her toward the servants. "Murphy, get her away through Wharf's rooms. Don't let anyone see her! Wharf, hide those two green silky things."

It was hard to worry about her reputation when Adam had almost been murdered in his bed, but she turned and bolted through Wharf's door, Murphy right behind her. As the groom pulled the door closed, she heard Randall's voice as he burst into Adam's sitting room. "Ash!" It sounded as if others were on Randall's heels.

She and Murphy moved through the dressing room and into Wharf's bedroom. It was a sizable chamber with a bed in disarray. "Best rest here and catch your breath, miss," Murphy said. "The corridors will be busy for a bit."

A wisp of smoke trickled from the barrel of his pistol and the acrid smell of black powder clung to him. She realized that though he and Wharf had been swift and competent in their response, the men were half dressed and disheveled. She glanced at the bed, then away. "A good thing you were both here and ready."

Murphy looked uncomfortable. "With the threats against his grace, Wharf thought we should be ready and armed, just in case. We were both army."

Mariah's erratic upbringing had made her more worldly than most young women. She had a fair idea of the real reason why the men were together here, but there was no need to discuss the matter further. Like her, Murphy had good reason to avoid being seen by others in the household. "Ashton is fortunate to have you in his service."

"The duke has been good to both of us." Murphy went to listen at the door that opened to the public corridor. "It sounds quiet now. Ready to risk going back to your own rooms, Miss Clarke?"

"Please." She smiled ruefully. "I feel foolish in this blanket."

He opened the door warily and peered out, then beckoned for her to come. She moved past him and darted barefoot through the corridor. Murphy followed. At her door, she said softly, "The outside guards should be checked. The assassin might have injured one to get onto the grounds."

"A good thought. I'll look now." He hesitated. "No need to worry about Wharf and me talking, miss. We'd never do anything to hurt you or the duke."

She guessed that the groom was an expert on forbidden love. "Thank you, Mr. Murphy. The less said by any of us, the better."

She slipped into her room, where she'd left a lamp burning, and headed straight for the clothes press. A flannel nightgown, her heaviest wool robe, and slippers replaced the blanket. She was braiding her hair when Julia rushed into the room. "Mariah, what happened? Was that a gunshot?"

Mariah realized that bare minutes had passed since the attack. After swift thought, she decided to tell the truth. "I was with Adam when a knife-wielding killer broke into his bedroom. Adam fought him off bare-handed while I pulled the bell rope. Wharf rushed in with a pistol and shot at the man, who went out the window like a rat racing down a gutter pipe." No need to mention Murphy.

"Good God." Julia caught her breath. "Ashton is uninjured?"

Mariah nodded. "He was . . . remarkable." If he hadn't been cat quick and had amazing fighting ability, they'd both be dead. She tied a ribbon around the end of her braid. "I'm going to his rooms, since it would be surprising not to investigate a gunshot."

"I'll go with you. We shall look most respectable."

Mariah hoped so, because the appearance of respectability was all she had left.

Chapter Thirty-Five

Not surprisingly, Adam got no more sleep that night. By the time he had his banyan on again, what seemed like half the household was in his rooms, drawn by the gunshots. Randall was in a murderous mood when he learned what had happened and promptly went outside to see if he could find any traces of the intruder.

Mariah and Julia arrived a couple of minutes later, heavily swaddled in robes and looking exactly as upset as one would expect if they'd been woken from sound sleep. Mariah's gaze met his for one intense moment before she purposely looked around the room and asked, "What happened?"

"A man broke in, but he's been routed. No damage done," he assured the women, trying not to think of how Mariah had looked lying in his arms.

"Thank heaven you're all right." Mariah shuddered. "If this is London, I look forward to the peace of Hartley." She took Julia's arm and they left.

He wondered if he'd still be alive if Mariah hadn't been with him. The assassin had been very silent. If Adam had been sleeping, that knife might have ended up in his heart. It was Mariah who had spotted the intruder, and her kick had given them the instant they'd needed to escape. He had a horrible vision of lying dead from knife wounds while the assassin raped and murdered Mariah.

As Wharf shooed other staff members, Randall returned, wet and grim. "One of the guards was knocked unconscious and tied up. The heavy rain covered up the intruder's approach over the wall. He somehow managed to scale the house and drop a rope by your window."

"Is the guard going to be all right?" Adam asked.

Randall nodded. "He was lucky. Did you get a clear view of your attacker?"

"He had a skull tattooed on his hand," Adam said tersely.

"So it's Shipley, and he's alive." Randall exhaled roughly. "At least now we know who we're looking for."

"The trick will be catching the devil." Adam frowned. "From what he said, he would enjoy killing a filthy heathen like me, but he's also being paid to murder me. So the underlying question is, who's paying him?"

"Which means that when we get Shipley, we need to keep him alive long enough to learn who his employer is. This is *damnable*." Randall headed for the door. "I'll go to Rob Carmichael and let him know."

"No need to wake Rob up at this hour," Adam said. "I doubt Shipley will be back tonight."

Neither would Mariah, alas.

After breakfast with Randall, who left to find the Bow Street Runner, Adam reluctantly headed to his office to face the unending paperwork required of a duke. The last thing he wanted to do was read dry legalistic papers after the passions and perils of the previous night. Plus, tonight would be his family dinner party, which was a distracting thought. "Formby, am I ever going to get caught up on this work?"

"You're making good progress, your grace," his secretary said in his most formal voice, the one that suggested he wasn't going to allow Adam to escape today.

"Shall I hire an assistant for you? Someone to help with the winnowing and basics, giving you more time for matters requiring experienced judgment."

Formby looked startled, then intrigued at the thought of having an underling to order around. "That might be helpful, and ultimately reduce the amount of material that you must deal with."

Trying not to look indecently relieved, Adam said, "Excellent. Please start seeking someone qualified and acceptable to you."

Formby beamed. "Thank you, your grace. I have a nephew who might be suitable."

The door opened and a harried footman said, "I'm sorry, your grace, but this gentleman insists on seeing you."

He was brushed aside by a well-dressed man in his early forties, his right arm in a sling and his face tight with controlled fury. Planting himself in front of Adam's desk, he snapped, "What are you doing with my daughter?"

Good God, he had Mariah's brown eyes and blond hair. This had to be Charles Clarke. For a stricken moment, Adam felt as if the man was aware of the glorious, life-affirming things he had done with Mariah the night before. But Clarke couldn't possibly know about that.

Under his breath, Adam said, "Summon Miss Clarke, Formby. Immediately."

As the secretary nodded and withdrew, Adam rose to his feet. "You must be Charles Clarke."

"The Honorable Charles Clarke Townsend," the newcomer spat out. "I may not be a duke, but my family is not without influence, and you will not be allowed to confine and ruin my daughter."

"I shouldn't wish to," Adam said mildly. What he and Mariah had done wasn't ruination, but generous, openhearted love. "Your daughter saved my life when I was near death by drowning. She is an honored guest in my home, along with her friend from Hartley, Mrs. Bancroft, who is a most respectable chaperone." If not necessarily a strict one. "By the way, I wore your clothing for several weeks. You have fine taste. What made you think I've ruined your daughter? She is a very independent young woman. Not easily ruined, I think. And is it Mr. Clarke Townsend, or Mr. Townsend?"

"Townsend will do." The visitor frowned, his anger blunted. "I have just come from my lawyer's office. Granger says that Mariah visited him with the Duke of Ashton. That Mariah believed I was dead, and that you were watching her like a hawk. Like she was your prisoner. She has replied to none of my letters for weeks, which has to mean that something dreadful has befallen her. Is she your honored guest, or your captive?"

Despite Townsend's pain and anger, Adam had to smile at the absurdity of the situation. He nodded toward the door, where Mariah had just appeared in a graceful peach morning gown. She looked far too delicate and ladylike to have kicked a man in the groin the night before while she was in the midst of passionate, illicit lovemaking. His matchless Mariah.

As Townsend turned, Mariah's shock turned to blazing joy. "Papa!" Weeping, she hurled herself into his embrace. "I thought you were dead!"

He winced as she crushed into his damaged arm, but he locked the other arm around her hard. "I was so worried, Mariah! What happened?" He glared at Adam. "Has this man ill-used you?"

Mariah laughed. "Not at all. Oh, Papa, so much has happened!" A grouping of leather-upholstered furniture was arranged on one side of the office. She drew her father down on the sofa and sat next to him, so close they were touching.

Adam left his desk and took the chair opposite the sofa. "You said you're the Honorable Charles Clarke Townsend. Are you a son of the Earl of Torrington?"

Clarke nodded. "I was the youngest and the black sheep. My father died a few weeks ago. We managed a deathbed reconciliation." His expression was wry. "It's perhaps as well that the reconciliation wasn't tested over a longer period of time. We were like chalk and cheese. But . . . we were both glad to part as friends, I think. My eldest brother is the new earl."

Mariah gasped. "I thought perhaps you came from the gentry. I didn't imagine your rank was so high."

"The Townsends have some of the bluest blood in Britain, which made my disgraceful behavior look all the worse," he said. "Legally, your name is Mariah Clarke Townsend. I simplified the name to Clarke after my father disowned me."

Adam frowned. "That is not the action of a decent parent."

"He was not without justification, though perhaps he overreacted." Charles sighed, then said to Mariah, "I was considered wild even before your mother and I eloped to Gretna when we were seventeen and eighteen. Both families were scandalized. I didn't start to grow up until I became responsible for you, and even then, I needed Granny Rose's help."

"Where have you been these last weeks? George Burke said you were dead, and he forged a letter from Granger and showed me your gold ring as proof. We learned that he was tampering with the post, but that didn't prove you were alive." She touched the sling. "Were you injured and that's why you didn't return to Hartley when expected?"

"Part of the reason. But what about you?" His glance at Adam still contained suspicion. "Why are you here, in this house, in London?"

Adam let Mariah tell the story, suitably edited. She ended with, "Julia and I have planned to return to Hartley tomorrow, since Ashton has kindly offered a carriage. I'm sure he wouldn't mind if you accompanied us. Are you ready to go home?"

He smiled mischievously. The charm he used to become a welcome guest at many homes for many years was clearly visible. "Remember I said my injury was only part of the reason I was delayed? More of the reason is only a few streets away. Will you come with me so I can explain more fully?"

She chuckled. "You never could resist a surprise. Do you want me to meet some of the relatives with whom you're now on terms again?"

"You've always been good at reading me. Yes, that's the case," he admitted. "My brother is far more tolerant of my shortcomings than my father was. But I'll say no more." He got to his feet. "Are you free now? I'd very much like to take you off."

"Very well." She glanced at Adam. "Will you come, too?"

Ignoring her father's frown, he said, "Of course." He tried to look innocent enough that he wouldn't alarm a protective father.

He doubted that he'd succeeded.

With Mariah's father giving directions, Adam's carriage driver took them to a house on the other side of Mayfair. When they stepped onto the sidewalk in front, Charles rather conspicuously offered Mariah his good arm. She suspected that he'd be much happier when she wasn't staying at Ashton House. He wasn't usually this protective, but he was very perceptive. She guessed that he sensed a connection between her and Adam.

The previous night's rain had washed the sky clear, and it was a lovely spring day. She saw that their destination was a typical Mayfair town house, well maintained with ivory trim and flowered window boxes.

Her father opened the door with a key, which was interesting. As he ushered Mariah and Adam inside, he called, "I'm back and I have her!"

He led them into the salon on the right, where

two women were embroidering. Both leaped to their feet. One was a petite, attractive woman in her early forties, and the other was . . . Mariah.

Mariah gasped, on the verge of fainting. Adam took hold of her arm. "Steady, Mariah," he murmured. "I think that like me, you have a previously unknown sister."

Mariah scrutinized the other young woman. Though they looked very similar, this stranger's face was a little thinner, her blond hair was styled differently, and her expression hinted at a different personality. But her fashionable morning gown was the exact same shade of peach that Mariah was wearing.

"Mariah?" the girl asked hesitantly.

Mariah had to swallow before she could speak. "Papa, have you been concealing a *twin sister* from me?"

"Well . . . yes." He sounded both pleased and embarrassed.

A wild thought struck Mariah. "Is your name Sarah?"

"Yes!" Her sister looked hopeful. "Do you remember me?"

"Not really. But please tell me—are you a paragon of all ladylike virtues?"

Sarah looked startled. "Absolutely not! As Mama will be the first to tell you."

Mama? Mariah turned to the older woman, who was staring at her hungrily. She was a bit shorter than Mariah and her dark blond hair was accented with strands of silver, but she looked like Sarah.

She looked like Mariah.

Mariah pressed her left hand over her heart, feeling as if it would pound out of her chest. "You're my mother? I've always assumed you died when I was only two!"

Her father cleared his throat. "I always said that we lost your mother. I never actually said that she died."

Mariah stared at him, amazed. "Don't tell me that you left my mother and split up my sister and me like a pair of puppies!" Beside her, Adam muffled a laugh.

"Legally, he had the right to take both of my daughters if he wanted to, so I felt grateful that he took only one." Her mother moved a step closer, her face earnest. "But not a day went by that I didn't think of you. My lost child."

Adam's hand tightened on Mariah's elbow as her gaze went from her mother to her father to her sister. She couldn't help herself. She dissolved into peals of laughter. "Papa, you *wretch!* All these years and you never told me!"

"It seemed simpler," he said uncomfortably.

" 'Simpler.' " Mariah shook her head. "I'm beginning to understand why your father disowned you." She turned to her sister. "For as long as I could remember, I imagined I had a sister named Sarah, who was always a perfect lady. She was my conscience and often my only friend. Now I see that I was remembering you."

"I certainly hope we'll be friends!" Sarah stepped forward and clasped her hand, her brown eyes yearning. "I grew up knowing I had a sister named Mariah, and I prayed that someday we'd meet again."

"I would have prayed that, too, if I'd known." Suddenly Mariah and Sarah were in each other's arms. Mariah extended a hand to her mother, and the hug turned into a three-way embrace. Though she had no conscious memory of her mother or her sister, she knew them on some soul-deep level. They filled holes she didn't know she had.

She finally disentangled herself and pulled her handkerchief from her reticule so she could blot her eyes. "Papa, there is still much of your story I don't know. To begin with, where the devil were you? And how did you injure your arm?"

"I'm very anxious to hear that myself," Adam remarked.

Mariah's mother glanced at Adam, a small furrow between her eyes. "We haven't been introduced to your friend."

"I'm sorry, my dear," Charles said, eyes sparkling. "May I present the Duke of Ashton? Your grace, my wife and younger daughter, Mrs. Townsend and Miss Sarah Townsend."

"How much younger?" Mariah asked with interest.

"About five minutes," her mother replied, her gaze at Adam becoming more approving. "There is much to be discussed. Let's all sit down and I'll ring for tea."

As they took seats, Mariah stayed close to her newfound sister and mother, but she gave Adam a grateful glance as he sat opposite. He more than anyone could understand her tumultuous emotions.

Her father said, "Mariah, I told you that I wanted to reestablish my connection with my family. In particular, I wanted to see my father, since I'd heard he was very ill. But even more, I wanted to see Anna." He gazed at his long-estranged wife, his heart in his eyes. "She was an heiress and everyone thought I married her for her money. They were wrong."

Anna sighed. "I was fool enough to believe those who told me not to trust Charles, that he was just a wild, fortune-hunting wastrel. One day when you girls were about two years old, we started quarreling. It started over nothing, but we said terrible things to one another and Charles stormed out, swearing never to return."

"And being a fool, I didn't," her father said sadly. "For too many years."

Mariah leaned forward. "Why not, Papa? Didn't you want to go home?"

"I knew I'd made a terrible mistake almost as soon as I left." He grimaced. "But I'd made such a botch of everything. I *was* a wastrel, a useless fribble. I decided I couldn't return until I had established myself independently. I wanted to prove to my father that I wasn't worthless, and to Anna that I was no fortune hunter."

"So you became a professional gambler," Adam said mildly.

Charles's mouth twisted. "Gambling wasn't a good way to build a fortune, but I didn't have any other abilities. I did well enough to maintain Mariah and me and Granny Rose in moderate comfort, but not enough to become a man of property. Despite my other flaws, I wasn't willing to cheat a young man out of his inheritance.

"Then I met George Burke. He was a grown man and a malicious fool. Since he seemed determined to lose his property, I decided he might as well lose it to me. After I won Hartley, I knew it was time to seek out Anna and beg her forgiveness." His gaze returned to his wife. "I didn't dare dream that she would take me back, but at the least, I wanted her to know how desperately sorry I was. There has never been anyone else."

Mariah knew that wasn't entirely true. But she'd never seen any sign that her father had fallen in love with any of the women with whom he'd had casual affairs. Her mother didn't need to know about those other females.

Charles's gaze shifted to Sarah. "I also wanted to see my other daughter. I was blessed with you,

Mariah. Whenever I looked at you, I wondered how my other girl was growing up."

"You should have come home sooner, Charles." Anna reached out to him.

He caught her hand and kissed it. "I know that now. It is the greatest miracle of my life that you have given me a second chance."

Sarah leaned toward Mariah and said in a mischievous stage whisper, "They've been like this ever since he returned!"

Mariah laughed. She liked the real Sarah much better than the one who had lived in her head and scolded her for so many years. Glancing at the sling supporting her father's injured arm, she asked, "Did Mama break your arm before accepting your apology?"

He grinned. "No, though she might have been tempted. I was traveling on a coach to call on her in Hertfordshire when we were robbed by highwaymen. I foolishly put up a struggle to save my gold ring. Anna had given it to me, you see. So my ring was stolen and my arm broken. I was lucky it wasn't my neck."

Anna picked up the story. "The local newspaper published an account of the robbery and the names of the victims. When I saw a Charles Clarke listed, I had a strange feeling that I should visit the inn where he was said to be recovering."

"So she swept into my room at the inn, as beautiful as the day we'd met, and said she wasn't surprised that I'd survived the highwaymen since I was born to be hanged." He laughed joyously. "I promptly agreed, and we went on from there."

They gazed at each other dotingly. Mariah said, "I feel as if I've wandered into a Restoration comedy."

Sarah gave her an understanding smile. "Strange indeed. But rather sweet. They can keep each other company in their old age."

Mariah guessed that there was a good deal more to her parents' reunion than holding hands in front of the fireplace. Given how young they'd been when they'd eloped, there was still plenty of time and strength for passion. Not that she wanted to think about that in too much detail!

Pulling his attention away from his wife, her father continued, "I wrote you, Mariah, explaining that I would be delayed and that I had a wonderful surprise for you. But you never replied. At first I was so absorbed in Anna and Sarah that I wasn't concerned, but as time passed, I became increasingly worried. Curse Burke for stealing our correspondence!"

"He has been dealt with," Adam remarked. "He decided to head for the colonies, where he could make a fresh start."

"Not voluntarily, I trust," Charles said hopefully.

"He was encouraged." Adam's expression was bland. He got to his feet. "You all have a great deal to catch up on, so I will remove myself. But I'm having a family dinner party tonight. Mariah had planned to attend. Will you all join me? There will be two other rediscovered families present, so a third will be even better."

"We are pleased to accept." Anna gave a pleased smile. "Sarah and I have lived mostly in the country, and we need to expand our acquaintance in London. This is my brother's town house, and he has suggested we visit more often."

"You're right, Ash, I wish to stay here and talk with my family." Mariah stood. "I'll walk you to the door."

They returned to the foyer, and she gave him a smile that was more intimate than she could risk in front of her family. "You understand this as no one else could."

"Discovering one's long-lost family is disorienting but miraculous." He leaned forward to brush a light kiss on her lips. "Be happy, Mariah. Your relatives aren't even dirty dishes."

As she laughed, he left the house. It still hurt beyond measure that they must separate, but now, thank all gods, she would not be alone.

Chapter Thirty-Six

It was almost time for Adam to go downstairs and greet the guests for his dinner party. He'd almost finished dressing when Wharf approached with a handsome bottle-green coat. Adam frowned. "I'd like one of the coats with a pistol pocket sewn in."

Wharf's brows quirked questioningly. "You expect trouble, your grace?"

"Having been almost murdered in my bed last night has left me wary," Adam explained. "Life has been unpredictable lately. Are my pocket pistols still in my desk?"

"They should be, sir." The valet looked thoughtful. "Soldiers talk about battle sense. The feeling something is wrong and extra care is required. Perhaps that's what you are experiencing. I shall fetch a suitable coat."

Adam crossed to his desk. The polished walnut case was in a bottom drawer, exactly where it should be. He opened the case and lifted out one of the pair of matched pistols. It felt familiar in his hand. The small but wickedly accurate weapons had been custom designed and built by Joseph Manton, who was considered the finest gunsmith in Britain. Manton had charged a small fortune, of course, but the pistols were worth it.

Adam examined the weapon for readiness before loading it. By the time he was done, Wharf had returned with a Spanish-blue coat.

The garment was more loosely cut than the other had been, and inside on the left was a reinforced pocket where the pistol could be carried safely. Since Adam was right-handed, he could reach in and pull it out easily.

A similar reinforced pocket on the right side held additional balls and powder and a small ram. He couldn't hug anyone without weapon and ammunition being noticed, but he didn't think this would be a hugging sort of evening.

After donning the coat and tying his cravat, he examined his image in the mirror. He looked exactly like the perfect duke who had tried so hard for years to be beyond reproach.

Yet so much had changed. He'd nearly died; he'd rediscovered himself, piece by piece; he'd found a family, and he'd fallen in love. Though the imminent loss of Mariah was like an anvil on his heart, his life was richer and more meaningful than it had ever been.

Wondering how well the Stillwells and Lawfords would get along, he headed downstairs. Though he'd never been a soldier, he could feel battle sense raising the hairs at the back of his neck.

Mariah was the only one in the salon. She sat on the sofa facing the fireplace, where flames flickered, because it was a cool evening. With her hair upswept and a golden gown falling in graceful folds, she looked like a princess, only more touchable. He suppressed the thought before he could act on it. "You look particularly lovely tonight."

She looked up, her smile radiant. "Adam, I have a sister! It's so wonderful that I can scarcely believe it."

Her happiness made him happy. "She looked equally delighted."

Mariah smoothed her hand over the shining gold

fabric on her knee. "Sarah lent me this gown. We had the most astonishing visit. In some ways we're very different, but in others, absurdly alike. We were finishing each other's sentences! Her clothes are new and fashionable and mine are often hand-me-downs, but her gowns fit me perfectly and we like the same colors. Did you notice that we were wearing the same shade of peach?"

He nodded as he leaned against the mantel, knowing better than to come too close to her. "The color suits you both. You have some of the same gestures, too. Does it bother you that she was raised in a more prosperous home?"

"Not really. Papa and I never went hungry. I do envy the fact that she had Mama, but she feels the same way about Papa." Mariah considered. "I think I'm more independent and adaptable than she is. I've had to be. She envies what she thinks of as my adventures. But she has a confidence about herself and her position in the world that I lack because Papa and I moved around so much and lived on the edges of respectability. Sarah and I decided that our lives have balanced out."

They were wise. "She's unmarried, isn't she? It's unusual that two such lovely sisters are unwed at twenty-five."

"She was betrothed, but he died." Mariah looked sad for a moment before changing the subject. "Isn't it a remarkable coincidence that you and I have both discovered unknown families? Random relatives returned from the dead? I don't know what to think, apart from happy. But I feel as if I've wandered into a stage play."

"The events haven't really been random," he said thoughtfully. "You and I were both removed from our proper places, you by your father, me by the all-powerful authorities. Through the efforts of your father and my stepfather, we have been restored to families that already existed. The timing is a bit coincidental, because it happened to both of us at almost the same time, but the events themselves are logical."

She considered his words, then said, "When I look at it that way, I'm not sure it's coincidence. More of a chain of events. If I hadn't thought my father dead, I wouldn't have performed Granny Rose's ritual and I wouldn't have been outside that night and I wouldn't have gone to the shore and found you. So we wouldn't have known we had mutual coincidences because we would never have met."

"Not to mention the fact that I'd be dead, and hence wouldn't have known about my long-lost family," he said dryly. "I think I'll take a Hindu view. We were fated to meet and become a part of the fabric of each other's lives. Though the Christian way also works, now that I think about it."

" 'The Lord moves in mysterious ways his wonders to perform.' " She quoted the hymn with a smile that was both wistful and loving. "Fated to meet. I like thinking that our friendship has meaning if not permanence."

The bond between them was so intense he felt that he could hold it in his hands. Mariah broke her gaze from his. "Your carriage won't be needed after all. Tomorrow I'll move to my uncle's house to be with my family. We'll head to Hartley in a fortnight or so, but when the time comes, we'll use my mother's carriage. For years, they lived in a house on her brother's estate. I gather it was lovely, but she's looking forward to living on her own estate, in her own house." Mariah laughed a little. "I had become used to thinking of Hartley as mine, so I shall have to hold my tongue when Mama makes changes."

Adam suspected that there would be some conflicts, given that Mariah had been in charge of her own life for years. But they'd managed with love to grease the wheels. "What about Julia? I'll be happy to send her north with an Ashton maid to bear her company on the journey."

Mariah shook her head. "Julia will also leave Ashton House to stay with us. Since she spends much of her time with her grandmother, she'll be an easy guest."

So Mariah would be in London, but he would no longer be able to see her every day. Even so, that felt better than having her hundreds of miles away. He crossed to the drinks cabinet. "I'm deficient in my duties. Would you like a sherry?"

"Please." She accepted the glass he poured, careful not to let their fingers touch. "With so many guests coming, you'll be kept busy serving."

"In a few minutes, Holmes will take over." He poured himself a small sherry, not saying that he'd come early in the hopes of having some private time with her. "About a quarter hour later, footmen will come in with trays of delectable little nibbles. That's Mrs. Holmes's idea. Many of my guests are strangers to each other, so it seemed a good idea to allow everyone a chance to move about and make new acquaintances before we must settle in fixed positions around the dinner table."

"A clever plan." Mariah raised her glass, barely sipping the sherry. "Food and drink will put everyone in a good mood."

Private conversation ended when Aunt Georgiana and Hal entered the room. Shifting his attention from Mariah to the rest of his life, he moved to greet them.

"Good evening." He shook Hal's hand and gave his aunt a respectful bow. She'd seen Mariah and seemed irritated that the interloper was still here. Adam asked, "Have you heard from Janey? I'd hoped she would have returned by now."

"She has been delayed by a slight relapse, or so she says." His aunt smiled fondly. "I think the truth is that she doesn't want to see you until her looks are recovered. The ague makes one look very pale and wan."

"She should know that wouldn't matter to me." Which was true, he realized. He was very fond of Janey. Perhaps he loved her. Either way, it didn't matter if she was pale. "I hope she comes back to London soon."

"I'm sure she shall," Hal said cheerfully. "It's not like Janey to miss excitement, so she's bound to turn up soon."

His mother frowned. "She mustn't risk her health. You and she will have years to enjoy each other's company, Ashton."

Conversation became general as Masterson and Kirkland arrived, having shared a carriage. Randall and Julia entered side by side, though not really together, since they neither spoke to nor looked at each other. Adam guessed that they had met when coming down the stairs from their rooms.

Next to arrive were the Townsends. Mariah rose and greeted them, her face glowing with pleasure. All the males present stared at Sarah. "Good God, there are two Mariahs?" Masterson exclaimed. He bowed deeply to Sarah and her mother. "How did the men of England become so fortunate?"

Sarah blushed while Mariah laughed. "Isn't it lovely? I've only discovered my twin sister today! Let me present my parents, Mr. and Mrs. Townsend, and my sister, Miss Sarah Townsend."

Looking suspiciously angelic, Mariah continued the introductions around the room. Georgiana

Lawford frowned at Charles. "Are you a connection of the Earl of Torrington?"

"He's my brother," Charles replied, looking every inch the aristocrat. "I've been away for some years, and I am happy to be home again."

Georgiana frowned more deeply as she glanced at Mariah, who was now established as the granddaughter and niece of an earl. It was a status that would be quite acceptable in a duchess and made Mariah even more of a potential threat. Adam's aunt didn't have enough faith in his sense of honor. He would not betray Janey.

He tried to remember if his aunt had always been so bad tempered. She'd never been particularly warm, but she'd treated him fairly. At least, until her husband died. After that, her disposition had turned more sour.

Last to arrive were the Stillwells, including all three children. Lucia, barely out of the schoolroom, was bubbling with excitement to be at a glamorous adult gathering.

Smiling, Adam moved forward and kissed his mother's cheek. She was also beaming with delight. In her gold-embroidered crimson sari, she looked very young and exotically beautiful. "My handsome son," she said softly. "Worth sailing halfway around the world to find."

After greeting the general and his brother and sisters, he turned to his other guests. "I have the great honor to present my mother, recently arrived from India, and my stepfather, General Stillwell. Also, my sisters and brother, Lady Kiri Lawford and Lucia and Thomas Stillwell."

Kirkland said fervently, "Ashton, how have you managed to find so many beautiful ladies in one place?" His gaze on Kiri, he bowed a greeting.

"The credit goes to two beautiful mothers who produce beautiful daughters. Let us have a toast to the ladies!" Adam raised his glass to Lakshmi, then to Anna Townsend. His gesture and words were echoed by the others.

Aunt Georgiana was quietly fuming, her narrow-eyed gaze fixed on Lakshmi. Adam recognized her distaste for having to meet socially with a person she considered inferior. He'd seen that expression in other eyes when they'd regarded him, but his aunt should have enough social sense to conceal her intolerance.

He took his family around the room to make the introductions more personal. Mariah was also quietly acting as a hostess, bringing people together. She and Adam worked together so naturally.

Soon the room was full of happy chatter. The young people drew into groups, with Sarah and Kiri and Lucia receiving enthusiastic attention from Adam's friends. More surprisingly, General Stillwell, Thomas, and Mariah's father were intent in conversation and Lakshmi and Mariah's mother looked as thick as thieves.

Adam scanned the room, checking to see that no

one was left out. Aunt Georgiana was a rather tight-lipped third to a discussion between Julia and Hal, but everyone else seemed to be having a good time. He should have included her in his toast even though Janey wasn't present.

He happened to be looking in the direction of the main door when it opened to reveal a tall, travel-rumpled woman who carried herself like a Greek goddess.

Lady Agnes Westerfield had arrived.

"Lady Agnes!" He crossed the room in a dozen steps and hugged her.

"Ashton!" She hugged him back, beaming. Her brows rose as she felt the pistol under his coat. Softly she said, "Armed in your own home, my lad?"

He grinned. This room contained his real mother and the aunt whose home he'd visited regularly in his growing years, but neither was more truly his mother than Lady Agnes, who had been the foundation of his English life. "I'll tell you about that later. For now, it's enough to say that I've regained most of my memory and I'm delighted that you're here, even though I remember every scold you ever gave me."

She glanced around the room. "Since my problem student recovered and is now mad for cricket, I decided to come up to town. I won't interfere with your party, but I couldn't wait any longer to see you." She chuckled. "On my way into

Ashton House I found someone else you'll want to see, but when she heard you had guests, she went to refresh her appearance. At my age, looking disreputable doesn't matter."

"You look wonderful, and you are staying for dinner." He took a firm grip on her arm. "You will start by meeting my mother, Lakshmi Lawford Stillwell."

"Adam! Truly?" she exclaimed with delight.

He explained briefly as he guided her across the room, accumulating other Westerfield graduates anxious to greet her. As they reached Lakshmi, he said, "Mother, may I present Lady Agnes Westerfield, who looked out for me when you were too far away?"

His mother rose from the sofa, then dropped into a deep curtsy, crimson silk pooling on the floor around her. "You have my heart's gratitude, Lady Agnes."

Mildly alarmed by the dramatic gesture, Lady Agnes said, "And you have my gratitude for producing such a fine son. He was the inspiration for my school."

Adam withdrew, leaving the women to talk, and made his way to Mariah. She stood a little apart on the far side of the room, watching the guests. She greeted him with a smile. "So many wonderful people in one place. I hope to meet Lady Agnes later."

"You will." The service door in a corner of the

room opened and several footmen entered the room carrying silver trays. One spotted his employer and immediately came to offer a tray filled with small flaky pastries, each impaled with a toothpick.

Mariah took one. As she daintily nibbled it from the toothpick, licking buttery flakes from her lips between bites, Adam had to look away. It hardly seemed fair that she was so alluring without even trying.

"Delicious," she reported. "There is a lovely cheese melting inside." She took another, then sighed happily.

Adam tried one, then another. And a third. When they refused more, the footman moved on to another group. A different footman headed toward them, his tray containing tidbits of roast sausage. His livery was different from the others, and after a moment Adam identified the fellow as a Lawford servant. He must have accompanied Hal and Aunt Georgiana and been pressed into service.

Mariah frowned as the man approached, as if something about him disturbed her. Then a buzz of voices sounded from the main entrance to the drawing room as several people exclaimed, "Janey's here!"

Adam looked across the width of the room and saw his betrothed poised in the wide doorway, her gaze scanning the group. She had to be the female Lady Agnes had mentioned as arriving at the same time. Though she wore a plain traveling gown, her fair hair was neat and her lovely face vivid with interest. "Hello!" she said gaily. "I just returned home from Lincolnshire and learned that everyone is here. I hope I'm not unwelcome, Ash."

"Of course not," he called across the room, his nerves clenching at the knowledge that her arrival changed everything.

Beside him Mariah cried, "Adam! Look out!"

His head snapped around at her urgency. While attention was on Janey's entrance, the approaching footman had pulled a wicked dagger from under the tray, and he was raising his arm to stab Adam.

The footman's tall, heavy figure was familiar, and so was his menacing snarl. "You won't escape this time, you heathen bastard!"

Adam dodged backward and grabbed for his pocket pistol. The knife sliced through his right sleeve. His forebodings had been correct, and now that the moment had arrived, he was steely calm. He drew the pistol and aimed it. "Drop the knife, Shipley!"

Shipley's eyes widened at the sight of the gun. "Damn you!"

He threw down the tray, sending sausage slices bouncing, and seized Mariah. Yanking her hard against him with an arm around her waist, he set the knife to her throat. "Shoot and you'll kill your pretty little whore!"

Gasps of shock echoed round the room as the

other guests saw what was happening. Hal exclaimed, "Shipley, what the devil are you doing!"

Randall swore and started to move toward the intruder. "Don't!" Shipley pressed the tip of the blade into Mariah's neck. A trickle of crimson rolled down her pale skin and stained the golden silk. "Or I'll cut the slut's throat."

His raging eyes were half mad. No one sane would have pursued Adam so relentlessly, risking a murder attempt in a room full of witnesses. Nerves taut, Adam lowered the gun to his side. "Release her and you can leave this house freely," he said, hoping he could persuade a madman. "She's done you no harm."

"She spread her legs for a filthy Indian duke," Shipley growled. "No decent Englishwoman would do that."

Sarah moved forward, her face white but her voice steady. "Are you sure it was her you saw? Or could it have been me? Let her go!"

Shipley jerked in confusion as he looked at Sarah, then at his captive. He began backing toward the service door, dragging Mariah with him. "Even if this is the wrong slut, I'll kill her if you come after me!"

Adam knew with devastating certainty that Shipley would murder Mariah as soon as they were out of the room. Full of hatred and frustration, he wanted blood.

Adam waited until Shipley's glance flicked to the other side of the room. Then he raised the pistol, glad the top of Mariah's head barely reached Shipley's chin.

Uttering silent prayers for perfect aim to all the gods he knew, he slowly squeezed the trigger and fired.

Chapter Thirty-Seven

Mariah's heart pounded like a frantic drum as Shipley dragged her backward. His knife hand jittered against her throat as he scanned for possible attack from one of the furious men in the room. Only the fact that the devil could kill her faster than anyone could intercede saved him from being torn to pieces.

She drew a shaky breath, trying to prevent fear from overwhelming her. Was she the only one who realized that Shipley would kill her once he was safely away? Four times he'd tried to kill Adam and failed, and his bloodlust could no longer be denied.

Adam realized. She saw the knowledge in his stark eyes. He was going to act, and she'd have only an instant to increase her chances of survival.

When Shipley's head was turned away, Adam raised his pistol and took aim. Hoping he was as good a shot as his friends claimed, she grabbed Shipley's wrist and shoved the knife away from her throat. Otherwise, even if Adam's aim was true, her captor's hand might spasm and kill her.

The blast of the gun numbed her ears as the ball smashed into Shipley's skull. Her captor collapsed onto Mariah, dragging her to the ground under his heavy body. She felt the blade slice into her throat as she fell. She lay on the carpet stunned, unable to breathe, fearing she was mortally wounded and just didn't know it yet.

"Mariah!" Adam threw Shipley's body aside and crushed her into a desperate embrace. "Are you all right?"

Freed of Shipley's weight, she gulped air into her lungs. "I . . . I think so."

She touched her throat and her fingertips came away scarlet. There was blood everywhere. She looked away from Shipley's shattered skull as she drew another breath. "Breathing would be easier if you loosen your grip."

He laughed shakily and complied while keeping a firm hold on her. She closed her eyes, shivering, grateful for Adam's warm embrace. He was all that was keeping her from falling into shrieking pieces.

Georgiana Lawford said in a horrified voice, "Merciful heaven! Is the villain dead?"

"Quite," Kirkland said grimly. "A death he richly deserved, but now we can't learn who hired him."

Julia dropped on her knees beside Mariah with a man's white handkerchief. "Let me take a look at that." Gently she blotted the blood away. After a moment, she said, "The cut is shallow. Bloody, but no serious damage done."

She folded the handkerchief into a long, narrow pad and carefully tied it around Mariah's neck. "Ashton, how badly is your arm hurt?"

"I hadn't noticed," Adam said, startled. "I don't think it can be serious, though."

Mariah glanced down and saw that his right sleeve was dark with blood. Please, God, don't let it be serious. He has endured so much already.

A woman took her hand, and she knew instantly it was her twin. "I was so frightened that I would lose you when I've just found you, Mariah!" Sarah said.

"You won't be rid of me so easily." Mariah smiled at her sister. "That was brave of you to try to distract him. In return, I've ruined your lovely gown." They squeezed each other's hands, needing no more words.

An unfamiliar female voice spoke. "Is this Mariah Clarke? I'd thought you would be much older."

Mariah raised her gaze and saw Janey Lawford in the circle of watching people. She was beautiful, with hair like polished golden oak and lively green eyes. Would Adam remember their betrothal now that Janey was here in person? Other women had triggered his memory on earlier occasions.

Mariah pushed herself into a sitting position. Since Adam's future wife had arrived, it was time for Mariah to leave his embrace forever.

Adam helped Mariah stand, since she seemed determined. "When I wrote you, I was trying to sound mature and disinterested," Mariah explained to Janey.

"You don't seem disinterested now." The other girl's gaze moved from Mariah to Adam and back again.

Ignoring that, Mariah said, "You're looking well recovered from the ague."

"The ague?" Janey said, startled. "I'm never ill."

Adam kept his arm around Mariah, still shaken to the marrow by how close she'd come to death. The horror of almost losing her cut through all the social strictures he'd been raised with. He couldn't let Mariah go, not now.

Catching his cousin's gaze with his own, he said gravely, "I'm glad you've returned, Janey. We must discuss our betrothal."

"Hal said your wits were scrambled, Adam, and here's the proof." Janey's brows furrowed. "Why do you think we're betrothed?"

"Since my wits were indeed scrambled, your mother told me about the betrothal and our plans to keep it quiet until we both returned to London." He winced as he recalled Janey's face. "The memory isn't clear, but I remember you and I embracing. You looked very happy. Wasn't that when I offered for you?"

"I remember the occasion," Janey said with a wry smile. "But you didn't ask for my hand in marriage."

Adam stiffened as new memories fell into place. "No, I didn't," he said slowly. "You were mad for a rather unsuitable man. Aunt Georgiana was flatly against it, but I'm your guardian so I could grant permission even if she disapproved. I said that if you felt the same way after six months, I would consider the fellow's offer."

Janey nodded. "I was so excited I kissed you. It meant so much that you were *listening* to me. Mama was furious with you for saying you'd grant permission if Rupert was who I truly wanted. But she was right—he would have been a dreadful mistake. I realized that when I'd been away from him for a few weeks."

"That doesn't explain why your mother claimed we're betrothed." Adam looked across the room to his aunt, not liking the direction of his thoughts. "I know you've always hoped we'd marry, Aunt Georgiana. Did you think to use my amnesia to persuade me to the altar?"

"You would have had to persuade me, too!" Janey exclaimed. "I adore Adam, Mama, but it would be like marrying Hal!"

"Once you got over that other stupid boy, I thought you might change your mind," her mother said defensively. "You and Ashton always get on so well. It would be an excellent match." She shot a venomous glance at Mariah. "I wanted to make sure that some fortune-hunting trollop didn't entangle Ashton before you returned to London."

Janey shook her head. "Even if I was willing, and I'm not, Adam has never seen me as anything but a little sister."

"Our mother might have had deeper plans," Hal said with an edge in his voice Adam had never heard before. His gaze locked on Georgiana. "You're the one who hired Shipley, Mother. The other servants despised him because he was such a brute, and his duties were never clear."

"I knew Shipley's family in Ireland," she snapped. "That, plus the fact that he had served in the army made me feel that he deserved a decent job."

"Did you hire him to murder Adam?" Hal's voice cut like a whip.

His mother arched her brows. "Don't be absurd, Hal! He was a footman, no more. How was I to know he would run mad and try to kill Ashton?"

"During a previous attempt, Shipley said that killing a filthy heathen like me would be both business and pleasure," Adam said flatly. "I think he despised my mixed blood, but he was also being paid to murder me."

Hal moved closer to his mother, his face despairing. "Mother, how could you? Adam was like your son!"

"He was no son to me! It was your father who insisted that he spend the holidays with us." Georgiana exploded with rage. "I did it for you, Hal! *You* should have been the duke, not a cousin's foreign by-blow."

She turned her poisonous glare on Adam. "My husband should have been the Duke of Ashton, and I the duchess, with Hal to follow. Instead, I was forced to accept you into my own household. I pointed out to my husband how easily small boys died, but he was shocked at the idea." She drew a harsh breath, her face twisted with fury. "If you married Janey, at least she would be Duchess of Ashton and my grandson would be a duke, but you wouldn't do it even though there's no more beautiful girl in England!"

"How did you find Shipley?" Adam asked, wanting to get all the answers while she was enraged enough to speak.

"His family was employed by mine in Ireland," she said sullenly. "When he came to me in London and asked for work, I realized that he was the perfect tool to get rid of you. He hated heathen foreigners and he knew how to kill. When I told him what must be done, he was delighted. He said he would try to make it look like an accident, but when that didn't work, he turned to a more direct approach."

Her words fell into the silence like stone. General Stillwell wrapped his arm around his wife's shoulders and Janey pressed her hands to her mouth, near weeping.

"So you chose to murder Adam to give Janey and me something we didn't want," Hal said bitterly. "You've disgraced us all. I am ashamed your blood runs in my veins." He turned to Adam, devastation in his eyes. "If you have her charged, she'll hang. Everyone here is a witness to her confession."

Adam, still numb with shock, studied his aunt. He'd had trouble believing that Hal might be behind the murder attempts. Knowing that his aunt was responsible was incredible in a different way. Though she had always been distant with him, he'd had no idea she could hate him enough to want him dead.

"Adam," Janey whispered, her eyes pleading.

Adam thought of how devastating a trial would be to Janey and Hal and made his decision. "Because of you, innocent men died in Scotland," he said to his aunt, his gaze unwavering. "Shipley almost killed Mariah. That and his own death are on your hands. You deserve to hang, but . . . there has been enough death."

What could be done with a murderous relation? He couldn't pack her halfway around the world, as he'd done with Burke, though the idea was tempting.

A solution occurred to him. "I don't want my cousins to have to endure your execution, but neither do I want to spend the rest of my life looking over my shoulder. I will put evidence of your crimes in the hands of a lawyer. You will retire to your family's estate in Ireland and never set foot in England again. If I die before you, the evidence will be turned over to the courts, and you can hang and be damned."

Hal drew an unsteady breath. "That is more generous than she deserves." To his mother, he said, "I shall escort you home now. Tomorrow I will take you to Ireland."

"I did it for you," she pleaded, looking up at her son. Now that her fury was burned out, she looked shrunken and old. "You deserved to be the Duke of Ashton."

"If you really knew and cared about me, you would know I prefer my horses to having a murderer for a mother." He offered her his arm, his expression set. "Madame, it is time to depart."

Janey came up to Adam, unshed tears in her eyes. "Thank you for not giving her what she deserves," she whispered. "What she did was unforgivable, but . . . she's my mother." She followed her brother and mother from the drawing room, making a gallant attempt to keep her head high.

There was silence after they left until Lady Agnes said, "After drama, dinner." She smiled wryly. "Raising boys has taught me that food does wonders for one's mood, and Ashton, you have one of the best chefs in London."

Recollecting that he had a roomful of guests, Adam pulled himself together. "It would be a pity to waste an excellent meal. And tonight, we have much to celebrate—restored families." He nodded toward his family, then Mariah's. "And also the fact that I no longer have to worry about being murdered. That was wearing on my nerves."

Mariah, who had been sitting on the sofa, said, "If you'll excuse me, I shall retire for the night. I'm not very good company at the moment."

"I'll go with you and bandage your neck properly," Julia said. She frowned at Adam. "Have Wharf take care of that arm."

Adam's gaze followed Mariah as she and Julia left. He wanted desperately to be with her to ensure she was all right. To tell her how much he loved her.

Before he could follow, Holmes approached and said, "I shall inform the nearest magistrate of the . . . unfortunate events since an investigation will be required. Dinner can be served soon, but it might be advisable to move your guests to the small salon until all is ready."

Adam agreed. A blanket had been laid over Shipley's body, but a corpse did rather put a damper on the mood. He raised his voice to get everyone's attention. "We shall adjourn to the small salon until dinner is announced." He glanced around the room, looking at each guest in turn. "The magistrate will be notified, and I assume he'll wish to speak with everyone who was present. I ask no one to lie. But . . . perhaps it won't be necessary to mention my aunt's role in the attempts on my life."

Heads nodded understandingly. Some things were best kept within the family.

As Adam ushered his guests from the drawing room, he realized that he really did have much to celebrate. His family, the removal of a lethal threat—and Mariah.

Chapter Thirty-Eight

Up in their rooms, Julia removed the handkerchief that had been tied around Mariah's neck and used a damp cloth to blot away dried blood. "The bleeding has stopped," she said after her examination. "I'll put on some salve and a lighter bandage."

"This is my opportunity to be very Parisian," Mariah said with brittle humor as Julia helped her out of the ruined gold dress. "They say that during the Reign of Terror, fashionable French women would tie a red cord around their throats as a frivolous reference to guillotining."

Julia shuddered. "I'm not ready for that much frivolity. Much better to wear scarves for the next few days."

Not feeling very frivolous herself, Mariah agreed. After Julia put a fresh bandage around her neck, it was a relief to change into her oldest, most comfortable nightgown.

Before going downstairs, Julia said tentatively, "The fact that Adam isn't betrothed changes everything."

Perhaps. Perhaps not. "I can't think beyond this

moment," Mariah said wearily, "or I will dissolve into strong hysterics." Tomorrow, when she was less emotionally and physically drained, would be soon enough to discover if she and Adam had a future. "Everyone in that room knows that Shipley found me in bed with Adam. I can see the caricatures now if he married me: the Slut Duchess."

Julia winced. "Most of the guests are related to one or the other of you, so they may well hold their tongues. If not—well, it's not uncommon for couples to anticipate their marriage vows."

"The anticipation is not the problem. Having everyone in London know is." She shuddered at the thought. "I do not want to face my father or mother or sister just now." Or to find out if a duke would marry a woman with no reputation.

"Do you want me to stay?" Julia asked.

"Thank you," Mariah bent to strip off her stockings. "For now, I want to be alone and sleep, and you're probably hungry. Go back to the party and enjoy yourself."

Julia studied her face. "As you wish. Don't be afraid to send for me if you need company."

When she was finally alone, Mariah slumped into a chair and buried her face in her hands, glad she no longer had to appear calm and in control. She would never forget the feel of that madman's grip, nor his knife against her throat. She had been sure she was going to die, and tremors of shock and fear still rippled through her.

Tomorrow she could manage to appear strong. Wearily she rose from the chair, climbed into her bed, and pulled the covers over her head.

For tonight, the world could go *hang*.

The dinner party was a mixture of enjoyable and strange. Everyone was making an effort to be cheerful, and by the second course the effort had become reality. Adam wanted to go to Mariah, but she needed rest, and he needed to achieve some degree of normalcy.

The magistrate arrived just as the meal was ending, which was a relief. The man was thorough but sensible. With so many distinguished witnesses agreeing that a deranged servant had attempted to kill the most noble Duke of Ashton, then been killed himself as he threatened a young lady, there was no doubt about what had happened.

Families and friends left after being questioned in the small salon. Adam encouraged the magistrate to talk to the Townsends first so he could avoid Mariah's father. Charles did not look pleased to know that his worst suspicions of Adam had been confirmed.

When Lakshmi and her family left, she patted him on the cheek. "I will have no more of these attempts on your life. I, your mother, forbid it!"

He smiled wearily as he kissed her. "I hope that the universe hears that."

Adam was the last to be questioned. When the

magistrate dismissed him with assurances that the unpleasant matter could be resolved quietly, he found that Randall was still up, waiting in the study and cradling a glass of brandy in his hands.

"Congratulations on surviving hell's own dinner party." Randall handed another brandy-filled glass to Adam. "If ever a man has earned a drink, it's you."

"Thank you." Adam folded into a chair as crushing fatigue descended on him. "I don't recall making a habit of getting blind drunk, but I may give it a try."

"I don't advise it. The price is too high the next morning." Randall sipped at his brandy. "Have you recovered the last of your memories?"

"I think so." Adam tested his mind. "I don't remember anything about the explosion. I have a feeling that's gone forever. Otherwise, the gaps have been filled."

"I'm glad your marksmanship proved to be as good as ever."

"So am I." Adam took a gulp of his brandy. His hands were shaking. "I keep thinking of how easily I could have killed Mariah."

"But you didn't. It was a calculated risk. If you hadn't made the attempt, she probably would have died at Shipley's hands. He looked ripe to kill."

"That's what I thought." He swallowed more brandy, trying not to remember what it looked like when a pistol ball smashed into Shipley's skull.

"You've never killed a man before tonight," Randall said softly.

"A record I wish I'd maintained." Adam's fingers clenched around his glass. "I'd do it again without hesitation. But I'm a coward. I'd rather not have shot him."

"That doesn't make you a coward. It means you have a soul."

Adam's tension started to unwind. "Painful things, souls. But better than the lack, I suppose."

Randall studied his face closely. Apparently deciding that Adam would do, he finished his brandy and got to his feet. "Get some rest, Ash. Tomorrow the world will seem a better place."

"Thank you for being here," Adam said quietly.

Randall gave a rare smile. "As you've always been for me? I'm glad for the chance to return the favor." He touched Adam's shoulder on the way out of the room. "Don't let the bastards win, Ash."

After the door closed behind Randall, Adam closed his eyes and sought the still, quiet center of his soul. True meditation was beyond him at the moment, but as his spirit calmed, he finally and fully recognized the great blessing born of the traumatic evening: he was free to marry Mariah. Nothing stood between them.

Except, perhaps, the lady herself. She might be having second thoughts about marrying a man who might get her killed merely by standing beside her.

But all his doubts were gone. He emptied his

glass and left the study to head upstairs. It was midnight on a shattering day, and he craved Mariah as he craved breath. They'd been through so much together in a short time. Too much perhaps. They'd had deception and forgiveness and passion. Oh, yes, they had passion.

He let himself quietly into her room. No lamp was lit, but open curtains admitted enough moonlight to reveal a small huddled form in the middle of her bed. She was covered completely, rejecting the world.

He pulled off his shoes and coat and lay down on the bed, careful not to wake her when he draped an arm over her waist. For now it was enough to be near.

Despite his care, she sighed and pulled the covers from her head. Her tumbling hair was flaxen in the moonlight, her delicate features more fairy than real. She gave him a tired smile of welcome. "Is the day over? I really, really want this day to be over."

"Midnight has passed, so it is now officially tomorrow. I'm too exhausted to do anything but sleep, but I wanted to do that with you." Tenderly he brushed back her hair, thinking it felt like moonbeams. "Will you marry me, Mariah? The sooner, the better."

His heart sank when she frowned. "The fact that you weren't betrothed to Janey doesn't mean you're obligated to marry me now." Her voice turned brittle. "I have been revealed as a wanton. If that becomes public, it will be a great scandal."

"Even if the betrothal had been real, I had already decided to break it." He found her hand under the coverlet and pulled it out so he could kiss her fingertips. "When I came so close to losing you, I decided scandal be damned. I'm relieved that Janey isn't heartbroken, but I would have married you anyhow."

She gazed at him searchingly. "So much has happened. Perhaps we should wait a few months. Normalcy might change . . . everything."

He laced his fingers through hers. "It won't change the fact that I love you."

She bit her lip. "Are you sure? Perhaps it's just that I was at hand while you struggled through a difficult time. You might feel differently when you have time to relax and look around."

Her uncertainty hurt until he reminded himself that Mariah's evening had been at least as shattering as his. She'd also had a lifetime living on the fringes of society. Now she needed reassurance and persuasion. "I spent years looking around London society and never found a woman I wanted to marry. You are the right one for me, Mariah. A love of a thousand lifetimes. I hope you feel the same way about me."

Her hand tightened around his. "Of course I do. How could I not? I . . . I just don't want you to ever have regrets."

Joy began to bubble through him, washing away the tension and grief of the evening. "Nonsense. I am a duke—fierce, powerful, selfish, and decisive. If I see something I want, I take it. And I want you." He leaned forward and kissed her. Her mouth was sweeter than honey, more addictive than opium. "Prepare to be overpowered, woman. You are mine, now and forever."

"In that case, my dearest love, I will most certainly marry you." She laughed with a joy that matched his. "Are you going to ravish me, my fierce duke?"

"Absolutely. Instantly. Over and over again. Unless you wish to ravish me. I'll happily cooperate in that." He brushed another kiss on her ear. "I will purchase a special license. Sarah will stand up with you. You will be my duchess before you can come up with any more foolish reasons to refuse me."

"You are far too powerful to resist. I resign myself to becoming a duchess." Her smile radiant, she laid her hand on his cheek. "I love you, Adam Darshan Lawford. You are my gift from the sea. I can't believe how lucky I am!"

"The luck is mutual. I owe my treacherous aunt thanks. I never would have met you if not for her." He slid his hand under the blanket and rested it on her warm breast, as perfect when covered in worn cotton as it had been in luxurious silk.

She caught her breath and slid her fingers into

his hair, drawing him down for a kiss. He felt as if he had come home for the first time in his life. "I suspect that I have loved you before," he murmured. "Hindus believe in reincarnation, you know. That could mean we've loved before and will again."

"I like the idea that we are bound together through time. World without end, amen." Her smile mischievous, she unfastened his crumpled cravat, then slid her hand inside the shirt to rest on his chest. "How tired did you say you were?"

Not as tired as he'd thought.

In fact, not tired at all . . .

Center Point Publishing
600 Brooks Road ● PO Box 1
Thorndike ME 04986-0001 USA

(207) 568-3717

US & Canada:
1 800 929-9108
www.centerpointlargeprint.com